Lawrence Smith came from a poo  nd.
They lived on and worked the land that be ....gton. They were paid nothing
but were given a small plot of land they used as their garden. Lawrence was the middle son.
Lawrence disliked working on the land with his father and older brother. He was called to
hunting.

The land around them was hilly and covered in great green forests. There were also
cleared farms all around them, but the massive forest still held countless deer and other animals
worth hunting. Lawrence thought it was the most beautiful land in the world.

The Smiths had to hunt to supplement their meager diet. It was a matter of survival.
Lawrence loved the smell of the damp ground under the huge, thickly packed trees as he stalked
his prey. The sun shined through the leaves and limbs and revealed the animals to Lawrence that
he was searching for. It took a very keen eye to see his prey, let alone hit it with an arrow.

Lawrence snuck away from the farm one day and was looking for anything he could find
to hunt. The family was in dire need of meat. He was stalking a great stag in the woods when he
heard a disturbance off to his left on the main road.

The sound of several men arguing spooked the animal he was stalking, so Lawrence, still
hidden in the thick green woods, walked slowly toward the road and the loud voices.

He could see a small group of finely dressed men who had been stopped and surrounded
by six or seven men with bows and swords. These highwaymen had stopped the entourage of
Prince George. They didn't know it at the time, but they figured it out soon enough. They had
already killed several of his well-armed guards from a distance with their bows. Those men were
lying dead at the feet of these rough-looking highwaymen.

Prince George had been trying to catch up to his grandfather's hunting party. He had slept
in that morning and was now trying to catch his grandfather, King George II, at one of their
hunting encampments.

Lawrence began inching his way closer through the trees and tall grass to see who these
men were and perhaps to hear their conversation. He could hear birds calling and chirping from
up in the trees.

It soon became obvious that the men were very wealthy and presumably were traveling
with a prince, who was in danger. Only a king or a prince and his entourage would be dressed so
richly and have so many guards.

He could see that these were important and wealthy men, no matter who they were.
Lawrence then heard the phrase "your money or your life." He knew instantly what he had to do.
There were three men on his side of the wealthy men's horses and another three men on the
opposite side. The presumed prince and his companions were trapped on either side by the
rough-looking highwaymen.

Lawrence thought that he might be able to hit the three closest men to him quite easily, but he wasn't sure about those on the other side. They were quite a distance from him.

He squatted down in the shadows of the large, ancient trees of this deep, dark forest to watch this event unfold. He then stood up slowly and moved quietly through the trees as if he were an animal himself.

He had done this nearly all of his life. He was seventeen years of age. The forest had become his home. This was second nature to him. He was like his prey, at home in this wonderful forest world. He knew where the crystal clear streams ran, and he knew that the animals of these woods came to drink water in them as he did.

He stood up and crept closer to the trapped hunting party. He felt the arrows in his quiver, counted them, and knelt down again. He was left-handed, so he held the bow in his left hand and drew the bowstring with his right.

He would target the men farthest away first and hope for a little confusion among the other three to give him some time to hit the other men. He pulled one of the long, deadly arrows his father had made for him from his quiver and placed it in position on his bow. Lawrence was ready.

Everyone in the county knew that Lawrence Smith was the best man alive with a bow. He was the quickest to find his target and had the sharpest eyes.

He could see his human targets now, close at hand, and he knew what he had to do. He shot three quick arrows at the men farthest from him. Two men fell instantly to the ground in silence. The third robber spun his giant horse around looking for an enemy but saw nothing. The third arrow had just missed him, flew across the road, and stuck into a large oak tree.

An old man on his way back to the village was standing near that tree watching all of this. The fourth arrow hit one of the men closest to Lawrence in the back and passed through his jacket and then his shirt and entered his heart. He was dead before he hit the ground. The other two men closest to Lawrence didn't know where to turn. The fifth arrow found its target as did the sixth.

All of Lawrence's arrows had found their mark except that one, which had nearly hit the old man running quickly away to Oak Junction.

The man on the far side of the group was the only man left alive. He slapped his horse with his broad sword, and the great brown horse bolted away. He left his five cohorts dead on the ground as he escaped. The highwayman was soon out of even Lawrence's range.

That man would live to kill again.

Lawrence walked out into the bright sunlight and addressed the group of men who had been held captive. "Gentlemen, are you hurt?"

"Why no, young man, thanks to you and your friends."

"I'm alone here in these woods, sir."

"What about all of those arrows flying past us?"

"I'm here by myself, gentlemen."

"What is your name?"

"I'm Lawrence Smith, sir."

"Well, I'm Prince George, and you've done a great service to your king by helping my friends and I survive this attack."

"My honor, sir," Lawrence said, unsure if he should believe the well-dressed man. The prince looked down at Lawrence standing in the deep grass beneath him and spoke.

"Hop up onto my horse and we will find my grandfather. He will want to thank you for your quick action and courage."

Lawrence grabbed the man's extended arm and swung his right leg up and onto the back of the large black horse and wrapped his arms around the waist of the prince as they quickly rode off to find the King.

This was the first time Lawrence had ever been on a horse. He held on for dear life with his bow slung over his shoulder.

When they finally found the king's party camped up the road a mile or so on the edge of his favorite hunting spot, the prince and his men dismounted and handed their horses over to several servants.

The servants walked away as the prince and the others were invited to sit in front of the king and told him what had happened. The king was most grateful to Lawrence for saving his grandson after hearing the account of what had happened. He could hardly believe it himself.

The prince and his friends told the king what had happened with great excitement and in precise detail. The men with the prince spoke of how Lawrence had saved the prince and the others from certain death. Lawrence was asked to spend the night with the king and his entourage, and he gladly accepted the invitation. How many times in his life would he have the opportunity to dine with a king after all?

The men drank well into the night and ate their fill of the animals that had been hunted in the forest. There were two great stags and several large turkeys and other game for everyone to feast on. There were more than a hundred men with the king, including eighty soldiers armed with more bows and arrows than he had ever seen before. Lawrence looked over the weapons with great interest.

Servants were serving food and drink to everyone, including Lawrence. He took a sip of the ale set in front of him in a large tankard and forced himself to swallow it. He preferred goat milk to ale, and goat milk was not his favorite.

A large group of men were sitting around Lawrence, and when they were busy talking he turned the tankard upside down behind him and poured its contents onto the ground. One of the king's guards saw him do it.

"Oh please, sir, don't tell anyone that I dumped this out. I just didn't like it."

"That's fine, Lawrence, I think it is an acquired taste. It took me years to learn to enjoy it myself."

Lawrence was relieved and ate a great meal. He was amazed at the amount of wine and ale that these noblemen and soldiers could drink.

In the morning, as Lawrence sat waiting to return to his family, he was given a parchment at the request of the king. A very tall, thin man with a sharp nose and deep-set blue eyes handed it to Lawrence with a forced smile after it had been written by a scribe recording the king's own words.

It was a deed to three large parcels of land far to the west of where they were camped. The king pointed several times in that direction as he spoke to Lawrence.

"You have done your country a fine service that will help change the course of history, Lawrence Smith. I will not forget you or what you have done. This deed is your reward for your bravery."

"Thank you, sir," was all Lawrence could think of to say.

"I will be here if you ever need me for anything. I am in your debt, Lawrence Smith."

Lawrence didn't know what to say. He didn't know what a deed was, and he couldn't read. He was just a young, uneducated man. He was a poacher and a reluctant farmer with nothing except the clothes on his back and his bow and arrows.

"Thank you, sir," was all he could say. The king seemed pleased with that response and walked away to more important things.

Lawrence was eventually dropped off on the road near Lord Huntington's farm as the king and his entourage passed slowly by it on the way to one of his grand estates nearby for more hunting and merrymaking.

When Lawrence entered his small home, his family was very relieved to see him. They had no idea what had happened to him and were very worried. They were all quite surprised at his tale and would not have believed it if not for the parchment that he showed them. It had the royal seal affixed to the bottom in purple wax. Lawrence was not one to tell tall tales, but his story was incredible.

While he was working slowly in the hot, dusty fields the next day he saw an old nun walking by on the road near his small house and approached her, taking the parchment out from under his shirt as he walked toward her. He begged her to read the parchment to him that the king's servant had given him. She quickly agreed when he told her who had given it to him. She couldn't believe it.

He handed the parchment to the nun as they both sat on a patch of cool, green grass under a large tree. They were both awestruck after she finished reading it.

Her thin, wrinkled hands told Lawrence of her age and wisdom. Lawrence's gift was described in great detail, and the deed explained where the parcels were and described in great detail the landmarks nearby so they could be easily found. There would be no mistakes as to where they were and to whom they now belonged.

This document freed Lawrence and his family from the land of Lord Huntington. It gave Lawrence the opportunity to take his family off the land when he was prepared to do so. He was amazed by the king's generosity.

The skinny old nun spread the word quickly when she returned to the village. She was quite the gossip even though that habit did not put her in a good light with her mother superior or God. It was intriguing news to everyone who heard it.

When Lawrence Smith was befriended by Prince George and the king, it changed his life overnight.

He had been living with his mother and father on the lord's land in one of the lord's peasant houses with no future and little material wealth. Lawrence was not a great farmhand, and his parents and friends had many humorous and quaint ways to describe his relationship with work in general.

His true love was hunting. He was a good tracker, like his father, but he was the best archer this part of England had ever known.

Anxious to see this great gift from the king with his own eyes, Lawrence packed his meager belongings into a small bag made of skins the next morning.

He had two shirts without buttons, two pairs of britches kept up with drawstrings, and a wooden bowl and spoon. He wore the high-top boots his father had given him years ago, his large hunting knife, and his bow and quiver of long, straight arrows his father had made for him.

He was now bound and determined to go off to find his new home and start his new life. He had never been more than a few days' walk from his childhood home before, and then only with his parents.

This is going to be quite an adventure, Lawrence thought as he prepared to leave his small family.

He had been given the name of the nearest village to his new land, Oak Junction, but had no idea where it was.

There was nothing keeping him tied to this land now. He was just an extra mouth to feed for his family, and times were hard. He knew that it couldn't be any worse for him down the road than it was living with his parents on one of Lord Huntington's farms.

They were a happy and close family, but he knew that there was nothing there for him except hard work and poverty. Lawrence hoped that his future might lay three days' walk from his home and west on the main road and that it would be better than his life on this farm.

His mother gave him two small, lovely loaves of fresh bread and a chunk of lamb wrapped in a small piece of cloth as he was about to leave. He was off to start his new life. "Be careful, son, the world is full of evil," his mother said as he hugged her. "I will, Mother, believe me. I will come back for all of you in time, I promise." His mother didn't think she would ever see him again.

"Keep your wits about you, son, and your knife close."

"Yes, father, I will remember everything that you taught me. I won't forget." He turned and looked at his two brothers. His throat was closing tightly and tears were welling up in his eyes.

"I will bring all of you to my land as soon as I build a proper house. I love you all. He hugged and kissed all of them and wept just a bit.

As he walked away, he thought that this might be the last time he would ever see his family. He was leaving his mother, father, big brother John, and little brother Sam, perhaps forever.

He created a mental image of them to carry with him into the future. He was walking off into the unknown, and he had no idea if he would ever see his beloved family again. His family feared for his safety out in the cold, cruel world but wished him the best as he walked away down the narrow little path that led to the road and his future.

Lawrence walked for several hours and then decided to rest and look for some food. He killed two rabbits on his walk. One was a small female and the other was a larger male. He had walked off the main road and waited in the bushes near a small pond.

"You can always find game if you can find water," his father would always remind him. His father had trained him well.

Lawrence gathered his second kill and placed them both in the bottom of his bag. He left quickly. If he had been seen hunting here, he would surely have been hung.

This was his life now. A lowly serf-turned-wealthy landowner with hundreds of acres of land and just a few pennies in his pocket. He had a parchment in his shirt that said he owned several hundred acres of land. He had a bag with two dead rabbits inside of it and a few pennies to his name.

He walked along the dirt road, lined on both sides with thick, green forest. Sometimes it was as thick as a forest could be and dark as the night. Other times it would thin out a little and open up just enough so that Lawrence could see acres of rolling farmland off in the distance. He wondered about the families that lived on those farms. *Were they tied to the land and poor?* He had no idea.

This land was all new to him, and he was eager to know it. He walked slowly, watching the other people walking past him until he could walk no farther, and it became dark.

He had passed many people on the road, but no one seemed to notice him. He was just a peasant. No one would ever try to rob him. It was obvious that he had nothing worth stealing. He started to relax as he thought about his appearance and his circumstances.

Soon he saw a fire off to the side of the road and ventured deep into the woods to investigate. He hid his bow and quiver in the bushes where no one would find them on his way into the woods. Thankfully, he still had his knife hanging at his side. There were three dirty men seated around a small fire trying to keep warm ahead of him in a clearing. Their clothing was in tatters.

"Hello, gents, may I sit at your fire?" They didn't speak but waved for him to join them. Moisture hung off their breaths as they exhaled. It was a very cold early evening. They were eating bread and some kind of gruel from a pot.

"I have a rabbit in my sack. May I cook it on your fire if we share?"

The mood changed instantly. Three smiles appeared out of nowhere on the formerly glum faces.

"Oh please, come and join us, young man, certainly," one man said as he gestured for Lawrence to join them with a large, dirty hand.

The haggard men were starving for meat, and even a small piece of meat would be an unexpected pleasure. Lawrence walked away from the fire with his bag and reached inside it. He still had enough light from the fire to skin and gut one of the rabbits without the men seeing into his bag.

He had gutted animals hundreds of times before and was a quick hand at it. He soon came back to the fire with the dead animal, ready to cook it. He put the skin back into his bag before he returned to them.

The men had found a stout stick to roast the rabbit on. They ran the stick through its body and held it over the glowing flames and red embers. Two of the men held and turned the stick with great glee, one at each end of the branch. They hadn't had meat for days. Lawrence found his bowl and grabbed his knife again.

These men thought Lawrence was almost a king. He had a spoon, a knife, and a bowl, and he was sharing a rabbit with them. The three ragged men couldn't believe their good fortune.

When the meat was cooked just right, Lawrence cut it into four portions with his large knife and gave each man a chunk of it. They ate happily.

When they were finished, Lawrence stood up and said goodbye to his dinner companions. They seemed surprised that he was about to leave them.

"Stay the night, sir," they whispered together.

"I don't think so, I have several more miles to cover," he answered. Lawrence didn't want to risk his safety sleeping near three strangers. His mother hadn't raised a fool, after all.

He had heard of the problems in the world and the dangers on the highways. He had now seen it firsthand.

"Good luck, gents," Lawrence said as he walked away with his bag and knife.

"And the same to you, sir," the men shouted out together. Lawrence walked back to the dirt road and found his bow and quiver where he had hidden them in the bushes. He walked a short while on the main road again until he came upon a thick forest with a small path leading into the darkness.

He walked into the woods and soon found a place to sleep under some heavy brush surrounded by several large boulders. He thought that he would be safe there through the night.

No one will see me sleeping here, he thought as he cleared a little spot to lie on under the bushes and between the boulders. He laid some green twigs and grass on the ground as a buffer against the cold dirt.

"What do you think that fool has in that bag of his, my friends?"

The largest of the three men thought it over for several hours and decided to find out.

"I'm going to find that boy and take his belongings." The two other men looked up at him with evil, gap-toothed smiles.

"Whatever he has is surely more than we have."

"Right you are." He turned and walked off down the road and found the small narrow trail that Lawrence had followed into the forest.

He walked slowly and deliberately until he saw Lawrence asleep on the ground. He had picked up a large branch to use as a weapon. He walked toward Lawrence and had his arm raised when he stepped on a branch and Lawrence raised his arm instinctively to protect himself. The branch came down hard but Lawrence was able to deflect its force and rolled to his left. He grabbed his knife and plunged it into the man's ribs when the man came at him again.

He fell slowly to the ground with a surprised look on his face and was soon dead. Lawrence bent over him to make sure he wasn't breathing.

He gathered his belongings and walked to the road again and kept walking. It was nearly sunrise; some tradesmen were already on the road. He took out a small loaf of bread and ate it while he walked. He had no idea how far he would have to walk. He ate his breakfast just in case it was a long journey.

There were many more people walking in both directions on the highway as the morning passed. He asked several people on the road about the way to Oak Junction. Thankfully, he was heading in the right direction, which was a great relief to him.

He had never been this far from home before, so everything was very new to him. He had nothing but his wits and the kindness of strangers now to help him survive. He was a good-sized boy for his age and looked older than his years due to all of the years he had spent working hard under the sun and hunting. Still, the truth was that Lawrence was really just a child.

He had lived a very sheltered life away from any town or village. He had never seen a naked woman or a man killed until he had killed those robbers the previous night and then this man.

Many boys his age had seen men killed either by the noose or by the king's guards. He and his family seldom came to town or walked on the highway. There was little reason to do so.

They had no money, and all they needed they received from their hard work on the farm. Lawrence thought to himself as he walked down the road, *I might like to see a naked woman someday.*

He walked on for another full day. He walked up small hills and down small hills, through valleys, in long straight lines, and in long arcs as the road meandered through the forest. He thought that he had passed every type of tree that God had created.

In the early evening, he came across a tradesman on the road. The short man walked slowly. He had a dark beard and long curly hair. He was stooped over slightly from carrying the heavy items that he had been selling for so many years. They were mostly pots and pans and cooking implements.

"Good sir, do you know where the old oak at the fork in the road is?"

"Yes, young man, just up the road, a bit farther."

"Thank you, sir. Is there a village or a blacksmith nearby?"

"Yes, both, just past the oak on the right leg of the road. You can see it during the day from the rise in the road."

"Is it a large village?"

"Well, not yet, lad, but it's growing."

What a stroke of luck for Lawrence. He had nothing except two rabbit skins, his bowl and spoon, his knife, and his bow and arrows. But somehow he had survived and found his destination. He worried about what might happen when the man he had killed was found, but he could do nothing to change that night. He had only been protecting himself.

He had been worried since he left home about finding this new land that he now found himself in. He had had no idea what to expect once he arrived. But he knew what he needed. He needed to find a blacksmith.

He continued to walk until it was almost dark. Then he saw it: the great oak.

He walked past the tree to the rise in the road and saw the faint lights of the village down below him and on the right side of the road.

Candles off in the distance, he thought as he looked all around him for shelter. He had found his new home.

His great adventure was about to begin.

He walked to the left and into the woods behind the giant old oak and looked for a place to sleep deep in the brush and trees away from the road. He felt a little like the scared rabbits he had eaten for dinner the night before.

He had no family or friends around him now. He was just a young, poor farm boy who now happened to own several hundred acres of land at the junction of the two main roads where the giant oak tree stood and more land farther out to the west somewhere.

He knew that the king had given him three parcels of land but he knew nothing about them or where they were. He now lived at Oak Junction at the fork in the road. He didn't bother with a fire. He felt for the other loaf of bread in his bag and began to eat it. He would try to sleep, but he knew he wouldn't.

He had too many things to think about and to plan.

Chapter Two

In the morning Lawrence thought about his plan as he hunted for his breakfast. First, he needed an ax. Lawrence quickly found another rabbit as he walked his land silently watching and then waiting. There seemed to be plenty of rabbits about.

He used small dry twigs to start the fire as his father had taught him. It was difficult without a flint. That was one of the items on his mental shopping list.

He found some dry twigs under the oak tree and carried them down to where he had been sleeping. He removed some moss from the oak and gathered more firewood on his way back to where he had spent the night.

It was difficult, but like his father always said, "Life is difficult." No one in his family complained very much. In the time it took to complain about something, you could solve the problem facing you. "Use your head, son," his father would say.

He gutted the large brown rabbit, skinned it, and put it on a stick. Breakfast was served. He ate the rabbit and hid his bow and arrows deep in the brush again. No one would ever find them deep in this dark forest of his new land.

Lawrence walked west to the village after breakfast. It took about forty minutes for him to arrive. When he reached the village, he was aghast. More people were walking about in front of him than he had seen in his entire life. He had his knife, thank God. No one threatened him, but it was something from home and it made him feel safe. His father had taught Lawrence how to wrestle and how to use his knife to protect himself if he had to.

Lawrence could smell the smoke from the blacksmith shop before he could see it. It wasn't a cooking fire that he smelled, it was the smith's fire. Lawrence knew the difference between the two. He followed his nose and wound his way into the village. The great labyrinth of paths and small shops that he saw astounded Lawrence. Shops and people stood all around him. He worried that he may never find his way out of this place and back to his plot of land again. He was getting nervous as he walked deeper into the sprawling village.

Then he saw it again. It was the black smoke rising ahead of him around the next corner. Then he heard that familiar sound as he got closer, the sound of the anvil being hit by a hammer and then the hiss of the bellows.

The burly blacksmith looked up from his fire with a scowl as Lawrence approached him. Lawrence backed up, a little surprised by the stern face of the large smithy.

"What do you need, young man?"

"I would like two ax heads, sir."

"And how do you intend to pay for them?"

"With pelts, sir."

"How many have you, young man?"

"How many do I need, sir?"

"Three pelts."

"I only have two, sir."

"That might be a problem for you then, son."

"I could kill another two rabbits tomorrow and give you four pelts instead of three if you give me two ax heads today, sir."

"You make a good offer. But why should I trust you?"

"My name is Lawrence Smith, and I'm living down by the old oak."

"Why, there's no house or shack out there on that land."

"There will be soon enough if you trade me those ax heads for four rabbit pelts."

"What did you say your name was?"

"Lawrence Smith, sir."

"Wait here," he said as he walked away up the slight grade toward the church.

The smithy was a big man with strong arms created from working at his craft for many years. He had thick black hair hanging down on both sides of his head from a part that ran down the center of it. He had deep-set green eyes that seemed kind even when he spoke loudly over his work. Lawrence could see that he was not a man to be trifled with.

The blacksmith lumbered slowly up the hill toward the church. Lawrence looked around and now noticed the many small stalls selling all types of tools and supplies. It was a dream come true. He had never seen anything like this before.

The blacksmith returned quickly with a short, round-faced priest.

"Tell the Father your name," the smithy bellowed.

"I'm Lawrence Smith, Father."

"Are you the son of the archer Lawrence Smith who shot the highwaymen?"

"No sir, I am the archer who shot the highwaymen."

As Lawrence spoke to the Father, Lawrence reached into his shirt and fished out the parchment that gave him title to the land at the giant oak and two other parcels west of the village.

The two men were both astonished. They had heard the news of the killings, of course. In fact, a villager who had seen the altercation from the other side of the road had told everyone in the village about it as well as the old nun.

The old man spoke of the great skill of the archer and of how he, the witness, had barely escaped with his own pitiful life when an arrow missed its intended target and struck the tree that he was standing by.

People soon began gathering in the area around the smithy's shop as they heard the conversation between Father Magnus, Lawrence, and the blacksmith. Word soon spread throughout the village. The blacksmith couldn't believe it, but it was true. This young man was the hero of the entire county and perhaps soon the entire country, yet they were talking about trading ax heads for rabbit pelts.

The Father whispered something to the blacksmith and he brought down two large axes from a shelf above where he was standing. "Lawrence, give Don the two pelts."

"They aren't cured yet, Father, so I'll just lay them here on the anvil."

The blacksmith handed Lawrence two ax heads as well. Lawrence placed them in his bag. Then, Father gave Don, the blacksmith, a handful of coins. The blacksmith put them into his leather pouch and placed it back on the ground near his stool, deep in his stall.

"Thank you, Father, I am in your debt."

"We'll worry about that later, Lawrence. Now be on your way and finish your errands." The other two men stayed behind, talking together as Lawrence left to find some vegetables. Lawrence felt rich beyond measure. He still had one pelt and more equipment than he could dream of.

He believed in God—more than ever before if that was possible.

Lawrence was able to buy a squash, some potatoes, and some corn with some of the few pennies his parents gave him when he left home. As he left the village, he could sense people watching him. They were whispering among themselves and pointing at him. He didn't yet understand what was happening.

Lawrence still had a little money in his pouch for the first time in his life, and he liked the feeling that it gave him.

Chapter Three

On his way back to the old oak, Lawrence came upon a young boy crying under some trees on the side of the road. He had a large wound on his face and head.

"Hello, son." The boy looked up and asked, "Can you spare some food, sir?"

"Where is your family?"

"Dead, sir."

"How?"

"Bandits, sir. We had nothing. They killed my mother and father and took my older sister."

"You're on your own then?"

"Yes sir, they bashed my head and left me for dead, I guess."

"Do you have any family left?"

"No, sir."

"What are your plans then?"

"Don't have any, sir."

"You'll starve soon enough then."

"Probably so, sir."

"Can you swing an ax?"

"I can learn, sir."

"My name is Lawrence. Come with me if you want. I can't promise you anything except hard work and rabbit meat right now."

"That sounds good to me, Lawrence, sir. I'm in your debt."

"Call me brother."

"Yes, sir."

"What is your name?"

"Lawrence Junior now, sir."

"How old are you?"

"Twelve, sir, maybe thirteen."

"Let's go then. Home is just around the corner at the oak."

"Oh, I know that tree, sir. I passed by it yesterday with my family."

"You live near there?"

"You could say that."

"Didn't see any houses there, sir."

Lawrence laughed.

"Right now we eat rabbits and live like rabbits in the bushes and under the sky. In eight months, we'll freeze to death if we don't build a house."

"Then let's build a house, big brother."

They walked east, and at the rise in the road, they saw the giant oak at the junction. Lawrence turned right and into the field, perhaps a hundred yards before reaching the old oak, between two of the large trees that lined the road, and Junior followed.

He had been Tommy Farmer before, but now he was Lawrence Junior. Each of the young men carried an ax. Lawrence was all the family that Junior would ever have now, or so he thought. It was early April 1770, and the weather was mild for this time in the spring.

Lawrence and Junior had an enormous task ahead of them. They had to make preparations for the coming winter. Lawrence had all the necessary skills for survival, thanks to his mother and father. He could farm, he knew how to hunt and track, and he could cook a little. That was the positive side of his mental ledger. And he now had help.

This young boy was going to be a great asset. He wasn't a horse, but he could follow instructions and he would only get stronger—if he lived. There were no guarantees about that. A man could die any number of ways in an instant if he wasn't careful or wasn't paying attention to his surroundings.

The new Lawrence Junior had seen his family destroyed right in front of him. They had done nothing wrong, worked all their lives, raised their children as best they could, and went to church regularly, and yet they were dead, or worse in his sister's case. He was afraid to think of what might have happened to her. He was lucky just to be alive himself. He had been left for dead just the day before.

The villagers hadn't found his sister's body yet, but they were still looking. *Perhaps we will meet again in heaven,* Junior thought.

Lawrence thought for a moment about the negative side of the ledger. They had no flint, no rope, no hunting nets, and no farming tools. They had no pots or pans or furniture either. Lastly, they had no shelter. Luckily, it was April. It could get very wet and cold, but they had time to build something.

Lawrence showed Junior how to cut the lower branches off the nearby trees with one of the new axes. They would use these to make a lean-to. While Junior went about that task, Lawrence went after more game. Lawrence knew he had plenty of rabbits on his land. He just had to find them. Lawrence had made camp about a third of the way down from the road on his first plot. He wanted to be away from the road. He knew that only bad things happened there. Lawrence slept with his knife and bow next to him. Without them, he could be dead in a moment if trouble came his way.

He walked up to the main road in the morning and surveyed his land below him.

He could see Junior off to his left in the tree line cutting limbs from the trees needed for the lean-to. To his right was a small stream that ran along the western edge of his land. It wasn't a river, but it might be large enough to contain some fish.

Lawrence was happy to see that at least they had fresh water nearby. This stream marked the western boundary of his land and ran across the main road from the village to the south under an old wooden bridge and down past the end of his property. Lawrence could see the stream as it meandered down his property and off into the distance until it fell off of a high ledge and into a great, green valley below him.

Lawrence and Junior could eat rabbit soup forever if they had a cooking pot. Lawrence had hidden his vegetables down where they slept in the thicket. They would eat them soon enough, but what he really wanted was the seeds and potatoes to dry so he could replant them in his garden. *And maybe soon,* Lawrence thought, *the corn that he bought would be dry enough to plant.*

He had to make dinner somehow tonight, but he wasn't sure what it would be. Lawrence walked along the river and down the length of his land. He was looking for tracks and droppings. He saw plenty. He saw many small animal trails coming through the brush and ending at the stream.

He could eat rabbit every day, but that would not be his first choice. He would kill rabbits and take some of them to market to trade or sell for needed supplies. He could sell pelts or trade them for tools as he had done a few days before. He was already rich. He had two axes now, two ax heads, and two more arms to help him clear his land and plant a garden.

Lawrence left for a few hours of hunting while Junior cut branches from the trees as Lawrence had shown him. He had been warned not to injure himself with the new sharp tools. Lawrence walked south along the stream looking for more evidence of animals.

He found what looked like a promising area and hid behind a thicket of brush facing the stream. He sat there for a good long while until a large male rabbit appeared. He shot it, grabbed it, and ran back into the bushes.

He laid the rabbit on some branches and watched the stream again. After some time, another rabbit appeared. He shot it as well. He couldn't believe his luck. He crossed the bottom end of his parcel, walking in deep cool grass shaded by a huge outcropping of rocks, and saw deer tracks as he bent over looking for signs of animals. He saw lots of tracks near a rock outcropping. It was a perfect place from which to shoot. He could climb up into the rocks in the evening and be there when the deer passed through again while looking for something to eat.

He reached the bottom east corner of his land and turned left or north, away from the tall waterfall, and followed the thick tree line until he came back to Junior, still cutting branches. Junior had a good pile of limbs cut. Some were two to three inches in diameter, and a couple were even larger. They carried them over to their little hideaway in the center of the thicket and laid them down in a neat pile. They would clear some more of this brush away and build a lean-to for shelter in the center of it. But first, they had to return to the village.

Lawrence had two fresh rabbits to trade. He needed a skillet and a flint to start with. If they had those, the two young men could cook many different things, and starting the fire would be so much easier. So off they walked, up and across their field and west onto the main road to the village. They talked on their way to the village.

"How is your head today, Junior?"

"Oh, it's much better. The swelling has gone down some, I think."

"Yes, I can see that. I think you will be alright, after all."

"Yes, I wasn't sure last night, but the sleep has made me feel much better."

The young men continued on their way.

There was a lot of excitement in the village as they entered.

Lawrence and Junior walked among the shops as he had done the day before. He and Lawrence Junior smelled the blacksmith smoke and then saw the black smoke plume, just as before.

"Is that the bow that you used to kill the highwaymen?" a little boy asked Lawrence.

"Yes, it is. It's the only bow I've ever owned."

The villagers were all watching Lawrence and talking to each other about him as he talked to the little boy and then walked away from him.

The smithy was much friendlier this time when Lawrence approached him. Lawrence had brought his bow with him on this visit to the village.

"It's beautiful," the smithy said, pointing at the bow. Lawrence smiled. His father had made him this bow when he was a young boy.

"I need a skillet, blacksmith, do you have any?"

"My name is Don, Lawrence, and yes I do have skillets." Lawrence was surprised when the blacksmith spoke to him so kindly and told him his name.

"I'm just a poor peasant, Don. Thank you for being so kind."

"A peasant with three-thousand acres," Don said with a pride that almost made it seem like he was the one who owned the land instead of Lawrence.

"What are you talking about?"

"There's talk all through the village; we just heard the whole story."

"What are you talking about, Don?"

"Everyone knows about your land now. The whole village knows. Information like that can't be kept secret for very long, Lawrence, not around here anyway."

Lawrence knew the king had given him some land. He had papers to prove it. But Lawrence couldn't read so he wasn't aware of the magnitude of the king's gift. The nun had not been entirely clear due to her excitement while reading the document. She had never touched such a document created by the king or his secretary before and had left out some important details, it seemed.

"I need many things, Don. I have come to my land with nothing. I also need a pot, but I've only one fresh rabbit today."

"One skillet and one pot for you, Lawrence. One rabbit is plenty for a trade, and you might even have some credit left over."

"That's wonderful," Lawrence said, standing in near shock.

"Thank you very much, Don."

Lawrence looked at Junior, pulled a rabbit out of his trusty bag, and handed it to Don. There was still one rabbit left inside.

"Here you are, smithy." The smith gave Junior the cauldron and the skillet. Junior placed them in the big bag and hung the heavy bag over his shoulder. It was almost too much for him to carry.

"Who is this lad with you, Lawrence?"

"He is my little brother."

"Oh," said Don with a broad smile. Lawrence was puzzled by the smithy's reaction.

This village was a mystery to him, and he thought that maybe he would never understand these people as long as he lived here.

"Thank you, smithy, can you send me to the flint-maker's stall now?"

"Yes, go back down the way you came from the main street to the fishmonger's stall, and then turn right up the hill. It's not far."

As they left, Lawrence and Junior both noticed the villagers watching them. If Lawrence or Junior were anyone of importance, it would have explained why they were being watched by everyone. But both of them knew that they weren't.

They found the turn at the bottom of the path and went up the hill again to the flint man's stall. "I will gladly trade a flint for a rabbit," he said when Lawrence asked him for a flint. Lawrence immediately thought he was getting the short end of that deal, so they found the butcher and sold the rabbit to him for six silver coins. Then they went back to the tall, thin flint man.

He sold them a large flint for two silver coins. He did not smile as they made the transaction. He gave them two smaller silver coins in change with the flint. The flint man thought that the butcher had told Lawrence the price of his flints as he saw them talking and was not happy about that.

The two boys still had four large silver coins and two smaller silver coins left. Going back down the main village path, they saw the spice merchant and bought a bag of salt for a large silver coin.

Lawrence had often heard his mother speak of the cost of salt. He didn't understand what she was complaining about then, but he did now. Salt was very dear indeed.

Lawrence and Junior had three large silver coins and two smaller ones left. They had turned a rabbit into a small fortune as far as Junior was concerned. Now they had a skillet, a pot, a flint, and a small bag of salt.

As they were leaving the village, Father Magnus approached.

"We all know about the child, Lawrence."

"What child, Father?"

"Lawrence, you oaf."

"What do you think you know, Father?"

"That his family was killed and his sister was taken."

"What else, Father?"

"That he was nearly killed and half-starved, and you found him on the road and fed him, and you have taken him under your protection."

"What else could I have done?"

"Nothing, Lawrence, except that everyone in the village knows it, and you deny it to me now."

"I'm a simple man with nothing, Father. He reminds me of my brothers, whom I'll probably never see again until and unless I am in heaven."

"Well, do you want his sister as well?"

When Junior heard that statement from the father, he jumped like a wild animal.

"Is she alive?" he yelled.

"She is, and she is in my chapel now."

"How?" Junior asked breathlessly.

"God's will, my son."

"Will you save her too, Lawrence?" the Father asked.

"What choice do I have, Father? They will be my new family now that I am here and all alone."

"I thought you'd say as much. Sit here on this bench under the tree and wait for me to go fetch her."

Lawrence sent Junior back down the main street of the village with all the coins as he sat down on the makeshift bench. It was just two stumps with a wide plank running over them.

"Get three small loaves of bread."

"I'll be right back," Junior shouted as he quickly ran off.

"Don't run off with all of the money," Lawrence shouted over his shoulder as Junior ran down the hill.

"I hadn't thought of that," Junior shouted back as he turned up a small lane into the heart of the village.

Father Magnus came back before Junior returned. Lawrence saw him walking across the grass in front of the village church and coming in his direction. With him was a tallish blonde girl of fifteen or sixteen years of age. She had some scratches on her face and two black eyes. She was wrapped in a black cloak soaked in blood, and she carried a small bundle in her arms.

As this young girl and the Father approached Lawrence from the front of the church, Lawrence could see Junior running as fast as his bare feet would carry him. Junior had the bread with him and tossed the loaves on the bench next to Lawrence when he arrived. Junior and the girl ran together and embraced. They were both crying and talking rapidly to each other.

Several people were watching from the stalls that lined the path near the church. It was very emotional for everyone watching.

Most everyone thought that the young woman had come to the end of her days like her parents. The children eventually wandered over to the bench where Lawrence was seated; they were still holding hands. They had been embracing for some time.

Lawrence got up and looked at Father Magnus and the two young people.

"She's lucky to be alive, Lawrence. Some of the villagers found her naked and beaten near Owl's Pond. She was covered in mud and filth. It looks like they tried to drown her and left her for dead. Perhaps they thought she was."

"What can we do for her now, Father?"

"Well she's back among the living, and she has her brother. That's a good start, son."

"Do you think she'll be alright with us in the field?"

"What she needs most is love and kindness, Lawrence. I think she'll find it with her brother and you."

"I hope you're right, Father. I'll do my best by the both of them."

"I know you will, my boy, and you can come to me or the nuns if you ever need anything."

"Thank you, Father. What I really need is about two weeks without rain. I'm going to build a lean-to today and then start on a small house in time. We can't be sleeping outside much longer."

"You're right about that, Lawrence. I'll pray for continued good weather, son, and hope for the best."

As Lawrence finished talking to Father Magnus, the children came closer to him.

"Lawrence, this is my sister Catherine. Isn't she grand?"

"She is rather, Junior. Nice to meet you, Catherine," Lawrence said as he put out his hand. Catherine immediately stepped back and away from him, fear showing in her deep blue eyes.

"Don't worry, Sis, Lawrence is our big brother. We are under his protection, and he's the greatest archer in the country. We have land, a place to sleep, and even a frying skillet and a pot. We are rich beyond measure." As they walked home, Lawrence began making a mental list of projects he had to complete before winter.

First, they needed to start and finish the lean-to. That would be simple enough, but it would need to be larger now. There would be three people living at Oak Junction, not just two.

They also needed a few more tools to start a garden. They had the potatoes and squash seeds to plant. The corn was still not dry enough to plant.

Lawrence had never seen himself as a farmer before. Now that was exactly what he needed to become. He didn't enjoy farming very much. His family often chastised him for his lack of interest in it. It was peasant drudgery as far as Lawrence was concerned. But now that he was going to farm his own land, it was a completely different story. He relished every cold morning now.

Junior had cut many small limbs for the lean-to, and the next day, after Lawrence found some game, they would start to build it in the center of the large spread of shrubs and thistles they now called home.

They slept on the ground in this clearing in the lower portion of his parcel for several days. No one could see them from the highway, so they felt fairly safe. But Lawrence found himself hearing every sound at night, as did Catherine.

Lawrence wasn't a fool. There were plenty of wicked men out and about looking for victims just like Lawrence and his two charges. All one had to do to understand the dangers around them and everyone else was to ask Junior and Catherine about what had happened to them. The two of them had lost everything in a few short moments.

Lawrence had also nearly fallen victim to an evil man he had tried to help. He had little understanding of any of these things.

This wouldn't happen to them again if Lawrence had anything to do with it. He had learned his lesson. In the morning while Lawrence was out hunting near the river, Junior and Catherine moved more limbs into their clearing.

When Lawrence returned with two rabbits, the fire was already going strong.

It was a cool April morning. Lawrence skinned and gutted the rabbits while Catherine put the skillet on the fire. The rabbits cooked quickly. It was a wonderful breakfast.

Chapter Four

The next day, Lawrence and Junior went out to hunt while Catherine built a fire. They were starting to create a routine. The boys walked along the rushing stream and soon spotted a beautiful large turkey. It strutted along the bank with its colorful feathers shining in the bright sunlight, looking for its breakfast of worms and seeds. Its head was bobbing from side to side looking for a small meal.

Lawrence and Junior stayed back in the bushes and waited for it to come closer to them. It was busy gobbling and scratching at the soil. Lawrence released his arrow, and in an instant the bird was dead. The bird didn't know what hit him. The arrow struck him in his chest as it tried to fly away, but it was finished.

Junior used to feel a bit sad when his father had killed an animal, but he understood that those animals had to die for them to survive.

Junior placed the turkey in their ever-present bag and hung it over his left shoulder. They walked farther along the stream until they could see the giant rock outcrop off to the left of them that marked the southern boundary of their land. The river rushed past the outcrop on the right. The crashing water could be heard far below.

Junior was now beginning to feel that this was his land as well. He was the adopted son, or brother, of Lawrence Smith after all. The young men didn't talk about it, but they were together every day and understood what that meant. The three of them were truly becoming a family now. The two could see the deer again, three of them, eating grass in front of the rock outcrop as they crouched in the brush. Lawrence looked at Junior as they squatted quietly behind the brush and small trees. "In a few weeks, we're going to kill a fine buck right here."

Junior didn't understand why they had to wait. "Try to get closer to the deer, Junior. Junior slowly walked a few yards towards them, crouched low and as silent as a cat. But somehow, they knew he was there and bolted. "Your scent is being blown right to them, Junior. They can smell you." Junior had no idea that his scent could give him away at such a distance. "You have to be downwind; the wind has to blow into your face when you're stalking or hunting," Lawrence explained to Junior as they started walking again.

They walked back to Catherine at the lean-to laughing and joking about the deer and their fine noses. Lawrence suggested that Junior might need a bath. Junior said the same thing about Lawrence as they reached their camping spot.

They were going to build the lean-to today from several of the limbs that Junior cut. They dug two deep holes in the ground six feet apart and placed two good-sized limbs in the holes standing upright. They filled the holes with dirt and tamped it down hard around the two tall posts. They laid a strong branch across the two uprights. It was then just a matter of placing several limbs from the cross member to the ground, covering them with finer branches and weaving them together. This would keep the sun off them during the day and help to keep them warm at night.

They ate the second rabbit from the day before at breakfast. They were happy to have it. Times were hard these days for everyone, but they were among the fortunate. They had shelter and food. It was mostly rabbit, but they could fry it or boil it in the cauldron with some herbs that grew around them, and they had salt now. Catherine's mother had taught her cooking and cleaning. She also helped in the fields and was a willing hand. The meals were much better after Catherine arrived in the camp.

In the afternoon the following day, Lawrence and Catherine left for the village while Junior cut more firewood and brought new boughs to sleep on into the lean-to. Catherine was very shy and spooked easily as they walked. Lawrence noticed the people walking around them on the road. He noticed the men especially and the weapons that they carried. Catherine noticed those things now too, more than in the past, but she also saw the beauty of the countryside and the little church and even the way the produce was displayed in the market. Her memory of the terror that she had endured was slowing retreating.

Lawrence noticed everything as well, but he saw everything through the eyes of a man. He looked for possible danger everywhere while he walked on the road and in the village. Before he had met Catherine, he saw less of the beauty around him. She helped him to see that more clearly now. He still saw the places where men might hide and then ambush them, but he was also seeing the beauty around him more, thanks to Catherine.

Lawrence had to see Don the smithy again on this visit to the village. He needed a shovel and a pick to start the garden. Lawrence had used his knife to dig the holes for the lean-to, and he wasn't happy about what the digging had done to the blade of his knife.

He had the turkey in his bag to trade or perhaps sell. He knew his way around the village now.

When I got to the fishmonger, I turned right and looked for the smoke, he thought as he walked along with Catherine. Don was becoming a friend now. That was how Lawrence now saw it.

They had come into contact often to do business, and he was the person who Lawrence knew the best in the village. He trusted him. Lawrence had two large silver coins in his pouch, but he hoped he wouldn't need them to buy the tools. He had other plans for the coins.

He had noticed how Don treated his customers, and how he set a price and then let his customers haggle a bit. It was a good strategy, Lawrence thought. Don got the price he needed, and his customers felt like they had landed a bargain in the process.

Most of the town's wares were sold in the same manner. Sometimes there were hard feelings between buyer and seller, but most times both parties to the deal were left feeling satisfied. After all, the customer could always go to another stall or even to another village if they felt they were being cheated. Catherine and Junior had lived a two-mile walk from Oak Junction but on the northern side, opposite of where they now lived with Lawrence. Their family had also worked on Lord Huntington's land. They had lived in one of his peasant farmhouses just as Lawrence and his family had. They came to the village once in a while, and Catherine knew the fishmonger's wife, Jane, quite well. Catherine told Richard that she wanted to talk to Jane in private, so while the women walked a short distance away, Lawrence and Richard, the fishmonger, struck up a conversation.

Catherine explained to Jane that she had not had her monthly visitor arrive as she had in the past, and she didn't understand what was wrong. She asked Jane if she knew what the problem might be.

"Oh lass, did those men defile you?"

"Yes, Jane, one did. I tried to fight him off, but there were so many others holding me. They beat me, and I just don't remember much after that."

"It's just as well, girl. You're probably going to have a baby."

"Oh Jane, what am I going to do?"

"Let's go talk to Father Magnus and see what he says."

Jane whispered something to Richard and left with Catherine.

Richard looked up as Lawrence saw the two women quickly walk away.

"Go, Lawrence. Go about your business, and I'll have Catherine safely waiting here when you return."

Lawrence went to do his errands while the ladies went to talk to the Father. They walked up the hill and entered the side of the church through a narrow wooden door. And talk they did. The nuns and Catherine discussed what had happened to Catherine. She told her story in the mother superior's room. They soon came to a unified conclusion.

The Father had little insight into the workings of the female heart let alone their bodies. He was silent as a mouse in his office, trying to keep busy while the women talked about heaven knows what in the next room. The nuns talked with the two ladies for some time. When they all finally came into his office, Father Magnus was apprehensive, and rightly so. He was not privy to their conversation and had no idea what he would have to deal with. But he knew somehow that it wasn't going to be anything good.

"She's going to have a baby," said a short, pleasant-looking nun as Jane shook her head up and down. Catherine sat there quietly and looked at something on the floor, or so the Father thought.

"Is Lawrence the father?" asked Father Magnus.

The ladies all answered together: "No!" The Father was confused, and the ladies looked at him while his mind raced.

"Oh, the kidnapping. I see, I see."

"Let's bring Lawrence up here for a chat then," suggested Jane, the fishmonger's wife. When Lawrence returned from his errands, he was carrying a shovel, a pick, and in his sack, a cloak. "Don was in a generous mood today," Lawrence said as he reached Richard the fishmonger's stand.

"Where is Catherine?"

"They're not back yet, Lawrence."

Just then it occurred to Lawrence that he had no idea where all the fine fish came from that were arranged on the table in front of the fishmonger.

"Where do you get these fish, Richard?"

"Most come from the river right in front of us, of course. But some come from farther away on wagons from other towns nearby. There are many different varieties of fish, Lawrence."

"The river right here on the west side of the village has fish in it?"

"Yes, Lawrence."

"How do you catch them?"

"With nets, baskets, and hooks."

Lawrence remembered that the river continued down past his land. *Perhaps I might catch some fish in the river where it passes by my land,* Lawrence thought.

Jane appeared back at the stall, breathing hard from the quick walk down the hill.

"Lawrence, you need to go see the Father."

"Is everything alright?"

"Yes, yes."

"What has happened to Catherine?"

"Nothing. She is still in the church talking with Father Magnus. Just go up to the church. They're expecting you."

Lawrence walked back up the path to the church as he was told. He hadn't walked through the village this way before, and he discovered many other shops he hadn't seen on his previous visits.

There was a tavern, a shop that sold honey, and a shop that sold knives and swords. There was also a tavern with many men seated inside drinking and talking loudly.

As Lawrence reached the tall, ancient church, he was met by one of the same nuns who had talked with Jane and Catherine a few moments before. She showed him into the Father's office and led him to a chair. Her name was Mother Meredith. She was a nun of about fifty with the face and blue eyes that were perfect for her work. She was very pleasant and patient. She was the mother superior.

When the Father finally walked in and sat down behind his large, messy desk, he had a nervous air about him. He was not the usual self-assured man he normally was.

"We have a situation here, Lawrence. None of which is your fault; we are sure of that. We are quite sure of that. It seems that your charge, that is to say, Catherine, is with child. Lawrence stood up quickly and looked into the eyes of everyone in the room and started talking fast. His hands were down at his sides with the palms turned upward.

"Father, I'm completely innocent. I haven't touched the girl, Father, as God is my witness."

"We know that, Lawrence. Catherine has also made that very clear to us. She is not blaming you, Lawrence. It seems those men who killed her mother and father committed other ghastly sins upon her as well. It's a miracle that the girl is still with us."

"That be true," said the mother superior, who was seated in the corner of the Father's small office. She had stayed to support Father Magnus in this unfamiliar territory. He was a mess. He hadn't had to deal with this situation much before. Usually, women who were taken like this were eventually found murdered. But by the grace of God, Catherine had survived.

The question now at hand was what would happen to Catherine and the baby. Lawrence looked into Father Magnus's eyes. He stood up and walked toward the Father and his desk. He spoke slowly and deliberately.

"I'll make her an honest woman if she will have me, Father. The past will lie dead and forgotten. No one needs to know the awful truth."

"We thought you might suggest this since we know you and your character a little better now, Lawrence. But it may not be fair to you."

"I will do anything to protect her reputation and her virtue, but she may not want me."

"She may not, Lawrence, but it still might be the best path for her."

"Why don't we bring her in and let you two talk in private?" Lawrence agreed to that idea, and the nun soon brought Catherine into the room as the Father left. The nun followed quietly behind him and shut the door. That left Lawrence and Catherine seated together quietly in private.

Catherine sat on a small wooden chair across the room from Lawrence with her head down in her hands, looking almost like she was in prayer. Lawrence paced back and forth across the uneven stone floor of the small dark room.

Lawrence began, "I'm not very clever, but I know enough to understand your situation. I've known you less than two months, Catherine, but I can see your little brother loves you and that you are a diligent worker. Our lives together will be very difficult in the beginning, but I will marry you to protect you and this child. I want to help create a real family for Junior, for you and for this innocent baby if you are willing to take the chance.

"I think we can create a better life if we all work together. This ugly incident that brought you into my life will be forgotten. I give you my promise not to make any physical approach to you until you want or love me. I will be very busy for the next several months and will have little time for tender moments anyway. What do you think, Catherine?"

"I agree to this marriage, Lawrence, and like you said, it may not be for love right now, but I think it is the best for me and perhaps it will work to the advantage of all as time passes. I know you love my brother as I do. He has told me of your kindness to him. Everyone in the village has only good things to say about you. They all have great respect and praise for you." Lawrence was surprised at that comment. He had never given it any thought before.

"I know you have some parcels of land and next to nothing else. I am glad to marry you with an open heart and pleasant hopes for our future."

Lawrence called for the Father when they were finished talking.

Lawrence and Catherine told the Father of their decision. Father Magnus was both happy and unsurprised. Lawrence and Catherine decided that they would like a little private service in the chapel as soon as possible due to Catherine's condition.

Chapter Five

The mother superior was put in charge of the wedding. The nuns were sent out to ask everyone who was able to offer up something for the young couple. Everyone in the village was invited, but that was to be kept a secret from Lawrence and Catherine. The story used to explain the large crowd that would appear on their wedding day was that there was a christening of a nobleman's child at the church on the same day as their wedding. Lawrence and Catherine would enter through the small chapel on the side of the church and then be led into the church proper for their wedding.

They all walked home that cool evening with many questions in their hearts after deciding to marry. Catherine washed her best dress and Lawrence's best shirt and britches. They also bathed.

Lawrence and Junior were not happy or at least pretended not to be happy about that little surprise. The water was warmed in the kettle at the fire, and they washed themselves behind a large blanket hung across a wooden branch in the lean-to. Each of the three had the lean-to to themselves in turn for privacy.

In the morning, they put on their clean clothing and cloaks and walked to the village in the cool air. Catherine had the new cloak on that Lawrence bought her when he first met her. It had replaced the one that she wore the day that she was attacked.

As they passed people on the way to the village that bright sunny morning, everyone seemed to be unusually happy. A large crowd milled about in front of the church as Lawrence and his small family walked up to the small chapel on the south side of the beautiful ancient church.

"What do you suppose that is all about?" Lawrence asked no one in particular.

"I heard something about a christening, but I don't know the family. They are supposed to be quite wealthy from what I hear, boys."

As they entered the chapel, a nun was there to direct them the rest of the way in. She opened a large, arched wooden door, and they saw Father Magnus standing in front of them across the room. As they walked towards the Father, Lawrence and Catherine both heard and saw movement to their left but paid little attention to it. Neither of them had walked this far into the church from the side entrance before, so they had little idea that they had entered into the heart of the church.

They were already as nervous as two young people could be for obvious reasons. When they finally saw the whole village in the church, it couldn't make them any more excited or nervous than they already were. Junior walked behind them and was fooled as well.

The service was short and to the point, as they had requested. Father Magnus spoke of the magic of marriage and the power of love. He talked of the responsibilities and joys that came with the institution of marriage. Both Lawrence and Catherine felt that they were ready to take on those responsibilities even though their situation was unique. The party afterward was as grand as any nobleman's wedding party could have been. The newlyweds felt like the richest people in the county, maybe in the whole country, at that moment. They were now a family in the eyes of the church and the village. All of their friends were there to celebrate with them.

The married couple received a few gifts at the party from their neighbors and friends. They received a lid for the skillet, a bag of sunflower seeds, and some needles and thread. They also received some cloth. All of these items would be quite useful as their clothing was in constant need of mending due to the work they were doing at home and out in the fields.

The entire week after the wedding was spent preparing the garden and planting. Only time would tell what the harvest would bring. They hoped the weather would be kind to them in the coming months.

Lawrence hunted every morning. He would usually kill at least two rabbits for the three of them for breakfast. That would keep them satisfied until dinner. Junior would stretch and clean the rabbit skins right after breakfast and lay them out to dry, tied on branches to stretch them and keep them flat. Then they would work in the garden. They found many stones as they turned the soil and prepared it for planting. There were also many river stones along the stream's bank. These stones were another wonderful gift the land had given them. The three of them carried the stones to a pile near where the house would be built. The stones would become the fireplace in the house in the near future.

Lawrence thought that it would be important to teach Junior how to use a bow as soon as possible. Junior could protect himself and Catherine when Lawrence was in the village or away on the property. For several days while hunting, Lawrence worked on an ash limb. While he sat and waited for his prey, he carved and smoothed the limb with his large, sharp knife until it became a proper bow just like the one his father had made for him years ago.

The string would be made of rabbit gut. Making the arrows was time-consuming, but again, Lawrence had been well trained by his father. He often thought back to how much he had hated working wood and farming with his father. Lawrence wished his father were here now to see all of his accomplishments. He had everything a man needed in this world: food, family, friends, and soon he would build a proper house. Lawrence would do all of this with the help of his new wife and his stepson or brother-in-law, Junior.

Lawrence went hunting each morning. Sometimes he would have Junior in tow, and sometimes he went without him. Junior was a quick study and learned to use his bow in little time. He killed a few stationary rabbits easily, but a moving target was still difficult for him at first. That skill would come with practice as all difficult things do.

Catherine started each cold morning by building a fire. Then as the morning passed, she made the meals, eating with the men, and then cleaned up around their campsite and worked in the garden.

Lawrence asked Catherine to weave a few special baskets for him one day at lunch, and eventually, she found the right materials and the time to do so.

The baskets were cone-shaped, about a foot-and-a-half tall, and closed at the narrow end. The widest end was about eight inches across. They were made from the marsh reeds and cattails that grew near the banks of the stream. They grew on an inside curve of the river where the current slowed. Catherine had no idea what the baskets were for, but she made them for Lawrence nonetheless.

He had drawn pictures of them with an arrow in the dirt. Lawrence hadn't forgotten his conversation with Richard, the fishmonger. He knew there were fish in his little stream now. When he had talked to Richard, the conversation made him think that it was possible. Speaking with the fishmonger prompted him to make those baskets.

Lawrence's land was downstream from the village. Many streams flowed into the main creek between his land and the wooden bridge above his land. Lawrence thought that there must be fish that escaped the nets and traps of Richard, though perhaps just a few. They would add food to their table and silver to their future if that were the case.

Lawrence knew that his shelter, hidden in the tall shrubs, couldn't be seen from the road, but the smoke from their fire could be. They had little security, and Lawrence was worried constantly about that. He'd had a sense of unease for some time. He often felt that they were being watched.

Catherine was soon showing. Her beautiful stomach swelled with the new life that was taking shape inside of her. Soon she would have trouble easily moving around. She was young and beautiful, but she was also getting very pregnant. They needed to build the house, and quickly.

By the time Lawrence had been living on his land for about five months, he knew most everyone in the village. He had sold enough rabbit skins for silver to pay two men for three days' carpentry work, and he hoped to be able to trade labor for his pelts or meat. He knew he could kill a great stag down near the rock outcrop. He would need to if it took longer to build the house. He had only a little silver saved.

Lawrence went to see Father Magnus as he often did when he needed advice. Father Magnus had taken the place of Lawrence's father in situations where Lawrence needed the advice of a more experienced and older man. Lawrence explained his plan, and Father Magnus called in a carpenter who happened to be making repairs on the church.

Lawrence explained that he just needed help with the main frame of the house. Maybe six large upright posts and about five large cross members for the roof. Getting them up and into position would be the hardest part. Lawrence knew he would need extra hands for this heavy work. Father Magnus offered his donkey as well if needed. The carpenter had a younger brother, and Lawrence and the carpenter agreed that the two men would come and work for three days for two large pieces of silver. They agreed to the conditions in front of the Father and were bound by their word.

They would come to Lawrence in two weeks' time. Now Lawrence faced two deadlines. The first was to build a house and the second was to be ready for the baby's arrival.

Lawrence, Catherine, and Junior discussed where the house should be built on their land. Catherine wanted it facing the old oak and the crossroads. Junior wanted it near the stream so fetching water would be easier.

Lawrence thought they were both very clever. They walked over the land and found a level spot just above their lean-to and halfway between the east and west boundaries of the property, facing the old oak but not too far from the stream. They all agreed that this was a fine spot for their home. It offered both solitude and protection.

"The view from here is perfect, Lawrence," Catherine said.

"Yes, Lawrence, this is perfect," Junior agreed. "We are close enough to the river to fetch the water easily."

Lawrence thought the spot was high enough on his land to see strangers coming down the road and flat enough to build a house on.

Lawrence and Junior picked ten large pines for the corners of the house and the doorposts. They chose trees near the road and up at the top of their land. They could cut them down, trim all the limbs, and slowly roll them downhill to the building site. Junior and Catherine thought Lawrence was very clever when he described the plan. The two siblings, however, hadn't thought about the logistics of the actual building of the house.

The trees were cut and trimmed and rolled down to the building site. Lawrence and Junior used ropes that Lawrence had purchased to control the speed of the large timbers as they rolled them down the hill. They used the trees that stood near the road as a crude block and tackle, wrapping the ropes around some of the trees several times, and used their own weight to slowly slide them down the land. When all of the trees were in place in a pile, they started digging the postholes for the house. Lawrence stepped off the distance of the sides of the house under the watchful eye of Catherine.

"Yes, Lawrence, that looks about right. What do you think?"

"Oh, I think it's perfect," he added wisely.

They now had the proper tools to make their work easier. A shovel and a pick were all they needed. They had dug all six holes, each one two feet deep, before lunch of the following day. Four holes were dug for the corners of the house and two for the doorposts.

When the carpenters arrived at Oak Junction, Lawrence and Junior were ready for them. The holes had been dug, and the tree trunks were nearby, ready to be split into useable lumber.

The good news from the carpenters was that the tree trunks were bigger in diameter than necessary, so one trunk made several posts and beams. Lawrence thought that each corner needed to be a full tree trunk. He was no builder, after all. The two carpenters used wedges and axes to split several of the trunks. The two brothers had come with many of their own tools and knew their trade well. They created smaller timbers to complete the frame of the house in two days. They used hand braces to drill the necessary holes in all the corners and hammered pegs into them to hold everything together.

On the third day, the carpenters also made several smaller boards to create the rafters for the roof. Lawrence asked them to stay on an extra half day so they could show him and Junior how to shingle the roof. The carpenters were pleased for the extra work. They also made smaller, narrower pieces of wood to build the walls between the posts. Some small pieces were also cut to line the window openings. Lawrence would buy window glass when he could afford it later. For now, he was going to cover the window openings with shutters and skins.

Catherine had been sewing rabbit hides together for many purposes in the new house. She had the hides ready just as the walls were being built. The family would use them to cover part of the floor where they slept and to place over the window openings to help keep out the cold winds.

Lawrence and Junior used small branches from the trees to weave the waddle backing for the plastered walls. The house looked like a giant square basket when they were done.

Early one morning as the carpenters started on the rafters, Lawrence and Junior went down to the rock outcrop to hunt. By now, Junior was an accomplished archer. He had been training for five or six months. It was early September, but the mornings were still cool and damp. The deer came every morning to feast on the last of the lush green grasses and flowers at the foot of the rocks near the southwest corner of Lawrence's land.

The outcrop looked like it had been pushed up through the earth by some unseen force that left the smooth molded rocks lying at a forty-five-degree angle to the grass-covered ground around them. That made it easy to climb in the darkness of the early morning. Lawrence and Junior could hear the stream rushing over several small cataracts and the giant falls behind them as they reached the top. They could see the falls off in the distant mist.

Lawrence and Junior climbed up into the shady recesses between the rocks before the deer made their way to this pasture, and the two young men waited. They only needed one buck. Several deer arrived after a long, quiet wait.

Lawrence and Junior picked the biggest one to shoot. He was enormous, with a beautiful rack of antlers, and took a majestic stance as he surveyed his domain. Junior got off two arrows, as did Lawrence. One of Junior's arrows missed, but the buck fell after both of Lawrence's arrows found their mark. The other deer scattered as the giant buck fell, instantly dead. Lawrence was glad for that. No hunter wants to see an animal suffer.

The two young men skinned and butchered the animal where it fell. It was too huge to consider moving. Lawrence laid the skin on a small sled-like device they had made for this hunt, piled the guts onto the skin, and tied it closed. They each hoisted a rear quarter on their shoulders and walked home pulling the sled. They would be exhausted when they reached the house, but they still had to return to the sight of the kill and bring the rest of the meat up to the house just the same. The smoker would see some use tonight and for several more days.

The carpenters had just finished putting the last rafter in place when Lawrence and Junior appeared the second time. The men climbed down from the now nearly finished roof, and Lawrence paid the men with two pieces of silver and one of the hindquarters.

The carpenters were thrilled with the unexpected gift. That was much more than they had bargained for. The meat would serve them and their families well as winter approached. Lawrence asked the two brothers to return next spring if they wanted more work, and they eagerly agreed. Lawrence had a gift of making people feel important and welcome, and he never had any difficulty getting men to work for him. He always gave the brothers and other workers that he used a little more than they expected.

After Lawrence and Junior completed the shingled roof, they rested, satisfied though hungry until dinner. Over the next few days, Lawrence and Junior made plaster by mixing lime, sand, clay, and ash together. When that was finished, they mixed the plaster with water in a wheelbarrow they had borrowed in the village from Don. They built a small table to place the mixed plaster on and shoveled the plaster onto the table.

From there, they used wooden trowels to scoop the plaster onto their hawks and then applied the plaster over the twigs, or waddle. It wasn't easy, and it wasn't neat at first, but it sealed the house from the weather. Most of the 'mud' fell to the ground in the process when they first started. They started in the rear, worked their way around from the back of the house, and finished the first coat on the front.

After a week of this, their plastering skills had improved greatly. When they finished in the front of the little house with the final coat, the plastered walls looked passable. It was certainly a house now. It only lacked proper windows and a door. They had completed the most important task of the year. They now had a permanent shelter.

Lawrence, Catherine, and Junior were now safe to face the winter. The two boys were nearly men now, with great responsibilities, and winter would arrive soon enough to test them further. Lawrence was nineteen years old and Junior was thirteen.

Junior could now hunt and track and use his bow with the best of them. He had Lawrence as a teacher, after all. They shot enough turkeys and rabbits to last all winter. They made jerky, and smoked rabbit, deer, turkey, and pheasant. They saved the feathers from the turkeys and pheasants to repair their arrows and to use in new ones that Lawrence made.

Junior looked enough like Lawrence to be his brother, though everyone in the village knew that he wasn't. He was on his way to becoming a tall man like Lawrence, and his hair and eyes were similar in color to his new brother. Many strangers made the mistake of thinking they were brothers before they heard of their first meeting.

After the house was finished, Lawrence could safely take stock of his situation and go back to something he had thought about several months ago, the fish in the stream.

Catherine had wondered what all of those pointed baskets were for as she made them. They didn't stand up very well, and she couldn't quite figure out why Lawrence had her make so many. There were at least a dozen. Even Junior had asked Lawrence about them.

"You 'll see in the spring" was all that Lawrence would say.

The baby was due in January. Lawrence and Junior took turns staying with Catherine as the day of the birth approached.

Junior was skilled enough to feed all of them now with his bow, and the two young men traded off, back and forth, day by cold winter day.

Lawrence enjoyed his time with Catherine. Since they had been together, these last months had been the first time they had time to sit together and get to know each other. They both had been so busy preparing for winter and the baby that they seldom spoke during the day.

Catherine seemed more at ease now and had pushed all the horror of the attack into her past as best she could.

Chapter Six

Lawrence and Catherine talked to the midwife, Mary, several times about the pending arrival of their baby. Mary lived nearby in Oak Junction and knew the timeline, rough as it was. She had delivered many of the children in the village. Her mother had done the same for the previous generation. She anticipated few problems with the birth. She considered it a natural event and was not in the least bit worried.

"Look at the animals in the fields, Lawrence," she had said. "They do it with some discomfort but it usually turns out just fine. Pay as little attention as you can. Catherine is the one who will do all of the work." Lawrence was still worried, but her words comforted him some. She was the expert, after all.

Catherine sat quietly in the corner of the little house cooking dinner. She was worried but said nothing. In time, she would be doing what all mothers must do.

Lawrence started building the chimney with the river stones that they had moved up to the house in the northwest corner. It didn't take long to build it with the help of several friends.

The house was just one big room, about twelve feet square, which they decided was adequate for the growing family. The floor in the sleeping area was covered with reeds, cattails, and grass when all the work inside was finished. Catherine had sewn many rabbit skins together and placed them over the floor where they slept. They used rabbit skins for blankets to keep them warm as well. There seemed to be no end of rabbits on their land, thank God.

When the chimney was done, the room was full of warmth. Lawrence and Junior had started stacking firewood in the corner of the house long before the walls were even finished. When Junior first came to Oak Junction, Lawrence had him cutting firewood for a good part of each day, and he cut firewood every free moment that he had. When he wasn't dreaming of rabbits, he was dreaming of cutting firewood.

It was much easier to cut the firewood in my dreams than in real life, he often thought.

When Catherine's water broke, Junior ran off to get the midwife. Catherine soon started having contractions as Lawrence sat at her side.

"You'll be fine, Catherine, she is on her way. She'll be here in just a moment."

"Thank you, Lawrence" was all she said as another contraction occurred.

They had both seen many farm animals deliver their young and all seemed well, even though it was uncomfortable for Catherine. The midwife had explained to Lawrence and Junior what all of these things meant. They all knew the signs when they finally arrived and were prepared as well as two young men can be. Junior soon came back with the midwife just as the baby emerged from her beautiful young mother. It was an easy birth, and Lawrence was glad for that. He didn't want this birth to be more painful than necessary considering the evil and disturbing circumstances surrounding it.

The winter was mild when it finally arrived. They had planned for all the possibilities and had stored plenty of food and firewood for the long winter. The baby was healthy, and Catherine was soon her beautiful self again.

Of course, their lives were changed completely now and would never be the same. No one slept very well the first few months after Elizabeth arrived. She always seemed to be hungry. She was a good baby though. She cried only when she was hungry or in need of a change. Other than those times, she seemed quite content. She had dark eyes and seemed to watch everything that went on around her.

The garden had provided the family with a good harvest. It consisted of many different types of vegetables and herbs. The rows were neat and ran in straight lines for about fifty feet. There were more than a hundred rows in the garden and mounds for planting as well.

The family now had venison and rabbit, and an occasional pheasant or turkey. Lawrence even had some silver coins left over to purchase a goat in the coming spring. They would need more milk for the baby, and Catherine could make and sell cheese. Lawrence would buy a rooster and two hens as well.

During their long talks through that winter, Catherine and Lawrence grew closer and learned about each other's life in greater detail and made plans for the family's future.

Catherine had been trained by her mother in the skills of husbandry and cooking. She could do anything and everything that was needed around the house and on the farm. Lawrence knew his hunting and farming skills well. They were becoming the perfect couple. It took time, but eventually, they both realized that they loved each other and were truly married.

As the months passed, the weather became milder. One day, Lawrence and Junior finally took those strange baskets to the stream. Junior couldn't believe what they were. Lawrence explained to him that they were fish traps. It was incredible to Junior. He could now catch fish with very little effort while he worked somewhere else on the farm. He knew he would love fish for all of his days.

The weather grew warmer as spring came into full bloom, and Catherine and Elizabeth grew stronger. The family finally ventured to the village to see their friends for the first time since the birth of Elizabeth. The family needed several items. The white, winter rabbit pelts would bring a good price at the tanners. They also had several pelts to trade left over from the year before. They needed more salt, seeds for the garden, the nanny goat, the chickens, and some more cloth. They all needed new clothes, and now the baby needed new clothes as well.

They spent a lovely day in the village and visited with all of their friends. Don the blacksmith, Richard the fishmonger, and the others had all survived the winter to face a new year. But as they were walking in the village, a shudder blazed down Catherine's spine as she saw two strangers come into view. Two of the men who had killed her family and attacked her were now walking their horses through the village. They had tied up their horses near the bakery and were buying supplies. Catherine pointed them out to Lawrence.

"Lawrence, those are two of the monsters who killed Mom and Dad, and tried to kill me."

"Are you sure, dear? Could you be mistaken?"

"No, they are surely two of those evil men, Lawrence. I will never forget them and what they did to all of us."

"Junior, take Catherine and the baby to the church, and tell Father Magnus about what's happening. Don't let those men see Catherine. Put up your hood, Catherine. Bring back lots of help from the tavern, Junior."

Junior quickly did as he was told. He grabbed Catherine's hand as she put up the hood on her cloak, and the two of them with the baby walked quickly up the hill through the village to the church. They breathlessly explained to Father Magnus what was happening as they stepped into his office.

The Father left immediately with Junior and gathered up some of the men from the tavern as fast as he could. They left the tavern and stopped at the other stalls on their way, gathering up even more men. They soon had clubs and swords and gathered shovels and other impromptu weapons from the blacksmith shop. The shop was soon emptied of any implement that could be used as a weapon. The men hastily marched down the lane from Don's shop to where Junior had left Lawrence.

The two strangers were busy purchasing leather gloves. Then they heard a noise behind them and turned to see several well-armed men coming their way. Others soon joined the battle if you can call a one-sided affair a battle. The killers didn't have a chance to pull their weapons.

There was no doubt that they were the robbers and killers; Catherine was sure of that. She would never be mistaken considering the terror she had gone through. It didn't take very long to subdue the murderers. The men were outnumbered, and the villagers took out their anger on the two men with murderous glee.

Father Magnus was just able to stop the throng before they killed the men. He jumped between the killers and the townsmen and yelled at them.

"We are Christians! Stop now or you are just like them." The villagers stopped beating the two men in short order.

The two rough-looking strangers had items with them that had belonged to Junior and Catherine's father. They also had a ring that had belonged to Catherine's mother. Catherine identified everything when it was shown to her.

"Yes, those were my mother's," she cried softly. The villagers had made no mistake when they attacked and apprehended these awful men. There was no doubt of their guilt.

The men were rushed to the church and locked in a small storage room behind a thick oak door. Two men were immediately sent off to Chesterfield on horseback to notify the sheriff. It would take a hard day's ride for the men to reach the sheriff. People in the village were shocked when word got out about the encounter with the thieves.

Sweet Catherine would have her vengeance at long last. She was very upset for obvious reasons. She stayed away from the village until the men were eventually taken to the courts in Chesterfield a few days later. It was hard for her and for Junior to have those men nearby. The memories of the death of their parents had been fading slowly away and now they were brought to the fore again. It was a difficult time for both of them. It changed the family's routine, and everyone in the village missed seeing Catherine and little Elizabeth in the village.

It took three days for the sheriff's men to arrive back at Oak Junction. By then, the village was almost back to normal. The Father and the nuns had been busy organizing the care of these two monsters. A man was always on guard duty outside the door of the cell. Sadly, Catherine knew that there were still at least two more men out there somewhere. *God help anyone who crosses their path,* she thought.

Lawrence and Junior started setting the fish traps in the mornings before going to the garden to work. They turned the soil in the garden as soon as it was soft enough to dig. They had dug irrigation channels the previous year, and now they needed to be refreshed. The furrows were cleared of debris, and the sides of the irrigation ditches were repaired as needed.

Rabbits were still scarce this early in the season, but the men still had plenty to do. They caught several fish each day with the traps. They often ate fish for dinner. They gutted and salted many fish for the following winter and sold fresh fish to Richard, the monger.

As the men worked in the field one day, Lawrence saw strange footprints from someone who must have come onto their property. They were long shoe prints, a bit narrower than his. Horse tracks ran next to them. They came from the main road and then passed across his fields and damaged some of his new crop. He wondered who they might belong to and why they had come onto his land. He then remembered the man he had seen on the road. He told no one.

Chapter Seven

Lawrence had a new project on his mind for the spring. He wanted to add another room to the house to use for storage, among other things. The family could keep all the preserved meats and fish there as well as the goat. Lawrence didn't want to lose the goat to the wolves or foxes that roamed the fields nearby.

The garden was larger than last year. This year they would also have corn. The cobs had dried and the kernels could be planted. They had saved and dried plenty of seeds and purchased more in the village. They hoped that their new larger garden would attract even more rabbits. They set traps in and around the plants to try and catch some.

They planted the garden and started on the second room of the house. Two weeks passed before Lawrence went back to the village. They worked constantly every day to get the garden finished. Lawrence then went to talk to Father Magnus about the men who had helped him on the house the previous fall.

He walked through the village, stopping often to speak to the many villagers who he now called friends. The walk up to the church was always pleasant and reminded Lawrence of his wedding and his love for Catherine. He entered the church from the south side as always and knocked on the father's door.

"Come in," the father said quietly.

Lawrence stood and waited for Father Magnus to put his quill pen down.

"I need those carpenters back at Oak Junction, Father," he said after he was invited to sit down in the Father's office.

"I'll tell one of the nuns going up that way to leave word in their village."

"Thank you, Father."

"How's Catherine these days?" he asked.

"She's doing better, but she is in no hurry to come back here until those last bandits are found. She still likes having Junior or me close by."

The oak leaves were sprouting when two of the sheriff's men finally came to Oak Junction to look for Lawrence and Catherine. The trial of the two men would start in a month, and they wanted Junior and Catherine to testify. Catherine wasn't happy about facing those "evil bastards," as she put it. They had killed her parents, but she knew it was her duty to be a witness. It would be a three-day walk for them to Chesterfield, but she would do it. Elizabeth was just four months old now, and it would be difficult for them to travel with such a young child. Lawrence went to see Father Magnus about borrowing his donkey cart for the journey to Chesterfield. Lawrence knocked on the door and entered. He saw Father Magnus working at his desk as always.

"Father Magnus, I thought I might ask you for the use of the donkey cart for our journey."

"That won't be a problem, Lawrence, I will take care of everything. Anything else you need, son? How is Catherine?"

"She is fine. She is just a little worried about the journey."

"I'm not a bit surprised, Lawrence, it is a bit of a trip." Father Magnus smiled as Lawrence left his small office.

Lawrence and Junior cut down several more trees for the construction of the new room for the house in the following days. They rolled them down to the construction area as before. There were still plenty of mature trees lining the road that passed their farm. The trees were quite thick along that upper end of the property and gave them all of the privacy that they could ever want.

Lawrence met the carpenters at the small office of the church where Father Magnus did his daily study and writings. It was the same room where Lawrence and Catherine had their marriage discussion. It brought back sweet memories for Lawrence. Lawrence discussed the cost of the job with the carpenters again while the Father listened. They agreed on a price, and when the deal was completed, Lawrence walked back to Oak Junction.

As he walked, throngs of people passed him in both directions on the road home. He couldn't shake the feeling that he was being watched. The feeling had been with him since he saw those footprints on his land.

Soon, a small yellow dog joined him. Lawrence paid him little attention. He turned, stopped, and yelled halfheartedly to try to make it leave. It then occurred to him that having a dog around the house might not be a bad idea. By the time he reached his little house, he had a name. His name was Lance. He was long and thin and looked hungry. As they entered the house, Junior saw the dog.

"What have you done, Lawrence?"

"Nothing. This creature has followed me home on its own."

"I think it might be a good idea to have a dog around here, Lawrence," Catherine said as she worked in the kitchen. The issue was settled.

Catherine tossed the skinny dog a morsel of meat, and he swallowed it immediately. She tossed him another, and he did the same. He looked around the room and settled next to the baby. He spent the night there for the next two years. Over time, he became close to everyone, but the person he favored most was the one who had first ignored him. Lawrence was his favorite.

The carpenters were only needed for two days. They were glad to be working for Lawrence again. They hadn't done much through the winter, and they needed the work. Lawrence had treated them more than fairly the last time he used them, and they hadn't forgotten his kindness or that of Catherine.

They would build the walls and the roof of the new room. Because they were adding to the existing house, they would only have to build three walls this time. Seth and John, the same carpenters who had come before, would again sleep at the church during the construction.

Seth and John came on the appointed morning to start splitting the tree trunks into timbers. Lance barked and tried to chase the men away until Lawrence called him off. Lawrence made it clear that the men were welcome. Lance sniffed both of them and walked slowly away, looking back over his shoulder.

Lawrence and Junior explained everything about the work that the family wanted done. When they had finished talking with them, Lawrence and Junior left to go hunting for more game. Catherine sat in the house with the baby and Lance. She took care of her daily chores as Lance watched the men suspiciously.

"If you need a drink, just give me a shout and I will bring you some water," she said as the men set to work. "Don't get too close to the dog."

Unknown to anybody, two riders were rapidly approaching Oak Junction from the east. They were riding very hard, and their horses were covered in sweat. They were not the sheriff's men but two of the remaining bandits who had been free over the last year or so.

They were on a mission. They were coming to kill the only witnesses to their killing spree, Catherine and Junior. It was near lunchtime when the bandits reached the giant oak. They dismounted and slowly walked onto Lawrence's land. They were dressed in fine clothing and seemed harmless enough at first glance.

They pretended to be lost travelers.

"Come and join us for lunch, gentlemen," Catherine said to the two men as they approached.

"Have you eaten today? Join us before you leave if you haven't." She did this with most strangers who stopped at the farm. "It isn't much, but you're welcome to eat with us."

"Thank you ma'am" was their response.

Catherine had learned from Lawrence to always be gracious and share whatever they had with anyone who passed by Oak Junction. Catherine didn't recognize their faces, but their voices seemed somehow familiar as they started to speak to her and the carpenters. She wasn't sure why at first, but she was troubled by something about the men. They sat down with the carpenters at the table that was always set up outside while Catherine went back into the house for more food.

Catherine and Lawrence always ate outside when the weather was nice. The view from the house was beautiful.

"This view is fit for a lord," Lawrence would say, looking out to the three points of the compass that they could see from their lunch table. Rolling hills and forests could be seen to the south and more forests to the west, past the stream, where two more of Lawrence's parcels were waiting for him somewhere off in the unknown, miles and miles away.

Somewhere out there, in that beautiful land, was more of Lawrence's wealth, just waiting for him to discover. He hadn't seen it yet—none of the family had—but it was out there, waiting for them to conquer.

Catherine felt ill at ease as the two men sat outside. She put Elizabeth down on some skins in the back corner of the house and picked up the knife that she used around the house for cooking. The knife was six inches long and as sharp as a razor. She slid it carefully behind her back between her skirt and her apron strings.

There is something familiar about them, she thought, but she still wasn't sure what it was.

These men now seemed like trouble to her, and the carpenters seemed to feel the same. The carpenters had their hammers nearby, just in case, or so it seemed to her. The visitors were both wearing fine clothing with leather belts and had large knives in beautiful leather sheaths on them. They had left their swords hanging on the saddles of their horses nearby.

Catherine could feel the tension between the strangers and the carpenters at the table as she came out of the house.

Something must've been said between them when I was in the house, she thought.

All at once, the two visitors came at Catherine with knives raised. She was completely surprised. The carpenters tried to intervene, but they were on the far side of the table. They circled around the table after the two men as they turned and lunged towards Catherine. She knew instantly who these devils were. The sound of their angry voices and their movements brought back all those horrible memories of her attack. Lance came running from across the yard and started to bark furiously.

"We're going to kill you, wench, and your baby," they yelled at her as they charged with knives in their upraised hands. Catherine screamed before she even had time to think. She pulled her knife from behind her back, and the two assailants slowed their approach and separated. They came at her from both sides. The carpenters soon reached them.

Lawrence and Junior were headed back home with two rabbits and a pheasant when Lawrence heard the screams and the dog barking. They dropped their kill and ran toward the house. They could see people moving and running around the front of the house. Two men were wrestling in one part of the yard and two more were around Catherine. As they got closer, they could make out the carpenters struggling with two strangers. Lance had a stranger's leg in his mouth.

As Lawrence and Junior approached, they placed arrows on their bowstrings, and Lawrence screamed, "Shoot the man on the right, Junior, I'll shoot the man nearest your sister." They released their arrows at the same time. Junior's arrow found the hip of his target, and he fell to the dark ground. One of the carpenters finished him off with a blow to his head from his trusty hammer. It made a sickening cracking sound as the hammer found its mark.

Lawrence's first arrow missed his target and hit one of the large trees that lined the road. As he was about to shoot again, Catherine found the man's throat with her knife as he turned to look at Lawrence. The second assailant fell to his knees. Lawrence shot another arrow and it hit the man in his chest. He twisted back toward Catherine and fell to the ground.

He was dying from the wound to his neck before Lawrence's arrow struck him. He fell dead in the grass near the entry of their little house.

Catherine went to her knees and began sobbing as Lawrence comforted her. Junior went to check on the carpenters. The two carpenters were banged up, but no one suffered stab wounds or any other serious injuries.

"They were going to kill Elizabeth, they were going to kill Elizabeth," Catherine kept crying loudly. Lance was still yanking on one of the dead man's legs with fierce determination. Lawrence chased him off. Lance returned to Lawrence's side, and Lawrence patted him and scratched his chest. "Good boy, Lance, good job." Lance turned to Catherine.

"Calm down, dear. These men won't hurt anyone ever again. Who are these men?"

"These are two more of the wretched beasts who killed Mom and Dad and beat Junior and me."

"Well, they won't be bothering anyone again. Junior, go and get the Father, and bring his donkey cart. We have to move these bodies out of here."

"How many more of these monsters do you think are left, Catherine?"

"I can't say, Lawrence, but the one I remember best has not returned yet."

The carpenters looked at Junior and Lawrence with some relief. They picked up the dead men and moved them around the corner of the house and out of her sight.

"Thank you, Lawrence, for saving us," Seth said as he and his brother sat down at the table again.

"That wasn't my arrow, Seth. Junior shot that one in the hip."

"Thank you, Junior," John chimed in. Junior was still shaking as he ran off to the village.

"Let's take the rest of the day off, men," Lawrence said to the carpenters.

"We'll see you tomorrow morning. I think we all need some time to compose ourselves."

"Yes, Lawrence, this has been quite an ordeal. We are still shaking as we stand here in front of you. I wouldn't want to climb that ladder right now or work on the roof."

In a short time, Junior returned with Father Magnus and the donkey cart. The two brothers loaded the dead men onto the crude cart for Father to take back to the village and then later to the cemetery.

The Father walked over to Catherine and checked on her and the baby. He whispered something to Catherine, and then passed his hand over her head and blessed her and Elizabeth. Lance watched and followed Father Magnus as he walked.

"These men were going to kill us, Father."

"I know, dear, but Lawrence and the carpenters have saved you. All is well now. Try to relax, and be glad that The Lord has saved all of you."

Lawrence took all of the carpenter's tools and placed them in the deep grass out of Catherine's sight. They were covered in blood, as were both Lawrence and Catherine.

Before he left, the Father talked with Catherine again and checked on Elizabeth once more. The baby had been fast asleep through the entire incident.

"Your child is safe, Catherine, as you are. Lawrence is here to protect you, and God will watch over all of you." Father patted Lance on the head as he left.

Once again, Lawrence had to kill. He wasn't proud of it, but he had been protecting his family and had been left no choice.

This was the world at Oak Junction during Lawrence's lifetime. Nothing was guaranteed except hard work, suffering, and difficulties. Lawrence had seen many men killed and had killed some himself. He never wanted to hurt anyone, but life had put him in a position where he had to act or lose his family or his own life.

The highwaymen's horses stayed at Oak Junction. Their masters were dead now, and no one knew who might inherit them. After a few weeks, things returned to almost normal. It was now time for Lawrence and his family to go to Chesterfield to give testimony against the two remaining bandits.

Lawrence went to see Father Magnus about borrowing his donkey cart again for the long journey to Chesterfield. After walking to the village and visiting with some of his friends, he came to the side entrance of the church. The Father's office was just inside.

There was a fine carriage parked there with the driver and a guard sitting against the side of the church on the grass. They were leaning up against the wall and smoking long pipes. They wore large brimmed hats to keep the sun off their faces and out of their eyes while driving. They wore heavy gloves to protect their hands from the reins that controlled the team of four beautiful black horses. Lawrence sat down on the grass near the door with them and started a conversation with the two men who came with the carriage.

"Where do you come from, and who owns this grand carriage?" One of the men blew smoke from his nose and then answered Lawrence.

"It belongs to Lord Sydney. We come from Lime Town, where the lord lives."

"What's he like?"

"He's a fair man. He treats the help well and kindly."

"Why are you here?"

"Don't rightly know; something about going to the courts." Lawrence thought that sounded interesting.

"Maybe the carriage is for Father Magnus." As Lawrence finished his sentence, Father Magnus and a very tall, well-dressed man emerged from the church.

"Lawrence, why didn't you come in to see me?"

"I could see you were busy, Father, with some important matters. I didn't want to interrupt." Lawrence stood up and brushed the grass from his simple cloths.

"Lord Sydney, this is Lawrence Smith, of whom we just spoke."

"I'm honored to meet you, your lordship."

"Thank you, Lawrence, the pleasure is mine."

"I've come about the donkey cart, Father, for our trip to Chesterfield."

Father Magnus looked at the lord, Lord Sydney looked back at the Father, and they both smiled for reasons unknown to Lawrence at that moment.

The two men who had been talking to Lawrence had no idea that they had been talking to the best archer in the land, the man who had saved Prince George. Lawrence had seemed like a simple farmer to them.

"This carriage is for all of us to go to the courts in Lawrence," Father Magnus said.

"You, Junior, Catherine, Elizabeth, and I will travel in it together." Lawrence was stunned.

"The lord wishes for all of us to travel together to the courts in some comfort and has furnished us with this fine coach. We're all riding in it to Chesterfield to the courts together. His Lordship has given us this carriage to use along with his driver and a guard."

"But why the coach and the men, Father?"

"The lord, who is close friends with the king, and even the king himself remembered that you did him and the lords—and the village, for that matter—a great service."

"What service is that, Father?"

"You killed several men who put all of us, the lords and the king included, in great peril. You surely didn't think the lords and the king would send you and your family to Chesterfield, so far away, on a donkey cart?"

"I had no idea, Father."

"Have your family here in the morning, Lawrence, and we will start on our journey."

"What about my goat?"

"You will be gone for about three days I think, Lawrence. I will arrange for one of the nuns to check on her twice a day."

"Thank you, Father," Lawrence said as he walked away shaking his head in disbelief.

"You aren't going to Chesterfield with me looking like that, you two," Catherine said after she learned of their journey tomorrow. You will take another bath before the journey, or I'll go alone."

The two young men both found bathing a waste of time, but Catherine insisted. They heated the water and washed near the fire. The bath was near a fireplace in their warm house and seemed almost pleasurable to the two young men. Catherine then gave them clean clothes and fed them when they were done.

Catherine's feelings for Lawrence were changing and becoming stronger. She didn't understand how she felt about Lawrence. She loved Junior and her parents, but this feeling for Lawrence was something different. She no longer feared Lawrence. He had proven to her that most men were good and wholesome. The men of the village, for the most part, had also shown her that. There were those who made remarks to each other when she was walking in the village. She even heard some women whisper about her at times. But she now knew that most people were good, not evil—not like the men Lawrence had killed.

Her feelings for Lawrence had changed and grown more complicated after he saved her from humiliation in Oak Junction. She was still confused. After all, she was just eighteen and had no mother to talk to.

She was married now in name only but had lived with Lawrence for almost two years, and he had kept his promise not to accost her in any way. He had never attempted to touch her or kiss her. She never saw him lurking near the stream when she bathed in the summer, even when she wished he might be there in the thick bushes somewhere. She never saw him there, watching her.

In the morning, Lawrence and his family took that walk to the village that they had taken so many times before. But it was different today. Today, they would travel by carriage like the wealthy. Lance followed them at a distance and smelled most of the vegetation that grew along the road. They were off on a great adventure, though with sad overtones. There would be no hunting or feeding or milking the goat for several days. The carriage traveled much faster than walking or going by donkey cart. They reached the halfway mark to the courts that evening.

Catherine had brought some smoked meat and bread, wrapped in a cloth. The Father laughed at her as she started to pull the food from her bag.

"You don't understand, do you?"

"What do you mean?"

"We're spending the night at an inn. We're going to have people serve us now. It will be wonderful. You two will have your own room." When Lawrence heard this, he instantly wondered about what it meant. "Junior and I will have a room to ourselves as well. There will be wine and ale tonight. It will be quite pleasant, I think."

Lawrence, Junior, and Catherine had only ever slept with their own family members or with each other at Oak Junction, under the stars in the beginning and then on the floor of their little house. They had never dreamed they would ever be able to stay in a proper inn.

They eventually pulled up to a fine large building surrounded by many smaller structures. Junior could see out in the darkness that one large building was a barn. He saw horses inside and several men feeding them. He couldn't believe it. He had never seen such a barn before. The building was just for animals. The barn was almost as large as a church. Lawrence couldn't believe it either.

Junior's family had never owned horses. Only the wealthy owned horses. Lawrence and his mother and father tended several goats and cows on their land, but they all belonged to the lord. Everything belonged to the lord. *They* even belonged to the lord if the truth were to be known, though they never spoke of that. It was too grim a thought to ponder. Some of the animals slept in the house with Junior's family to help keep them warm and to keep the animals out of danger. This was common practice with all the families that Junior had ever known.

The driver and guard would sleep in the carriage to ensure that the horses and the carriage would be safe throughout the night. Catherine tossed the food that she had brought to Lance. He picked it up and slipped under the coach. He had run behind the coach with ease as they traveled. He would not leave their side.

"I wouldn't get too close to the dog, gentlemen. He is not fond of strangers or anyone who approaches him," Catherine mentioned as she entered the inn.

Lance was not a vicious dog. He was quite calm and predictable. He was satisfied to rest at the feet of any Smith and watch his surroundings. If a stranger approached, he became a different dog. No one understood his behavior but assumed it was due to his mysterious past and lineage.

The innkeeper showed everyone to their rooms so that they could get settled before dinner. They had little luggage. They only had small bundles of clothing. The men had two white shirts, drawers, and one clean pair of britches each. Catherine had a clean dress for court and one more for the trip home.

Lance watched the family nervously as they entered the building. He walked over to the front door with his meal, walked in a tight circle out of the path of the humans, and settled in to wait.

After some time, the family came back downstairs to eat a fine dinner off of pewter plates and spoons to use. It was like a dream. They had chicken, bread, vegetables, and wine. Catherine had never had wine before. She drank several glasses. Lawrence found that surprising. All of this was beyond their wildest dreams. Father Magnus smiled with satisfaction as he finished his meal.

When they finished dinner, Father Magnus touched Junior's shoulder to get his attention and they left for their room. Father had to practically push Junior up the stairs and away from his sister and Lawrence. Lawrence and Catherine sat for a while and listened to the music being played in the room where they had eaten. Catherine reached over and touched Lawrence on the hand. He was surprised and glad. He had fallen in love with Catherine long ago but had resisted the urge to tell her for fear of her not wanting him in that way.

"Isn't this wonderful, Catherine?"

"Oh yes, Lawrence, I can't believe it. This is all happening due to the death of my family, and I feel a bit ashamed to enjoy all of it."

"Don't be ashamed, Catherine. You are on your way to do your duty by them. We must eat and have some rest on the way. They would not want you to live your whole life in sadness, would they?"

"No, they were fine people, and I understand that I am supposed to make the best of the rest of my life. It would be dishonorable to them not to."

"Exactly, Catherine."

Music was playing in the background in this wonderful, foreign place as their hands touched. They had never had an experience like this before, and they didn't want it to end. Finally, as the night passed and their eyelids became heavier, they decide it was time for bed. They climbed the old wooden stairs to their sleeping quarters, hand in hand.

They reached the old door, and Lawrence opened it. The little room was cool and dark inside as they entered. Lawrence lit the candle that sat on a small table. The two saw that their room had only one bed, and it was grand. It was high off the ground with real blankets and a rich quilt. The room was perfect.

Lawrence was looking for a place to sleep on the floor somewhere. He thought that perhaps he could fold up a blanket and place it under him on the floor. There were plenty on the bed and one would not be missed. While he was thinking about all of this, Catherine had removed her clothing while under the covers of the large, comfortable bed.

"Come to bed, my dear husband," she said softly. Lawrence smiled and wondered if this was a dream or real. He was not expecting this to happen. He turned and blew out the candle.

They were truly married at long last. He had finally seen and touched a naked woman, even if the room was quite dark. He was now a man in the truest sense of the word.

In the morning, everything was different and yet the same. Lawrence and Catherine came down the stairs holding hands after the Father had knocked on their door to awaken them. Junior had never seen them hold hands before, and he mentioned it to the Father.

"Yes, son, it's amazing what a good night's rest can do for two young people," the Father said to Junior as they followed Lawrence and Catherine down the narrow wooden stairs.

Junior looked at Lawrence and Catherine with suspicion. He didn't understand what was going on. They all ate a wonderful breakfast and then left for the courts.

It was a three-hour journey to finally arrive in Chesterfield. Lance followed close behind the carriage. Everyone entered the court and sat in the gallery, waiting. Lawrence, Junior, Catherine, and Father Magnus sat in the very back. There were so many people crammed into this large room that the Smiths felt uncomfortable. Lance sat close by outside in a shady spot of grass. His bright eyes closed slowly now and then as he waited.

Finally, after many people had spoken regarding this tragedy, Lawrence was asked to come up and sit in the witness box.

The tall barrister dressed in black asked Lawrence about the original incident with the highwaymen and Prince George. He was also asked about his life at Oak Junction and about his friends there. They all wondered how this poor former serf now owned a farm. One of the judges read the deed from George III, which gave Lawrence all of his land. Father Magnus had made sure that Lawrence brought it with him. The judges had no idea who Lawrence was until the deeds were read. They had heard the stories, of course, but he had no idea that this Lawrence Smith was the same Lawrence Smith who had saved the prince.

That was when Lawrence finally began to understand why the villagers treated him the way they did. It all became very clear to him after the judge had read the deed. It was astounding. He was rich. He was richer than he had ever dreamed he could be. This little piece of paper from the King had given him rights and wealth that few men could ever gain no matter how hard or how long they worked.

The defendants sat in their chairs with what seemed like little interest in their case. The judges asked Lawrence about the circumstances of the apprehension of the men in the village, and Lawrence explained what had happened there as best he could remember. Lawrence was also asked about the items that were found with these men that had belonged to the murdered parents of Junior and Catherine. Again, Lawrence answered the questions the best he could. When the judges and the barristers were finished, Lawrence asked for permission to speak.

The judges allowed him to do so. Lawrence stood up in front of the judges and looked at them sitting high above him.

"I speak to the court as a husband and a father today. The evidence I gave is surely strong enough to prove these men guilty without my poor wife having to come forward and testify and face these monsters again here in this court. Her parents were murdered, her brother was attacked and left for dead with a serious head wound, and my Catherine was beaten and defiled. Has she not already suffered enough? These men also tried to drown her. It is a miracle that she survived, and a blessing that she has very little memory of what she went through. Please let the other witness's testimony, mine, and the physical evidence speak for her, and let her be at peace at long last. Thank you."

Needless to say, he did not mention how Elizabeth was conceived. That was too awful and sad to mention, and better left a secret to only those few in Oak Junction who knew it.

Lawrence was then seated, and Father Magnus was called to testify. He spoke of Catherine's parents, whom he knew slightly, and he spoke of Junior and Catherine, whom he had known a bit better as they had been to Sunday school occasionally. Father was then asked to speak about Lawrence.

"He is an honest man who is bound and determined to make a life for himself and his family. If he tells you something, it is so."

The court had heard enough. They decided not to call Catherine to the stand. That was a great blessing for her. When Lawrence and Junior told her the news, she was carried away with relief. She was more than ready to go home.

The only thing left was the verdict of the court, and it came quickly. The three judges talked among themselves for a few moments and then one of them wrote something down on a piece of parchment. The other two judges looked at the parchment and shook their heads in agreement. The parchment was handed to a short bald man nearby who loudly read the verdict from behind a large desk. His voice echoed off the high ceiling and wooden walls of the large courtroom.

"We the court, on this day, March 17, 1771, find the defendants Ronald Gray and Edward Jones guilty of murder, rape, theft, and other felonies too numerous to mention. We will show you the same mercy that you showed your victims—none. You shall both hang on April 1, 1771, at sunrise. If it were up to us, you shall remain in hell for all eternity. May God have mercy on your wretched souls."

Father Magnus was heard softly saying "amen" in the rear of the court.

"As for your belongings—the weapons, saddles, and horses—they will all go to the Smith family for what little compensation that they may bring." Court was then adjourned.

Lawrence could care less about the swords and other belongings from these criminals. But the horses would change their lives beyond measure. He would now have horses to plow his fields, and he would now be able to visit his parents more easily. And perhaps more importantly, he would be able to travel to his properties in the west. Depending on that land's fertility and location, he might be able to farm more land and raise more animals.

Lawrence often thought about his life and how he had been given his new family. He felt God had given him much more than he had ever deserved. He had a little house, some land, ample food, and best of all, this wonderful family and all of his friends. He really was a wealthy man in many different ways. Lawrence often wondered why he was so very fortunate while others were not. He needed to ask Father Magnus to explain it to him someday. It was a complete mystery to him.

Junior and Lawrence rode home with Catherine in the carriage along with Elizabeth. Father Magnus stayed behind for some church business in Chesterfield. The family stayed in an inn again on the way back to Oak Junction. Junior had his own room this time. Father had given

Lawrence money to pay for the rooms at the inn on their way home. It had come from Lord Huntington.

Lawrence and Catherine were on their much-belated honeymoon. Lawrence was also busy making another list in his head. First, they needed to make a real door for the house. It would be made of thick oak planks held together with three huge, forged-metal straps. It would hang on three stout iron hinges made by Don the smithy. It would have an iron bolt that would slide into a long metal bar with a hole in it that ran from the bottom to the top of the doorframe. It would be as strong as possible. Elizabeth would be walking soon enough, and a real door would make Catherine's life easier and safer for everyone. Lawrence also decided that Junior needed to learn to read.

Chapter Eight

The ride from Chesterfield back to Oak Junction was very pleasant and uneventful. Lawrence, Junior, and Catherine noticed all the new growth in the plants all around them. Having lived on farms for their entire lives, they were always aware of the changing seasons. The city folk were less interested, or so it seemed to them.

Lawrence now understood why the villagers had stared at him when they first discovered who he was. They knew more about his new life and wealth than he did. The gossip was fairly accurate. In some stories, he had more land than in other people's stories, but most of the tales were pretty close to the truth.

Some people thought that Lawrence had killed several more men than he actually did. But those who gossiped needed some excitement in their humdrum lives, and Lawrence's life story provided that for them. Lawrence didn't see any harm in that, and he couldn't stop them even if he wanted to. Lawrence now had a better understanding of his real wealth. He now realized that Junior needed to learn to read to protect the family and their future if something happened to him. They now had gained something in this life that they could lose if they weren't careful. Once Junior learned to read, he could then teach the entire family how to read for their protection from all manner of thieves and swindlers.

The family got back to Oak Junction by late morning, and Don had kept his word. The goat was fat and seemed as content as any goat can be. She was tied up and straining on her rope trying to eat the grass just beyond her reach.

The horses were still hobbled, and there was plenty of manure for the garden. Don had made another water trough for the horses from a long log, split in half and hollowed out. They still had plenty of water to drink on this beautiful day. While Lawrence and Junior were checking on the rest of the animals, including the rabbit traps surrounding the garden, Catherine started making lunch.

Lance walked the land and sniffed for any evidence of strangers passing across his domain. He smelled all of the animals to make sure they were still fit and healthy.

Catherine started a fire in the fireplace and had Junior fetch fresh water for a stew. She didn't have to cook outside anymore, thanks to the boys. She had a new house and a proper fireplace to cook in now. She took some dried venison, potatoes, and squash, and grabbed some very dry bread. The bread was tossed into the pot, which hung from a bar that swiveled in and out of the fire.

There were potatoes already in the pot. She would add the squash at the last moment. While the water boiled, Catherine played with Elizabeth. She was a lovely, happy baby. Catherine loved her Elizabeth more than anyone or anything else in the world in spite of how she was created. She loved Lawrence nearly as much for accepting the three of them as his family. They now were living the life that most married men and women took for granted.

Lawrence and Junior wandered over to the new room when they returned. In one corner, they found the hardware, bridles, and saddles that came with their two new horses. They were of fine quality with rich tooling on the leather of the saddles and bridles. They were very expensive and surely had been used by a wealthy man, but only God knew where the saddles and horses came from. What fate had befallen those who had owned all of these things in the past was anybody's guess. The court had given the lot to Lawrence, so now they were his responsibility. Every time he used them, he would be reminded of their former owner's imminent fate.

Junior was going through the handsome saddlebags when he came upon a few silver coins tucked into the crease of the bag.

This money could help several poor families in Oak Junction, he thought. Junior immediately showed Lawrence what he had found.

"That money isn't ours, Junior, we will give it to Father Magnus when we go into town in a few days."

The Smiths had plenty of food and clothing, but Lawrence needed the blacksmith to make several hinges and the metal straps for their new front door and shutters. The door wasn't built yet, but that wouldn't take long. Don would also have to make the nails Lawrence needed and a latch. Catherine soon called them in for lunch. She had a nice rabbit on the fire as well as the stew. It was nice to be home again at Oak Junction.

"Sit down, you two, and eat before it gets cold."

"But we need to go to the village, dear."

Junior looked at Lawrence and Catherine with a surprised look on his face.

"You can go after you eat. Not another word."

In the afternoon, as Lawrence left the house for the village, he looked to the south. He could see two-thirds of his parcel from where he stood near the road. The garden was one-hundred yards south of the house. He could see the new rows of turned soil under the warming sun. In a few weeks, they would see new green shoots coming up. Lawrence decided that Junior needed to come down with a shovel and throw more fresh manure on the garden just in case.

Lawrence swore an oath as he looked out over his land that he would never cut down the forest at the bottom of his property. He knew that if he did, the animal life there would suffer and be diminished. Lawrence knew that the family depended on those animals for life itself and that he would be a fool to disturb their environment. Lawrence was many things, but he was not raised to be a fool. He gave Catherine a kiss as he left their little house. "I'm leaving, dear. Do you need anything from town?"

"No dear, just be safe and come home as soon as you can."

Junior was still uneasy with the new intimacy between his sister and Lawrence, his "big brother." Lawrence asked Junior to split some large logs into four-inch-thick fence posts before he left and to toss some more fertilizer on the bottom half of the garden.

"It's a little thin down there, Junior," Lawrence said as he passed him on the way to the road and town.

"Alright, Lawrence, I'll do that first. It will be done before you return."

Lawrence wanted to build a split-rail fence along the north edge of his property near the main east-west road. There were plenty of people passing by day and night, and he wanted to keep strangers away from his family. The fence wouldn't keep people out, but it would let all of the travelers on the road know that the land belonged to someone.

As Lawrence left to see Father Magnus, he began to watch all of the people riding by him on horseback. He had never paid much attention to how they controlled their horses before. But now he could use his newfound horses as they did. If only he could learn to master the art of the wealthy, horseback riding.

He had ridden a donkey once as a small child and understood the mechanics of guiding and stopping a horse and making it run. But he had never done so himself. He had been bringing carrots and other treats to the horses since his return to Oak Junction from Chesterfield. He wanted the horses to know and trust him. He often thought that he understood animals much better than he understood people.

He could not understand the evil in men. He knew that most men came into this world with nothing and left the same way. Lawrence knew that most men tried to live their lives honorably. Whether they were successful at that or not was a different matter. Only God could make that final decision at the end of their lives. Lawrence knew there were wealthy men who had virtually everything a man could want who were nonetheless unhappy, mean, and cruel. And he knew that there were poor men as well who were mean and hurt people to acquire wealth. It didn't make any sense to Lawrence. He wanted to ask Father Magnus about this troubling reality.

The men who killed, robbed, and violated Catherine were young once, rich or poor, and had made choices that put them at the end of the sword or the gallows. Lawrence was bewildered and thought that this was perhaps some evidence of God and the Devil working in people's lives. Lawrence thought it might be God working in the good men and the Devil working in the others.

Lawrence reached the village after about half an hour of walking. The road went uphill to the rise that Lawrence had looked over that first day he'd arrived in Oak Junction. The land then rolled pleasantly down to the village. Some of the pastures were turning green again with new plants and others were a rich brown color from being freshly plowed. The view opened up into a wide vista in front of him.

He could see the village the entire time after passing over the ridge. There were turns in the road, and trees along both sides of it, but you could see Oak Junction and wonder what was happening there from up on that little hill that stood above the valley.

Oak Junction was becoming a larger village every day, engendering many stories of success and failure. Lawrence stopped to visit with Richard the fishmonger and Don the blacksmith on his way to the church. They were both his friends now and in a good humor.

Lawrence had his bag made of rabbit skins with him as usual with a few cured skins tucked in it. He stopped to sell them to the tanners and received his silver coins and then went on his way. It was a beautiful day with large white fluffy clouds and a blue sky overhead. He could smell the dampness in the soil left from a light morning rain. It was his favorite time of year. There was promise in the breeze, and he could sense that better times were coming.

It had been very difficult for the farmers and the tradesmen through the long cold winter, but now there seemed to be more opportunity in the wind. Lawrence could see it in the faces of the villagers and their customers, and he was getting a bit more silver for his pelts now.

Something was happening in his England, this land that he loved. Lawrence could see all the shops lined up along the wide winding pathway as it climbed up to the hill to the church. It was almost a road now. The trees were beginning to put on their broken cloak of green, and people were standing under and around them talking business and buying everyday items. Leather, meat, cloth, wine, and lumber were now available in the village market again after the long quiet winter.

There were wooden carts pulled by men and donkeys everywhere. If a child got lost here, it would take a long while for their mothers or fathers to find them if they got separated, so the women held their children close. A child or even a grown man could get hurt quickly if he didn't have his wits about him. Wagons and animals were passing by in every direction.

The nuns were busy this morning as Lawrence walked into the central aisle of the church. They were sweeping, dusting, and singing to themselves. Lawrence seldom came into the church this way, but when he did, he was reminded of how large, beautiful, and quiet it was. It was a sanctuary for those who were in need of one.

He knocked on the Father's door and was asked to enter as usual. The Father was behind his old desk reading a letter.

"How may I help you, Lawrence?"

"I need to ask a favor, Father."

"Yes, what might that be?"

"Junior found some silver in the saddlebags that were on the horses from the court. I didn't work for that silver, and I want to give it to the church."

"Yes, that seems like the proper thing to do, Lawrence, we will use it for the poor."

"And I need your help with my property deed."

"Yes, what do you need me to do?"

"I have horses now. I can travel to my other parcels with Junior and see what value they might have."

"I can help you with that quite easily. I will read the deed and find out exactly where the parcels are and write down directions to those parcels with the information from the deed. I don't remember all the details from the court proceedings. I can send Sister Ruth with you. She can read as well as anyone here." Lawrence handed Father his deed. It was all the proof in the world of Lawrence's wealth. He had no fear that Father Magnus would take the deed or cheat him. He was like a father to him now.

Father Magnus began reading and then writing something on another sheet of paper. Lawrence watched and saw a map beginning to take shape in front of him under the fleshy right hand of the Father. It was amazing for Lawrence to see the letters appear and become words and then sentences. Lawrence also watched the map that was developing in front of his own eyes on the table. Each time the Father dipped his pen into the ink and returned it to the paper, more of the world unfolded before him. He still couldn't read what was written, but he could read the map, and with the help of a person who could read the words, he would be able to find his land.

Lawrence's whole world had consisted of one small lane and several farms around his parents' dilapidated shack just a few years ago. Now he knew the way to Oak Junction and Chesterfield.

Father Magnus had probably traveled all over England in service to the church, or so Lawrence thought. He was pretty sure of that. He might have even been to London, but Lawrence never asked. When the Father was done with the map, he looked up and handed several papers back to Lawrence.

"There's a map here and several descriptive notes regarding your land's locations. There are two parcels that belong to you beyond this one. They have neighbors on either side. When you reach the Monroes' land, the land to the west is yours until it reaches the Jones'. It is on the main highway, like here at Oak Junction. Your land runs south for about a day's walk to where the river turns east. That is the southern boundary of your property. Everything inside those boundaries belongs to you: the forests, the lakes, and all the animals. You will be surprised at how vast it is. Your third parcel is another day's ride to the west. That land is next to Lord Huntington's estate. You shouldn't have any trouble finding it. You own the land west of his as well."

"I think I'll only go to the second parcel. I don't want to keep Sister Ruth away from her duties for too long."

"She's a little downhearted, Lawrence. Her mother just died, so the trip will do her good."

It was interesting to Lawrence to know that one of his parcels was next to Lord Huntington's estate. It showed how far Lawrence had come. His whole family once belonged to Lord Huntington, and now they owned neighboring properties. Lawrence smiled with some satisfaction. He now understood that his life was not limited by the expectations of others. It was only limited by his dreams and willingness to work for them to become reality.

"Thank you, Father, but there's just one more thing."

"Yes?"

"I would like Junior to learn to read and study mathematics. He's going to be a man of means someday, and he'll need those skills to survive."

"You can't read, Lawrence, and you've done well."

"Yes Father, but you were here to help me, as well as Don and Richard. They showed me how to trade and how much to ask for my pelts and so forth. I want Junior to be able to protect his family with his brain as well as a bow."

"You are a wise man, Lawrence. I'll see what I can do."

"Thank you, Father."

Lawrence forgot to ask Father about the good and evil in men, but he had other things to do. First, he stopped at the smithy's shop to order hinges and hasps on his way down the hill from the church. He decided to build the shutters and the door for the house before he left on his journey to the west as he wanted his family well protected. Junior had cut many planks using their wedges and ax. They had purchased a handsaw, too, so there were no excuses not to build the front door now. Lawrence understood that the door and shutters couldn't stop intruders, but it might give them second thoughts about trying to break into his little home, and they would help keep their little house warmer at night.

The Smiths' little house looked like many of the houses that dotted the countryside. It had a shingled roof, the walls were covered in whitewash, and smoke floated from its chimney. But this house was special due to the family that lived inside. They were people who had learned the secret to success. It turned out to be very simple. Treat all people with dignity, be honest in your business dealings, and work as if you were going to conquer the world. No one who ever conquered their little part of the world did it without work and heartache. A bit of good luck helps as well. Lawrence never forgot that.

When Lawrence returned home, he put Junior to work making the garden bigger than the year before. Junior turned the soil and mixed in the manure while Lawrence was away looking at his other property in the west. There was plenty of food in the larder, and Junior was getting bigger and stronger. He was nearly fifteen years old now, Catherine was nineteen, and Lawrence was twenty-one.

Lawrence laughed to himself as he imagined Junior finding and moving more stones as he dug in the garden. There was no end to the stones that lay buried in the soil, but they too turned out to be a gift. Rather than complain about them, when they found one, they added it to the pile that stood near the corner of the house. They used them as building materials. They built the fireplace in the house with them, and one day they would be used to build a wall around the farm.

They built the doors and shutters before Lawrence left.

Chapter Nine

In the morning, Lawrence left Oak Junction for the church on horseback. He brought the second horse for Sister Ruth. He wasn't as confident as he had hoped to be about riding, but he felt better the longer he did it. By the time he reached the village, he was quite at ease on his horse.

Everyone in the village knew the story of how Lawrence received his horses. They also knew that Lawrence had never ridden before, and they watched him with apprehension as he practiced. They didn't want him to fall, but some were certain that he would. He was fine, however, and he made it to the church without mishap. He had imagined himself falling off in many different ways for many different reasons. He surprised himself as well as the many people in the village who watched him pass by.

Perhaps the time he spent feeding the horses and talking to them had helped them be relaxed around him and to trust him. They were calm, strong, and relaxed. He groomed and fed them every night and in the morning. He talked to them quietly as if they were his own children. The horses certainly knew who Lawrence was by the time he began to ride them. His favorite horse was the black one with three white stockings and a white blaze on his head. The other horse was brown with a golden tail. He thought that they were both magnificent. The three of them reached the church after a lovely, if not cautious, trip. Lawrence helped Sister Ruth place her sidesaddle on the thick brown horse and Lawrence cinched the saddle tightly.

"What have you named the horses, Lawrence?"

"The horses haven't been named yet, Sister. I have been waiting for Elizabeth and Catherine to come up with their names," Lawrence answered. Father Magnus had made arrangements for them to stay in the church at their destination in Themstead with Father Gregory.

It took most of the day at a slow walk and a trot every now and then to reach the village of Themstead. The nun was an excellent rider and coaxed Lawrence on once in a while to put his horse into a gallop and then into a run. Lawrence tried it when she asked him to, but he wasn't as comfortable as he thought he would be. Time and practice would change that. Lawrence and the nun found the church easily and settled in for the night. It was getting dark when they arrived, so they decided to eat and get up early in the morning to scout Lawrence's land. Lawrence learned a lot from Sister Ruth on their journey. She had come from a large, poor family, and several of the sisters had left the family to become nuns as she had. Most of the nun's siblings had left home early for lack of food as Lawrence had. She didn't know her parents well because she left home when she was quite young, but she saw them and now knew them as adult friends. Her brothers worked the land with her parents and their own families. She had many nieces and nephews and saw them as often as she could.

Sister Ruth was still troubled by the untimely death of her mother, and this trip had given her something else to occupy her mind and her time. Lawrence and Ruth talked for most of their journey to Themstead.

Sister Ruth believed in God, of course, and knew her mother would go to heaven at some point. But she still missed her and had a heavy heart. She had never loved a man and was completely happy in her life. She read the Bible daily and knew it all by heart. She could not explain the death and misery of young families or their children or why there was evil and disease in the world. She believed that God had a plan for all of us and that we should all pray daily. She believed Christ died for our sins and that we should all be baptized.

By the time Lawrence reached Themstead, he knew Sister Ruth very well. He knew his Bible stories even better. She knew all of them and told many of them to Lawrence in great detail as they rode to the town of Themstead.

In the morning, they had the wonderful warm potato soup made by Sister Susan, a young, short nun at the great church where they had spent the night. They thanked Father Gregory for his hospitality.

They were about to leave when he came up to Lawrence and held out his hand to shake Lawrence's again as he had done the night before. He spoke to Lawrence once more before they left.

"We all know of your bravery and kindness to others, Lawrence. As you no doubt have already discovered in your life, Lawrence, goodness does not go unrewarded. We all can see that in you and your life story."

Lawrence was taken aback. He had no idea that people would know of him so far from home. He wondered what would have happened if he had done something wrong or evil to someone. Would that news travel as far and as fast? It made him think about his life and how he would have to live it.

Lawrence and Sister Ruth headed west on the main road, sometimes sheltered in the shade of huge trees that hung over the road like giant mushrooms. Sometimes they were in the bright sunshine and had trouble seeing the road ahead because of it.

There were many traders and families walking on the road and riding by on horses. Sometimes a horse and rider would come running through the throng of people with what seemed like little regard for the safety of those walking in front of them. It seemed like a miracle that no one was injured, or so Lawrence thought.

In time, they came upon an old woman and her crippled daughter. They were walking slowly down the edge of the road in the shadows of the large trees.

As Lawrence and Sister Ruth came upon the two women, Sister Ruth recognized the pair in front of them instantly and slowed her horse to a slow gait. She could never forget the horrible accident years ago when this child was nearly crushed by a falling tree during a sudden windstorm.

"Hello, Rebecca, how does God find you today?"

"Judith and I are very well. Thank you very kindly for remembering us, Sister Ruth."

"Judith is very often in my heart and prayers, Rebecca. Do you know of the Monroe family? Do you know where we might find their property?"

"Just up the road a little farther on the left side. The road here is at the northern edge of their land."

"Thank you, Rebecca, for your help."

They soon reached the west corner of the Monroes' property and the beginning of Lawrence's parcel according to the Father's map and Rebecca's help. The land was lush with many trees standing among some open spaces ready to farm.

It sloped away to the south from the road, like Oak Junction, but it was mostly a thick, deep, dark forest. Lawrence knew right away what he must do. A river ran through the land, cutting it into two parts. He would create a clearing in the forest near the main road and build a sawmill. Maybe not today, maybe not tomorrow, but in his lifetime, he or Junior would be a great dealer in lumber. They would sell lumber for houses, wagons, and large sailing ships. There was a forest of ships masts below him on his land as far as he could see.

He looked at Sister Ruth, and she smiled back at Lawrence.

"There is a God, Lawrence, and some of us are rewarded in this life too," Sister Ruth said with a warm smile.

On the way back to Oak Junction, Lawrence asked Sister Ruth about the old, deserted village near Oak Junction but farther north. She described its history for him. It had been where many quarries were located in the distant past. The village was built because of those quarries. The church had been built as an outpost on the way to the north from Nottingham and to the sea in the west with the stone from those quarries.

Farmland had eventually been carved out of the forest over time as the population grew. Lawrence's early family had been a part of that rich history, but none of them had ever been educated and he knew very little of their family lore.

Sister Ruth was aware of many horrible stories from the past when highwaymen ran wilder than they did now, and she relished in telling Lawrence many of them. Lawrence felt relatively safe on the roads today, as did Sister Ruth. She was a fatalist and knew her life was always in God's hands. Lawrence had his bow and knife because he thought exactly the opposite was true.

Chapter Ten

Junior had done his chores while Lawrence was off to Themstead. He had enlarged the garden, turned the soil, and carried many rocks up to near the house. This fall, they would build a second fireplace and chimney in the new room and hoped they could sell enough skins to the tanners for silver to pay the carpenters. Rabbits were still so plentiful that at dinnertime, they often joked about renaming their place Rabbit Junction. Everyone thought that that was very funny and quite true.

In the evening after everyone was asleep, Lawrence and Catherine finally spoke about their family life and hopes to each other. Lance lay near both of them with his ears twitching as though he were listening. "Catherine, my dear, the land to the west is larger than we could ever have hoped for. It is many times larger than this parcel at Oak Junction. The soil is as rich as any I have ever seen."

"Will you and Junior be up to the task at hand?"

"Yes, but there is no hurry. The land here will feed and clothe us until we can make the move farther to the west. If we never leave here, we will be very comfortable all of our long lives."

"That's all that I ask, Lawrence. I don't need much as long as we are together for a very long time."

"I feel exactly as you do, my dear, but there is a possibility that our children will be more comfortable and secure than we could ever dream of."

"I'm sure you're right, my dear, but I don't want you to take on too much. I want you here at my side forever."

"I feel the same, Catherine, but we have a chance to do something great, and I think we must try."

"I know you, Lawrence, and I know that I cannot stop you once you have a dream. Just be mindful of your health and safety, for all our sake."

"I will, my dear."

When the conversation ended, they kissed and soon drifted off to sleep in each other's arms. But not before Lawrence had formulated a rough plan of what he was going to do. It would take time, but he was a patient man. Maybe not as patient as he thought he was, but he was smart enough to know that this plan would take several years and that he couldn't rush it even if he wanted to.

The carpenters started building the walls of the new room soon after Lawrence returned from Themstead. They had plenty of timber and more experience than the year before. Soon there was another room, equal in size to the first, attached to their house. The carpenters then plastered the walls and finished the roof. The smoked venison and other food items could now be moved into the second room. It was also used to store all the tools and to keep the goat safe at night.

The family now had twice the space and had room for a couple of proper beds. Lawrence and Junior started on the frames as Catherine worked on the mattresses and pillows. The main ingredient for the beds was dry straw, and they had plenty of that from the previous year's harvest, which had dried in the eaves of the roof.

They knew it would be nice to get up off the floor and sleep on a soft bed of straw. It took a day to build the bed frames and about the same for the mattresses. There was a large mattress for Lawrence, Katherine, and Elizabeth. Junior had a smaller mattress for himself. They were all still in the same room together, but at least the goat and the horses now had their own shelter from the weather in the second room.

The next day, a beautiful spring day, it finally arrived. Lawrence hoped for rain now that they were inside, and rain it did. There were some small issues, but they were soon solved by Lawrence and Junior's hard work. The main task at hand now was to kill enough rabbits and fowl to fill the larder. It had been depleted in large part through the winter.

The deer were still passing through at the rock outcrop and eating the fine grasses that grew there. Lawrence didn't want to kill one until fall came. They would have plenty of root vegetables and rabbit to get them through the next winter. If they shot one large buck, it would be the end of a perfect year. The garden did well, and they had plenty of extra vegetables to sell at the market this year. Food was not a problem, nor was shelter.

The animals were out of the weather now in the shed when the weather turned bad, and so were Lawrence and his family. Catherine had a proper hearth for cooking and all the pots and pans she needed. It was going to be a great Christmas. There was even a little silver hidden away just in case.

As life became easier, Lawrence thought that come the middle of spring, they would start regularly going to church. They hadn't had the time before with all of the building and hunting, but now they would have more leisure time. They all thought it was a great idea. Catherine didn't have her normal cycle in December, but this time she knew what that meant.
She waited for Lawrence to come to bed before she told him the news.

"We are going to have another child, Lawrence, isn't that wonderful?"

"Of course it is, my dear. I am so glad that we will have a playmate for Elizabeth. I just hope that you will have an easy delivery like the last time. That was a blessing."

"Well dear, I've talked to the other mothers, and most agree that the second child is easier to deliver than the first."

"I hope they are right, dear. I suppose they are the ones who should know. My knowledge of these matters is limited to the farm animals. I will just hope for the best. I love you, dear."

"I love you too, Lawrence, and I thank God for you every day of my life."

"I feel the same, dear. I know I don't tell you often enough about how strong my love for you is."

"I know, Lawrence, be sure of that. I know and love you more each day."

Another baby was coming sometime around September. They would be ready. They had planned everything as well as possible, and the midwife was notified.

This was going to be the year of the plow. Lawrence and Junior were getting tired of working the garden with the shovel and hoe. It just took too much time, and the size of the harvest was still very small. The plow would change that. The horses had made all of that possible.

Lawrence had been saving his silver coins and rabbit hides for this great event in their lives. Yet it came much sooner than expected. Lawrence had thought he would have to save for at least two years for a horse. But now he had those two horses that he had so badly needed, and still had the money and the skins he was going to use to buy them. He could use that money now to buy the plow this spring.

The family prayed every night at supper with full hearts and full stomachs. Lawrence was very excited about the new baby coming. Elizabeth was two years old now, and she was becoming much easier to care for. Lawrence was even able to offer some help with Elizabeth at times, limited as it was.

There were many preparations necessary for the second baby's birth. The house was quite comfortable, and small though it was, it was airtight against the wind and rain. It was the year 1772, and things looked quite good for the family and their future.

As the weather improved, Junior set the fish traps and brought back fresh meat. Lawrence walked up the tract from the house to the main road almost every day. There was a clear dirt pathway through the grass and bushes on their land now that led to the road.

The last of the snow had melted. He walked on the side of the road away from the tracks of the wagons on the main road. They were often still filled with slush or water from the melting winter snow. He tried to keep his feet dry and warm, but he wasn't always successful.

Catherine had made him a new set of clothes: a pair of britches, a shirt, and a jacket made of rabbit hides. The jacket worked wonderfully against the early spring wind. Lawrence reached the village in forty-five minutes. He wanted to walk and build up his strength again. He felt weakened from his winter of leisure. Winter often brought a malaise that the walking also helped to end. There wasn't much to do through the winter and so Lawrence hadn't had much physical activity. Dumping the chamber pots and garbage was all he had done for the most part.

Junior had done the rest of the winter work and was pleased to get out to do it. Most people were still inside their homes and shops now as Lawrence walked through the village.

Don, the blacksmith, loved this time of year for obvious reasons. Lawrence could smell the now-familiar aroma of the blacksmith's shop, and in the early mornings such as this, he could often hear the hammer on the anvil.

Later in the day, the talking and rushing about of people would drown out the sound, even in early spring when fewer people were in the village. Lawrence and Catherine weren't the only people near or in the village expecting a child. Jane, the fishmonger's wife, Don's wife Mary, and several others were expecting. It had been a very long, cold winter.

Lawrence walked up toward the church and found Don in his shop, on the right side of the path, as usual. He was stoking his fire, and at his happiest when the air was cold and fresh like it was at the moment.

"Good morning, Don."

"Good morning, Lawrence, how does God find you today?"

"I'm fine, Don, thank you."

"I see you brought me those pieces of lumber that I had asked for, Lawrence."

"Yes, just as you had asked."

"Fine, son, fine."

Don was a big man. He was not as tall as Lawrence, but he was as strong and almost as large as an ox. You couldn't see many of his muscles due to a thick layer of fat that covered his entire body. He wasn't round and fat like Father Magnus, however. Don was taller and well known for his love of meat, potatoes, and beer. He could eat and drink with the best of them.

"I can fix you up with the plow in a few days, Lawrence. I have some parts on hand, but I'll have to make most of the others."

"That's fine, Don, the ground is still too hard to even begin to think about plowing. I'd say maybe four more weeks or so, and then I'll be able to start in the garden."

"I think you're right, lad."

"Have you seen Father Magnus, Don?"

"No, it's still too early for him to be up and about. He eats a late, slow breakfast and doesn't care for this cold spring air. It's a blessing to me, I must say."

"How's your family, Don?"

"Oh, the girls are fine. Mary is cooking something as always, and Ginger is right next to her. They're two peas in a pod."

"How old is Ginger now?"

"Oh, let me think a moment. She's fourteen. I think she's a woman now."

"Anyone showing a proper interest in her yet?"

"Not really. She spends most of her days in the house helping her mother."

"How is your wife feeling now that she is expecting?"

"She's fine, just happy to be with child. It's been a long spell without a pregnancy. We are still hoping for a boy, but only God knows about these things I suppose."

"Has Ginger talked with Junior at all?"

"I don't think so, why?"

"Well, Junior's nearly 15 now. He'll be wanting a wife soon enough."

"You don't say? You're probably right, Lawrence. I hadn't thought much about it."

"Just a thought, Don. You have a fine family and have always treated my family fairly. One good turn deserves another if you understand my meaning."

"That's something to think about Lawrence, that's for sure."

"Catherine and I would love to have her in the family if she's of a mind."

"What about Junior? Has he said anything about Ginger?"

"I'm not sure what he might have said to Catherine or anyone else, but let's have them see each other once in a while, and we'll see what happens."

"Let's have the wives set it up then, Don."

Don couldn't believe his good fortune. Junior was a fine young man with unlimited potential. Don's wife would be beside herself when she heard the news. Lawrence had hoped that Junior might work with Don and learn a valuable trade. Besides, if they were going to build a lumber mill, it would be helpful for Lawrence if Junior understood the art of the blacksmith.

Don had no sons of his own, and Junior's help would be a blessing to the smithy. It could also give Junior and Ginger a chance to get to know each other in an easy and natural way.

"Don, do you ever need help with the shop?"

"Absolutely. If I had a dependable lad to help around here, I could do more than twice the work I'm doing now. I've been looking for one, but I have little free time these days or so it seems."

"Do you have enough work to keep two men busy?"

"I could use help two or three days a week, most certainly. I send a lot of work to the village of Themstead now."

"What if Junior came to work for you a few days a week and helped you out? You could teach him your trade, and he could visit with Ginger?"

"What about you and your farm, Lawrence?"

"I have two horses now, Don. They can pull a plow. I can hunt enough by myself to feed all of us. Once we've planted the crops, I won't need Junior until harvest time."

"That's a good point."

"I want Junior to spend more time in the village now, and to learn about business and make friends with all of the merchants. This could be the start of that."

"I see your point, Lawrence."

"He could still live at Oak Junction and walk to your stall on the days that you need him, Don. I'm sure if there was a pretty young girl at the end of his walk, he wouldn't miss many days' work."

"Right you are, Lawrence, right you are."

Don's father had been the blacksmith in the village until he had to retire, as his father had been before him. Don was the only son, and if he had any dreams of sailing away to a different life, his father, also named Don, made sure that they didn't come true. He had to teach his son his craft so all of the generations of smithies before him would not have died in vain. The village was always in need of a good blacksmith, and Don's family had always filled that need. That wouldn't change if Don could help it.

Don the blacksmith and his family were highly respected and had a fine income. They lived in a proper stone house, old though it may be, behind their shop. Don's grandfather, Jonas, had built this house when he came to Oak Junction many, many years ago. Don always knew he was to take over his father's shop. He had no choice in the matter. It was a small village without a smith when Jonas's father arrived with his family those many years ago. Don's father became the smithy as he was the only son and as his father had been before him. Then Don became the blacksmith, and he still had no sons. They did well enough, but Junior's help would make a difference in his and Mary's life, especially now that she was expecting.

Don had another chance for a son now, but a healthy baby and a safe delivery was all that they prayed for. If they had a son, he would grow up to become the new blacksmith. They still had time; Don was thirty-nine and Mary was twenty-nine. They had been waiting a very long time for God to give them another child and another chance.

If they had a son, their old age would be more comfortable. If God gave him another daughter, they would make the best of it. They had a small garden in the back of their home, and chickens and plenty of eggs. They wouldn't starve, that was for certain. They also had a small room they could rent. It wasn't their first choice, but they would be fine either way.

Eventually, Father Magnus made his daily appearance in the lane. He walked through the village after morning prayers and his breakfast. He felt the importance of his responsibilities as the church's representative and was a genuinely warm and caring priest. He knew of many clergymen who were not, and so did the villagers. Father Magnus had only been there for six years and was a welcome change.

The previous priest was a problem from day one. He had a very high regard for himself and very little for anyone else. He was a tall thin man, and he looked down on everyone in a literal sense because of his height and in a stern manner because of his ego and pride. He wasn't the best fit for his type of work.

He alienated himself quickly, in fact, from most everyone. His first great mistake was to complain about his food. There was never enough and it didn't suit him, or so he said. The nuns, who prepared his meals, were not very happy with him about that, and the food did not improve. It was the same food that everyone else had to eat, and it was fine. But nothing was good enough for Father Alfred.

He had created the worst possible set of circumstances for himself at the outset of his tenure in the village. The nuns disliked him, and not without reason. They disliked him because he was rude and bossy. If there were any issues with the meals, those that were of less quality, quantity, or freshness always went to Father Alfred due to his constant complaints. The nuns were only human after all, and their good nature had been pushed well past its limit.

Church attendance dropped off. Father Alfred's attitude did not go unnoticed in the small village and was reflected in the donation box and the volunteers. It didn't take long for his superiors to send someone out to Oak Junction for an informal chat. "How are things going in the village? Why have the donations dropped off?" And so on.

The Father disliked his accommodations, his staff, the nuns and monks, and the villagers. He complained that they were all cold and distant. He came from a large diocese where he had served for many years. Things had been going downhill rapidly for a number of reasons, and finally, the diocese thought a change would be good for everyone, so he had been sent to Oak Junction.

It was great for Stanton, the town that he left, but terrible for Oak Junction. He lasted in Oak Junction for almost a year, and it was a disaster. He was lucky to get out of the town with his life. The village had great expectations for their new clergyman, and he fell so far short that the gap was insurmountable, as were the hard feelings.

There was actually a celebration when he left. It was near Easter, but everyone in Oak Junction knew what was really being celebrated. When Father Magnus came to replace him, he faced a dubious group of parishioners coming back to church to see what he was like. But he was the complete opposite of Father Alfred.

First, Father Magnus was younger and could relate to village life. Alfred had come from a large town, where his personality was less important. In this village, small as it was, Father Magnus's personality, made all the difference in the world. He walked the village every day and became well acquainted with most everyone. The nuns and monks loved him soon enough, and that was vital for his survival there.

Everyone was much happier, and that showed in the church, the village, and the donation box. Father Magnus wasn't interested in power or prestige. He was a true servant of God. He had no interest in the politics of the church, and he would be quite happy to stay at Oak Junction until God called him home.

Lawrence was unaware of all this history in the village. He was only interested in finding some way for young Junior to learn to read. He had hoped Father Magnus would allow Junior to spend evening prayers with the monks and then study more reading with them.

The father agreed and had spoken to the monks. They were all eager to help another person to learn to read the Bible. So that part of Lawrence's plan had been accomplished. Junior knew that Lawrence wanted him to learn to read, and he was willing to give it a try. He realized what an advantage that would be for him in the future, and he was very eager. He did not, however, know about the blacksmith job or about Ginger yet.

Mary and Catherine did talk a few days after Lawrence and Don the blacksmith had spoken to each other. Mary said she would make sure that Ginger would be outside with her father whenever Junior was in the village.

Lawrence and Junior came to the village at least twice a week in the early spring with fresh fish from their traps, and rabbits or skins. As the weather got warmer, they would come more often. This would be the perfect way for Junior and Ginger to meet and get to know each other.

One morning at breakfast, Lawrence spoke to Junior, who was sitting across the table from him. "We've been talking, Junior, Catherine, and I, and we want you to start working with Don the smithy. There's not much for you to do around here this early in the year, and Don needs a hand."

"I can see where that makes sense. Will he pay me something, Lawrence?"

"A little, perhaps, but you will become richer with the knowledge he will give you. I have no more to teach you. You can fish, hunt, and farm now. In the village, you will learn to read and create things with iron. You will have all the tools to become a successful man."

"What about the mill?"

"This *is* about the mill and the family's future plans, Junior. You will make all the iron parts for it, nails, hinges, straps, everything. Between you and me, we will build the mill. We will need more laborers, of course, but we will design and build it ourselves."

"Are you willing to do this for your future?"

"Absolutely, Lawrence, I can see that it is to my advantage."

"If anything ever happens to me, Junior, you will be able to take care of our family," Lawrence said very seriously.

"And besides, I think Don has a sweet young daughter," Junior added.

"Really, how'd you know that, Junior?"

"Oh, I've seen her and even talked to her in the market once or twice. She and her mother are often at the fishmonger's stall."

It seemed that Junior was one step ahead of Lawrence regarding Ginger.

Junior was smarter than most people realized. He could even read a little already. He had started to learn a bit from his late mother.

Chapter Eleven

Lawrence and Junior finally started to build the fence on the north end of the property along the main road as Lawrence had planned. They split tree trunks for days. They ended up with rough two-by-fours of lumber about six feet long. Some of those were cut in half to create the uprights or supports. The men dug deep holes along a centerline, placed the support pieces into the holes, and filled the holes back in while someone held them at a forty-five-degree angle and nailed them together. Then long pieces of wood were laid across the crossed posts that had been partially buried in the ground. It was quite simple. It was a long boundary line, perhaps three-hundred feet or so.

It took several days, but when it was completed, there was a proper fence that ran along the side of the road that everyone could see. The fence would stand there for years. It marked the private property of Lawrence Smith.

The family ate lunch at their outside table every morning as the weather warmed. It was where they had fought and killed the two highwaymen with the help of the carpenters, Seth and John. The area held sad memories for the family, but those would pass in time.

Elizabeth was almost three now, and she tried to help with the cooking and serving of the meals. She would always know Lawrence as her father, and she was his daughter in his heart.

For Junior, his family life was a little more complicated. Lawrence had started out as Junior's savior. Junior sometimes saw him as a father figure, and he often saw him as a big brother as well. And now, almost four years into their life together, he was his brother-in-law. It was complicated, but they had little time or need to discuss it.

With winter now gone, and the earth warming, it was time to plant the fields again. They needed the plow, and Junior was beside himself with expectation. This year was going to be very special indeed. Their farming life was going to be much easier now. They would plant nearly four times the land than in the past year. Lawrence and Junior had both seen men working with a horse and plow before, but they could never dream that they would ever own a horse or a plow themselves.

If Don had kept his word, and he always did, the plow was waiting for them in the village as they sat eating their breakfast. It was the middle of March now, and weeks had passed since Lawrence had given those pieces of wood to Don.

Lawrence and Junior packed their new bags with pelts again to take to market. Catherine had made new bags for them out of hides and cloth. They were large backpacks. They could stuff them with anything they wanted to take to town to sell: fish, turkey, rabbit, meat, or vegetables.

If they had a large harvest this year, Father Magnus might let them use his donkey cart to bring all the vegetables into the village to sell. Oak Junction wasn't a town yet. But with its great location and a growing population, it would be a large town in time.

Lawrence had not seen his parents for four years but had often sent word to them through traders or Father Magnus or the nuns who would travel through the villages looking for converts or fulfilling their normal church duties.

Lawrence was planning to visit them very soon with silver from all the pelts and the fresh fish he would sell at the market. Silver money was easier to hide and carry on horseback. He thought he could make the journey to his parents' shack in one long day's ride on his horse when the time came.

As Lawrence and Junior walked to the village in the morning, they made plans for the year. It was a cool morning with bright, white fluffy clouds floating above them. Birds flew back and forth in the trees building nests. They worked constantly, not unlike Lawrence and his family.

Lawrence, a man now, talked about the challenges ahead of them and about the new life Junior was about to begin with Don and the monks. Lawrence wasn't worried about Junior. Lawrence knew he was smart and a hard worker. Junior would be the best apprentice any blacksmith ever had. There was no doubt about that as far as Lawrence was concerned.

Lawrence and Junior walked along the new fence they had just finished under the giant trees that lined the main road and marveled at how long and straight it was. It had taken them a week to complete. They had done a great job. It ran under many large ancient trees along the winding road to Oak Junction. It was a beautiful boundary for their property. The boundary was made up of the giant trees and the new fence that would last a lifetime or maybe more. Parts of it were in the shade for several hours of each day. People walking on the road would be able to lean up against the uprights to eat and rest. It would become the perfect spot for lunch on a day's journey and a reminder of the fact that on the other side was private property.

As they reached the rise in the road, Junior could see across the valley straight ahead to the fields where he had lived with his parents. Off to the right, he could see the church where Father Magnus lived and the growing village around it. It was quite beautiful this time of year. New growth was sprouting again in that endless cycle that humans follow for such a short, hard time.

It was sometimes sad for Junior to look out over the village to the other side where he had lived with his parents and be reminded of them. But it also reminded him of the blessings that he now possessed.

He had a man in his life to go for help and advice, and he knew that he was loved by all of his family. He had a roof over his head and a purpose in life that he hadn't had before. Perhaps he had to mature too soon, but that was life. He had no choice. As Lawrence had said, "If you don't have a plan, you will starve."

Junior loved his life more than he could express. He looked at Lawrence and remembered that little starving boy he had been on the side of the road where the fence now stood. He thought about how Lawrence had promised him nothing except hard work and rabbit dinners. He thought about how Lawrence had saved Catherine from ridicule and loneliness by marrying her and how much he loved Elizabeth, the child of a murderer and rapist. Junior would slowly begin to understand the relationship between Lawrence and his sister as he matured over the next year.

Junior also thought about how much Lawrence had taught him and how he had changed his life forever. Junior was well respected, sheltered, and well-fed. He owed all of this to

Lawrence, and Lawrence asked only that they be a family. And now he was going to learn to read and to be a blacksmith and maybe find his future wife.

Lawrence noticed that the morning was still a little cool. Lance walked behind the two young men and looked at the birds above him flitting in the trees.

Lawrence liked to walk to the village along this beautiful length of road. It gave him time to think and be at peace. He also liked to listen to the voices of all the travelers on the road. Lawrence heard different accents and even different languages now and then on the now busy road. It was his time, too, to contemplate his circumstances.

He was completely happy but still wanted to accomplish more. He had discovered a drive in himself that he didn't recognize. It had only manifested itself when he needed to survive on his own. He often wondered if he was different from other men.

He had decided up to this point in his young life that the differences between men were all created by need and the circumstances that they found themselves in. Anyone would do what he had done or die trying, or so he thought. There was no other good choice, as far as he could see. He wanted to ask Father Magnus about this when he saw him again.

The two young men reached the village and visited with Richard and his wife, June, as they did most every time they came to town. She had morning sickness now and was very pleased with herself for being pregnant. They were thrilled about having their first child, and at the same time, worried about all the changes it would bring to their lives. She gave most of the credit to her husband for her condition. She often told Catherine with a warm smile, "We would have a thousand children if it were up to my husband."

Lawrence and Junior walked farther up the hill to the far side of the village on the winding path they traveled so often. At the tanner's, they showed their pelts and struck a deal quickly. The tanner was a fair man with a good reputation in the village. He made a good living and had no need to cheat his clients. He was a tall thin man with piercing grey eyes and white hair. He reminded Junior of an eagle, though he never mentioned it to anyone.

The white winter pelts were highly prized. Lawrence had several of them to trade for silver now. Junior was learning the art of trading from watching Lawrence, just as Lawrence had learned by watching Richard and Don. It was a valuable skill to develop. Everyone in the village knew that they would always come to a fair deal with Lawrence.

The two men walked back through the village and turned left up a lane toward the church. Then they turned right at the butcher's stall. Don was just past the candlemaker on the right pathway leading to the church of Father Magnus.

Many crooked little paths ran up the hill to the church through the village. It sometimes made Lawrence think about life with all its choices that had to be made.

Don had the plow sitting in the front of his stall when the men arrived. He was very proud of what he had created. Everyone in the village saw it as they walked by Don's shop. Ginger and Mary were both there with him.

"Good morning, Lawrence, Junior."

"Good morning, Don, ladies," Lawrence and Junior answered.

"The plow is done," Don said, pointing to it with pride.

"It looks quite stout, Don."

"Yes, Junior, this needs to be as strong as possible to turn the heavy earth."

The plow had one large curved blade that Don had hammered into shape from a single piece of flat iron on his anvil. It was attached to a long thick piece of timber that was six inches thick and four feet long. It had a couple of steel rings bolted into the large timber to attach the horse's ropes near the bottom of the plow. It also had rings near the top to run the horse's reins through so that it could be driven in the direction the plowman wanted. It was a fine piece of the smithy's art.

Junior looked at Ginger, and her eyes smiled back at him. She and her mother had several long conversations about this moment. Their lives could be changed forever if Junior thought he might want to get to know Ginger better than he already did.

"How has your journey been to the village today?"

"Perfect, Ginger, it's a beautiful day," Junior replied.

He had been interested in Ginger for some time but had been afraid to push the matter. He thought that she was quite pretty.

Lawrence and Don wandered to the back of the shop to talk. Lawrence counted out the silver for the plow and also produced a rabbit. Don and Lawrence could hear Junior and Ginger still talking in the distance behind them.

"This rabbit is for Junior's dinner tonight, Don."

"Thanks, Lawrence, but we have plenty."

Junior was talking with Mary and Ginger in a quiet voice. Junior was calm and at ease as Lawrence handed Don the plump rabbit.

"You don't have to do this, Lawrence."

"I know, Don, but humor me. It will make me and Catherine feel better if we contribute to Junior's meals."

"So be it, Lawrence, but don't fret over this."

The two men could still here Ginger and Junior talking behind them as they finished their business.

"When do you start to work with daddy, Junior?"

"Today's the day."

Ginger seemed genuinely interested. She already knew all of what was to happen, but she showed a genuine interest.

"Would you like a drink of water?"

"Yes, thank you, Ginger."

"I'm off to see the Father, Don," Lawrence said as he started to walk to the front of the stall.

"Fine then, Lawrence. I'll send Junior off to the church when I'm done with him here."

"Goodbye ladies," Lawrence said as he headed toward the low door. He ducked under a tree branch as he walked out into the lane and turned right toward the church and Father Magnus.

Lawrence was quite pleased with himself as he walked up the lane. He had put his stepson on a course that might improve his life immensely.

If Lawrence were to look back over his shoulder, he would see most of the village now below him as he climbed up the hill to the church, but he did not. Lawrence would have seen throngs of people walking up and down the paths between the stalls, buying or looking at products that they needed but perhaps could not yet afford.

Most people in the village were wealthier than those who came into town to purchase items at the stalls. Some visitors, however, were large landowners who had worked to improve their lot over many years and had done so quite successfully. It was not impossible to become wealthy from a humble beginning, but it was not easy. Lawrence would also have seen Junior and Ginger, still talking casually. Lawrence had other matters on his mind today.

Lawrence went into the church and found Father Magnus at his desk as usual after knocking and being invited in.

"It has all been arranged, Lawrence. When Junior finishes with the smithy today, he will come here for evening prayers and Bible study. He will come every night he is in the village."

"Thank you, Father. I just talked with Don. After we've planted our crops, Catherine, Elizabeth, and I will come to Bible study twice a week. That is, at least for as long as Catherine can make the journey up to the church. I may put her on the horse once in a while, but I'm a little leery about that."

"I can understand that, Lawrence, as those horses are quite large and nervous. I'd hate to see her thrown off and hurt."

"My thoughts exactly, Father. I'm off to see my parents and brothers tomorrow, and I'll spend one night with them, at least. Could you send one of the sisters to stay with Catherine while I'm away?"

"Of course, Lawrence, I know just the nuns to send."

"I don't expect any harm to come to them, but we do live near the main road, and many people pass by there day and night as you surely know."

"I'll send a couple of the younger nuns. They'll enjoy playing with Elizabeth as well as giving Catherine some company. They can help her with dinner. It must be getting more difficult as she progresses in her condition."

"Thank you, Father."

The journey to Riverside was easy on horseback the next morning. Lawrence saw the spot where he had shared his rabbit with the three men at the fire. He was amazed at how different the world looked from the back of a tall horse. The forest was still thick and green, but somehow it looked smaller and shorter than when he was on foot.

He rode for several hours through open countryside with large green fields and trees lining the road on either side. Many people on horseback passed him as he went on his way and smiled "the smile of the rich" at him. It took him some time to understand what was happening. They all assumed that he was wealthy because he rode a horse. It was one thing that helped people tell the class of a man or a woman. Lawrence had never given it much thought before.

He could smell the farm as he got closer to home. A large herd of cattle created that familiar aroma, and he could hear the birds up in the trees making their nests as he rode comfortably on his horse. The land was much more beautiful than he remembered. Perhaps it was because he was a free man now with land of his own.

Lawrence thought about the animals and how they never seemed to give up hope as he saw the birds rebuilding their nests. Soon enough, he could see the little house he had grown up in. It was nothing more than one small room, like his own new home. He was surprised at how much they looked alike. He had forgotten how small it was.

His parents couldn't believe it when they saw him ride up on a horse. They had watched him with suspicion as he approached. Then they finally recognized him. Lawrence dismounted and handed his mother two rabbits for dinner.

"He actually has a horse!" his brother cried out. They didn't even recognize him at first sight. They expected him to be walking, like most poor people. The Smiths had heard stories about their son from the nuns and Father Magnus, but they dared not believe any of them until they came from his own lips.

"Mother, Father, I'm so glad you're well," Lawrence greeted them. His big brother Willie came running in from the fields and received a hug when Lawrence was finished hugging his parents. Then he jumped on his little brother and slapped his back.

"It's all true then."

"Calm down, brother, calm down."

"You have a horse! We're rich, father."

"Now, now, son, give Lawrence a chance to catch his breath."

"You don't know the half of it," Lawrence whispered.

"You are all coming to live with me this winter. I'm building a new room on my house just for you."

The family embraced again, and Lawrence's mother cried in happiness. She wanted the family to be together again but knew that she couldn't intrude until invited, Lawrence being married now and with a child. She couldn't wait to see the child, and there was more good news.

"We are having another baby in a few months, Mother." She sat down and took a deep breath.

"Heaven above, dear," she said as she looked at her husband. "It's more than I ever could have asked for."

"We heard you had a daughter, Lawrence."

"Yes, Elizabeth, and now with the new one on the way, we want all of you to be with us. My brother-in-law lives with us also. His name is Junior."

"How will we manage, Lawrence? There will be so many to feed."

"Don't worry, Mother, we have good land, plenty of game, and a plow."

"You have a plow?"

"Yes, father, I have a plow and two horses. Life will be easier for you from now on, I promise."

"He has two horses and a plow," his mother repeated in wonder.

"I heard, my sweet wife, that he has two horses and a plow," his father repeated.

"Who works on your farm then, Lawrence?" His father remembering Lawrence's aversion to farm work.

"I do, father, along with my brother-in-law and my wife, Catherine."

"Well, things have certainly changed, that's for sure."

"Yes, Father, I am a different man from when you last saw me."

"You were just a boy when you left us, Lawrence. I'm just happy that you survived."

After a long visit, they ate a meager dinner of barley soup with chicken and bread. They would save the rabbits for dinner the next night. It was nice to be home again even if it was all of them in one small room.

The land looked the same. It was green and lush, except that the trees looked a little bit taller and his parents a bit older. All of this land belonged to the lord and not to Lawrence's family. If they stayed here, they would never own anything. Lawrence was going to change all of that. As Lawrence lay by the fire in the evening, he remembered his life there. He remembered how everything was owned by the Lord of the Manor, Lord Huntington. He remembered how little the family had for all their hard work.

They had a room and any food they could manage from their small garden. But the crops they worked so hard on and most of the animals around them belonged to the Manor. They had chickens and eggs, of course, but little else. Their only thoughts were of survival. They never looked further than Sunday dinner, when they might have a chicken if it was a feast day.

Lawrence would show them what hopes and dreams could create if you were free and had some land of your own. He found a chance to speak quietly to his father later that night.

"I'm so sorry, Father, for not working as hard as I should have on this land with you."

"You were just a boy, son, and full of dreams and energy. You have nothing to apologize for. It is I who should be sorry for trying to keep you on this land as a farmer and not seeing what you were made of. I had dreams when I was younger too, Lawrence, but back then there was no hope of a better life. It was worse than it is now."

There was no rift between father and son, but they both felt better after they had had the chance to talk in private. Their bond had not been broken by distance or misunderstanding.

In the morning, Lawrence left for Oak Junction and his new family. He gave his parents the silver coins he had brought for them, and they were thrilled. His family gave him a bit of bread and a jug of water for his journey home. He would continue to send word to them often, and they would come to live with him in the fall or early winter. He was very glad to see them all in good health, especially his father, who worked so hard for so little in return.

Lawrence rode home content with the future that he had planned, but he couldn't help but feel a little uneasy.

Up the road and behind a large tree, a man sat on a fine horse and watched Lawrence. He rode away before Lawrence could possibly see him. He had followed Lawrence from Oak

Junction. He was an evil man, and Lawrence had met him once before. This man had plans, and they were not good for Lawrence or his family.

When Junior had finished his first day with Don, he had dinner with Don and his family.

They had a nice two-room house behind the blacksmith shop. It had stone floors, and the windows had proper window glass. Junior liked Don's wife Mary, and Ginger seemed very sweet. He didn't find anything disagreeable about any of them. He thought that he might be happy with them as family.

Junior went to the church after dinner and spent an hour or so studying after evening prayers. He started to remember the bits and pieces his mother had taught him from the Bible when he was quite small. After his studies at church, Junior walked home.

This time of night, it was a beautiful walk back to Oak Junction. He thought about his feelings for Ginger and whether he felt that she could be the person he might spend his life with. He didn't know her well enough yet, but she was pleasing to his eyes and she seemed even-tempered.

Sometimes he saw her get upset with her parents, but she never raised her voice or misbehaved. Junior saw the flash in her beautiful green eyes when she was a little angry.

He remembered being mad at his parents when he was younger, and he wished they were still alive so he could apologize to them. He would talk to Ginger about these regrets the next day. He was so much more mature and smarter now. He was sixteen.

Ginger seemed interested in him, and he thought that she was easy to talk to. But there were some things in his heart that he could not talk to Lawrence or his sister about. Ginger might be the one person he could share those feelings with, or so he hoped. He looked forward to seeing her and working with her father and learning more about the family.

Lawrence got home in the evening on the same day he had left his mother's house. He couldn't believe how soon he was home again at Oak Junction. He was getting more comfortable riding his horse and the journey went quickly. He even ran his horse a bit to get used to the speed and the feel of the ground moving fast underneath him. He rode both horses around Oak Junction, but the black one he rode out to his parents was his favorite.

Junior's skill as a blacksmith was growing daily. He learned about building a proper fire and how to keep it at the right temperature for working iron. He was soon making simple items and learning the tricks of the trade. He turned out to be a natural.

He liked the heat of the fire and swinging the large hammer as well as the smaller one, used for finer detail on the small projects that Don started him on. Junior wore his apron with pride, and when people walked by him, he felt respected and knew that people understood that he was not just a farm boy, though there was surely nothing wrong with that. All trades are needed to make the world, and he never would forget that. In no time, he was doing real work for Don and making him more money than Don had ever hoped for.

Lawrence decided the brown horse with the golden tail would be Junior's after riding the black horse for several weeks.

They would use both horses to plow the fields, so if one horse died or was stolen, the other would already be trained. When the day came, they used the Father's donkey cart to bring the plow and all the hardware home. Everything would be there: a bridle with long leather reins and the harnesses that the horses would wear around their powerful necks. They were now finally going to be real farmers.

In the morning after breakfast, Lawrence and Junior walked to the village to get the plow. Lawrence told Junior about his visit with his family. Junior told Lawrence about work, Bible study, learning to read, and especially about Ginger. When they reached the church, Father Magnus had the donkey harnessed to the cart, and he was waiting for the two of them.

"I see you're working with Don now, Junior."

"Yes, Father, I'm learning the trade. I think I like it and might make it my life's work."

"Well, you could do a lot worse, that's for certain. How do you find Ginger?" Father Magnus asked with a smile.

"Oh, I like the whole family, Father Magnus. They're a fine Christian family."

"Alright, boys, off with you. Give my love to Catherine and Lawrence."

They thanked him and walked back down the short distance to Don's shop. Don watched proudly as the two young, muscular men loaded the heavy plow onto the wagon.

"Thank you, Don, for this beautiful tool. It will change our lives forever."

"I'm glad for you and your family, Lawrence. Use it in good health. I hope it will make you a richer man than you already are."

When the plow was brought home on the donkey cart, there was a great deal of excitement in the small family. Lizzie loved the horses and was around them whenever possible. She stood nearby as the two men came back to the house. She ran out to meet them as she always did, except when she was napping. Lawrence knew the dangers of having horses on the property and they all watched her closely. Catherine kept her distance as well, for fear of the horse bumping into her or knocking her to the ground. Lance placed himself between Elizabeth and the donkey.

"How are things in town, dear?"

"Fine, Catherine. Father Magnus sends his love."

Lawrence and Junior were able to hook up the plow to Junior's horse in short order. Lawrence and Junior had both seen plows being used in the fields before, as they were growing up but had never used one themselves.

The brown horse was well behaved, and they had a pretty good idea of how to hook up the plow. There were only so many ways one could do it. Once that was accomplished, Lawrence gave the command to the horse to move forward. He smacked his lips and shook the reins softly and the horse moved slowly forward. It was a miracle.

Elizabeth sat at the table and watched quietly with her mother as the boys started plowing the field. It was a wonderful sight. The rich brown earth curled over as the horse walked slowly forward.

The plow required no effort from the horse as far as they could tell and little from the man behind it. All one had to do was to walk and direct the horse in whatever direction you wanted it to move.

Catherine thought that even she could plow the fields if need be. Junior was thrilled. He would still have to irrigate and weed, but the hard digging with the shovel was going to be a thing of the past. It would soon be a distant memory.

The amount of land used for planting increased once the plow was in use. It was a farm now. On the eastern half of the farm, away from the stream, they would grow wheat, oats, and barley. All of the grain crops they grew could be eaten by the Smiths and by the horses as well.

It required a large amount of land and hard work to keep and feed horses. In the past, Lawrence grew very little wheat. They bought most of their bread in the village. But now they planted wheat and hoped to sell it to bakers as flour. They would have to pay the miller to grind their wheat, of course. No one works hard or very long for nothing.

The gristmill was along the side of the river near Tom the tanner. Lawrence had talked to the miller and his wife a few times in the past, just in passing. But when the wheat was harvested, Lawrence would be spending much more time at the mill. Richard had explained to Lawrence about the grinding process and how the miller was to be paid.

A portion of the crop was given to the miller to grind the wheat or he gladly took silver. Lawrence realized that this mill was a perfect example of what to build in the future on his second parcel of land. As his wheat crop grew in size, he spent more time at the mill and visited with Samuel and his wife Martha, who both lived in a part of the large two-story building. It was a stout building made in the post-and-beam style. Huge beams held the roof up as they ran across the giant posts.

It was a large puzzle to put together, Lawrence thought as he walked through the building over and over.

Lawrence studied the mill very closely every chance he got. After some time, Lawrence could see the mill with every piece of lumber and iron in his mind's eye. He watched and learned how Samuel engaged and disengaged the workings of the miraculous machinery. The water wheel turned constantly, but by moving some long levers, you could stop the motion inside the mill to clean or repair it.

The grinding was done on the second floor, and the flour fell from the stones through a hole and onto the floor beneath it. The miller then shoveled the flour into large cloth bags. Every job or trade has its dangers: fire for Don the blacksmith and the baker, but the miller had to deal with the fine dust constantly in the air around him. Even the area where he lived with his family was covered in a fine layer of flour dust. It seemed like fog sometimes. Lawrence's mill would use large saw blades to cut wood, not grind wheat, but the power source would be the same.

The machinery would be very similar too, so Lawrence had Sam watch closely as the mill was working.

Martha, Don the blacksmith's wife, was Mary's sister. Most people were born, grew up, and died in the same small village. This was not unusual. Sometimes a man would travel in his work if he was a merchant or a tradesman, and perhaps meet a woman from a different town or village and bring her back as his wife. But that was not the norm.

Lawrence had been saving his silver for four years now. He put a little in a leather bag as often as possible and hid it in a hole under a stone on the hearth of his fireplace.

After the planting was completed, Junior spent a few days working on the third room of the house with Lawrence and a few days working with Don. Junior and Lawrence cut several trees down and split them into timbers. They dug the holes for the corner posts again, and then the carpenters arrived. Lawrence and Sam had been learning from the carpenters, so they did as much work as they could to make the carpenters' work go faster.

The process was the same as before. The third room was almost exactly the same as the first two but larger. There would be four people living there: Lawrence's parents and his two brothers. The room also had its own fireplace and hearth for cooking. It was practically a separate house.

In the early fall, the new room was completed, and Lawrence borrowed the Father's cart once again. He didn't need the donkey, however, using Junior's horse to pull the cart to his parents' house instead. It was a much faster journey. When Lawrence arrived at his parents' home, they piled what little they had onto the cart and came back to Oak Junction.

They owned nothing but their clothing and a few chickens. There was no sadness as the family left their old home. That life had been filled with drudgery and disappointment for many years. They barely escaped starvation even during the best of times. Lawrence rode beside the cart. He sat tall and proud in his saddle. It was one of the happiest days of his life. To be able to bring his family all together, under one roof, and for all of them to work their own land together was a miracle.

Lawrence's father, Charles, felt a huge burden lifted from his shoulders. He would now be the master of his own future, just like his son. And he would be rewarded in proportion to his hard work and skill as a farmer. He might even put on a few needed pounds. Their old shack slowly disappeared over the horizon as they made their way to Lawrence's land and their new future. With all of the family working together now, their crops, their wealth, and their comfort would only increase. None of this would ever have been possible but for the fact that Lawrence had saved the life of a man who turned out to be a prince.

Lawrence now had a special relationship with the king and all of the men under him. He didn't see the king, but he knew he had the ear of someone close to him if he ever needed it. Lawrence was never in need of favors, but it was comforting to know that there was someone out there to turn to in a time of crisis.

Lawrence hoped this would never be needed.

Chapter Twelve

Lawrence's little brother, Sam, was very handy, and he soon made more chairs and stools from all the small bits of useless scraps of wood around Oak Junction. While Lawrence and Lawrence's father, Charles, worked the fields, William made a new and larger smokehouse. Now with his family back together, Lawrence could spend less time farming and more time hunting and learning about how to build a lumber mill.

The Smiths began attending church regularly. Lizzie would sit with her mother and father, and listen to Father Magnus preach and lead Sunday school. It was a wonderful time to have everyone together again.

Soon it was time for the new baby. Lawrence sent for the midwife again, and the birth went well. Lawrence's mother was there to help this time. Lawrence and Catherine had a new son, who they named Eli. Meanwhile, Richard and his wife had a lovely new daughter, and a week later, Don and Mary had a son. He would be another Don. There were babies everywhere in the village. As the times got better, the babies came.

Junior was working with Don and going to read with the monks at night. He tried to help everyone in the family learn to read in the evenings when they had the time. Lawrence and Junior were still working and hunting, but with more of the family there, the work was soon shared by many hands. Junior's skill as a blacksmith was increasing all the time. Don was being well rewarded for the time he spent teaching Junior the trade.

Don and Mary were over the moon about their new baby boy, as was Ginger.

Junior and Ginger were getting to know each other better as the months passed. Junior's reading skills were becoming very strong. He reached a point where he was leading a small Bible class once a week.

At sixteen, he could read almost as well as the monks. He had worked as hard at learning to read as he did learning to be a blacksmith. The family was very proud of him. The world was now opening up for him, and he could become a successful merchant or tradesman because of his ability to read and his blacksmithing skills. It was only limited by his ambition and his desire to work. Lawrence had big plans for Junior. As for his new son Eli, he was happiest at his mother's breast.

Junior was learning the lesson that all men must eventually learn. Life is hard at best, and you must learn to work in order to eat. This was the natural order of things for most people at Oak Junction. Junior again remembered his first conversation with Lawrence.

"Do you have a plan?"

"No, sir."

"You'll starve then."

"Probably so, sir" had been his answer. It still held true.

Junior had learned this lesson well.

Chapter Thirteen

Jason Jones was a lovely child. He was almost too beautiful to be a boy. He was the first child of Thomas and Lydia Jones. Thomas Jones had grown up in northern England, near the Scottish border. His family owned a very old inn and tavern and many acres of farmland there.

He worked there every day, all day, and most nights. It was a lovely old building with great charm and a colorful history. His family had owned it for generations, and he loved it. He loved the work, he loved the local customers for the most part, and he had loved working with his parents.

Jason was Thomas's eldest son. He hated this life for all the same reasons that his father loved it. He hated the work, he hated the people, and he hated the buildings. He just hated his life. For Jason, it was just an isolated, creepy old building that sucked the life out of him. It was like a jail for him. He hated working with his parents and his siblings as well. Sometimes he felt like he hated everyone and everything. Jason thought he had good reason for these troubling feelings.

One of the tavern regulars had molested him, and more than once, in the dark, cold, and unfriendly place. It started when he was twelve. He had been alone cleaning a room upstairs when he was attacked. He was reminded constantly of that dreadful event by the building and the people who came there. He was always afraid. He carried two painful, powerful secrets in his heart at all times.

First was the fact that he had been abused by someone he and his parents knew. He carried that pain with him all of the time. Second was the fact that he wanted to kill the man who had abused him. He saw no other escape. He knew that he couldn't tell his parents about the event because of the threats that he kept receiving from the man, a tavern regular.

Jason had been cornered by this large, ugly, vicious man and was made to do things that he was just starting to discover and understand. They were turned into evil, powerful, and demeaning acts by his attacker.

These acts were no longer loving acts between husband and wife but had been changed forever into his own private, lurid nightmare. This had happened to him more than once, and Jason knew it would never end unless his tormentor was dead. One cold winter night, Michael, the man who had molested Jason, came in for a few pints. Jason was cleaning and helping his mother in the kitchen, as usual, when he saw Michael seated at the bar.

He was rude, as always, to Jason's father when he served him. But this time, something happened to Jason as he watched this man verbally abuse his father. Something stirred in his chest and his mind. He knew he was going to kill Michael that night. That thought made him happy for the first time in years. He was now fifteen, but he felt like he was eighty. He was worn down, angry, and mean. His parents had noticed the change in him, but they hoped and thought that it might pass. It did not.

Michael had sold some livestock that day at the small market in town and now had more money than usual in his pockets. He lorded that over the other men at the tavern in his usual way.

Most everyone in the village hated him, for many different reasons. Several of them would have killed him themselves if they thought they could get away with it. Not just to rob him but because he was such a nasty bastard to everyone he encountered. He was the one man in the village everyone knew but for all the wrong reasons.

He drank several more pints over several hours. He drank much more than his usual quota. He became more disagreeable as the night wore on and was asked to leave several times by Jason's father. He refused each time. When he became even more insolent and disrespectful than usual, some of the men from the inn had had enough and grabbed him by his arms and legs and took him outside. They tossed him to the ground and hit him several times. They kicked him as well. When he finally went down the final time into the cold damp dirt, he laid still on the ground, unconscious. He was covered in mud and looked as though he had crawled out of a deep cold grave.

After a short time, Michael came to and staggered his way toward his home down the lane. Jason had seen the ruckus and wanted to join in, but he thought it better not to interfere. He had another idea soon enough.

"I'm going outside, Mum, just for a minute."

"Alright, boy, but don't be long. It's near closing time, we have plenty to do in here now, and I'm not doing it all alone again."

She said this to him from another room as he picked up a very large, sharp knife that he often used in the kitchen. He used it to cut meat for his mother's meat pies. They were very good pies; everyone in the county agreed on that.

Jason left by the rear door of the house. He walked through the large bright kitchen and watched the men kick and beat Michael from behind some overgrown bushes at the rear of the inn. Jason was elated and felt emboldened as he watched. When Michael got up and staggered away, Jason followed behind him, behind the tall bushes and in the damp cold grass.

Jason soon began to enjoy tracking Michael, his prey. Jason's true nature was emerging at long last. The longer he followed Michael, the more powerful he felt. He knew that he was in control of the situation and what the outcome would be. He was filled with a rage that made him feel like he could tear the earth in half. But Jason was the one torn in half: half loved by his parents and siblings and the other half hating himself and everyone else.

He wasn't sure why he felt this way, but that was the way he was. He didn't have any empathy for people around him and never would. He had tried to change, but it was impossible. Michael was talking to himself as he stumbled down the path. He was laughing loudly and singing as only a drunkard can. Jason heard his name come out of Michael's mouth as he staggered down the road and snapped.

He jumped out of the bushes and stabbed Michael from behind in the lower right side of his back. Michael didn't know at the time that he had been stabbed. He was so drunk that he thought he had perhaps scraped the low-hanging branch of a tree or bush. He turned around to see Jason standing in front of him with a large bloody knife in his pale hand. But it still didn't register with him that he had been injured.

"Come for a little tickle, have you, boy?"

Without thinking, Jason quickly lunged forward and stabbed the now mortally wounded man in the stomach several times. Michael tried to retreat out of Jason's reach. Michael then started to say something again but lost his breath. Then Jason stabbed him in the chest as Michael bent over to catch his breath, blood running from his mouth.

Michael again started to say something when Jason sliced his throat with enough force to make him stand straight up, then he stabbed him in the groin.

Michael fell backward, dead at Jason's feet. Jason knelt down over the large, dirt-covered man and went through his pants. He made sure that he took all of Michael's money and walked back down the lane to the rear of the family's large two-story white house. The altercation had been unseen. He had a feeling of comfort in his heart that he hadn't felt for a very long time. He felt free and satisfied for the first time in years.

Jason washed his hands and the knife in the bucket outside the door to the kitchen and splashed the water into the grass. He then entered the house. His mother was cleaning the last of the tables and talking to some new customers who had just come into the dining room.

"Sorry folks, we're done for the night, but do come to see us again."

She turned and walked into the kitchen after locking the front door.

"What were you up to outside, dear?"

"Oh nothing, Mother, I just thought I heard footsteps in the garden."

"That's a good boy, always on the lookout for trouble."

She was right in a way. Jason was always on the lookout for trouble, but not in the way that she thought.

Jason looked down at the knife in his hands and started cutting the beef for his mother's pies again with a smile. His life would never be the same.

Chapter Fourteen

Over the following years, Jason was often in trouble but it was nothing he couldn't handle. He still worked at the inn for his parents. They thought that he seemed happy again, and for the most part, he was. He had gathered a few young men around him who were kindred spirits—a little rough-and-tumble, maybe even a little dangerous. His parents weren't always certain how dangerous they might be. They were often worried about Jason's future. No one ever connected Jason to Michael's murder, and no one was ever tried or hanged for it. There were far too many people who might have wanted to kill him, and the fifteen-year-old was not on the list of suspects.

Jason was a little different from most criminals who start out hurting animals and stealing their parents' small coins. His first crime was murder. He was a natural leader and soon talked his cohorts into several ventures that made them quick money and little notice from the law.

That was a bad mix for any young man short of money and time on his hands. By the time Lawrence was sixteen, Jason was twenty and had left a trail, along with his fellow criminals, of robbery, mayhem, and murder from the north of England down to the Midlands. Then Jason and his men stopped a small group of men to rob or worse. Those men turned out to be Prince George and his companions out on a hunt. This was when the paths of Jason Jones and Lawrence Smith crossed for the very first time. Jason was the lone survivor of that encounter, but he had many different men who traveled the highways with him off and on, and he would gather another group together soon enough. Over time, Jason heard about Lawrence, his good fortune, and his life at Oak Junction, and it made him sick to his stomach.

Jason escaped alone after Lawrence killed his men. He survived the best he could. He robbed and killed many men and raped their women on the country roads to the north of Chesterfield. He stayed away from the south until he could rebuild his gang. He lived in the woods when the weather was fair, and he went home to his parents when the winters arrived. His family had no idea what he was capable of or what he had been doing so far from home.

He often returned with several fine horses that he kept in their pastures. His parents were in awe of his fine clothes, and he often gave them money when they needed it. They thought he dealt in horse trading and selling. Jason did in a way. He was a thief and a killer. He would kill riders on the roads, kill their women, steal their horses, and sell them if and when he could. His parents had no idea who their son really was or what his life was like away from the inn. Jason had a fire in his belly again, and the cause now was Lawrence Smith.

He would lie awake at night and hear the fanciful stories over and over in his head about Lawrence and his successes. It made him want to spit bile.

As soon as the weather permitted it, he got a new group of outlaws together and went south to Oak Junction and the villages in the region. He had never seen Lawrence, but he knew he would find him eventually. Having not been this far south for some time, he knew that he wouldn't be recognized. He thought it would be easy to find money and women on the roads around Oak Junction. He was right, but he would pay a very high price for his deeds.

His group robbed, killed, and raped for many months. They had money and adventures galore. That was until they met the farmer's family.

They let a little boy and a young girl survive after killing their parents and after Jason raped the girl. They thought they had killed both of them with hard blows to their heads and drowning the girl in a small lake. But the girl and the little boy survived, and that would be another setback for Jason.

When he got word of this, he sent his men back to clean up the mess, and they never returned. Then he heard the new stories about Lawrence Smith, his family, and of course, the trial of his men. He heard how Lawrence had killed the other two men and was reminded of how the king had given Lawrence all those acres of land for his bravery and for killing Jason's band of outlaws.

Their paths had now crossed again. He was the man on horseback who watched Lawrence work in his fields with his now large family. Jason was sick with envy and anger.

Jason would kill them all once he got a gang together again. Jason swore an oath: "I will kill all of them, children included." He would even kill little Lizzie. He didn't know it at the time, but Lizzie was his own daughter. She was as beautiful as he had been, and she even closely resembled him.

Chapter Fifteen

Lawrence had several tasks to accomplish before he could leave again for his second parcel of land at Themstead. Now that he had his horses, he needed to buy a strong wagon to carry his produce to the village in the autumn and to help him transport his tools and provisions to his second piece of land.

He still had many pelts in storage from the previous year's hunts that Junior had cleaned and cured over the winter. He would sell them to Tom the tanner and have the wheelwright, Kyle, construct a wagon for him. It shouldn't be too dear as it only needed to be a rough wagon and not a fine carriage like the one Lawrence and Catherine had ridden to Chesterfield.

Lawrence hadn't saved as much silver as he had hoped, but he had saved some, and the family never went without food. He had very little need of money at this point as he and Catherine had made nearly everything they needed or traded game or pelts for what he couldn't make himself.

Lawrence hadn't changed over the years, but sometimes he felt that the villagers looked at him differently now. Instead of the simple farmer and hunter that he still felt he was, he felt that the villagers now saw him as one of the wealthy elite. He felt that he was the same because he used little gold or silver in his day-to-day dealings with the villagers. But the villagers couldn't forget about all his landholdings and the choices that he had compared to them. He wanted to ask Father Magnus about the greed and envy that some people felt in this world.

He knew that he had been given a great advantage over the other villagers in some ways, but he couldn't understand people feeling that they deserved what he had. He felt that perhaps they should work a little harder or smarter rather than focusing on what he had created through his hard work and planning. Granted, he was a special case. Few men had ever had their lives changed by the flight of an arrow. He was thinking about this as he walked through the village to order his wagon.

He stopped to visit with Richard, the fishmonger, as he entered the lane that would take him up to Don and then to the wheelwright. Richard was a tall man with a slender body and long hands and feet. He had straight blond hair with reddish highlights that people teased him about. His temper had gotten the worst of him in the tavern more than once. Many thought he was from Viking stock and tried to stay on the good side of him.

Richard was very glad to see Lawrence. His business was doing better now, partly due to his dealings with Lawrence and partly due to the growth of the village in general. When Lawrence started with his fish traps, he was catching few fish. They were mostly for his own family. Eventually, Catherine made more traps, and they had extra fish to sell to Richard. Lawrence stopped for just a moment to drop off more fish and to say hello to Richard.

"I see by all the fish that you are now bringing me that you have learned how to catch fish quite well, Lawrence. I'm glad you've figured it out."

"Well, Richard, you showed me the secret, and I just used the information from you to start making better use of my time. Those traps are wonderful."

"Well, I'm glad to be of help to you. Those fish of yours have helped the both of us make a bit more money." Lawrence left with a few more pieces of silver in his hand. As he left and started walking to see Don the blacksmith, Lawrence realized that both men had benefited by their fair dealings with each other. Every person Lawrence had dealt with in business was better off than before, and Lawrence was as well.

It occurred to Lawrence after he left Don and while he was walking to the wheelwright that those who complained about not having money or food were usually those who didn't actively pursue work or commerce and who didn't really understand how business or commerce worked in the first place. He didn't understand people with no motivation or desire to better themselves and their family's position in life.

He knew there would always be those who, for one reason or another, would fall outside of society's norms whether it was a lazy wife or husband, or the town drunk. They simply would rather complain or felt that they couldn't improve their own circumstances. Why that was, he had no idea.

It was no accident that Lawrence was the finest archer in the area. He had spent most of his youth practicing with his father. He had no idea of the luck that would come his way because of that skill. But life's results were always a bit of luck after all, and Lawrence happened to be one of its benefactors. He would have to ask Father Magnus about that, too, when he had the time.

Lawrence walked for some time and eventually arrived at the wheelwright's shop.

"Kyle, I need to talk with you."

"Yes Lawrence, how are you? What might I do for you today?"

"I have saved just a little silver and need a rough wagon to haul my produce to the village. Nothing fancy, Kyle, but something strong and built to last."

"I know just what you want. Look at that one going down the road right now. What do you think?"

"Oh, my lord, that looks a bit more expensive than I might be able to afford. It's way too large."

"Alright then, Lawrence, how about that one over there?"

Kyle pointed to a slightly smaller wagon passing down the lane, filled with lumber, but large enough for Lawrence's produce. Lawrence thought that it was just what he needed.

"Yes Kyle, that's just what I want."

"Well, Lawrence, that would cost you around two pounds."

"Oh my goodness, Kyle. I don't know if I can afford that."

"Well, Lawrence, I might be able to do it for a few pennies less, but not many."

"Alright then, Kyle, I'll trust you to make me a good wagon at a fair price under two pounds. I know you need to make it worth your while."

Kyle the wheelwright was very happy to build a wagon for Lawrence. He knew exactly what Lawrence wanted and could make one soon enough and still make a profit at the agreed price.

Part of the wheels would come from Don's shop as well, so once again, Lawrence was immersed in this lovely cycle of commerce, and everyone benefited. Between the pelts that Lawrence had from last year and the silver he had hidden and saved in his hearth, he had just enough money to have his wagon built for a little less than two pounds. If it was a little less, that would be a blessing. It would be a rough wagon but perfect to carry all his goods in that he needed for his trip to Themstead or to carry his produce to market in.

Lawrence loved to walk through the village and see silver changing hands. He had never thought of himself as a businessman before, at least not like the other merchants. He was just beginning to participate in the economic cycle. In the past, he had never had enough silver to consider himself part of village commerce. He felt like an outsider looking in. He saw himself watching the village function without him. Now he was part of it, and with a larger harvest coming in the autumn, he would very soon have more silver than he could have ever dared to dream of.

Lawrence wandered back to Don's shop and stopped to talk with him a bit. It was getting late, and Don was finished for the day and cleaning up.

"How are things working out with Junior?" Lawrence knew exactly how things were going with the two of them, but it was an opening for a conversation with Don.

"Lawrence, I'm doing a third more work since Junior started with me."

"Is he behaving himself?"

"Oh yes, he is a proper gentleman, he is. Just like his father, or brother, or whatever," Don said, clearing his throat.

"I know it's a strange family situation, Don, but it seems to be working."

"That it does, Lawrence."

"How do the young ones seem to be getting along, Don?"

"I think they fancy each other a bit, Lawrence, but only time will tell."

Lawrence then changed the direction of the conversation.

"You know I'm leaving shortly for my land in Themstead?"

"I know, and I will be sad to lose Junior when you leave."

"Well, I've been thinking about that, Don. I'm thinking of taking my little brother Sam instead."

"Why is that then?"

"Well, Junior still has much to learn from you and the monks, and there is Ginger. Sam is now the same age as Junior was when I found him on the road. I think he will be fine with me in Themstead."

"I see, I see. So I haven't lost him yet?"

"I don't think so, Don. I want Junior to learn mathematics, and he and the monks seem happy with each others' company."

"Well, I'm very happy to hear that, and I'm pretty sure Ginger will be too."

"I'm going to tell Junior tonight that he is staying here in Oak Junction, Don. My parents and older brother can take care of Catherine and the kids here at Oak Junction for a few months.

I still need to decide what I'm going to do with that land in Themstead. There's plenty of timber there, and I might be able to farm a little as well. That's why I need to go back there and look it over carefully."

"You're not one to run away from hard work, Lawrence, that's for sure. The whole village knows that."

"I know your father is very proud of all that you have accomplished here. He and I were just talking about you the other day."

"Really? What did he have to say then? I'm curious."

"He was just saying how grateful he was to be able to bring his family back together and have a chance at a better future because of your hard work and generosity."

"Well, they are my family after all."

"Junior wasn't your family, and you helped him and his dear sister too."

"But that was the right and proper thing to do, Don."

"That's the whole point, Lawrence, that's who you are. Not everyone would do the same, given the chance."

Lawrence and Don talked for some time. Finally, they said their goodbyes as the conversation finished after about half an hour, and Lawrence left the little shop and headed for home.

Lawrence started walking home down the hill from Don's shop and thought about their conversation. *Why didn't everyone want the best future for themselves and their families?* he wondered. It was true enough that some folks just didn't seem to care. Lawrence saw them all around him. What caused one person to settle for less than what a little hard work could bring them? He would have to ask Father Magnus about that.

Lawrence couldn't shake the feeling that he was being watched as he walked off the main road and climbed over his wonderful, long straight fence that he and Junior had built. As he walked down toward his house, he could see across the land for miles. It was virgin forest with more types of trees than he could count. The land was full of animals that would feed him and give him an income as long as he lived if he wanted to take the time and make the effort to hunt them.

I may be one of the luckiest men in the world, he thought as walked slowly down to his house. *No, I know it.*

Chapter Sixteen

That night before dinner, Lawrence and Catherine talked about Junior staying at Oak Junction instead of leaving with Lawrence for Themstead. They both agreed that it was for the best given the circumstances. When they sat down, Lawrence broached the subject with Junior.

"Catherine and I have thought carefully about you coming with me to Themstead, Junior. We think you should stay here for the time being."

"But Lawrence," he protested, "I want to help you with all that hard work. This schooling is often boring, and I feel like I might fall asleep sometimes."

"I know, Junior, you and I are cut from the same cloth. But our future depends on the both of us. I will do the heavy labor for a time with young Sam, and you will learn to read and do mathematics. That route will serve our family best."

"Sam is just a babe, Lawrence."

"He is nearly as old as you were when I found you on the side of the road."

Sam watched the two men talk about him as if he wasn't even there. Junior laughed and then agreed with Lawrence.

A part of him felt glad that he wasn't leaving. He had thought he might miss Ginger and didn't want to leave her. He was growing fonder of her by the day. He had a strong love of adventure as Lawrence did. He had hoped that he could go to Themstead and help start the next part of their dream, but as Lawrence explained it to him, the new plan made perfect sense.

Junior still needed to improve his blacksmithing skills and work on his education. That was all nearby in Oak Junction. And again, there was Ginger to think about. Junior and Ginger had been talking about their feelings for each other. Both felt there was hope that a marriage might be in the offing sometime in the not too distant future.

So it was settled.

"Sam, are you up for a little trip down the road to the west?" Lawrence asked as they finished dinner.

"Yes, Lawrence, as long as I won't be missed here on the farm."

"We'll manage, Sam," said William, Sam's oldest brother.

Lawrence's mother and father exchanged a worried look. They feared for Sam's safety. Lawrence saw the worry on both of their faces.

"He will be fine, Father, Mother. I promise."

Sam was thrilled that he would go to Themstead rather than Junior. He had been hearing about "the west" for some time. He was up for an adventure as much as Junior had been, and he was now fourteen and almost a man.

Lance followed the conversation with his eyes closed, but his ears twitched as each man spoke. His eyes opened as Lawrence explained his reasoning and narrowed as Junior spoke. He listened until they were finished talking and had strained to hear every word. Lance agreed with Lawrence.

Chapter Seventeen

Lawrence thought back to when he and Junior first came to Oak Junction and how hard they had to work. If Sam were half the man that Junior was, they would be fine in Themstead. Sam was a hard worker, and Lawrence had forgotten something. When Lawrence came to Oak Junction just a few years before, he was just a child himself. He didn't know it at the time, thank goodness. He was far too young to be afraid and had been too stubborn to quit. Lawrence had now grown into a man himself. Lawrence explained to William and Junior what he wanted the two of them to accomplish in the coming months at Oak Junction.

He made it very clear to them that Charles, Mary, and Catherine were in charge. The ground would be soft enough to plow in a few weeks, and the planting would begin again. When that was finished and there was enough fresh meat in the shed, Lawrence, Sam, and William would leave for Themstead.

Catherine and Mary were busy gathering up all the household items that the boys would need. The wagon would be finished soon enough, and William would transport Lawrence and Sam to Themstead, along with Lawrence's horse, and bring the wagon back home.

The men got busy making a list of tools that Lawrence and Sam would need at their second parcel, far to the west. It was the beginning of spring in 1773.

That night, Lance was restless. He growled and puffed and sniffed the damp night air. He thought that he heard something and walked to the door and barked. Lawrence didn't stir. No one stirred. He barked again, twice.

Lawrence finally woke up.

"Lance, go lie down, or I'll put you out in the cold." Lance barked again.

"If you don't lie down, Lance, you'll be outside with the goat."

Lance came back to his spot next to Lawrence, walked in a tight circle, and laid down.

"Good boy, Lance. Go to sleep now, and let us all get some rest."

Lance did not sleep. There was danger nearby, and he knew it. These humans were just too lazy to listen to him.

Chapter Eighteen

In the morning, the goat was gone.

"What could have happened, Lawrence? She never leaves the yard."

"I don't know, dear. She's around here someplace. She'll turn up."

Lance sniffed the ground and walked towards the edge of the forest. He smelled a stranger on his farm. He walked some more, and then he saw it and barked his urgent bark. Not the "come play with me bark" or "the hungry bark" but "the urgent, danger bark."

Lawrence walked over to the spot and saw the goat dead in the tall grass. He thought a fox had killed it. Lance barked twice more. Lawrence knelt down and saw the slice of a sharp knife across her throat and was stunned.

"What monster would do this to a defenseless animal?" Lance looked at Lawrence with the face of a dog saying, "I tried to warn you last night, Lawrence." Lawrence looked at Lance and said, "Sorry fella, you were right, and I was wrong. I will never doubt you again."

Lance was satisfied with Lawrence's apology and hoped that he had truly learned his lesson.

"The goat is dead, Catherine. The foxes must have killed her," he lied. Lance agreed with Lawrence's lie.

No need to worry the woman, Lance reasoned.

"I'll go into town and get another goat this morning after breakfast, Catherine."

After breakfast, Lance and Lawrence walked across the farm and saw a horse's hoofprints in the ground. They were close to the garden and ran directly to where the goat had been tied. Then they went to the road. Lawrence and Lance walked back to Oak Junction, and Lawrence bought another goat. Lawrence talked most of the way back. Lance just listened.

Catherine and Lawrence had spoken many times about his leaving as only a man and wife can while they lay in bed together. They knew this time would come, but it had come quicker than they had expected and with dangerous undertones. Their good fortune had made it easier for Lawrence to leave Oak Junction and begin the next part of their life. Once again, luck had helped Lawrence and his family. But the death of the goat left a foreboding feeling in the air. This was not the way Lawrence had wanted to leave his family.

Two separate thoughts tugged at Lawrence's heart as the days passed. He knew his wife and small children would be safe with his parents and brothers there, but he would miss them terribly even though he would only be a day's ride away.

He loved and surely would miss Oak Junction and his family and friends. He also felt that he must go. He had no control over matters such as moving and how to press forward, or so it seemed to him now. He was being pushed by something that he didn't understand. He was also very worried about who might have killed the goat and why.

What was the meaning behind it? he wondered.

When Charles and the family lived on Lord Huntington's land, they weren't allowed to hunt deer legally. Charles had been young once himself and was very good with a bow. His father James had taught him just as Charles had tried to teach Lawrence. William was often left to the farm chores as his father and Lawrence went into the woods to hunt.

William enjoyed farm life and spent many happy days with his mother Mary and younger brother Sam working in the fields. He thought that he was more like his mother Mary than his father in that regard.

He had his turn with the bow and was quite good, but it held little interest for him. He loved the land and the woods even though they belonged to someone else. William didn't have the strong desire to change his circumstances that his brother Lawrence did.

William thought that he would have been very happy to live the life of a serf until he died.

Chapter Nineteen

When the earth was soft enough to plow, the whole family attacked the fields. They switched back and forth between the horses as they plowed, and it went quickly. The boys plowed as the women and Charles followed behind and planted the seeds or potato pieces. They had many different seeds that would grow on their land. They had sunny areas and areas in partial shade, and they planted accordingly. They were finished in a week.

When the planting was completed, the boys, William and Sam, started to build a proper henhouse and a fenced area for the new goat.

"We aren't going to lose another animal to these foxes," the boys said with determination. Charles and Lawrence went out to hunt while William and Sam worked in the fields. Charles and Lawrence had little time to hunt together on Lord Huntington's land. They were expected to work in the fields all day long.

Charles sometimes would let Lawrence go off into the woods and hunt as he had done when he was a young boy in his distant past.

"There was more to life than farm work after all," Charles would tell his wife. Charles's father had been a fine archer in his day, and so it was no accident, that Charles was able to pass that skill onto Lawrence. They had not hunted together often. Lawrence had little idea of his father's talent with the bow. It turned out to be in their blood.

Charles and Lawrence had worked several evenings together in the winter, repairing and making new arrows and creating three new bows for Charles, William, and Sam. The men had no bows when they left Lord Huntington's land.

Charles quickly put that right as soon as he had the time. Sam had not used a bow yet, so it would soon be time for Charles to teach him as he had taught Lawrence. He wouldn't have the time that he had with Lawrence to properly show Sam how to use a bow because he was leaving soon with Lawrence. But he would do his best with the time they had. Learning to use a bow was not only a valuable skill for hunting game but also for use as a weapon to protect their family.

When Charles and Lawrence left the house carrying their bows, it was midday. The air was still as they walked along the stream. They could hear the birds chirping happily and see them flying back and forth with bits of straw and grass in their beaks.

The spring nesting had started again. Charles saw the tracks of large game birds, probably pheasant and turkeys, along the stream just as Lawrence had seen over the years. Lawrence was starting to realize how much he was like his father as he watched him.

Their friends and neighbors had often mentioned that "there be no doubt" who Lawrence's father was, and they were right. He could see himself in his father's face. That was clear enough. He saw himself in his father's movements as well.

They walked quietly together as Lawrence took his father to the rock outcrop. They sat down on the warming earth and watched the deer eating grass in the distance in front of them.

"We should come out here early tomorrow morning and climb those rocks, and wait for a fine buck."

"My thoughts exactly, Father."

Once more, Lawrence saw how he was his father all over again.

"We must never cut these trees, or we will lose these fine creatures."

Lawrence couldn't help but be amazed at what his father had said.

"Someday, I'll have to tell you more about your grandfather and what a hunter he had been." Lawrence knew his father didn't have to tell him about his grandfather. He was already looking into his grandfather's face as his father spoke to him.

They walked back to the house after a few hours of hunting. They found three rabbits and a pheasant on this outing for dinner.

The boys were finished with their chores when Charles and Lawrence returned to the house. Charles spoke to them as he placed the game on the ground near the entrance to the house where Lawrence now lived.

"Tomorrow, very early, almost tonight, we will all climb the rock outcrop with our bows and shoot a fine buck. Sharpen your carving knives, my sweet ladies, we are going to have a fine feast tomorrow," said Charles.

Very early in the morning, the men all quietly climbed the rocks and waited for the giant buck to appear. When it did, there was no doubt which one it was. There were several does around him, but he was impossible to miss. He was enormous. They could tell by his bearing that he knew he was the king of all his pride.

The men had settled in for some hours in the lofty rocks before the sun had risen above the treetops. They waited for the buck to arrive as he always did. He walked slowly across the meadow with his nose in the air and his large eyes surveying his land. Then he slowly walked toward the Smith men hiding in the rocks. They were downwind and invisible to the stag. The men waited for the sign from Lawrence. He nodded his head, and the four men shot their arrows into the calm air and waited for the results. The fine buck was hit with three arrows near the heart. The fourth arrow hit him in the flank. There was some joking about the arrow in his rear and who might have shot that arrow. It turned out to be Sam's, but it was one of the first times he had shot at a live, moving target. He was satisfied that at least he had hit the animal. The beautiful animal died instantly and did not suffer. The men were very glad for that. God had given man dominion over the animals of the earth in order to survive but not to hurt them needlessly. Nothing made a real hunter sadder than to see an animal suffer for no reason.

They slaughtered the animal where it fell. They used the sled again to bring the innards and the head to the house. Sam pulled the sled for a while and then William joined in to help carry part of the stag. Charles and Lawrence each carried one of the hind legs. Lawrence left his father and brothers behind and went off to invite Don, Richard, their families, and Father Magnus to join them in their feast when he reached home.

It would be one of their last meals together for a while.

Chapter Twenty

While Lawrence and Lance were headed to the village, the boys built a slow-burning fire in the smokehouse. After the animal was butchered and skinned, they loaded the smokehouse, hanging the meat from the roof. Lawrence gave a small bit of meat to Lance when they reached the village. There was still plenty of fresh meat left to cook on the open fire for all the guests who would arrive. Mary, Catherine, and the other ladies and girls all helped to prepare the meal. It was meant to be a celebration of Lawrence and Sam leaving, but it turned out to be much more.

All the friends' babies and their mothers were at the feast as well. Father said a wonderful prayer and set the mood for the evening. Everyone had a wonderful time together, eating and drinking.

Near the end of the evening, Junior and Ginger stood up and asked permission from their parents to be engaged. It was sooner than expected, but no one was surprised. Young love has little patience, and they proved that to be true once more.

Later, when the men were together at the table without the women, Father Magnus asked for their complete attention. He had heard through some traveling nuns and some of the sheriff's men that there was an increase in robberies and problems on the roads in the outlying areas again. Several people had been killed and their belongings stolen not too far from Themstead, and the news would soon reach the village. This was bad news for the village because of the loss of trade it might cause. Even more importantly, however, it might mean added danger for Lawrence and Sam on their journey back to Themstead. Lawrence wondered if the death of the goat was connected to this.

Why didn't the thieves take the goat to eat if that was what they were after? he wondered. Lawrence had no good answer for that.

Chapter Twenty-One

Jason had no trouble finding men willing to enter the lifestyle of a highwayman. Times were very hard for everyone these days. He gave them horses and weapons. Many of them felt important and powerful for the first time in their lives. They had nothing and nothing to lose. Jason knew that he had to accept the consequences of his evil actions, and he had always been prepared for whatever they turned out to be. He always knew how he would meet his end and was unafraid.

It was easy for Jason and his small band to rob and kill merchants and travelers on the roads at will. The sheriff's men might come days later, if at all, to investigate these crimes, but they were often busy elsewhere. Times were improving, and there was plenty of gold and silver moving from farmers' markets to small towns and villages. This made it all the more enticing for Jason and his men to venture out onto the roads.

Jason's victims, for the most part, had no training in self-defense. Those wealthy enough to have guards were not accosted often, and Jason's men stayed hidden in the forests as those men passed by. Jason's men always tried to have surprise on their side. That was usually enough to succeed against the unsuspecting merchants with few or no guards for protection.

Jason had several men riding with him again. He knew the sheriff could always send out many more men than he could fight off, but he was clever and could easily disappear into the woods with his small band of thieves. They had a central camp deep in the forest, and several prearranged meeting points picked out on the roads to the north. When they were going to attack a group of people on the road, they always had a plan of action and an escape route well planned ahead of time.

There was one major distinction between victims for Jason, and that was when it came to women. The women were often taken into the woods and horribly murdered. Their bodies were seldom if ever found. Jason and his men tried to never leave a living victim. They had seen the results of that. If or when Jason and his men were caught, they knew there would be no mercy from the sheriff's men or the courts. It would be the sword or the noose.

Jason had left his men in their camp deep in the woods south of Oak Junction several times to travel there. He watched the traffic on the roads like a vulture as he rode past the village. Jason never ventured into the village, but he could ride the highways to see what was happening with all of the tradesmen, Lawrence, and his family. Jason would tie his horse deep in the woods and then walk back on the narrow animal trails around the village to a high vantage point and watch the Smith family. There were many hills around them where he could watch them as they worked on the farm, far out in the fields. He often talked to people walking on the roads in the area and was able to stay current with village gossip.

Jason's hatred for Lawrence only grew with the passing of time. While Lawrence was looking into the future and working on his farm, Jason was content replaying the past and trying to formulate a plan of action that would place Lawrence's head on a pike.

Jason had made his choices early in life and knew he would have to live with the consequences. He had been dealt some difficult times as a child, but so had many others, and they didn't end up as killers, or worse, as he had.

There was something else in his makeup that made him who he was. He came from a family of some means. His family owned an inn and had some land and animals. He never went hungry or wanted for anything. He had loving parents and a large family with uncles, aunts, and cousins. There was no explaining why he turned out to be such an animal.

Lawrence, on the other hand, never had anything of his own except his family and his bow. As far as he knew before he had killed the highwaymen and saved the prince, he was bound to the land and would never own anything.

Lawrence might have been happy to stay on the lord's land like William, but he was adventurous from the day he was born. It didn't take a genius to know what his future was going to be if all had remained the same. Yet he never took anything that wasn't his and never hurt anyone unless it was for his own safety.

Lawrence didn't know who Jason was and would never recognize him if they had met face to face, but Catherine had seen him up close and would remember his face forever. There was still some confusion about how many of her attackers were still alive and at large. She took no chances. She never went to the village without a male escort, and she was hyper-aware. She had seen those two men in the village only because she was always on alert.

Once Lawrence had his supplies at Themstead, he would be able to come home whenever he wanted or needed on horseback. It would take two days to drive the wagon there, but only one long day on horseback to go to Themstead or to come back to Oak Junction. Lawrence wasn't going to be that far away, but for Catherine, it might as well have been France.

This would be the first time they were apart since they had met. She was quite worried about Lawrence's safety, but the family at Oak Junction would be perfectly safe. After all, Catherine had Charles, William, and Junior there to help protect her and her children and her mother-in-law, Mary. It would take some time to adjust to taking care of the children and the animals without Lawrence. Even now, with the help of Mary and the remaining men, it would be different and difficult.

Catherine's days were full, and she would have little time to miss Lawrence. The nights, however, would be different. She could put the children in bed with her, but she loved having Lawrence next to her to feel protected and loved. She was nearly back to her old self, the Catherine so full of happiness and joy that she was before she lost her family. Father Magnus had done his best to listen to her and try to explain why God didn't save her family. Of course, those things can ever be explained away, and only time can heal the sharp pains of loss and the sadness that she felt.

Finding and eventually loving Lawrence had helped soften that pain, and then the children came. For Catherine, the joy was complete. She got over her tragedies as well as she could. How Lizzie was conceived was no longer important. Her daughter brought Catherine back into the world again. The way Lawrence took to this little girl also showed Catherine where her future lay. This man who worked so hard every day to secure their survival and who stood by his word and never tried to touch her in a sexual way had proven that his word was not to be taken lightly. How could she not fall in love with him? It took her longer than she expected, but that was only because she was damaged and had to learn to trust and love all over again. The longer it took her, the more she loved Lawrence. When they made love that first time when she asked him to come to her bed, she knew how lucky she was and that she would love this man forever. She gave herself and her heart to him without holding back and with no reservations. Catherine knew that only death would separate them, and maybe not even that.

She and the other women at the feast that evening knew full well what was happening around them in the countryside and what the men were talking about. The traders and the merchants who came to the village talked about the robberies and murders constantly. What did the menfolk think that their wives talked about all day out in the fields, the weather?

She was rightfully worried about her husband and young Sam going off to live in the woods again. She was older and wiser now. She was more aware of the dangers that always lurked in the darkness away from hearth and home. She knew she couldn't stop Lawrence from finding or at least searching for his destiny, but she would make sure he was safe. She would have to ask Father Magnus for his help in protecting her husband and his brothers.

Chapter Twenty-Two

Catherine needed a plan as much as Jason did. She was not going to let Lawrence travel to Themstead with Sam and William without protection. Lawrence may be the best archer in the county, she thought, but he was still open to ambush on the road to Themstead. She wanted to make sure her men would have protection. She went to see Father Magnus to formulate a plan. Catherine walked into the village with Junior on his way to Don's blacksmith shop. As he left her to work, she continued up the now wide path past the tavern and entered the side of the church where she had entered on her wedding day and so many times since. She held her skirt with both hands to keep it out of the damp mud on the path as she walked. She wore a hat to keep the sun off her white skin. Catherine worked out of doors daily, but she always wore a hat to keep her skin smooth and white. Her hands told the true story of how hard she worked. She knocked on Father Magnus's office door. The Father answered and asked her in. She sat down on the same chair where she had been seated when Lawrence had asked her to marry him. Father Magnus saw her looking around the room with a slight smile on her face.

"This room brings back many memories for us, doesn't it, Catherine?" Father Magnus asked as he looked up from his large desk.

"Yes it does, Father. Some sad and some very happy."

"I'm sure of that, child. Now, how may I help you today?"

"I'm concerned about Lawrence, William, and Sam heading off to Themstead with all these troubles on the roads."

"I'm sure you are, my dear, so am I. That is why I've sent word to the sheriff and Lord Huntington. This isn't just about your loved ones, Catherine. Everyone in the county is up in arms about this matter. We're going to formulate a plan that may catch the highwayman and protect your family and everyone else as well."

"What are you planning, Father?"

"I'm a priest, not a warrior, but I'm sure the sheriff and Lord Huntington have come up with something. I may even play a small part in the plan. I'm going to travel to Themstead behind Lawrence on my donkey cart. From what I have been told, there's going to be a story spread about in the village and the outlying areas that there might be some gold on my cart. There might be a surprise for someone instead if they come at me with robbery on their minds. Let's just hope they do."

"But Father Magnus, what about your safety?"

"I am protected by something more powerful than these evil men, my dear, you can be sure of that. I know that I am going to see my maker when and if anything ever happens to me. I hope to have many more years here with you and the other villagers, but I have no fear of death. When I leave this earth, I will be with the Lord."

There was gold under that tarp, or so the story went. It would look like several large boxes were on the cart. It was said to be a rather large treasure under the cover. Unknown to anyone, several of the king's guard would be riding out of uniform on different parts of the main highway along with several of the sheriff's men.

The men had discussed where the best place for an ambush was and placed themselves accordingly. Some were on horseback, some on foot, and some hiding in the woods and tall grass. They would have the element of surprise and the day of their choosing to attack the highwaymen.

It wasn't hard for the date of the gold convoy to leak out and eventually reach the ears of Jason and his cohorts. The sheriff and his men, Lawrence, and the soldiers had a week to prepare the attack. Jason had just five days' notice, but that was plenty of time for him and his men. They were experts at this type of crime.

In that week, Lawrence and Catherine made many difficult discussions while talking in bed. They knew there were many risks in this venture, but they had to try something, and this seemed to be the best plan that they or anyone else could come up with. At least they would be in control of the situation. Everyone knew Lawrence and his brothers were leaving, and it was only natural for the Father to go with them for his protection if he was going to go with a load of gold to the church in Themstead. The story suggested that many gold items from some churches in the area were being gathered up and brought to Themstead and then sent on to London in the south. The secret seemed reasonable to those few people who heard it. It wasn't a great quantity of gold, but it would be tempting enough for the highwaymen. The roads were busy in the early spring, so a few more riders and pedestrians around would seem normal enough. The wagons would travel slowly because a donkey would pull it and the heavy loads on both wagons. The roads were still soft and muddy in some places as well.

Jason could care less about the gold. It was Lawrence he was after. His men were very excited and felt very sure of themselves. Lawrence was coming from Oak Junction, heading west, and Jason was coming from the west near Themstead. There was going to be trouble on the road somewhere in between. Jason had decided to attack the wagons as they were making a tight turn and heading uphill. They would be slowed by the incline, making them easy targets. The sheriff's men, the lord's men, and Lawrence had come to the same conclusion. It was somewhat difficult to get everyone into the proper places, unseen on both sides of the road, but eventually, it was done, long before the wagons arrived.

The Father's wagon stopped, and several men were inspecting the wheel in the rear on the side closest to the edge of the road as if it were broken or impaired. There were archers on both sides of the road in the woods, waiting for the highwaymen. There were weapons lying in the tall grass along the road as well where Lawrence and many others were standing or walking, looking like simple onlookers.

Soon enough, a small group of riders approached from the west. It was the middle of a beautiful afternoon. They stopped and asked about the apparently broken wagon and its contents. Father Magnus started to answer something about food for the poor when one of the riders laughed, pulling out his sword.

"Get back and away from here if you know what's good for you, or die where you stand."

He put his sword to the throat of Father Magnus who then naturally stepped backward toward Lawrence.

The bandit raised his sword closer to the Father's throat and then waved it at Lawrence, who had backed up into the tall grass as he'd been asked. Lawrence quickly knocked Sam over into a culvert behind him, knelt down, and picked up his bow. Father moved to the side and gave Lawrence a clear shot at the bandit.

That was the signal for the beginning of Jason's end. Lawrence shot an arrow into the throat of the man who was threatening Father Magnus and then several other men appeared from beneath the tarp with swords and bows at the ready. All of a sudden, several men then came out of the woods and more horsemen converged on the two wagons with swords and other weapons.

Two highwaymen in the rear of their pack tried to turn and run, but the lord's men who emerged from the forest started shooting arrows and blocking the road. The two men in the rear, who had tried to escape, were shot dead. Four men were left in a tight knot near the wagon and tried to turn their horses and run, but men stood along the road with their bows at the ready. One of the four made a dash for it, and he was hit with several arrows and fell to the muddy road. The three remaining men instantly put their hands in the air. None of the sheriff's or lord's men were injured. Lawrence and William were fine. Sam was muddy and shaken up, but Lawrence's quick action ensured that he remained safe. The dead men were placed in the Father's wagon, and the wagon was turned back towards Oak Junction with the Father and all of the sheriff's men. Lawrence, William, and Sam went on toward Themstead with Lord Huntington's men after they all congratulated themselves on their planning and the outcome. They reached Halfway Farm without incident and made camp, deep in the forest, in the evening. The lord's men would go to Themstead and then home with William when he returned. William would return home the following day once they unloaded the wagon in Themstead. The next day, they continued their journey and reached Themstead.

The boys made a fire and ate smoked deer and turkey. They also enjoyed their bread and some beer they had brought. Catherine had packed them a fine dinner. Sam was still shaken a little by the events of the day before, as was William. Everything had turned out perfect, though, or so they thought.

When Father Magnus reached the village at Oak Junction, he sent one of the sheriff's men to fetch Catherine to the church. She wanted to see the men who had been killed or captured. "No, Father, I recognize none of these men" was all that she said when faced with the dead and the survivors of the incident on the road.

She wanted to see a very dead Jason, but it wasn't to be. He wasn't there, and not one of the prisoners would talk. They would all probably go to the gallows in silence. They would rather die quickly than risk a visit from Jason. They had seen him in action and wanted no part of his wrath.

The nuns fed the prisoners and lingered in the hall outside the impromptu cell. They could hear some talking, but it was low and hard to understand. Mother Meredith thought she heard something about Oak Junction and Catherine, but she wasn't sure. Mother Meredith went immediately to talk to Father Magnus about what she had heard.

Jason wasn't sure about the story of the gold in Father Magnus's wagon. It was plausible, and yet there was something about it that didn't ring true to him. His men would not listen to his objections to the story. They would have none of it. They knew that there was gold coming up that highway, and they wanted it.

They heard the story in a tavern near Themstead from a crafty old fellow who lived on the edge of the law and society. He was often accused of minor crimes and had spent some time in prison. Jason's men thought his story was true.

Jason only entertained the whole idea because Lawrence might be involved. He only had a few days to plan the robbery. The veracity of the story was clouded by haste and greed. Jason had seen this kind of thing before, and it seldom ended well. But his men weren't going to listen to him, so he tried to plan this assault as well as possible.

Jason and his men picked the same portion of the road for their attack where the sheriff expected it because of the steep grade. The wagons would have to slow down due to their weight. Jason's men didn't realize that there was so much cover on both sides of the road for the sheriff's men to hide in. They thought the thick forest was to their advantage. They thought they had surprise on their side, but they were wrong.

They wouldn't listen to Jason's warnings. He went along but laid back a bit, just in case. As his men went over the rise in the highway, he stopped his horse, led it into the woods, and changed his clothes. Jason came back out into the bright sunlight in a dirty cloak and broad black hat. He walked with a staff, slower than his usual pace, and came over the hill as the sheriff's men closed off the escape route of his men and killed several of them. He sat down in the shadows at the side of the road and witnessed the whole ambush. He had rubbed dirt on his face and tried to disappear into the crowd of people that soon appeared.

He tried to present himself as older and slower than his twenty-five years as he slowly ambled down the road, bent over like an old man. It worked because no one noticed him or even looked his way.

Jason was mad that Lawrence had won this small battle. That's what Jason felt it was, just a small battle. They were locked in a war now, and this was just one small meaningless encounter. Jason was angry to have lost those horses, however. The men could easily be replaced; that wasn't going to be a problem. He cared nothing about them. They were just a means to an end for him. But he loved those horses. He could remember every man he killed and which horse belonged to which victim. Then Jason noticed the horse Lawrence had been riding and the one pulling his wagon. Those had been his horses not so long ago. Jason remembered the wealthy couple he had taken into the woods and murdered. He had made them strip and then killed them not far from this very spot.

He was wearing that dead man's boots at this very moment and still had most of their clothes at his parents' inn. He had never hated Lawrence more. Lawrence had Jason's most prized possessions, his horses. Everything on this earth belonged to him, Jason thought. was All possessions were only temporarily in the custody of someone else. That was how he saw things. He was becoming quite mad.

After the ambush of the highwaymen, Lawrence and Sam got right back on their wagon and headed to Themstead. Once they arrived in Themstead the next afternoon, they walked around their new land and found a high spot where they would build a lean-to.

Chapter Twenty-Three

Lawrence and Sam wanted to stay as dry as possible when the rains came again. They had brought several deer hides with them for covering the lean-to. They cut firewood and stacked it inside to keep it dry, just in case the weather turned to rain.

This plot of land was twenty times larger than Oak Junction, and it was covered in timber. There were areas where crops would grow, but this was mostly a vast, virgin forest.

William helped them plow a large area in the morning before he left for home. He would camp at the farm halfway back to Oak Junction along with Lord Huntington's men.

They had spoken to a farmer on their way to Themstead, and he was more than happy to have William spend the night on his farm. They unloaded the wagon after the field was plowed, and then William left for home with it.

This was the first time that Sam had lived out in the open. He was prepared for the worst, but it turned out not to be too bad. They had a small shelter, food, and plenty of work to keep them occupied and warm.

They planted many different crops on the newly plowed part of their land. They had corn, barley, oats, squash, carrots, and turnips. They planted the garden close to the river. It was a proper river at their new parcel, not just a stream.

It would be perfect for the mill. Lawrence showed Sam how to dig the trench for the irrigation canal from the river to the garden. The plow came in handy for this as well. The land was not as rocky as at Oak Junction. The soil was a rich dark color and beautiful. They worked for several days before they took the time to investigate this great new land where they now lived. It was going to take several days to see all of it, but that would have to wait until much later.

On the Friday before they left for Oak Junction, Lawrence and Sam rode to Themstead together on horseback. It took them an hour to get there at a slow pace. It was easy to find. There was a grand church on the high ground, and the town spread out around the church like a lace tablecloth with lots of streets and smaller pathways. Sam was beside himself. He had never seen such a large town in his entire life. His blue eyes were open wider than Lawrence thought possible. They were both very surprised at the size of the town and very happy about it. Lawrence had seen little of it when he came to Themstead the first time. While Lawrence and Sam were in Themstead, Catherine and the rest of the family went about their usual routine in Oak Junction.

William had arrived home safe and sound. He had made friends with the farmer and his daughter at Halfway Farm, where he had spent the night on his way back to Oak Junction. William was surprised at how much the farmer knew about Lawrence and their family.

William had been treated as an honored guest, not as a stranger. He had never paid much attention to how others felt about his family before, but this farmer changed all of that.

William saw how he was respected because he was Lawrence's brother. It was hard for him to understand. He soon began to realize that his behavior would always be a reflection on Lawrence and the rest of his family just as Lawrence's behavior had reflected on him.

He had never thought of what it was to be respected when he was a serf. He was nothing then. Now, he was a free man. He was the brother of Lawrence Smith, a respected citizen and landowner. He liked how that felt. He realized now how much he benefited from his brother's accomplishments. He felt for the first time in his life that he was more than just a farmer. He felt that he was from a special family and that all of them had a bigger role to play in their village. They were not rich yet, but they were well respected.

When Lawrence and Sam finally reached home after that first week, there was a big celebration. The family was fine, and Lawrence's parents were happy that Lawrence and Sam were safe at home once more. It even looked to Lawrence like his father, Charles, had gained a few needed pounds. Everything seemed perfect. Lizzie was old enough now to miss her daddy and gave him a big hug. Eli was there with a big smile as well. All seemed perfect at Oak Junction.

Several people from the village were invited for dinner with Lawrence and the family when they returned. Don and his family came as well as Richard's family. Father Magnus and the nuns who helped Catherine while Lawrence was away were there as well. Everyone was thrilled about the capture of the highwaymen, and they prayed that everyone would be safe on the roads now. Late in the evening when everyone had left or gone to bed, Lawrence and Catherine finally had a chance to talk. Lawrence could tell that something was bothering Catherine.

"What is it, my love, why are you so downhearted?"

"The leader of that gang that killed my parents was not among those who were captured or killed on the highway. That animal is still on the loose, Lawrence."

"He may be in a different county, Catherine. He may even be dead and buried in a dark, cold forest somewhere. The crows may be picking at his bones as we speak."

"I can sense that he is still about, Lawrence. I won't be at peace until I know he is dead. Look at Lizzie. When you see that face on a dead man looking up from a deep, cold grave, I'll be completely happy."

"I promise, Catherine, that one day we will know how the end of that man's life comes to an end."

"Perhaps it will be me who takes care of that," Catherine said.

"No, Catherine," Lawrence said as he hugged her with affection. "I have no doubt that you could do it, but certainly it should be me instead. My hands are already covered in blood."

Chapter Twenty-Four

Lawrence stayed two days at Oak Junction. He visited with his father, mother, and Junior. His parents were quite content with their new house, grandchildren, and daughter-in-law. Lawrence was well on his way to a bright future if he continued to work diligently. He went to speak to Father Magnus following the church service on Sunday after he sent the rest of the Smiths home to work at the farm. Father Magnus was working in his office when Lawrence knocked on his door.

"Come in, come in, Lawrence."

"Hello Father, I've come to ask for some guidance."

Lawrence sat down quietly across from the Father's large old desk and waited quietly for him to look up.

"Go ahead, son, speak up."

"Themstead is a very big town, and I'm not sure how to proceed with my plan there."

"What do you want to do, Lawrence?"

"Well, I want to sell lumber and build a mill there."

"Then do it."

"But how, and where do I start?"

"Lawrence, you are forgetting something."

"What is that, Father?"

"You are Lawrence Smith, and you can do anything. Everyone in Themstesd knows who you are already. You just don't know them yet. You can do anything you set your mind to. Just go to the wheelwright. He'll buy your wood, and then he'll tell someone about you, and then that man will want some of your wood, and so forth."

"Is it really that simple?"

"Yes, if you believe in yourself and in God, all things are possible."

"Are you sure, Father, is it truly that simple?"

"No Lawrence, it isn't simple, but you've done it most of your young life already. You've proven you can do anything. Now get out of here and continue to do what you have always done. There's nothing to worry about. Besides, worrying will accomplish nothing." *Where did I hear that before?* he thought with a smile.

As Lawrence left the Father, he was remembering how things had started for him in Oak Junction. Living under the sky and stars, having nothing and no one.

Perhaps Father Magnus is right, he thought.

Catherine agreed with Father Magnus as well when Lawrence spoke to her about his fears. Catherine knew that Lawrence could do anything. Lawrence and Sam left for Themstead Monday morning. This time they rode both horses back to Themstead.

Sister Meredith spoke to the Father about what she had heard from the prisoners. The intent wasn't clear, but the victims were surely going to be the Smith family. The Father spoke with Mother Meredith and asked several questions that neither of them could answer: "Who is left to carry out these evil deeds, what were they going to be, and when would they occur?"

The men in custody weren't talking, so the Father hatched another plan.

Why not place a stranger in the cell with them, a drunk perhaps, to listen in on their conversations? he thought.

First, he sent one of the nuns to ask Charles to come to the church in the morning for a chat, and then he walked over to the tavern.

No one in Oak Junction could remember why the tavern was built so close to the church. There were many theories. Some thought it was to make the drinkers feel guilty about all the time and money they spent there instead of being with their families or doing something constructive. That didn't seem to work, though. Some thought it was perhaps to make it easier for the intoxicated to get to church early on Sunday mornings.

Father felt deep in his heart that somewhere in heaven, someone knew that he would someday be serving at this particular church, and they also knew how much he loved his ale. So, the tavern was built near the church for his convenience and pleasure. Father Magnus could remember many passages from the Bible regarding the pleasure of alcoholic consumption, but not drunkenness. They were among his favorites.

To his knowledge, there were no passages that prohibited drinking, only the advice that its consumption is moderate. Thus, he believed the tavern was built by divine intervention for his pleasure and convenience. But the tavern could always be struck by lightning or burned down if this pleasure was abused. He was fine with that interpretation.

Father went to the tavern to speak to the owner, Theodore. Father wanted someone to volunteer to stay in the cell overnight with the captured highwaymen and pretend to be very, very drunk. Theodore thought his son was just the man for the job. Theodore Jr. loved his ale, just like Father Magnus, and had some every day, as did most adults and children during this time.

"Hello, Father, how are you today?"

"Fine, Theodore. I would like an ale, please."

"Sure, Father, what brings you in today?"

"Other than my need of a drink, you mean?"

"Well not exactly, Father."

"I know what you're trying to say, Theodore. I need some help from you."

"What can I do for you, Father? I'm just a tavern keeper. I have little experience in the matters you must be concerned with."

"Well, that isn't exactly true. I need you or your son to come and keep the bandits company for a night to listen to their plan against the Smiths. You are men who might be able to take care of yourselves if the need arises, and they have already seen me. They won't talk in front of a clergyman. But if a common thief were in their midst, they might brag or at least tip their hand."

"Well, I need to stay here and run the tavern, but I can spare my eldest son to take that matter under consideration. He loves Lawrence, after all. He has helped us often when we needed it, and we have not forgotten that. I'll talk to Theodore and see what he says. Just a moment."

The large tavern keeper disappeared for a moment and then returned with a smile on his face.

"He'll be glad to do it. Whatever you ask, he will do."

"Have him drink some ale before he comes to the church tonight. I want him to smell of the tavern and pretend to sleep next to these awful men. I want him to listen in to their conversations if they will let him. Or perhaps he may need to somehow befriend them first."

"Consider it done. He will be there at sunset."

Theodore Jr. was especially fond of the Smith family and would gladly play drunk for a night and listen in on the prisoners. So that evening, Theodore Jr. was taken into the cell with the three monsters and belched and snored the night away as best he could, trying to listen to them all night long. Sadly, he didn't gain any information, but he did annoy them to no end and had a thoroughly good time doing it. They couldn't fall asleep once he finally dozed off. His snoring was horrendous.

Theodore's parents thought he should sleep in the church every night. They hoped Father could find him some kind of job there, which would keep him there every night.

"Perhaps he should learn to read with Junior," they mentioned to Father Magnus.

But Theodore Jr. would have none of it. He couldn't care less about reading. His parents had their best night's sleep in years while he was away in the church storage room that had temporarily been converted into a prison cell. Father Magnus was against that idea because he had also heard Theodore snoring all night from his bedroom, not far from the cell where Theodore slept. Many people knew of the Father's sleeping habits, and many thought they were related to the tavern's location, but no one ever mentioned that. Some villagers even thought that he enjoyed his ale a little too much on some occasions.

Charles arrived late in the morning to see Father Magnus. The air still carried a chill, and he had been up early, getting the boys up and feeding the animals. He worked for more than an hour before going to see the Father.

He was now aware of the Father's routine, so he didn't rush into the village too early. A nun had made it very clear to him that it was of great importance that Charles speak with Father Magnus but that she didn't have a clue as to what the meeting would be about.

Catherine would go with her father-in-law into the village as well. She needed to buy some bread and perhaps some fruit. She was thinking of making a pie. The boys were already starting a fire to smoke some fresh game they had killed when Catherine and Charles left the house.

When Lawrence and Sam returned to Themstead, all was well. No one had touched their supplies. They had found a small cave for storing their most valuable tools and disguised the entrance to keep anyone from finding out. It seemed to have worked perfectly. It was also big enough for both of them to sleep in if the weather became too wet or cold.

They irrigated the garden and then rode into Themstead. Sam was uncomfortable on horseback, but Lawrence watched him closely and rode in front of him. When they reached Themstead, it was very much like it had been on those first days at Oak Junction. Lawrence could see that people were taking notice of the two of them. Lawrence was more comfortable communicating with the locals now after talking to Father Magnus. They all knew of him at least, and some would even speak to him as they rode by. "Good morning, Lawrence," they would say. "Good day, sir [or ma'am]," he would reply.

Lawrence had met Father Gregory once before on his first trip there, and he went directly to that beautiful church to renew their acquaintance. Father Gregory had asked Lawrence to join him and some other townsfolk for lunch on this day. Lawrence accepted and was now led into a vast hall when he reached the giant church. When he entered, he could see thirty or so men who were about to eat. He was led to the head of a great table by Father Gregory and shown where to sit down. Lawrence, to his surprise, was seated at the head of the table.

All of the men's eyes were upon him. He didn't understand what was happening. Then Father Gregory began to speak. "Lawrence Smith, we're very glad to welcome you and young

Sam here to the town elders meeting. We were all wondering what your plans might be and how we might help those plans come to pass. Father Magnus has instructed me to have all of us meet with you today, so we are at your disposal."

Father Magnus, what a rascal, Lawrence thought as he tried to gather his thoughts.

"Well, gentlemen," Lawrence began as he stood up at the head of the table, leaning on his hands. "This is the first time I have ever spoken to such a group. I usually speak only to my family and my farm animals, and I'm not sure that they always listen." The men all laughed at that comment.

"I was given a very substantial piece of land with many trees and fine soil on it just down the road. You all know the place. I want to cut down some of those trees and build a sawmill. It will, in turn, create an income for myself and my family, and should draw more commerce to Themstead. I know the value of forested land, and I will leave ample woods there. I intend to farm all of the areas that I clear. I will need men to help me, and I am prepared to pay a fair wage. I think my venture will benefit me and my family as well as many, many people here in town and well beyond the city walls."

Everyone in the meeting applauded Lawrence at the end of his speech. He had all these incredible plans but didn't have any idea, of course, how many of them would ever come to pass in his lifetime.

He thought he had handled the discussion of his plans with the town elders rather well considering that it came as a complete surprise to him. By the time he was finished, he had talked for almost an hour and in great detail about how his dream would help the town of Themstead.

Sam was astonished at what he had seen. He didn't recognize the Lawrence standing there at the head of this long, long table and speaking to this group of fine gentlemen. Lawrence could work all day in the fields and never say more than "Hello" and "Hand me the hoe, please." Sam had never seen this Lawrence before, and he was so proud of him. He had seen a little of what it was to be respected and it affected him in the same way it had affected William.

Several of the men came up to Lawrence and Sam after lunch and spoke to them about who to contact about what, and how much they would pay for certain products, and so forth. Lawrence thought that he was clearly blessed, and still he couldn't understand why. He took care of his family as most men did, treated everyone the same, with respect, and like most men, was fair with everyone. He would have to ask Father Magnus about why he was so blessed.

On the way out of Themstead after lunch in the great hall of the church, Lawrence could see the wealth that existed in this growing town. The houses and shops were a little bigger and nicer than most of those in Oak Junction.

It wasn't that the people were showing off. They were just more comfortable because more money passed through the town. Life wasn't always about being smarter than everybody else; Lawrence was proof of that. It was about being in the right place at the right time and taking a risk, and not being afraid. Lawrence made his own luck as most successful people do, and he was unafraid of doing something that might lead to failure. He was not afraid of failure. He knew that failure taught powerful life lessons. He knew he would not stop until he succeeded. Failure was not an option for him.

Charles had wanted to teach young Sam how to use his bow and how to hunt, but Lawrence had taken Sam with him to Themstead. Charles had to find comfort spending time with William now that Sam was gone. He spent many happy hours hunting with William. Junior was away working or learning to read with the monks most of the time now.

William and his father now had a chance to get reacquainted. Their lives were still filled with work, but they found time to hunt and talk together often.

The Smiths had little money left to speak of after Lawrence left for Themstead. Catherine had a bit, and Lawrence had taken some with him to Themstead. William and Charles wanted to get Lizzie something for her upcoming birthday. Lizzie and Eli were the only family members who had known the exact dates of their birthdays and that was only because Junior had learned to read and write.

Charles and William decided to get Lizzie an animal as a birthday gift. They would keep a small portion of the rabbit pelts aside from this hunting season and buy a male goat for her. They had the nanny goat already. Lizzie was so very fond of it, and they had the pasture, so why not buy a male goat and let nature take its course? It wouldn't take the men long to kill enough rabbits to trade for a nice ram. If he grew up healthy and did his job as expected, they would have plenty of goats for Lizzie to love and care for, and goat milk as well.

Lawrence and Sam came home every Saturday on their horses. They ate dinner with the whole family, visited friends, and went to church on Sunday mornings. The first Sunday, after Lawrence's meeting with the town elders in Themstead, he took time to speak with Father Magnus after church services. He knocked on the Father's door and entered as he had hundreds of times before.

"How are things in Themstead, Lawrence?" the Father asked as Lawrence entered the Father's small, warm office after services.

"You know exactly how things are going."

"Not at all, Lawrence, I'm stuck here helping these village folks stay on God's path."

"Well, everyone surely was helpful when I reached Themstead last week."

"I'm sure they were, Lawrence, it's a wonderful town. Did you see Father Gregory again?"

"Of course I did, you clever fellow." Lawrence answered. "I went to see him for lunch as you had arranged."

"I don't know what you mean, and you're being a little disrespectful to me, I might add."

"Sorry Father, but you are a rascal, after all."

"That may be, Lawrence, but I'm a very useful rascal at times."

"Yes you are, Father, and we thank you for your kindness."

"The future is always in your hands, Lawrence. I only grease the axle once in a while."

"I brought you a fat turkey for dinner, Father, because one good turn deserves another."

"Quite right, Lawrence, so let's go have a pint."

This was the Father's way. He was always unassuming and yet wonderfully helpful. What could he have accomplished in the outside world away from the confines of his church? Why had he chosen to live this life of strict morality in this monastic way? Was he hiding a deep secret, or was he just born to be a role model for all of Oak Junction and those beyond its boundaries? Lawrence would have to ask him about that sometime, but tonight they were just going to share a few pints.

Chapter Twenty-Five

On their way back to Themstead the following morning, Lawrence and Sam discussed their plans for the coming weeks and years. They needed to cut down several trees so they could dry them and eventually cut them into timbers. They would have to dig a giant hole for their future pit saw and build the wooden frame needed to hold the tree trunks in place as they were cut.

The first thing they would buy with the proceeds from their farm was the two-man pit saw. Then they could start cutting planks and beams to sell to the people and businesses in town.

While the boys were heading off to Themstead, the women were busy cleaning the rooms and cooking in Oak Junction. There was still plenty of work to do around Oak Junction. They checked the rabbit traps daily. They caught some but not as many as they had hoped. It seemed that the rabbits weren't so easily trapped.

Catherine and her mother-in-law, Martha, had lunches to prepare, children to care for, and dinners to plan. There were few idle moments. They still had seven people to feed and care for every day and nine or more on the weekends. They also worked in the fields and took care of the animals. All these things didn't happen by accident. Charles and the women talked every morning to discuss their plans for the day.

One virtue the Smith family possessed was that they had become very good at planning and preparing for any eventuality. They always had plenty of food preserved in the pantry, and they kept the boys and Charles busy with hunting and fishing when the planting was finished. It was just a matter of weeding and watering now on the farm.

It was an easy walk for Mary and June to come to Oak Junction from the village with their babies. Catherine had news from Lawrence in Themstead, and the ladies brought news from the village. They always enjoyed any chance to be together to visit and to share their burdens and their joys. They had few burdens lately and many joys. Life had been very good to all of them.

The sheriff's men finally came and took the highwaymen to Chesterfield without incident. The nuns were sorry that they didn't get more information for Father Magnus, but they did the best they could. There was always a nun sitting at the door on the other side of the men, silently listening in the dark. The nuns took turns, all through their captivity, but to no avail. They were very glad to see them leave. They were dangerous men, and they interfered with the routine of the church. They were always one nun short while the men were locked up. Father Magnus never noticed any changes while the prisoners were at the church. He was busy with his work and didn't appreciate all the extra work the nuns had to do while the prisoners were confined in the building. But that was the lot of nuns and wives in that time. They had that in common at least.

The fact that men, be they priests, farmers, or merchants, were seldom aware of how valuable their female partners were until they were gone or ill was always very clear to the women of Oak Junction and everywhere else throughout most of human history. That was just the way the world was. At least one's duties were clear and well defined then. The women took care of their families in both the cities and on the farms and also helped in whatever business matters their husbands were involved in. It had always been this way, and would, they thought, always remain so.

While nearly everyone looked up to Lawrence as a hero of sorts, Catherine was just his wife and the mother of his two children. But Catherine was fine with that.

Lawrence loved her and treated her very kindly, and she loved him and was content with her position in the universe. Besides, she was much too busy to be jealous or to even give her situation in life much thought. If she did, she would be quite pleased. She had a man who loved her and would do anything for her, and she had her lovely children to love and care for. She wanted for nothing except for Lawrence to be home more often and safe.

After the ladies finished their outside work, they all came into Charles and Martha's room. The new room was bigger but very much like the one Lawrence and Catherine shared. They started a fire as soon as they entered. It was still cold outside, and the warm fireplace was very inviting. They were going to make Lizzie a dress for her birthday. It would be a fancy dress for church and other special events.

They had made several garments together for the children, of course, and they always enjoyed working on them together, but this one would be different. While the women were busy in the house, Charles and William went hunting. Junior was still at the blacksmith's and with the monks at night. Junior, on most days, had dinner with Don, Mary, Ginger, and the new baby, Don Jr.

Lawrence often brought fresh game to Don's home to help feed Junior. Don's income was much improved since Junior had come to work with him, but Lawrence always wanted to help with some extra food. After all, Don was helping Junior learn a trade and to interact with the customers who came to see him. That was invaluable, and Lawrence understood that better than most. Lawrence had an innate understanding of cause and effect.

He wanted Junior and all of his children to understand that the only way to survive for certain was to be the master of your own destiny. When the family worked the land for the lord, they received nothing more than food from their garden and the chickens and their eggs for payment. Right now they had little silver, but they had more than enough food, and in the fall they would be able to sell their crops anywhere they chose and for whatever price someone was willing to pay them. Lawrence and his family could decide the location, time, and price to sell their crops. Their lives had become more complicated, but they would learn to deal with a more complicated life as time passed with the help of their friends and, of course, Father Magnus.

Lawrence now realized that they wouldn't fail at their venture. The worst was far behind them. He thought about this as he and Sam started chopping down the largest tree they had ever seen in their lives. It was April 1, 1775, and someone was celebrating a birthday on Saturday.

Lawrence would invite everyone, including Father Magnus.

Chapter Twenty-Six

Lawrence and Sam cut down several trees around the garden. This let more sunshine onto the land and would allow them to create a bigger area to plant next year. They stripped limbs from the trees and brought some of them into the lean-to for firewood. In a few weeks, they would cut some of the smaller trees into two- or three-foot sections to sell to the wheelwright. He would shape them into spokes or hubs, or the pieces for the outer rim of the wagon wheels he made.

It was getting close to lunchtime, so Sam and Lawrence went out to hunt. What they would eat for lunch was usually a surprise until they caught something. They never knew what they would come across on these outings. As they walked south along the river, they soon saw turkey and rabbit tracks in the soft soil.

They walked slowly on and eventually heard a turkey in the brush. They stopped, listened, and waited, hiding behind the bushes that surrounded them. Eventually, a turkey came out into a small clearing near them, and Lawrence killed it in a flash.

Sam was always amazed at how fast Lawrence could size up the situation and decide exactly what he needed to do. This was one of Lawrence's traits that made him so formidable. If he had been a warrior in the true sense of the word, he would have been unsurpassed.

They placed the beautiful turkey in their bag. They continued to walk farther along the river to the south, listening to it tumble and crash over stones and boulders. The noise from the fast-moving water hid any sounds that the hunters might have made. They walked deeper into the woods and waited. "It's your turn, Sam. If you want to eat today, make your shot count."

They waited for a very long time. Sam was tired, sore, and hungry, but he was responsible for lunch today. Lawrence had other plans for the turkey.

Finally, a large rabbit appeared heading to the river. Sam aimed and hit the rabbit. It was a clean hit, and the rabbit died instantly.

"That's the way to do it, Sam. We can eat lunch now. Great shot."

"What about the turkey, brother?"

"We can sell that in town for a few pennies and start our savings, Sam."

"What are you talking about, Lawrence?"

"We need silver to buy more tools and supplies."

"Why not just trade like at home?"

"We will do that too, Sam, but sometimes it's easier and to our advantage to use silver."

"Oh, I think I understand," Sam replied.

He remembered buying the flint and was reminded of how Lawrence had changed a rabbit into silver coins on one of their trips into the village.

In the morning, Lawrence and Sam headed back to Oak Junction to be with their family. The week had passed very quickly for both of them. Sometimes Lawrence felt guilty that he was away from his family so much, but he knew it was only for a relatively short time.

Charles and William's relationship had always been a good one, but since coming to Oak Junction, they had more time with each other and more time to reconnect. They were both older now and were able to express their feelings more clearly and on a deeper level. William began to understand his father better now, and he took more of an interest in doing things with Charles and learning from him.

This included the time they now spent hunting when they weren't working the fields. It gave Charles an opportunity to talk with William about his future. William loved farming and being outside. And now that they had some land of their own, he thought that he would be quite content to stay on their land and watch over it. William always seemed to be closer to his mother Martha and was very protective of little Sam, but he hadn't been very close to Lawrence.

Lawrence was the middle child and was always very independent. That was one of the reasons he was able to feel comfortable leaving their home when he did. William wasn't sure what the future held for him, but he knew that farming would be a part of it. William could see himself working on their farm with several hired men as it grew. He was quite happy with that prospect. Even Charles, who had little imagination of his own, could see the potential of the land at Oak Junction. Lawrence had enough imagination for the whole family. All these people had to do was be brave enough to follow Lawrence and his dreams.

William had felt left out sometimes and was drawn to his mother in the past. Since the family had come to live with Lawrence and Catherine, they had all become closer. Charles was much happier and so his relationship with his wife, Martha, had improved greatly as well. Then there was Catherine and the grandchildren. Charles and Martha were over the moon about all of them. They had worried, like most parents do, about who their children would marry and what their future held.

They were all very much relieved now, especially Lawrence. Catherine was very smart and a very good mother and wife. Most importantly for them, she had given Lawrence's parents two wonderful grandchildren. If that was all she ever did, it would have been quite enough for them.

The fact that they now had a chance at a bright future and weren't tied to someone else's land was incredible. To be able to be part of something larger than each family member and to be able to create something that might live on beyond them gave them the focus and the energy to make it come true.

At first, Charles was a little sad that Sam was with Lawrence, but Martha helped Charles see that this was a second chance to regain that closeness with William that he craved. Charles was able to tell William all the stories about their family history that he had been keeping to himself for all the years that they were on the lord's land. In turn, William not only felt closer to his immediate family but also to his family in the distant past whom he had never met. He was now also becoming attached to the land that he worked and lived on.

When Lawrence and Sam reached home again at the end of the week, there was a festive atmosphere all around them. It was late in the day, and several of their friends were at Oak Junction for Elizabeth's birthday party. Father Magnus and the nuns who had stayed with Catherine were there again, along with Mother Meredith and Sister Ruth.

Lawrence had thought Sister Ruth was rather serious when they rode together to Themstead. But she was in great humor at the party. Perhaps it had just been that she was still mourning the death of her mother on that trip they had taken together to Themstead. In any event, it seems that everyone was in high spirits as the children ran out to meet their father and Sam. The children were still too young to understand where their father went off to every week, but they were always thrilled when Lawrence and Sam came home.

Theodore, the tavern owner, and his wife were at Lawrence's home for the first time. Theodore Jr. was now old enough to mind the tavern alone, so his parents took the opportunity to visit with the Smiths. They had become closer after Theodore was involved with the capture of the two bandits in the village and the battle that preceded it.

Theodore was a force to be dealt with, most certainly. He was very well built and had been in many a battle in his tavern and elsewhere. He was seldom on the losing side. He never went looking for trouble, but he didn't run when he felt he was in the right. In this way, he was very much like Lawrence, and they had hit it off instantly when they first met.

Lawrence and his father weren't people who frequented the tavern, but there was no doubt that Theodore was a good man, and he had many a story to tell. He saw nearly all of the men in the village in his establishment more than once a week. He was the first or second person in the village to see any strangers who passed through the village as well. He often saw people behaving at their worst, but he tried to keep an open mind about them until proven wrong. Theodore was very aware of his role in the community, and he was very careful to keep any stories from becoming public knowledge if he could help it.

He would tell a story once in a great while if he had enough ale in him, but strangely, he wasn't a big drinker. He inherited the tavern from his father, who was its best customer according to many of the old-timers.

Theodore never spoke ill of his parents, but he didn't have the drinking habit that his father was born with. Most of the people on the south side of the village where Theodore and his wife lived were part of the merchant class and had larger plots of land with bigger gardens and many animals behind their shops, as well as larger dwellings. They were self-sufficient and would eventually become the wealthier members of the town when it became one.

Theodore knew many important and funny things about his customers. He would never tell a story exactly the same way twice, and he always left out the names of the guilty parties. He would simply use the saints' names when telling his stories. Father Magnus didn't always appreciate that, but sometimes he did.

Even if the stories were about the person hearing them, he would disguise them enough so that even the listener wouldn't recognize himself in them. Lawrence loved the stories like most everyone else, but he was never interested in the real people except one. That was Father Magnus. Lawrence knew that there had to be a great deal of history that came with the Father. Lawrence didn't like gossip, but he was intrigued. He had a great desire to know this man who had helped him so much in his life.

Chapter Twenty-Seven

There were people who knew more about the Father. Among them were those who volunteered at the church, the nuns, and the monks. Lawrence didn't have much day-to-day contact with those people. Now that he was at Themstead most of the week, he saw the villagers even less than before. Junior, however, had a great deal of contact with the monks now. But the monks didn't have much to say about the Father's family history.

Father Magnus's history was hidden in the past somewhere, out of sight from all but his family, if he had any. Everyone held Father Magnus in high regard, and rightly so, but Lawrence wanted to get to know Father better. Father Magnus knew more about Lawrence than Lawrence knew about Father Magnus, just as the villagers knew more about Lawrence when he first came to the village than Lawrence knew about them. He wanted to change that.

Lawrence and his family went to church every Sunday now. But that was a very formal affair and did not lend itself to long personal conversations with Father Magnus. Lawrence still didn't even know Father Magnus's first name. He doubted that anyone in the village knew it.

Father Magnus wasn't aloof. He was just the opposite, and his warmth and ability to get close to people made a first name unnecessary. His title was enough to calm and reassure his parishioners. That made him a bigger mystery to Lawrence. Here was this man who had played the largest role in Lawrence's life other than his own father, yet he didn't even know his first name. Lawrence wanted to change that if he could. He needed to talk to Father Magnus about this.

After the party on Saturday night, when all the guests had left and the children were put to bed, Lawrence and Catherine had time to talk more in private. They talked about everything that was happening at Oak Junction, and Lawrence brought Catherine up to date with his plans at Themstead. Lawrence listened as Catherine told him about how his parents and the children were doing. He watched her lovely face in the candlelight as she told him about how Junior and Ginger seemed to love each other and about the young couples' sweet courting. Their courting was quite different from the way Lawrence and Catherine had met and became a couple. There was no doubt about that. Sadly, their union had begun with a tragedy.

Lawrence and Catherine were married first, after courting and eventually falling in love, even though they were already man and wife in the eyes of the law. Sadly, they now spent a great deal of time apart, but they both realized that it was for several months at most. They would soon be together in a new house at Themstead. That was most important for both of them. Catherine and Lawrence kissed, and Catherine blew out the candle at the side of the bed. She hoped their courting would never end.

That night, Lance was restless. He sniffed and walked the room slowly. He licked Lawrence's hand to waken him. He had heard something.

Lawrence rolled up on his side and looked at Lance, and then he heard it.

"What was that, Lance? Come on, we'll take a look." As Lawrence opened the door, Lance was off like a shot.

Lawrence looked up after smelling something. It was smoke. There was a burning arrow lodged in a shingle just above the door. Lawrence ran to the bucket of water that was always kept at the front side of the house and tossed it on the roof. It put the fire out.

While he was putting out the small fire, Lance was running after a black horse with a tall rider. The rider looked familiar, but most humans looked alike to him. This one had a nasty smell about him, however, and he'd remembered it. It was the sheriff that he was chasing.

Eventually, after running a great distance, Lance gained on the horse and made a desperate leap. He missed the rider with his jaw but tore away a piece of the saddle blanket as he fell. He tumbled on the ground but was uninjured. He was not as young as he had once been, but he was still in his prime, or so he thought.

He walked and ran back to the house and family with a red piece of fabric in his mouth. It was smooth to his tongue and smelled of evil and many different horses. He dropped it at Lawrence's feet and went to the horse trough for a well-deserved drink and to lay down.

"What is this, boy? Good job, Lance," Lawrence said as he examined the fabric closer. It was a rich, red silk fabric.

"Good boy, Lance, this shouldn't be too hard to match. Not many people can afford such a fine cloth on their horse blanket." Lawrence went into the house and reemerged with a leg he had torn off a smoked rabbit that was hanging in the room and tossed it to Lance.

On Sunday, the entire family went to church. They all walked together on the main road. They were quite a sight. The two little ones were leading the way, one willing to walk just so far out in front of her parents and the other tucked into a blanket and held by Lawrence, his face appearing occasionally when they passed into some shade. Elizabeth looked back often to be sure that Lawrence and Catherine were still close behind her. She was soon tired out, and her parents had to carry her the rest of the way to the church.

Don and his family sat next to Junior, with Ginger between Don and Junior for all in the village to see. Of course, everyone knew that Junior and Ginger were engaged and that the wedding was only a matter of planning now.

Elizabeth was wearing the new dress that her mother and grandmother had made for her. She was quite proud of it. The Smiths were quite a handsome family. Catherine was always very concerned about keeping a neat home and having her family looking their best. Eli was just starting to walk now, and his mother or grandmother always had a firm grip on him.

Father Magnus had a great gift in writing his sermons. His viewpoint and understanding nature always came through. Lawrence tried to understand the Father by examining the content and the viewpoint of his sermons. Lawrence wondered how Father Magnus was able to understand and convey feelings of loss and sadness to everyone or hope when that was called for, without experiencing the normal events of a family man and marriage.

There were many times that Lawrence moved forward in his life without knowing what would happen next, but he took the chance nonetheless. Lawrence wasn't sure that God would have time to watch over him constantly, so he left as little to chance as possible. It did seem like a paradox. You were told to work hard, struggle, and even suffer and to do all you could to be successful, and then you are told that God will provide. Lawrence had learned to plan and keep going forward, no matter what. He would be the master of his future or die trying. There would be unforeseen events coming, certainly. That was life, after all. But those unforeseen events weren't always bad. That appeared to be the story of his young life up to this point as far as he was concerned.

Lawrence wondered, *What was it about Father Magnus that gave so many of the villagers the confidence they had in him and his words?* Father Magnus was older, but what gave him the ability to anticipate and to answer Lawrence's and the villagers' questions so well? Lawrence wanted to understand how the Father could do this. He was determined to talk to Father Magnus. He had been thinking about it for years but never had the time.

"Go on home, Catherine, I need to talk with the Father about some things."

"Is everything alright, Lawrence?"

"Yes, dear. I just need to talk with him for a few moments. Be careful going home, dear. Keep your eyes open for trouble, brothers," he added as he left and walked around to the side of the church. Everyone in Lawrence's family left for home together down the road back to the old oak. They all had many chores to attend to before the day ended. There were animals to feed, children to care for, and work to complete in the fields while Lawrence walked to the Father's office.

Lawrence waited in the dark hallway for the Father to come to his office in the rear of the lovely old church. Soon father approached his office carrying several large books, and Lawrence spoke to him.

"May I speak with you, Father Magnus?"

"Yes Lawrence, of course. I always have time for you."

This was another part of the mystery of Father Magnus for Lawrence. How did he develop that gift of his to make everyone feel important?

"I need to talk to you for a few moments. I have something that I need to show you."

Father Magnus fussed with the heavy door and eventually got it to open. He pushed it into the room, and they both entered.

"I know, Lawrence, I can see the worry on your face. Sit down here and relax for a moment."

Lawrence sat down on one of the hard wooden chairs in the Father's office while Father Magnus put his books and papers away on the large wooden shelves behind his desk. Father Magnus was usually a very neat man. He tried his best to keep his office neat and orderly even with all the very large old books that filled the room.

Lawrence started on his long list of questions for Father Magnus after he settled into his chair.

"How is it that you are able to answer all these difficult questions that we bring to you, Father? You always seem to be three steps ahead of everyone else."

"The fact that you are now asking me that question tells me that you may be able, or nearly ready, to hear my answer, Lawrence."

"What gives you the knowledge and the confidence to lead us in our little corner of the world, Father?"

"First, it is my position, obviously. You come expecting me to have the answers to most of your questions. Your expectations of me and our common beliefs and your trust in God already have prepared you to accept my answers as the truth. I have a great resource here in the Bible and in all the monks and nuns who help me. There are many here in this church, men and women who know the Bible better and have studied it far longer than I have. We discuss these issues together all the time. These questions of life and morality, and God, are mysteries to all of us.

"I am, after all, just a man, older than you, surely, and perhaps a little wiser due to my age and experiences, but just a man like yourself. I have not always been protected and nurtured by the church, and I have lived out in the world."

"May I ask you about your life before you entered into the clergy?"

"I don't think you are at the point where you know the right questions to ask me yet. That will come with age and wisdom. But let me tell you a story."

Father Magnus started to tell a tale to Lawrence.

"There once might have been a young handsome lad named, let's think for a moment, Jerome. And perhaps this young lad came from one of the wealthiest families in London. He would have gone to the best schools and would have been one of the brightest students.

"Let's understood these facts to be true, at least in this story. He would have had many advantages over his compatriots. Jerome would have perhaps entered into the family business. And it might have been one of the most important in London. And if that did happen, and let's say that it did, he surely would have been meeting many wealthy and beautiful women and their families who would have seen Jerome's promise. And all of those families would have wanted to benefit from that in some small way.

"Due to his apparent wealth and connections, many might have sought him out as a potential husband for any number of prominent, wealthy, and beautiful young women. If that were the case, and let's say that it was, it would follow that all these wonderful things would come to pass. So Jerome soon had a wonderful family, wealth, happiness, and maybe even some little respect in the community.

"Just as you do, he might have had a couple of children, a boy and a girl. Jerome and the love of his life might have married young and had a wonderful few years and thought that their entire life together would continue as it had started out. That it was to be absolute bliss, forever."

Lawrence sat impatiently, listening to this story.

"Let's suppose, however, that just four years later, the entire family was destroyed, except the father. It doesn't matter what happened to them, but they are gone. What might you expect the father to do then?

"He could defile the memory of his family in any number of ways, or just drink himself to death. The choice was his, Lawrence, what would he do? Perhaps he could try to find some purpose in his small pitiful life by helping others instead of destroying his own life. Maybe helping those who had experienced the same type of disasters in their lives might help him survive as well. Let's suppose he was forced to leave the wealth and the society that he knew due to circumstances beyond his control. He could shake his fist at God and curse him, or grow over time and develop the ability to empathize with and help others. Perhaps in the end, by doing that, he might actually help himself heal.

This is the story of all of us, Lawrence. In time, if we live a long life, we will lose everyone, won't we, Lawrence? This is what life has in store for us. Helping others helps with our own healing and survival, Lawrence. You think I have all the answers, but I don't. Your children will think you have all the answers for a while, and then they will realize that you don't.

"Perhaps together, Lawrence, you, God, and I can come up with enough good answers in the short term to help us live a decent life. We will all suffer loss and pain, but how we react to those losses will be what people will remember about all of us."

"I see, Father."

"Do you have any more questions for me?"

"Yes, Father. Look at this."

"Where did you get that?"

"It was from Lance's mouth. Someone tried to burn my house down last night. I put the fire out after little damage. But Lance chased the man and horses and brought this back to me. I think it is important. It is very fine cloth, I think. Perhaps you might find out who might have a saddle blanket made of this."

"Yes, Lawrence, I will look into it before I say anything, but I think I know where it might be from. I will look into this, but don't speak of it to anyone."

"I brought you a rabbit for dinner."

"Thank you, Lawrence, you're a good man."

Lawrence walked home wondering about all that Father Magnus had said. As he walked onto his land, a man on horseback came toward him and stopped. He was tall and slender as he sat on his beautiful black horse. He had a regal bearing. It was the sheriff. The man who had first handed the document to Lawrence that changed his life.

"Lawrence, you have been a lucky man so far. I have plans for you and your family. They won't make you feel very safe, I'm afraid."

Lawrence said nothing about the cloth and wondered why the sheriff was on his land, so far from his own home.

"What are you talking about?"

"These parcels that the king has given you were to be mine. You have taken them from me. If you do not leave here after signing them over to me, you will suffer the consequences."

The sheriff pulled a rolled-up parchment from his saddlebag and held it in his hand.

"You will sign this and leave the county, or you will all pay the consequences." Lawrence knew that it was a deed to his land.

"Sign this or your family will perish. I might even let you live to suffer their loss," he hissed as he spoke.

"I will never leave my land in fear and especially not from fear of you."

"I have the resources and power to destroy you and your family, Lawrence. Don't trifle with me. You will suffer the consequences if you do."

"You are a fool to think that you can chase me off of my land, sheriff."

"I have warned you, Lawrence, you will not win this battle. I will have all of you killed, and there is nothing you can do about it. And no one would believe your tale if you told them about our little conversation here. We are quite alone at the moment." Lawrence looked around and saw that he was correct. All of the family was working far away in the fields.

"I knew you were watching us from the forest, you coward. My family and I will never leave here unless I am old or died a natural death. You will have a very long wait, I'm afraid."

"I don't think so, Lawrence. You have been warned. You might die sooner than you think."

"Not likely, sheriff. Not by your hands, at least."

"I have tried to save you a great deal of grief, Lawrence. You are a fool. You deserve nothing that you have now. I will take all of it away, one way or the other."

"I should kill you now as we talk, sheriff."

"Yes, that would be ironic. If you were to do that, you would hang and lose all of this land and I would gain nothing, but you won't. No one would believe your story."

The sheriff turned his horse away abruptly and rode slowly away. He looked back at Lawrence once and shook his head. Lawrence now knew that he had a powerful enemy. One, perhaps, who he could not win over in any way other than a physical battle. The man had political power, wealth, and connections beyond this little village.

Lawrence didn't tell Catherine about what had happened as they sat down together in the afternoon to rest. He had been thinking what to do all afternoon as he worked.

"I need to talk to Father Magnus, dear."

"What about, Lawrence?"

"I just remembered something I need to ask him. I won't be gone long."

"Alright dear, but be back for dinner. I don't want you to leave for Themstead without a proper meal.

Lawrence grabbed his quiver of arrows and his bow as he walked to the front door.

"Why are you taking your bow, dear?" Catherine asked him.

"You never know, dear. I might see something on the way to the village that I might want to kill." Lawrence walked to the village and was seated in the Father's office again in a short time.

"Why are you back so soon, Lawrence? I thought you were leaving later?"

"I am, Father, but I just had a visit from the sheriff."

"Oh, interesting. Was he there to talk with you about the bandits? What did he say?"

"He wants my land, Father. He has threatened to harm me and my family if I don't leave after signing my land over to him."

"Why would he do such a thing?"

"He was there when the king gave that land to me. I could see that he was not very happy about giving me that deed then. I could see it on his face. I didn't know who he was at the time. I guess he's been thinking about it all these years. Now he has decided to act against me."

"Well, Lawrence, this is not out of character for him. He has been known to put his own interests before those of the people he serves. He has acquired a good deal of land over the years. He is quite rich now. I am not unaware of his activities, but I dare not speak of them without more proof. I will look into the matter and contact some people who might be able to help us."

"Thank you, Father. I have no idea how long he will wait, and I don't want my family injured or worse. I will take matters into my own hands if nothing comes of your inquiry."

"I understand, Lawrence, but give me a little time to sort these issues out. I'm sure I will get some action after I talk to some people who are close to the king. I do have some influence with him as you do."

"Surely he has forgotten about me as that was long ago. He might think of me when he hunts nearby, but that is the only time, I'm sure. I will keep quiet about all of this, Father. I don't want to worry my family. Please do the same when you come to my home."

Lawrence was home in time for dinner and said nothing about his visit with Father Magnus. Later on Sunday, Lawrence and Sam left for Themstead once more. The family stood on the side of the road as the two men and their horses disappeared over the rise in the road. This week, they were going to kill another buck. Lawrence and Sam would use it to help pay for the new house they needed to build.

A man stood deep in the forest and watched as they left.

Lawrence and Sam rode hard through the night and reached Themstead as the sun came up behind them. Lawrence kept a wary eye on the highway ahead and on the forest as they rode quickly to Themstead. He now knew that he and his family were in mortal danger. He now knew that he had two enemies to watch out for.

Chapter Twenty-Eight

Lawrence and Sam had already cut plenty of trees, which were drying in the field. They had sold several pelts before they left Oak Junction, and Lawrence gave several silver coins to Catherine again. He also kept a few for himself and Sam. When the new house was built, Catherine would come with the children and live at Themstead.

On Monday, Lawrence and Sam irrigated the garden and went into Themstead for more supplies. The crops were beginning to send up their fresh young shoots again. The men walked through most of the town and saw several of the business owners they had met at the church lunch, now working in their respective shops. Lawrence talked to each of them for a short while as they worked and then walked on to the next stall. He did the same thing again at the next stall and so on.

Lawrence traded some pelts for silver and then bought some salt again for use in their new camp. It wasn't a home to them yet, but it soon would be. Lawrence hid some of their silver in a hole in the floor of their cave. They thought it would be safe there after they placed a large rock over the silver just in case. It took both of them to move the rock to its new position over the silver. They smoothed out the marks in the soil around it that told the story of it being moved.

Lawrence was more confused about Father Magnus than ever before. Most of what he had said made sense, but what about that story? Was it the story of his life, or was it just an allegory? He still didn't know Father Magnus's first name. He would have to ask Father Gregory about Father Magnus when he had the chance.

Lawrence and Sam dug the giant hole for the pit saw for several more days after returning to Themstead. They also hunted and watered their garden as needed. They had plenty to eat and fresh, cool water nearby to drink from the river. They had it much easier than Lawrence and Junior had it in the very beginning at Oak Junction.

They had tin cups and plates and all manner of items that were needed to live a fairly comfortable existence. They were still sleeping in the lean-to, but the weather was nice, and they had the cave to sleep in when the weather was wet or too cold to be comfortable. They were completely surrounded by trees, and no one would ever suspect that anyone was living in these dark mysterious woods.

The land was so vast that they hadn't had time to explore any of it. They were still busy just doing the day-to-day work that kept them alive.

Lawrence wanted the pit done well before the carpenters arrived to start on the house. He laid out lines in the dirt with a stick several different times, trying to get the location of the sawmill just right. He would build their house at the end of the sawmill just like the miller. There would be no flour dust in his home, only the sweet smell of newly-cut timber. This building would be a proper one and look much better than his little house in Oak Junction.

Over the next week, Lawrence and Sam cut many logs into three-foot lengths and then split them as the wheelwright had shown them. They had many small lengths of wood for the wheelwright by Friday. Lawrence and Sam put them in their bags and carried them into town. They sold them to the wheelwright for silver and then walked over to the church to see Father Gregory.

They found Father Gregory in his office. It was bigger than Father Magnus's office with a much larger window as well. But the stonework and stones of this building were the same as at Oak Junction.

Father Gregory was going over some notes when Lawrence and Sam entered his office.

The door was ajar, and they could see him seated at his desk.

"Hello Father, we are here with a gift for you, the monks, and the nuns." Sam took a turkey out of his sack when Lawrence looked at him and laid it on the grey stone floor near the door of the office.

"Thank you, Lawrence, who's this with you?"

"This is my younger brother Sam, Father. He is living here with me at Themstead now."

"Oh yes, I remember him now. He was at the town meeting. Nice to see you again, Sam. You know you have a very famous brother?"

"Yes sir, I know I do," Sam said quietly.

"We are all very happy to have you and your brother living here now."

Sam looked down at the floor as Father Gregory complimented them.

"With all the plans you have, I know you are going to be very successful here. Lawrence, if you need anything, call on me at any time."

"Thank you, Father," Lawrence answered as the two young men stood up to leave.

As they turned toward the door, Lawrence turned back around and spoke to Father Gregory.

"Do you know where Father Magnus was born?"

"I think he comes from London, Lawrence. Yes, I'm quite sure of it. I think he still has family there."

"Thank you, Father, God be with you."

"And with the two of you." As Lawrence walked back through town with young Sam, his mind was racing.

Had he heard correctly? Father Magnus had family in London? That was very interesting. As Lawrence and Sam walked slowly through Themstead, looking for their supplies, many of the shopkeepers acknowledged them and Lawrence reciprocated, though he was still thinking about Father Magnus.

Father Magnus was right that everyone in Themstead knew of Lawrence. He just had to take the time to talk a little to all of them now and then. He didn't know where he would find that time, but he would. Themstead was a large village with were many people Lawrence would end up doing business with. This was going to be his new home and the beginning of his fortune.

When Lawrence and Sam reached their lean-to, it was already late morning, and the sun was rising still higher in the east. Now their morning work would begin. They still had plenty of the log sections to split for Kyle, the wheelwright, but that could wait. They ate some smoked meat that Catherine had sent with them and then checked on the horses. These were the most valuable assets that Lawrence had except for his family and his land.

The horses had plenty of grass and water, but Lawrence decided to give them some oats as well. Lawrence always had plenty of work to do on his land, and thankfully, he had learned to enjoy it. He had learned to receive pleasure from simple accomplishments.

He had many responsibilities to his family, but he never felt burdened or unhappy because of them. This was his life, and he enjoyed it for the most part. He couldn't always be with his family at this point, but everything he was doing was meant to improve their lives. His absence was just part of the cost they paid for their current and future success. Lawrence didn't take much time thinking about those things as he worked, but he was intrigued by Father Magnus's past.

Lawrence and Sam took some time after lunch to explore their land for the first time. They had been here at Themstead for almost a month now, going home on weekends and then returning.

The land was too vast to even begin to explore on one short adventure. They would only cover a very small area south of the garden next to the river on this short outing. They had little time to waste before winter came again. As they began to walk toward the river with their weapons, they soon hear the sound of the rushing river racing over stones and debris.

Soon they came across the ruins of an old footbridge that had fallen into the fast-moving torrent years before. The land sloped away from town and caused the river to rush rapidly over the many rock formations that created small waterfalls and cataracts.

The river ran to the south and then disappeared into the forest again. As Lawrence and Sam reached the river, they turned south and walked along it for some time. *If anyone were to fall into this river, they would surely die,* Sam thought. Lawrence warned Sam to stay away from the river's edge as they walked. Neither one of them could swim, but it wouldn't matter here as the water moved too fast to worry about that. They would be gone in seconds if they fell in.

After a short walk, they turned east and walked deeper into the forest. The land soon leveled out and became flat once they were twenty yards from the river. They could hear the crash of a larger waterfall somewhere on the river below them, but looking into that would have to wait for another day.

The forest was very thick and dark, and after a few steps away from it, the sounds of the river were soon gone. Looking back the way they had come, Sam could only see trees. There were giant trees of every shape and shade of green. The river had vanished behind them as if in a dream. The forest became quiet except for the sounds of the wind blowing through the distant treetops and the many animal and bird calls.

There were ancient paths through this forest, but who knew where they would take them. They didn't venture far into this dark green mystery. They weren't afraid, but this was not the time for a long adventure.

The aromas and sounds reminded Lawrence of his life on the lord's land with his father and all the fine days he spent hunting as a child and as a young man. He was reminded of how lucky he was to have been born in the country and not in a large city. They followed the narrow trail in front of them. It had most likely been created by animals and then enlarged or beaten down by the king's hunters or poachers in this gigantic forest. There were no signs of human habitation or harvesting of the enormous trees in this minute part of Lawrence's land.

As they walked back to the river, they saw several more deer tracks. "This is what we wanted to find. We will kill a fine buck near here and sell it to the butcher in Themstead. With the silver, we will receive from him and the wheelwright, we will have Don make a pit saw for us." They walked back to their campsite as the sun began to drop behind the now almost black trees.

They started a fire and ate some smoked rabbit and bread they had brought with them. Sam dreamt of cutting oak again that night. Tomorrow, Tuesday, would be a long day. Lawrence was determined to split all the sections of oak into long thin blocks for the wheelwright. Lawrence and Sam had a huge pile of wood to cut. Sam told Lawrence about his dreams of the night before, about cutting the oak. Lawrence laughed. "You weren't dreaming, Sam, you were just seeing into our future."

On Wednesday, Father Magnus came to Themstead on church business and stopped to see Lawrence on his journey. He found Lawrence and Sam hard at work as usual. Luckily for Lawrence, Father had come on his donkey cart. Their wagon was back at Oak Junction now. Father Magnus brought Lawrence and Sam up to date regarding the events from Oak Junction and their family while he joined the two men working.

There had been no news of problems on the roads lately, which brought them some relief. Lawrence explained to the Father what all the pieces of oak were for, and the Father offered his cart. Father Magnus was going to see Father Gregory. Lawrence and Sam loaded the cart and rode to Themstesd with Father Magnus. Lawrence sat next to him and talked while Sam rode in the back with the wood. It was a pleasant ride. The weather was perfect, and there were many people on the highway. The road was dry. No rain had fallen in a week or so, and they hadn't had to sleep in their secret cave. Lawrence had made Sam promise to keep the secret, even from Father Magnus.

Father Magnus took Lawrence directly to the wheelwright's shop, passing many other shops and townsfolk as they went. Many people waved as they passed by. Sam wasn't sure if the people were waving at Lawrence or the Father. Father Magnus noticed this too but knew who the people were waving at. He knew very well that it wasn't him. He was just a visiting clergyman. Lawrence was Lawrence, after all, and everyone wanted to show their respect and catch his eye.

When they reached the wheelwright's shop, Sam and the wheelwright's young helper started to unload the cart while Lawrence and Kyle talked. Father walked on to the church. He knew Lawrence would end up there eventually with his cart, and he had business to discuss with Father Gregory.

Lawrence and Kyle talked for half an hour at least. Kyle could use all the wood that Lawrence would bring him, including the cedar. He used many cedar pieces in the wagons that he built. The wood was strong and held up to the wet weather for years. The cedar wood made Kyle's wagons last almost forever.

Business was very good now in Themstead, though no one knew what might come in the future. The merchants knew they had to do well while the times were good. Lawrence was assured of a steady income for the time being, from Kyle at least. And his coming harvest in Oak Junction looked like a good one this year. When the boys were finished unloading the cart, Lawrence and Sam drove it to the great old church. They stopped at the baker's stand on their way and bought a large loaf of bread.

Lawrence and Sam entered the church to find both of the Fathers talking in Father Gregory's office. They waited outside the office in a large hallway that led into the church. Sam wandered into the church proper and studied the huge space all around him.

Sam was a big boy for his age just as Lawrence had been. He still had a fair complexion as the sun hadn't yet darkened his face as it had for his brother Lawrence. He hadn't worked in the fields long enough yet. He had bright blue eyes and blond hair. Lawrence had blond hair when he was younger as well. But like many things in life, the hair of the child would soon turn dark and then grey as youth turns to middle age and then old age.

The small church at Oak Junction was the only church Sam had entered, and that had seemed very large to him at the time. This church at Themstead was three times the size of the one that Father Magnus led.

Sam couldn't understand how it all stayed up but was very glad that it did, even if only for the time that he was in it. As he walked across the stone floor, he could hear the echoes of his footsteps from across the giant room. He looked up to the ceiling, and it looked to him like he was outside under the night sky. It was so high. He thought that there must be a God for this building to be built by mere men and continue to stand for all these years. The church was more than two-hundred years old.

When the Fathers had finished talking, Lawrence knocked on the ancient oak door.

"Come in, Lawrence. Welcome. Sit down here."

"Thank you, Father Gregory."

"How can I help you today, Lawrence?"

"I'm just here to let Father Magnus know that I have brought his cart back to him."

"Thank you," Father Magnus answered.

"Are you sure you don't need it any longer?"

"No, Father, but I have a favor to ask of you."

"What is it, son?"

"I would like to give you some silver coins to pass on to Don the blacksmith for me."

"Of course, Lawrence. Is there a message to go with the silver?"

"Yes Father, there is."

"Then give it to me, my son."

"Just let him know that I am ready for the pit saw, Father."

"Well done, Lawrence, I'll tell him as soon as I reach home."

"Thank you again, Father."

"What are you doing on your land at the moment, Lawrence?"

"I'm cutting down some oak trees. You saw the pieces on the wagon on the way here. Those are going to be used by the wheelwright, and I've cut down some cedar for him and myself."

"There are many furniture makers here in Themstead, Lawrence, and not many oaks left close by except on your land. They might buy your wood as well," Father Gregory chimed in.

"Thank you, Father Gregory. I will talk to some of them and see what comes of it," Lawrence answered.

"You already have, Lawrence, at the lunch here just a few weeks ago. They're just waiting to hear from you. You may have the last and the best oak trees left in the area."

Lawrence realized when he heard this that he would have to stop and talk to the furniture makers on his way out of town that day. He had already seen several oak trees on his land, and there was a gigantic area still to explore. He would focus on the oaks and cedar to raise the needed silver to build his mill. The mill would be of stone and wood and would be a small fortress compared to his home in Oak Junction.

He needed to show his intention of staying in Themstead for a very long time by building a proper building. With the ability to sell his wood to the craftsmen in Themstead, he would have the financial means to build his new home and the mill there. The brothers would first build a strong stone mill with a proper door and strong shutters. And in time, they would build the house next to the mill on the river. Lawrence's mill would be visible to everyone passing by on the main highway, and everyone would come to know it and, he hoped, use it.

The next morning, Father Magnus left for Oak Junction on his small cart after a fine late breakfast with Father Gregory. He was at ease on the main highway, heading home on a clear, crisp spring morning. He didn't mind the cool weather; his simple garments were ample, and the results of his eating and drinking habits kept him warm enough.

He passed several travelers on his way home and eventually stopped to pick up three elderly people who were having difficulties walking along the rough road and carrying their meager belongings at the same time.

Their house had been damaged by fire, and they were hoping to stay in Oak Junction with some distant family members for a short time while their house was being repaired. They were too old to live out of doors and hoped their family could help them.

"Who is your family in Oak Junction then?"

"Charles Smith, Father. They have the farm at the junction east of the village."

"I know them well. How are you related?"

"Charles is our nephew, but we haven't seen each other in years. We have been separated by much geography and ill health. We just found out that they had moved. We had lost track of them, but then some kind soul told us where they had moved. We are his father's last remaining siblings, Father."

"Well, I'm sure they will help you. They have helped many others, even strangers, whenever they have been asked."

"That is what we have heard, and so we are traveling to Oak Junction. We have no one else to turn to."

"I understand, friends, I understand. Please come to me if you need anything the Smith family can't help you with."

"Thank you, Father. We have some children, but they are barely getting by and don't have enough, even for themselves. There are so many of them now." The Father drove on and wondered how this would all turn out. He continued past the village and eventually pulled in to Lawrence's farm.

Father Magnus climbed slowly down from his perch on the cart and knocked at the door of Lawrence's home after his old wagon had come to a stop. The donkey instantly started to eat the tall grass that grew at his hooves.

Catherine opened the thick, heavy door slowly.

"Father, how nice to see you. How are you?"

"I'm fine, my dear. I've brought you some company. I'm afraid they're in some distress."

"Who are they, and what do they need?"

"They have no place to stay in Themstead at the moment, and they say they are part of Lawrence's family."

"Yes, young lady, our house burned some, but it will be fit for us to return to in just a fortnight," one of the old men announced.

"If we could stay, it would be a blessing."

"You are welcome, of course. We have plenty of food, but the lodgings may be a little tight. We just have the two rooms."

"We are fine with that, young lady, and we will help in the fields or with the animals if you might let us. We are farmers by trade. We live one day west of Themstead. Father saved us for sure."

"Charles is in the fields with his son William. I am his daughter-in-law, married to Lawrence. These are my children, Elizabeth and Eli. Please come in and rest. I'll bring you some water." Catherine waved for them to follow her as she entered the house. Catherine brought water for everyone, and they drank heartily. She could hear them talking quietly as she returned to them.

"I'm off, Catherine, give everyone my best," the Father said as he climbed back up onto his cart with some difficulty. He turned his brown shaggy donkey to the left and back up the road to the village and his church, which he had passed to bring these old people to see Catherine.

It was a beautiful early evening when he reached Don at his blacksmith shop and gave him the message from Lawrence and the silver coins.

Father wondered how it was that the folks he happened to rescue were Charles and Lawrence's family. Of course, he knew most of the families in Oak Junction, but why or how was it that the people he stopped to help were relatives of Charles and his family? The Father had always felt a special affection for Lawrence and now his entire family as well.

Perhaps it was God reminding Father Magnus of His presence, showing him that He still cared and could intervene when it was least expected. The Father's faith, like most people's, ebbed and flowed over his lifetime. He always believed in God, but sometimes it was easier than others. And when things like this happened to him, he was always pleased and surprised. He didn't have all the answers, and he was often frustrated by his congregation, and sometimes even by God.

He knew his duty was to lead his flock to see and feel God in their lives, but sometimes it was just easier than others. Father Magnus saw Lawrence as the son he might have had if his life had gone in a different direction. He wasn't complaining, he was just thinking about what he had and didn't have.

Chapter Twenty-Nine

Catherine sent Lizzie out to bring her grandfather and uncle back to the house. When they returned, they saw that they had three elderly visitors. They all sat down to talk with them. Their relationships were all worked out eventually as they made the necessary accommodations for the two old widowers and one old widow.

Catherine and the children would move in with Charles and Martha, and the new family members would stay in Catherine and Lawrence's room. It meant more work for Catherine and Martha, but it had to be done. These people had no one else to turn to. This long lost part of the Smith family was now reunited by a fire. They would stay for several days after many years of not seeing each other. There were the two brothers and their sister. They had all lost their respective spouses over the years and had ended up living together in one house on one of the brother's farms.

It was one day's ride west of Themstead. After a good night's sleep, these three older folks seemed very fit and had hearty appetites. They had lived on farms all their lives and were up and waiting for Charles in the morning, tools in hand. There wasn't much to do, but they helped with glee. They hadn't been away from home for years, and they were revitalized. The sister collected the eggs with Lizzie in the long hen house and fed the animals while the brothers went into the fields to weed.

Just before lunch, a lone rider on a beautiful black horse rode slowly by the farm. He looked into the fields and couldn't believe what he saw. Charles, William, Junior, and three more tall figures were standing together, talking and leaning on their tools. He decided not to stop or come back in the evening. He would ride on to Themstead.

He looked older than his twenty-six years. He was slouched in his saddle and his head hung low under a large dark hat. After he passed the farm, he sat up straight and held his head high. His bright blue eyes stared straight ahead revealing no emotion. It was Jason looking over at the Smith family. He had plans for them. But those three extra silhouettes made him think twice. He couldn't see that those three forms were older people who would have been no threat to him.

Junior came home that night to find these long lost family members at Oak Junction. Father Magnus had mentioned to Don that "the Smiths" had company. Junior helped move some items to make room for them with the help of William.

Everyone talked at length through the night and learned of many other family members still alive who lived far away from Oak Junction and Themstead. It was very interesting for them to discover that they had many unknown relatives still living in close proximity but to the west.

Lawrence and Sam cut down several large, straight pine trees over several days of hard work. They also chopped down more cedar and oak trees. They stripped the small limbs off the trees for firewood and cut the trunks and larger branches into three- and four-foot sections. Some of the larger oak trunks would go to the furniture makers and the smaller oak pieces to the wheelwright. The cedar wood was sold to both craftsmen.

In the afternoon on Friday, Lawrence and Sam went into the town to visit some of their new friends and clients. They would be leaving Themstead for the weekend. They would bring the wagon back from Oak Junction on their next return trip. It was needed in Themstead to carry all the heavy wood into the town to sell to the furniture makers who Lawrence had made contact with.

It wasn't hard to close the deals with them. They needed all the wood they could get right away. Lawrence wouldn't need the wagon back at Oak Junction until the harvest in the fall. When Lawrence was riding home, he felt wonderful. He had customers for his wood, he had ordered his pit saw, and he even had some silver in his pouch for Catherine. He couldn't wait to see her and everyone else. As it turned out, there were more surprises than he could have hoped for. Lawrence knew that life was always full of surprises.

When Lawrence finally arrived home at Oak Junction, there was a crowd in front of his little house to meet him: Charles, Martha, Catherine, William, Junior, Lizzie, Eli, and three older strangers.

They were all seated out in front of the house around the long table where they usually ate their lunches. The three old people wouldn't remain strangers for long. Lawrence heard the story of the fire and their circumstances and understood their plight completely.

"There is ample room for everyone. We have plenty of food, and we are family, after all," Lawrence said after he heard their story of the fire.

Jason gathered up some new men to ride with his remaining group and rode southwest from Themstead to find gold and adventure. He still had plenty of horses, and desperate men were plentiful. After a few days of riding and camping in the forests, they eventually came across a wealthy family heading north to Chesterfield.

They were very rich merchants on their way to visit family and to do some business in the north of the country. They didn't stand a chance.

They had a driver and one guard, but they were both killed by one of the new members of the gang. He had a longbow and used it at quite a distance to kill the guard and then the driver. He killed both men with ease and no remorse. He thought that he was quite good with his bow, and so did his compatriots.

The group of highwaymen then came in for the merchant and his wife. They encircled the family with their horses while Jason climbed down from his horse and approached them. He stabbed the man without warning as the woman and her two children huddled in fear. He looked at the newest member of the gang and at one who he knew the best among them and nodded his head. They dismounted. The newest member killed the woman with a knife to her throat. The veteran then killed the two young children. Jason had said nothing to the two men. They knew that no witnesses could be left behind to tell of their crime. They dug through their belongings and took all that was worth anything. They tossed the bodies into the forest and took the carriage and horses.

When the bodies were found shortly thereafter by a traveler, there was great anger and disgust throughout the county. They had all died brutal deaths and had been tortured by the bandits. It was the worst of all the recent crimes that had occurred on the roads in these counties to date. The citizens were in a foul mood and wanted to take matters into their own hands after this terrible act had been discovered.

When Lawrence got back to Themstead, the news was all over the town. It wouldn't take long for it to reach Oak Junction and Catherine. He worried about Catherine and his family when he heard the news. Lawrence would be coming come back with the wagon at the end of the week, so he would have to spend the night with the farmer on the main road to Themstead again. He would not be home as quickly as had been his practice, and he was worried.

The old farmer's name was Joseph. He enjoyed the occasional company of Lawrence and his family. Joseph lived a simple life with his daughter on their farm. It was impossible to make the journey home in one day with the wagon. This farm was at the halfway point of the trip when he used the wagon, so it became the logical location to camp on the way home.

Chapter Thirty

Lawrence took several loads of wood into Themstead over the next few days with Sam. On one of his visits, he ran into a stranger buying a large number of supplies. The man was very well dressed and had a beautiful black horse with a very expensive saddle.

When that man turned to look in the direction of Lawrence as he rode deeper into town, Lawrence saw it. It was the face that he hoped one day to finally see. The man looked just like Lizzie, with a handsome face and those flashing blue eyes. There was no doubt about who this man was. *This is Jason, and he must be the one responsible for the recent robberies and murders in the area,* Lawrence thought.

Lawrence was in his wagon and had wood to deliver. He stopped the wagon on the side of the road and jumped down to the ground. "Sam, stay with the wagon, but watch that man." Sam raised his arm and pointed to Jason as he stood by his horse talking to a shopkeeper. "Don't approach that man; he is very dangerous. Just watch him and stay here. I'm going up to the church."

There were people crowded in all the lanes and pathways in the town. As he ran up the hill to the church, he wondered how many of them were with that murderer and which ones they might be. He locked eyes with some of the people around him but couldn't get any sense of them. *Were they just townsfolk, or were they murderers?* he wondered.

When Lawrence reached the church, he saw Father Gregory talking with one of the sheriff's men. He asked them both to follow him inside.

"I have seen the highwayman here in town who killed Catherine's family."

"How do you know it's him?"

"Believe me, Father, I know what he looks like. Catherine has described him to me a thousand times."

"What do you suggest, Lawrence?"

"Send this soldier back to his master with the news so he can bring back help."

"But that will take days!"

"We can do little else, Father, except follow him and see if he is alone or with others. We don't want to endanger the town. I left Sam watching him near the gates. Come back with some nuns, and we will track him through the village."

"Good idea, Lawrence, we're invisible to men like him. The nuns can wander by and try to listen in if he speaks to anyone. I'll leave Sam in your care with the wagon, ride out to the highway, and wait in the forest. I will need to borrow a horse so that I can follow him." Father Magnus sent one of the nuns to the tavern to borrow a horse from Theodore. She came back quickly with it and walked it down toward the city gates. She waited there as Lawrence had instructed. Then everyone else quickly left the church to go get help.

When the Father and the nuns saw Sam, he was calmly talking to the stranger near the wagon. He had remained seated on the wagon as he had been told. The man had walked towards Sam, who was in front of the bakery. The man had walked farther away from the city gates and up higher into the village. Father Gregory walked up to the stranger and started talking to him and Sam. The nuns fanned out and told the shopkeepers what was happening just in case. They were all on alert soon enough. Lawrence left Themstead through the city gates as the Father distracted Jason and kept him looking at him and Sam.

Lawrence rode quickly down the road and entered the forest. It was very thick and difficult on a horse. It was dark and smelled of the dust that he and the horse had disturbed on the trees they had to pass through. He dismounted and walked his horse deeper into the shadows. He turned his horse around and sat in the silent darkness, waiting for Jason to appear. He could see the sun's rays hitting the dust particles floating in front of him, gleaming in the partial darkness.

"He seemed nice enough, Father," Sam said to Father Gregory after the man had left them and disappeared into the crowd.

"Evil comes in many disguises, Sam. He is one of the worst that I have ever seen. He has killed so many innocent people and ruined their families just for what little money they carried with them."

Jason left Themstead through the same gate as Lawrence after purchasing several items and rode down the highway to the west. There were several sacks containing food tied to his saddle and hanging on both sides on his horse's flanks. Jason carried enough food to feed several men for some time.

Lawrence stayed concealed in the forest for several moments and just watched. Jason was riding his horse at a slow pace and Lawrence wanted to keep as much distance between them as possible without losing sight of him. If he got too close, he might be recognized. He surely didn't want that. Other riders and people walking on the highway offered some cover for Lawrence, thank goodness. In a few more moments, he walked his horse out onto the road and climbed on him. He bumped his heels against the horse and began to move slowly forward.

He was sure that Jason had been watching the family from a distance for some time. After about a mile down the road, two riders came out of the forest and joined Jason. Lawrence followed them on his horse until they turned into the thick forest again, a few miles farther up the winding road.

Father Magnus was still talking with Sam in the village about good and evil as Lawrence walked his horse into the woods and dismounted. Lawrence tied his horse in the trees and walked toward where Jason had entered the woods. He soon was hiding behind their excited horses and could hear Jason's men talking in front of him. He had his bow with him but soon realized that there were far too many men there, even for him.

Back in Oak Junction, things were going better than expected. The three elderly visitors were very helpful and full of the families' history and eager to tell it. They didn't know Lawrence had land in Themstead until Catherine mentioned it to them.

They seldom went into Themstead, mostly just working on their farm and staying at their home. They lived one day's ride on horseback west of Themstead. They had fourteen children among them, mostly boys. They were all grown and lived around them in the countryside. They were good children and kept a close watch over them. They were good hunters like all of the Smiths, too, and were all honest men. The three old siblings had decided to go to Oak Junction instead of burdening their own children after the fire.

When Lawrence returned to Themstead after following Jason on the road, Father Gregory was very anxious. He sent a rider off to the sheriff's office, a day's ride away. He feared for the townspeople and the travelers on the roads, but there was not much they could do. The nuns had already done a good job of informing most everyone about the situation. As more people came to the town, the news traveled among them.

Most everyone who didn't live in Themstead cut their shopping and trading time short and headed to the safety of their homes and other villages before darkness would fall over them. For some, it was a long journey home, and they wanted to travel to the safety of their own homes and villages before sunset. Lawrence returned the horse to the nuns and walked back to his wagon and Sam. They still had to sell all the wood to the wheelwright before going back to their plot of land.

Lawrence had wanted to follow those men, but there was nothing he could do on his own. Some of the folks in town wanted to go after them, but Lawrence knew that that was a fool's errand. None of these townsfolk had the skills needed to attack Jason and his men. It would have been suicide for all of them.

The wagon was hastily unloaded, and Kyle paid Lawrence his silver.

"Do be careful on your way back to Oak Junction, Lawrence. God only knows where those men will strike next."

"Thank you, Kyle, we will do our best." When the conversation was over, Lawrence snapped his whip over the horse's head, and the wagon and the two men were soon on their way out of the village. The roads were empty of travelers now, as was Themstead.

The soldiers arrived late the next day after a long, hard ride. Lawrence took the soldiers to where he had seen the men the day before. There were remnants of a campfire and some chicken bones, but little else. Lawrence had counted twelve men in all. The soldiers didn't seem very excited about trying to find them.

The soldiers were fourteen strong, plus Lawrence. The odds weren't bad, but the soldiers didn't have their hearts in it. They seldom seemed to. They would rather be back in the big city with their women and their ale. They weren't paid enough to go looking for their own deaths. They were mostly for show, and the townsfolk and the farmers all knew it.

The highwaymen knew it as well. The people had given up on the lords and the king at this moment of desperation. All the king and the lords did was tax them into ruin and make their lives miserable as far as they were concerned.

That was one of the reasons Lawrence was such a hero to them. He was one of them, and he was unafraid. They felt stronger when he was around, but they weren't ready to take the law into their own hands yet. Lawrence knew this, but he had to do something. They saw the tracks of the highwaymen leave the forest and join the highway going west but soon lost the trail. It was getting dark, and there had been too many people, horses, and carts on the road to follow their tracks any farther.

Everyone rode back to Themstead disappointed. Lawrence talked with Father Gregory and explained the situation to him. It was decided that Father Magnus would have a talk with the sheriff about the number and willingness of the sheriff's men.

Lawrence went back to his camp to make some important changes. He knew his cave was going to be much more important now with Jason and his men in the area. Lawrence had to use the cave now to prevent his and Sam's demise. Lawrence and Sam would be easy targets if Jason and his men ever found them out in the open in their camp.

When Lawrence arrived at camp, he looked it over very carefully. He looked for signs that others had been there and discovered their secret. It wouldn't be long before he might have visitors, and Lawrence wanted to be prepared. His horse seemed impatient and scraped the ground as Lawrence walked quietly around the area and into the woods for a short distance.

He was satisfied that they'd had no visitors by the time he returned to Sam.

Chapter Thirty-One

After twelve days had passed, the three elderly family members were ready to go home. Father Magnus took them on his cart, but not alone. Charles and William rode with them. They all spent the night at the farmer's house again. Joseph was very pleased to have so many visitors. There were more people visiting him now than ever before.

The farmer's young daughter talked at length with William at night, and they seemed to enjoy each other's company. They had talked several times before whenever he came to spend the night at the farm on his way to Themstead or on his way back to Oak Junction. This family was isolated living out and away from town. The farmer was happy to see someone take an interest in his daughter. She was of marriageable age, and he was losing hope that he might have grandchildren at some point in his life.

William left early in the evening to reach Lawrence. When William got to Lawrence's camp, the only thing there that he could see was the wagon. It was late evening, and William thought there should at least be a welcoming fire for him. He was instantly concerned.

He climbed down from his horse, tied it to a tree limb, and began to start a fire. A hand was on his shoulder before a spark could fly from his flint. It was Lawrence.

"Follow me," he whispered. William followed Lawrence, and soon they were standing in front of a very large bush. It was at least six feet tall and just as wide. They walked behind it and found the entrance to the cave. There was just enough space between the plant and the rock face to slip a horse and his rider behind it to enter the cave.

"We are sleeping indoors for a while. Jason and his men are nearby, I'm sure of it."

"I'm sure you're right, Lawrence. Everyone else is safe at the farmer's house tonight. Our uncles and aunt, Father Magnus, and Dad are all there."

"We will meet them when they leave the farm in the morning. We'll have to get up early to protect them on their way to their farm west of Themstead."

"They have many sons who might help us, Lawrence."

"That would be a great help, but first things first, go and get your horse. We'll hide it in the cave here with ours. Sam, go help William. Make sure he doesn't get lost."

They went for the horse and returned shortly. Sam walked it behind the bush as Lawrence held it back and away from the cave entrance. Sam then walked the horse to where the other horses were tied up deep in the rear of the cave. They ate a dinner of smoked turkey and bread. They had a bucket of water and two cups.

"Just like home, my brothers, just like home," Lawrence said with a grim look on his face. They all sat around a small fire near the entrance to the cave, finishing their dinner and trying to get warm. The smoke from the small fire was nearly invisible as it drifted through the large plant in front of the cave. It was a very dark night, and the moon had not yet risen. They slept lightly.

In the morning, they rode east, back to what they now called Halfway Farm, to meet everyone with the cart. They met them there and slowly proceeded west on the journey to their newly reunited uncle's farm. It would be a long journey.

They all spent the night at Lawrence's new farm in Themstead. It was very exciting for the newly found family members to see how large the parcel was. As farmers, they could see that the possibilities were endless. The next morning, they left for their uncle's farm. It was the first time any of them had traveled this far from Oak Junction.

The three lean old folks seemed to hold up fine on the long journey. It was a fine adventure for them. They didn't understand the danger that Jason presented to those who traveled on these roads now. They were too excited to be out on the road and in new surroundings with family to be worried. The land looked familiar to all of them, and they were at ease despite the danger of Jason lurking in the back of their minds. Lawrence, his brothers, and their father watched the forest along both sides of the road for trouble as they returned to Themstead.

There were many heavily armed men with their families in the yard of the three elderly relatives' fine house when Lawrence and all of the family members reached their uncles' and aunt's farm.

"Who are you?" the well-armed men yelled to Lawrence and his group before they got too close. Their wives and all of their many children quickly left the area and entered a large stone house that stood behind them for protection in case something happened.

"I am Lawrence Smith, your cousin. I have your parents here with us." Their weapons were soon lowered and were pointed to the ground.

"Thank God, we couldn't find them anywhere. We just returned from looking for them again."

"We are sorry to make you all worry about us, but we didn't want to burden you after the fire," one of the old men said as he walked toward his many children.

"We decided to go to Oak Junction and meet Lawrence, Charles, and the whole family," the oldest uncle yelled out from the wagon where he was still seated. We stayed with them until the house was supposed to be finished. Is it done now as promised?"

"Yes, Father," one of them said as the old man climbed down from the wagon and walked in his direction.

Lawrence and one of the men in front of the house slowly rode their horses toward each other to get a closer look at each other's newfound cousin. The resemblance was astounding. They could have been brothers. They looked so much alike. Both men had slender faces with rugged features and broad shoulders. They were taller than most men of their day as well.

"My name is Langley, and we are all in your debt, Lawrence."

"Not at all, you are family—long lost perhaps, but family nonetheless."

"We thought our parents might have been hurt by the highwaymen or worse."

"I completely understand, Langley."

Everyone soon stepped out of the wagon and dismounted from their horses, and the family members all went into the huge stone house and sat in the great room and visited. The old uncles and aunt went to see that the repairs had been finished properly. They were soon satisfied and settled back into their three great leather chairs near a giant fireplace with a warm fire burning that awaited their safe return.

"Langley," Lawrence started off saying as they sat down in the grand room. "I have received some land from the king near here in the west. Do you know of it?"

"Yes, but we had no idea that we were related to you, so we paid little attention to all the stories. It's just half a day's ride from here to the west."

"Perhaps you could show it to me before we go back to Themstead."

"That would be our pleasure. You will spend the night, and in the morning, I will take any or all of you to this land of yours."

They ate a fine supper of turkey, rabbit, venison, fish, and vegetables. There was plenty of wine and ale, too, more than a hundred men could drink. The house was grand, and as they talked, Lawrence and his family learned that the family had plenty of wonderful farmland nearby, divided among all the brothers and brothers-in-law. If the uncles and cousins were struggling now, they surely must have been very rich in the past.

Lawrence soon learned as he spoke to Langley on their way to Lawrence's third parcel in the morning, that their parents were very poor when they were growing up and never changed their habits of living off the land. They were one of the richest families in the area now but lived very humble lives. "They are a little slow to be sure because of their age," Langley mentioned, "but we watch them as best we can." The three old folks had bought up every parcel of land that came up for sale around them over the years and now had the biggest farm around other than a lord who lived miles away.

The third parcel of Lawrence's was larger than the rest. It was far from a village or town, but it was the best land yet. They rode their horses up a great hill and could see below, their land spread out before them. It was like heaven. Rivers and lakes could be seen from where they sat on their horses on the high knoll. It was covered with trees as far as you could see.

Lawrence had his map with him that Father Magnus had drawn, and he had his deed. He showed them to Langley, and Langley smiled. "I thought *we* were well off, Lawrence, but you make us look like paupers."

"I have a plan, Langley, and I want you to be a very big part of it. It will include all of your siblings and mine. Let's talk in a few days at my camp in Themstead." Langley agreed. He too had an imagination and a desire to create something for his family that would last long after he was gone.

After everyone left the home of the elder Smiths, things returned to normal for a time. Lawrence and Sam stayed in Themstead while everyone else returned to Oak Junction.

Don's wife and Catherine talked over the plans for Junior and Ginger's wedding many times into the late evening while the men sat across the room and played chess. They also talked about their future grandchildren. The two women had already had a long and close relationship, but this coming wedding would cement it all the more. They had grown up in the same area west of the village and had many childhood friends in common. That was how it was in Oak Junction. Everyone would eventually find connections from their past with others in the village or make new friends and new connections as their lives unfolded.

Lawrence was still very interested in Father Magnus's past, but there were more pressing issues at hand.

One afternoon while Lawrence and Sam were cutting timber in their saw pit, a large cloud of dust appeared west of their land on the main road. He and Sam gathered their weapons and walked a short distance into the woods where they could remain unseen in the dark forest as the ominous cloud grew larger and the sound of several horses could be heard.

Lawrence and Sam sat quietly in the dark as a large group of well-armed men rode onto their land. To their relief, it was Langley and several of their long-lost cousins. The horses strained at their bridles and dripped saliva onto the ground with excitement as all the men came to a dusty stop in Lawrence's camp. The men, too, were excited and seemed anxious. Lawrence and Sam came back out of the woods when they saw who the men were.

"We have come for a visit, cousin Lawrence. I have brought all of my men with me. We have about thirty, all good bowmen and brave."

"Fine, Langley, come and sit with Sam and me," Lawrence said as he appeared, coming out of the woods with Sam.

"What's the plan then, Lawrence, what are we to do?"

All of the men dismounted and several of the younger cousins followed Sam into the woods with the horses. They would be fed and watered while the older men talked over Lawrence's plan. All of the men walked over to the center of the camp and settled around the camp's fire after releasing their horses to Sam and their sons or cousins.

"We know that we are under almost constant surveillance here, Langley. It's just a matter of time until we are attacked. I think that we need to regularly send some of your men deep into the forest around our camp and wait for our common enemy. Perhaps we can outsmart them."

"That might just work, Lawrence, but when will they come?"

"That is the difficulty, Langley. That is what we must discuss."

Chapter Thirty-Two

Father Magnus was in his office writing another letter. It was again addressed to a house in London. Mother Meredith now knew the address by heart. She had sent more than a few of these letters out over the years for the Father to the same address. She didn't know who the letter was for, but she had her own theory. She thought perhaps they went to a sibling or some other relative, but she never asked.

She felt that there was an old wound in the Father's heart, but she didn't know what it was. Perhaps the reason was a lost lover or an old friendship that had gone bad. There was never a reply as far as she knew.

Lawrence and Sam had taken many loads of wood to Themstead. Both the wheelwright and the furniture makers still wanted all the wood that Lawrence could cut. The silver was adding up at long last for Lawrence and Sam.

They would soon go back to Oak Junction for the harvest. Lawrence was worried about getting Sam home safely. Lawrence had talked to Langley about several things, one of which was safety on their way back to Oak Junction.

It was decided that at least ten men would ride with Lawrence and Sam back to their farm in Oak Junction. Langley had wanted to see the farm, and this gave him a plausible excuse. Several of the men would ride ahead of Lawrence looking for signs of trouble or unusual activity on the road. Catherine had made it very clear to Lawrence on his last visit home that he could not travel home or to Themstead without guards. She simply would not allow it.

Jason had been watching Lawrence as usual and knew about his entourage. He had nearly as many men as Lawrence and felt certain he would prevail under the right circumstances. He was dreaming up his plan as he walked past Lawrence's camp.

He was dressed as an old woman covered in layers of filthy old cloths, pulling an aged donkey. Jason walked into the empty camp and saw the fire ring and walked throughout the camp, looking for anything that might help him prevail in a battle against Lawrence.

He had waited until Sam and Lawrence left the camp on their wagon before he entered it. He saw where Lawrence and Sam slept on the ground near the fire and noticed their woodpile. He didn't see the most important feature of his camp, however, the secret cave. Jason bent down and rubbed the ashes from the fire between his fingers, trying to detect the last time it had been burning. He thought he had a good idea for an ambush. He was content, thrilled, and at ease. His blue eyes flashed with evil. He was going to be ready soon enough!

Lawrence and Sam had loaded up the wagon with wood again on Friday morning and went into Themstead once more. It was very early in the morning, and few people were about. They noticed an old woman and her donkey as they left their camp. Lawrence stopped at Simon's furniture shop, dropped off some of his load of oak there, and received his payment in silver. He then went deeper into town and turned north toward the wheelwright's shop.

The stalls were just starting to open as Lawrence met Kyle on the path outside his shop.

"Morning, Kyle, where's your helper?"

"He's under the woodchips somewhere 'round here sleeping, I think."

"I brought you the oak you wanted."

"Thanks, Lawrence, here's your money as agreed." Kyle handed Lawrence his money, and Lawrence dropped the coins into his money pouch. Kyle walked back into his shop while Lawrence and Sam started to unload the wagon.

Kyle came out again and spoke to Lawrence.

"Lawrence, do you need Sam today?"

"Yes Kyle, we're starting the harvest as soon as I get back to the farm in Oak Junction."

"Oh, I see. That's alright then. I'm sure my helper will show up sooner or later. I'll tan his hide for being late, you can bet on that."

Lawrence said his goodbyes to Kyle, and Kyle thanked him for the wood that he'd sold him. Kyle was left alone and looking around his stall under his tables and benches for his lost apprentice. Lawrence was now leaving Themstead and heading home.

Lawrence and Sam left the village and found his escort of cousins waiting for him at the main highway. He didn't like having all these armed men with him, but Catherine gave him no choice. The armed men made him feel like a prisoner. Catherine was now adamant that he wasn't to travel alone anymore.

As Lawrence turned onto the highway, his cousins fell in all around him. They were a small but very serious band of warriors. They all hoped that their numbers alone might deter any attack from Jason. They walked their horses slowly at first and then began to ride hard until they reached Halfway Farm. They ate with posted guards and then settled in to spend the night. The farmer was thrilled to see Lawrence again and asked about William. He was intent on marrying his daughter into this now large and powerful Smith family. The men slept in shifts, and very early in the morning went on their way with the best wishes of their hosts.

Several of the men had ridden onto the main road ahead of Lawrence and Sam and walked into the forest looking for their enemies with no results. Everything seemed peaceful and quiet. Lawrence and Sam reached Oak Junction early in the afternoon on Saturday. Lawrence's family had planned the harvest to start on Saturday and had many of the ripe vegetables in baskets ready to pile onto the wagon.

They had staggered their planting times so the crops would be ready to pick over several weeks. Catherine had met most of the men with Lawrence already, but some were still strangers to her and the rest of the family. Everyone was well aware of the problems that Jason was causing in the area. No one traveled on the roads alone these days without guards if it could be helped.

Lawrence walked into Oak Junction to see Father Magnus while his family settled in at the farm. He wanted to invite him to supper that night. The entire village was quiet due to the danger on the roads. The villagers weren't selling very much and were suffering. Everyone was locked up in their homes. Lawrence talked to Don and Junior and then walked up toward the church. Lawrence saw the Father sitting in the tavern as he walked past the door and entered to visit with him. Father Magnus turned around as Lawrence tapped him on the shoulder.

"Oh Lawrence, I have news for you. I have sent several letters to London asking for help and explaining the lack of interest by the sheriff's men in our situation. I haven't heard back as of yet, but I'm sure I will."

"I hope so, Father, but we may soon have to take matters into our own hands."

"Yes, the townsfolk are getting desperate, Lawrence. You may be right. How are you and your family?"

"We are fine, Father. The harvest will start in earnest tomorrow. We will bring our goods into town the following morning. I'm a little worried about the lack of traders in the village, but if all goes well, we should have enough silver to start a proper house in Themstead.

"I have looked into the matter of the cloth. I have my suspicions and will take a trip north in a few days to see what I might find out. I will let you know if I find anything interesting. Keep your wits about you and God will provide, son."

Lawrence gave Father some silver for the church and walked back to Don's shop to pick up Junior. They walked back home together talking about the mill at Themstead and Ginger. It was a beautiful afternoon. They could smell dinner cooking down the road at the farm as they drew closer. Lawrence and Junior raced home down the road. Lawrence won as usual.

The women made breakfast early, and the men were all in the fields before sunup. They took four wagonloads of vegetables into the market and received good prices for everything. There were few items in the market, so the prices were on the high side.

Some of Lawrence's wheat had already been cut and threshed, so it was taken to the mill in the afternoon to be ground into flour. They sold most of the flour on the way out of the village but brought a little back to Catherine.

Lawrence offered some money to his cousins for the work they had done in the fields that day, but they all refused to take it. They had just wanted to be part of Lawrence's plan to catch the highwaymen and worked in the field to keep from becoming soft. While they were in Oak Junction, things were happening in Themstead.

Lawrence knew that he was being watched most of the time now for some time, either by Jason or some of his men. There was a constant stream of strangers riding by his camp, many more than in the recent past. Something was going on, and he wasn't sure what it was. They were constantly riding past their camp or walking the paths through the forests. Lawrence could see that the paths in the woods were trodden down more. There was the same number of animals in the area, but the paths were becoming wider.

Half of Langley's men had been busy in Lawrence's camp while Lawrence was on his way to Oak Junction. Several of Langley's men were sent west, away from Themstead, but not far. They camped in the woods just past their farms. Several of the men in Oak Junction had left late Saturday afternoon and ridden hard to the east, back to Lawrence's camp. They had their horses taken down to the small lakes at the bottom of Lawrence's land to be tended to by some of the younger boys.

These men took up positions deep in the forest around Lawrence's camp as they had been doing for several weeks now. They were all well armed and had plenty of supplies. The newest trap was set by Saturday night. Jason knew Lawrence wouldn't be back to Themstead until late Sunday night.

Several of Jason's men took up positions around the camp in the woods, even up in the trees on Sunday afternoon, not knowing that Langley's men were already deeper in the forest, encircling them. As the day wore on, more of Jason's men came into the camp and hid in the forest, near the clearing in the camp, including Jason. They were finally ready. Langley's men saw the enemy set up their ambush but waited anxiously for the last part of their plan to fall into place.

Lawrence asked Sam to stay and help Charles with the work in the fields. Lawrence talked to Catherine and kissed her goodbye. They said all that needed to be said just in case the worst did happen. This was how it had been for several weeks. They knew something was going to happen, they just didn't know exactly when. William, Langley, and Junior rode with their remaining men back to Themstead.

Junior spoke to Ginger before he left. He knew he loved her now and told her again. They knew that he may not return, and she understood. She wouldn't be happy if he was hurt, but she understood the need for his actions.

Father Magnus never heard from the sheriff or anyone else in a position of authority about his letters or their lack of interest in the villagers' problems.

Mother Meredith handed the Father a letter on Monday morning. It was from London. Father looked very angry after reading it and was in a foul mood all day.

At a prearranged time early Sunday morning, Langley's men in the west broke camp and headed east, back to Themstead. They were headed for Lawrence's camp again. They had done this several times over the last month.

Lawrence and Langley and the rest of the men started for Themstead from Oak Junction at around the same time. These two groups of men would converge at Lawrence's camp at the prearranged time while the men deep in the woods would start their attack and drive Jason and his men from the camp clearing and hopefully out onto the main road. If all went according to plan, Lawrence, Langley, and their men would be waiting for them. They rode hard with expectation as in the recent past. This was the best plan they had come up with while considering all of the facts they had before them.

All of the men arrived at precisely the right moment from the east and the west, and the plan worked perfectly. They had practiced it several times. All of the parts of the plan were ingrained in their minds.

This time, Jason had set his trap and was waiting for Lawrence to arrive.

Lawrence's and Langley's men in the forest knew that Jason's men were in position around the camp and up in the trees. Langley's men shot their arrows at Jason's men from three sides at the appointed time. Jason's men were completely surprised and soon broke ranks and tried to run to the highway. They had to run, surrender, or die. Langley and Lawrence were waiting in the deep grass and forest on the other side of the road with their men to target those who made it to the road.

Jason's men didn't have a chance. They were caught in the crossfire, and there was no hope for them. It was like being in the center of a swarm of angry bees. Men were screaming and falling from the trees and dying out in the open as they ran to escape. Jason's men could see some of Lawrence's men on the east side of the camp on the road, but Langley's men, deeper in the woods, were invisible and could shoot at will and not be seen. They were hunters, after all, and Jason's men were easy prey.

Lawrence saw a man prepared to shoot Langley and shot him instantly. He fell dead to the bare ground near the fire. Then Langley saw a man in a tree aiming at one of his brothers and shot him through the neck. He died before he hit the ground. So it went for about twenty minutes.

Eventually, all of those who didn't die surrendered. Most of Jason's men were dead, as were a few of Langley's. William and Junior were unhurt and had proved themselves to be great archers and very brave in battle along with many of their cousins. There had been innumerable arrows flying in all directions, and they had remained uninjured.

It took several minutes to find Jason among the fallen men. Lawrence walked among the dead and turned all of them over, one at a time, looking for Jason until he finally found him. When Lawrence did find Jason, he knew that Jason was doomed. He had been hit several times with arrows, but he was still alive when Lawrence found him. Lawrence and Jason then spoke to each other for the first time on this bloody field of battle.

"Lawrence, you were the sharper one today after all."

"Jason, your treachery has given me a wife, a daughter, and a brother-in-law. The least I can do is make sure that you die in battle and not at the end of a rope. That little girl you saw on my farm is yours. I will raise and protect her as my own."

Lawrence stabbed Jason in the heart with Catherine's knife, and he was gone. Catherine didn't kill Jason, but Catherine's knife did. Lawrence then sent a rider to bring Catherine back to look at Jason before he was buried.

Of Jason's band of outlaws, eighteen died on the battlefield at Themstead with Jason and two survived to heal and be hung in Chesterfield. They showed no remorse for their evil behavior. Two of Langley's men were killed, one brother-in-law and one cousin. Others were wounded, but they all survived to tell their children and grandchildren about the part they had played in "the Battle of Themstead."

Chapter Thirty-Three

The letter that Father Magnus finally received from London was from his sister. No one in the government ever wrote back to Father about why the soldiers were always unavailable to protect the villagers or to investigate the crimes that they were constantly subjected to.

All of the highwaymen were buried in the forest in unmarked graves. Jason was buried at the edge of the main highway near where Lawrence's lumbermill would be built. Catherine threw the first shovel of dirt onto Jason's face in the deep, cold grave two days after the battle. She was finally completely happy with the death of Jason now that she could confirm it firsthand.

With the silver Lawrence earned from the crops from his two parcels of land, he ordered another plow from Don and bought seeds and supplies for the two farms and the family. The women always needed cloth to make and repair the family's clothes, and everyone needed new shoes. The children were growing quickly, and nothing fit them anymore.

Lawrence didn't need the horses in Themstead until the spring when he would have to plow the fields and plant his crops again. Even then he would only need one for a few days. He had decided this spring was the time to convert his garden in Themstead into a proper farm. As soon as the land had thawed and the weather had warmed a little, they cleared more trees and shrubs to create a larger area for farming.

Lawrence and Sam used their horses to pull the stumps from the ground after the large trees had been cut down and the men had dug down under the tree stumps as far as they could. It was hard work, but the boys enjoyed it. They talked and teased each other as they tried to outdo their siblings. Charles and William came to help them, and it became a family tradition each year as the farm grew. When they were finished, they brought the horses back to Oak Junction.

Lawrence had already cut nearly enough wood for the house at Themstead. He would eventually build the house and mill and move Catherine and the children there. Junior and Ginger would then be married and move into the house at Oak Junction. Lawrence seemed to be gone most of the time now, but the family would soon be together once again when the house was finished at Themstead.

Lawrence had already talked to his cousin Langley and all of his cousins at Themstead about helping him build the mill. They were eager to help build Lawrence's mill and get established there. It started out as just two rooms drawn in the dirt floor of their home in Oak Junction. It would be built of stone and wood. It would be two stories tall with a shingled roof. Lawrence had saved just enough for the laborers. He had a whole forest full of trees and piles of stone to build it.

Junior had been trying to teach his sister and the other children to read in the evenings when he came home after spending time with the monks. It was difficult for many reasons, but he was making some progress. Lawrence was seldom home so he was learning less than Catherine and the children, but they were very bright and were doing well. They would be there to help Lawrence in the future as the business grew.

The farm at Oak Junction was bigger this spring, and Lawrence was already selling wood in Themstead. He would have two farms producing an income while he started to build the mill. They would have a steady stream of silver from the lumber he was selling and plenty to eat. If the mill was never built they would be comfortable, but Lawrence dreamed a bigger dream with a bigger future. He couldn't help it. This was who he was now. He didn't know why, but he felt it in his bones. He wanted to ask Father Magnus about why some men were successful and others not, but he fell asleep and dreamed of the conversation instead.

In the morning, the entire Smith family walked to church. The road was full of travelers again, and the village was full of tradesmen and their customers. Since the news of the death of Jason and his small dangerous band, everyone came out of their homes again and the countryside came to life. Lawrence knew that he still had one very powerful enemy. Catherine was unaware of the threats from the sheriff.

Lawrence walked with the family as they looked at all the items in the market and purchased what they needed. Lawrence ordered the second plow from Don. They all stayed at the blacksmith shop and visited for some time after the church services were over.

The women visited in the house while the men talked in the yard and discussed the Battle of Themstead. Junior told his version of the story with excitement as Lawrence looked on and filled in some of the pieces that Junior wasn't sure of or failed to remember. They weren't happy about the deaths of all those men, especially their two cousins, but Jason had left them no choice. Because there was no help from London or Chesterfield, they had to act on their own.

Don was very happy with Junior's progress at the blacksmith shop. Don's earnings at the shop had doubled as Junior's skills increased, and Don would be able to pay Junior a wage now in preparation for his upcoming marriage to his daughter. When they had finished visiting, Lawrence's family headed back to their house and Lawrence went to see Father Magnus. Of course, Lawrence was the hero once more in the village, but he was more comfortable in the role that he had now been forced to fill.

On his short walk to see the Father, Lawrence thought about all that had happened in his life. He had many questions on his mind that he wanted answered. As he approached the side entry to the church, he saw Mother Meredith.

"How are you, Lawrence?"

"Fine, Mother, I've come to see Father Magnus."

"That's a good thing, Lawrence. The Father is a bit out of sorts today. Perhaps you could cheer him up."

"What seems to be bothering him?"

"That's for him to tell you if he will. Go knock on his door."

Lawrence walked into the ancient hall and knocked on the Father's door and was asked in as usual. Lawrence could see that Father Magnus was not his usual self. Lawrence sat in the chair that he and Catherine had come to know so well as the Father shuffled several papers around on his desk.

"Lawrence, nice to see you. I hope all is well."

"Yes Father, I've brought you a turkey. It's in the hall."

"Thank you, Lawrence, what can I do for you today?"

"Well, I've come to ask you about a few things that are on my mind."

"Like what, my son?" The sound of the Father's voice was somehow different as if he were in pain of some sort, and it caught Lawrence off guard.

"Perhaps I should come back another time, Father."

"I'm sorry, Lawrence, I'm in a bit of a situation myself at the moment. Perhaps you might be able to help me."

"I can try, Father, but somehow I doubt it."

"Well, let's talk a little.

You see, Lawrence, I've written several letters to the sheriff about our troubles out here with the highwaymen and the lack of a satisfactory response. They have not written back, and I'm quite upset about it. The village pays its taxes, yet nothing gets done."

"Well, Father, it seems to me that the problem has been solved."

"Yes, Lawrence, but not by our government officials. By you and several of your family members."

"That's true, Father, but wasn't that God's will? We know the sheriff is a thief and perhaps worse."

"Good point, Lawrence, good point."

"Surely that can't be the only issue that is troubling you, sir. The problem with Jason is at least behind us now. That just leaves the sheriff as far as I can tell."

"You're right, Lawrence, but my other problem is more complex. It's a family matter with a long history."

"Then we're finished, Father?"

"No Lawrence, I need your help with this. I know I can trust you to be discreet."

"If you see fit to ask me, Father, I cannot refuse to try and help, but my experience is rather limited as you well know. I'm just a young farmer."

"You say that, Lawrence, but you are unaware of your own strengths and talents. Everyone sees them except you."

"Go on then, Father."

"I came into the church through the back door, so to speak. All of the details are too troubling to mention now, but let's just say that I'm more like you than you could imagine. I did come from a very wealthy family in London, and I was married once. I had a wife and a young son; they were both taken away from me by a man as evil as Jason. Wrongly, I took my revenge. I killed him and several men who deserved to die, but in the process, I lost the respect and comfort of my only living family member and became a fugitive.

"My sister now has a son. I haven't seen my sister for years and have never laid eyes on her son, my nephew. They see no redemption for me, and they both judge me more harshly than I or any God could. I have written to her many times over the years and she never responds to me except to tell me that I'm bound for hell."

"Well, Father, I think I know you as well as anyone in this village. I don't know all your secrets or the personal circumstances that drove you to do what you did, but I know you love God and the goodness in man. I'm sure that what you did was for what you thought was a just cause.

"If you are going to hell, I will surely be there with you. I have killed many more men, none who didn't deserve death, and in so doing I have been rewarded beyond measure with land, a family, and some wealth. You and I are just men, but you are a priest as well. The good you have done surely has earned you God's forgiveness. You have saved countless people from evil and perhaps from hurting others. Where is the forgiveness of God for you in this situation? I have benefitted greatly from God, and you are being punished. This just doesn't make any sense."

"Perhaps it is to make me patient and wise."

"How patient and wise must a man be, Father?"

"I don't know, Lawrence, I don't know."

"You must go to London and talk to your sister. Perhaps there is a bigger misunderstanding between the two of you. Send her another letter."

"Perhaps you are right, Lawrence, perhaps you are right."

Father Magnus sent another letter to his sister in London and informed her that he would be at her door in two weeks' time come hell or high water. This mystery of the sister's hatred of her brother would perhaps be solved at long last. Father Magnus had decided before he left Oak Junction that this would be his last attempt at bringing the three of them back together.

Father Magnus had fled London after he took his revenge and had assumed a new identity. He left his sister and brother-in-law to help their father run the family business. His sister India and her husband had become wealthy as the years had passed. They had one son, and shortly thereafter her husband died. Mary and her son Zachary took over the business when her husband died.

They continued to prosper, and eventually, Zachary took over complete control of the company, but it was too much for him. India had wanted Father Magnus to be there to help her. Father Magnus knew none of this. His sister blamed the Father for the untimely death of her husband due to the stress of running the business and she felt abandoned by him as well. She only saw her losses and hurts and forgot about her brother's own sorrows and guilt. Perhaps this visit would bring them back together. Perhaps the long and uncomfortable carriage ride to London would be worth the trouble. Only time would tell.

Lawrence walked home from the old church and thanked God that his family was safe as he came down the hill through the village. He and Catherine argued as all couples did, but they were always able to come to an understanding eventually, and that would end it. The marriage of Junior and Ginger was one example. Catherine thought that Lawrence should be more interested than he was in all the preparations, and Lawrence knew from experience that he had nothing to bring to that discussion.

He loved Ginger now as one of his own children, of course, and was looking forward to the day of the ceremony and the joining of the two families. Lawrence was very happy with Junior's progress in his studies with the monks and his improving skills as a full-fledged blacksmith. He knew without question that they would be fine and give him some lovely grandchildren. Lawrence was busy thinking of his obligations to his family, as always.

He now had two farms to care for and was planning the design of the new house in Themstead and the construction of the mill. He had many things on his mind. They weren't more important than the wedding, but they were very important nonetheless. There wouldn't be a wedding until the mill in Themstead was nearly completed. Construction of the mill couldn't be started until next spring, and the crops still needed to be harvested.

Lawrence and Sam stayed in Oak Junction for two weeks. His cousins went home after the harvest was completed. Their help with the harvest was invaluable, and it gave the family some free time to enjoy their accomplishments. Many of the root vegetables were put into the storage room for their later use. The rest, along with some of the hay and some of the other crops, were sold in the village for a fine profit.

Prices were up, and most everyone seemed much happier than in the recent past. They had good reason, to be sure. Lawrence and his cousins had wiped out Jason and his men, and the weather had improved. Even those who began to see Lawrence as one of the elites in the village, and more comfortable than they were, knew he deserved everything he had. They began to understand that his family had truly saved all of them from some great difficulties they had been facing.

Lawrence and Sam went back to Themstead to close up their camp and to harvest their large garden. They had enjoyed a few days of rest with the family, but now the time had come to return to Themstead. They still had to cut more wood for the shops in Themstead and sell their crops there as well. They would spend the winter in Oak Junction. They hoped it would be their last. In the spring, they would build their mill in Themstead and start their new lives there. They would live in the mill until the house was completed.

Chapter Thirty-Four

Father Magnus returned to Oak Junction before Lawrence left for his camp in Themstead. His trip to London had been a success. It turned out that his sister was indeed somewhat self-centered, self-righteous, and spoiled and had suffered tragedies. This was no surprise to Father Magnus. However, they were able to work out everything between them to their mutual satisfaction. The Father was then finally able to meet his nephew, Zachary.

Father Magnus wanted to begin a relationship with his sister and his nephew, who seemed like a fine young man and appeared to be a hard worker. The family was reconnected and planned on growing closer over time. They all wrote to each other often and began to find out who and what the other people in the family were all about.

Their relationship grew and helped mend the siblings' relationship as time passed. The Father was quite happy about the way things had turned out. He felt good that at least he had tried to clear the air. He was thrilled when the meetings surpassed his expectations.

Lawrence and the Father found time to talk before Lawrence left for Themstead. Lawrence forgot to ask the Father, however, about the part that God played in success and failure. He had far too much on his mind at the time. He was just glad that he had played some small role in the affair and that it had all worked out for the best.

With the harvest over and Jason dead, there was no reason for Lawrence and his brothers to stay at Oak Junction. Lawrence was taking the wagon back to Themstead. They would spend the night at Halfway Farm, as always. They spent the night, and William saw "her" again.

He thought the farmer's daughter might be a good catch, and after some discussion between the two, it became clear that the feelings were mutual. Catherine would have to come in the spring and meet his family. It looked like soon the two families would be joined by love and grandchildren. William would stay at Halfway Farm and help with their harvest and join Lawrence a few days later in Themstead. In the morning, Lawrence and Sam left William behind and headed for their campsite.

The wagon ride was very slow, so the two brothers had plenty of time to talk and plan what they would do in Themstead and how long it would take them. When they reached the camp, Sam started a fire and brought water for dinner. Lawrence went out for fresh game and soon heard turkeys down near the stream to the south. Lawrence shot a large old hen. That was plenty and more for their dinner. They would be in Themstead for just a few days to harvest their crops and sell them in the bustling market there.

The plow and all their cooking equipment were placed in the wagon on the third morning with their blankets and all their clothing. William arrived late in the morning from Halfway Farm while they were hitching their horse to the wagon. They took a final load of wood into the town to Kyle and returned to camp for their produce. They returned to the market and soon sold all that they had.

They said their goodbyes to Father Gregory and all their other friends in the large town and left for Oak Junction. It was a time of mixed feelings for Lawrence and Sam. They liked their time together in Themstead without all the interruptions caused by family members and so many chores to complete.

They knew that they could hunt or chop wood or work in the garden at their own pace. Back in Oak Junction, two women were running the farm. There was no doubt about that. It was more regimented and orderly. It had to be, of course, with two small children and seven adults and countless animals to look after.

There were many chickens now and more eggs to gather, several goats to feed and milk, two horses to look after, and now one cow to milk and feed. There wasn't much time left for daydreaming or even thinking past the next meal. There were meals to prepare and clothing to make or repair as well as two children who needed love and attention.

Lawrence was a good father when he was at home, and with Charles and Martha's help, most things got done as needed. Catherine was able to spend time with the children when she wasn't working in the kitchen or out in the fields. The family members were healthy for the most part and as content as most families.

There were few squabbles among them, and life was good. Many of their friends had lost children, suffered the loss of parents, or had insufficient food. The church helped, and Father Magnus was very organized and sympathetic, but the church could only do so much.

There were many generous families around the area and in Oak Junction that gave aid to the church for the poor and the sick. Lawrence's family had always given something, and now that they had more, they gave more. Still, many families suffered from poor shelter, family drunkenness, abuse, and desertion.

Lawrence was glad to see the Father in a better mood since coming back from London, but he still didn't have the heart to ask him why God let these people around them suffer. Maybe he would ask him in the spring when there was fine weather and there was food in the markets again. Winter was a hard time for everyone.

With the winter closing in on the countryside, Lawrence and Catherine had more time together to talk about their family and their future. With Lawrence away most of the time during the year, they sometimes felt that they were drifting apart. But theirs was a deep, strong love, and it had grown stronger over the years despite being apart.

Once Lawrence was sure the animals were cared for, he had plenty of time to play with his children and reconnect with Catherine and everyone else. Lawrence never forgot that it was his duty to protect his family, whatever that took. Elizabeth and Eli were growing fast and were typical siblings. Fights started and ended in short order and were quickly forgotten. The children were never bored. With all the animals and the wild land around them, it was a paradise for them to explore and discover. It was very much like Lawrence's life had been except that they were free.

Catherine had great role models in her parents. They weren't educated, but they had common sense when it came to running a household. They were frugal when necessary and always loving. They were very much like Lawrence and Catherine. Catherine loved Lawrence because he was very much like her father, hard-working and honest.

She knew of many women in Oak Junction who could never please their inlaws, and it caused no end of difficulties in their families. There was none of that in the Smith family. Lawrence's brothers were always helpful and very respectful, and Catherine was well aware of how lucky she was to have such a wonderful family around to help, and of course, she had Lawrence.

He never drank and was never a bully to her or anyone else. She was so grateful that she was able to get over her fears from her attack and let him work his way into her heart. Lawrence walked to the village once or twice a week to see their friends and bring back any items that Catherine needed. He never refused her anything, and she was very aware of how very lucky she was.

Lawrence and Don visited each other often. They enjoyed looking forward to their grandchildren and watching little Don run around the shop or the yard. He already felt at home in the shop and around the furnace. It didn't take Don Jr. very long to realize that fire was a double-edged sword, a source of warmth and danger. His mother and Ginger spoiled him to some degree, but that was to be expected due to all the problems that preceded him.

Don and Lawrence both agreed that Ginger would make a fine mother. She had a pleasant disposition, and she was no fool. She was like her father in personality, but she looked exactly like her mother. She had those green eyes and red hair that could be seen for miles. And that white skin of hers was like the marble of the statues in the church.

Ginger got along with everyone and would be a strong and smart partner for Junior. She loved going to listen to Father Magnus in church with her family and Junior and knew it would be a big part of Junior's and her life together. Junior felt the same. After all, he spent many a night with the monks learning to read and understand mathematics and the Bible at that church.

He had been almost living the life of a monk for the last few years while he learned to read and understand mathematics. He enjoyed his time with the monks, but Junior was glad it was coming to an end. He was getting married soon, and they had the mill to build. His young life was going to go through some major changes, and very soon.

Lawrence and Catherine spent many winter nights discussing the design of the new house and mill. After nearly two winters drawing pictures in the dirt with a stick and changing their minds innumerable times, they finally came up with a design that they could both agree on.

The house and mill would be made of stone on the first floor. The material was as plentiful as timber on their land. The buildings would last almost forever. The family would be safe from the outside world. With thick wood doors and shutters, Lawrence could leave his family if needed, knowing that they would be safe.

There would be no windows on the first floor facing the main road. There would be windows on the ground floor facing the farm, but they would have extra-strong shutters as well. Times were better now, but Lawrence and Catherine both understood how fast that could change. They knew that from personal experience, and they still had a young family to raise and protect.

Once the spring planting was finished in Oak Junction, Lawrence and the boys would head back to Themstead and move into the secret cave until the weather improved. They would clear the land near the highway where the house and mill would be built and plant their crops in the fields that were already waiting for them. The house and the mill would be one large building with a breezeway between the two halves. There would be a strong wooden gate at the entrance of the breezeway. It would be closed at night to keep out intruders. It would be a small fortress.

Lawrence met with Father Magnus often during the fallow time. Lawrence didn't ask all those questions he had spinning in his brain, but he did ask some. Father didn't always have time for Lawrence. He had many duties to perform in the village. When Lawrence would spy the Father in the tavern at the end of the day, he would make a point to talk with him if he wasn't deep in conversation with someone else.

Lawrence was just another villager, after all, and didn't feel that he had the right to take up more of the Father's time than anyone else. But Lawrence did understand that they had a very special bond and could talk on a more personal level than most of the villagers. Father had made that very clear to Lawrence and Catherine more than once. He tried to create that same relationship with everyone in the village, but Lawrence and Catherine were likely the closest to being a real family that Father had in Oak Junction.

Lawrence had acquired some prestige and respect in the village despite his denying it. The same applied to the surrounding towns and villages. He always tried to see himself as a family man and a farmer. That's all he ever wanted to be. Circumstances had forced him into playing a larger role in his community than he had planned. He didn't desire wealth or prestige or power. He only came by them through the results of his hard work and doing right as he saw it.

Of course, Father Magnus, and the Bible were a road map to success. But luck ultimately placed Lawrence where he was—that and hard work. That was how Lawrence saw himself and his place in the world. Life for Lawrence was very simple: work hard, take care of your family, be fair to people, and keep your eyes and ears open. The world was still a very dangerous place no matter how well you planned for the future.

The winter wasn't terrible in 1776, and Lawrence was lucky to be living at Oak Junction. The winters were usually mild compared to other parts of England. It still was very cold, and some people died from the weather, but that was relatively rare.

It was usually the very old or the ill-prepared who died. Lawrence was neither. So as the weather improved, Lawrence and his family had a very clear plan and put it into action. Everyone knew what the plan was, and they were eager to get on with it. When the soil was soft enough to plant, they did just that. After the fields were plowed and planted, the boys worked to clear more of the land at Oak Junction for planting the following year.

Each year in the fall, they would clear more land. They cleared trees and shrubs and turned the soil, getting it ready to plant the following spring. After the planting was finished, William, Lawrence, and Sam left for Themstead to do the same all over again there. Their lives were a tapestry of routine and accomplishment.

Chapter Thirty-Five

This was going to be a very special year like the year of the plow but much bigger. This was the year of the wedding and the move to the new house in Themstead. Most of the plans for the wedding were complete now, and Lawrence was very relieved about that.

William was the quiet son of Charles and Martha, and he too would soon be married to Nancy at Halfway Farm. They had discussed it often, William and Nancy, and on this trip back to Themstead, they had made it "official."

Nancy's widowed father was very satisfied. He took complete credit for the union. As far as he was concerned, geography and circumstances had nothing to do with it. He felt sure that it was his clever planning.

His name was Joseph. He had married late and only had one daughter, and then his wife died giving birth to Nancy. He never got a second chance at fatherhood. Joseph and Nancy made the best of it. What else could they do? They had their land and some help from their fellow villagers at harvest time. They had some little help from a few family members down the road a long distance away, but mostly they did everything on their own.

Nancy learned to work the farm from her father, and as he got older, she took on more of the responsibilities. They had many acres of prime farmland and many animals to care for.

Everyone thought that she would make William a wonderful wife. William was a farmer at heart, and Nancy was smart and very good with the farm. She and Lawrence were close before the announcement of the marriage, and he was not surprised when it came.

William was a willing worker but not much of a planner. Nancy would fill that void in William nicely, and Lawrence and Catherine would always be there just in case they needed help or advice.

Lawrence talked at length with Joseph and Nancy. Lawrence made sure that they understood how pleased he and Catherine were for the two young lovers. The entire Smith family would come to meet them and make plans for the wedding as soon as they were able to get away from Oak Junction.

Right now, they needed to go to Themstead and start building the house and mill so Catherine could move there with the children to be with Lawrence at long last. The wedding of Ginger and Junior would happen as soon as the new house was finished. Everyone was fine with that timeline. William was twenty-five and Nancy would soon be twenty.

When the Smith men reached Themstead, they wasted no time. They set up their crude housekeeping schedule once again and planted the crops. Lawrence and William hunted as often as needed while Sam kept order in the camp. He had cut ample firewood in the past year, so that was already done. He needed to care for the horses and tend to the fire and water. When he had finished those chores, he would sometimes be able to hunt with his brothers.

They had brought some food with them from home, but not very much. They ate mostly off the land. They had silver now from the sale of their crops at the farm, so they could buy a little of what they needed in the town of Themstead. They had enough money saved for the craftsmen they would need to build the house, and they had an unlimited supply of stones and lumber to build it all around them. They had gathered stones over the past two years for the masons while clearing the land for their farm.

What little they had left in the cave when they left seemed untouched. Their secret appeared to still be safe. They slept out in the open and were content under the black, clear sky and the stars. They were young men, after all, and used to hard living. This was not the type of living that Catherine and the children should be subjected to. Soon Lawrence and the boys were back to cutting trees down and making cedar and oak planks and blocks for their customers in town.

Lawrence made the ride into Themstead as he had done at Oak Junction soon after arriving back at his camp. He went into town to speak with his many customers. Kyle the wheelwright and George, a furniture maker, to name just a few, listened to his plans and knew they would all come to pass.

The new spring also meant more orders from them. After speaking with most of his clients, Lawrence was sure that the year was off to a good start. After a short time, the silver was adding up, and Lawrence had talked to the craftsmen he would need to build his new house and mill.

Many things were different when Lawrence and his brothers came back to Themstead in the spring. It had been a big town in the past, but it had grown some and was busier than ever. Several more of the local merchants he had met at that first meeting were approaching him for trade and advice. There were many furniture makers in Themstead, and Lawrence had a vast supply of timber. It was a perfect match for success.

Because Lawrence had put his and his own family's safety on the line to eliminate Jason and his men, business was growing again, and the town's people had a much better appreciation of who Lawrence and his family were and what they stood for.

His workload increased rapidly as time passed, and he had plenty of money coming in for the house and mill. It happened much faster than he thought possible. The boys worked from sunup until sundown to fill their orders. The pit saw was seldom not in use. It was a wonderful spring. In April, the work started on the house and mill, and by July the house was done and the focus turned to the mill.

All of Lawrence's cousins came whenever possible, and they became more familiar with each other and started to become a real family again after years of separation. Two carpenters worked full-time on the buildings. Junior made all the iron pieces for the house and mill in Oak Junction and sent them back with Lawrence on the Mondays when he and Sam rode back to Themstead. They could make the trip on horseback in one long day. They no longer needed the wagon to carry large or heavy tools to the new farm. All of that was already there now or could be purchased there.

They would spend the night at Halfway Farm if they came by wagon with Catherine. Catherine came a few times to oversee the work, but it was difficult to bring the children and spend the night out in the open before the house was finished. Lawrence, William, and Sam had cut and shaped many trees into timbers and stored the timber in preparation for the building, so there was little wasted time in construction. There were times when the weather slowed their progress, but they didn't let that dishearten them. They kept at the work for months, until the end of fall. At that point, the work was finished on the house and mill, and the wedding of Junior and Ginger was at hand.

All of the men stopped to look around before leaving the farm that year. The Themstead parcel had become a farm now. It was still small, but it had become a farm.

With the construction finished in the fall and the crops harvested and sold in Themstead for a healthy profit, it was time to close up the house and head back to Oak Junction. The boys slept that last night in the great room as they had been doing for some time; it had a large fireplace and it was much more comfortable than sleeping outdoors or in the cave. The cave was still a secret from everyone except the family, and it would remain that way forever. It now was time for the wedding of Ginger and Junior, and everyone was needed at Oak Junction.

This was a time of mixed emotions for everyone. Lawrence and his family would be leaving and the newlyweds would be taking their places at Oak Junction. For Charles and Martha, they were losing their son, daughter-in-law, and grandchildren, but they were receiving Ginger and the chance for more grandchildren to come. Junior was like a son to them. There was no distinction between the boys in that regard.

When Lawrence and the boys reached Oak Junction for the final trip of the year, there was another grand feast. Each year as Lawrence and Catherine had improved their situation, the feast had become larger with more friends invited and more food. This year was a very special event indeed.

The wedding plans had been completed, no thanks to Lawrence, and on the first of April, the wedding would take place at the lovely church up on the hill in Oak Junction overlooking the green valley that they all loved so much. Once again Father Magnus would preside at the wedding of a Smith, just as he had a few years earlier with Lawrence and Catherine. Junior had different parents than Lawrence, William, and Sam, but he was as much a Smith now as any of them.

Father Gregory and Lawrence had become well acquainted over the years, and he was invited to the wedding as were several people from Themstead. Lawrence's family west of Themstead would be there as well. The two old widowers and widow, Langley, and all their children and grandchildren would be there too.

The church was full, and there was excitement in the air. Elizabeth and Eli walked ahead of Catherine as Junior stood at the altar trembling like a young tree in a strong wind. This was the antithesis of Lawrence and Catherine's wedding, but Lawrence and Catherine were not jealous. They both loved all of it.

Father Magnus spoke eloquently of the duties of the married couple to each other and God, and about the need to help those who were less fortunate. Not to make them dependent but to help them so they might stand on their own two feet and continue their life journey with their heads held high.

The ceremony was short as church weddings go, and Lawrence was glad for that. There was a great party outside the front of the old church when the wedding was finished. The church looked exactly the same as it had the day that the Father brought Catherine to be reunited with Junior and to see Lawrence so many years ago, that very first time. Lawrence sat on the same bench where he'd sat all those years ago.

Who could have dreamed that all their lives had turned out so well? Even Father Magnus admitted that he was a little surprised as he and Lawrence talked after the wedding ceremony about how well Lawrence and his family had done. The Father reminded Lawrence of all the blessings he had received from the Almighty, and Lawrence had to agree. The proof was in the pudding.

In the evening, when all of the Smiths except Lawrence walked home under a beautiful sky, they laughed and joked about the fun they and the villagers had had. Junior and Ginger were spending their wedding night at Theo's Inn, everything on the house—his gift to them.

The village had grown quite a bit, but it still looked like home to most of the people who still lived there. The old-timers could remember how it looked and sounded many years ago, but there were fewer of them around each year. Many of the villagers at Oak Junction had died over the years. That was the cycle of life, after all.

The main difference in the village now was the many new homes and shops that had been built and the families who had come there for a better life. Lawrence was thinking about all of this as he walked into the village for what would be one of the last times as a resident of Oak Junction.

He walked up the little streets and remembered how wide they had seemed as he looked for his friends. He hoped to see many strangers in town, buying and selling their wares. More people coming to the market usually meant better prices for his produce. Thankfully, the market was bustling with lots of friendly chatter among the shopkeepers and their customers.

This year would be the largest harvest for Lawrence if all went well. He was always amazed at his good fortune. His family was intact, his stepson was married, and he would be moving very soon to his new home in Themstead.

He knew he needed to go to church and thank God properly. Lawrence and Catherine entered the church and walked up to the very front. They knelt down and prayed and thanked their maker for all their bounty. When they stood up to leave, they saw Father Magnus. He looked a little older as did Lawrence. They had both filled out just a little with age and contentment. They had known each other for just six years or so now, but it seemed like a lifetime for both of them.

Chapter Thirty-Six

Father Magnus was talking with a woman of about forty and a young man of about twenty in the church. They had the same face as Father Magnus. A blind man would have known that they were related just by hearing them talk.

As Lawrence and Catherine turned to leave, not wanting to disturb their conversation, Father called out to them in a very happy voice and gestured for them to come over. They did.

"Lawrence, Catherine, this is my sister, India, and my nephew, Zachary," Father said with pride.

"Nice to meet you. I'm Lawrence Smith, and this is my wife, Catherine."

Once the introductions were finished, Father Magnus mentioned that this was the first of hopefully many visits of his only family to his home. His sister was nice looking with an intelligent face. She seemed a little quiet or reserved. His nephew was outgoing and had a pleasant manner about him—not brash but straightforward and self-assured. The nephew explained that they were there to see his uncle and that they were in the shipping business.

One more facet of the Father's life was revealed to Lawrence. He now saw before him the cause of all of the Father's long and recent pain. The fact that it had been repaired made Lawrence content. He knew that it had, and seeing these people made the life of Father Magnus more complete and real to Lawrence. They were all invited to Lawrence and Catherine's for dinner, of course. Lawrence would learn much more about them that night.

The dinner was a great success as always. More families came as people began to learn more about how modest Lawrence and his family were. In the beginning, the townsfolk didn't know Lawrence well enough to feel comfortable coming to his homestead. Over time, they realized that Lawrence didn't put on airs and only saw himself as a farmer and family man. Many people who didn't have firsthand contact with him thought he would be aloof due to his many accomplishments, but he wasn't like that at all. They soon discovered that once they met him.

This party was a time for everyone to forget about work and relax. Father Magnus's sister and nephew did come to the party on his ancient cart, pulled by his donkey, Daisy, as always. His sister, India, and her son, Zachary, were introduced to everyone there. Lawrence visited with most everyone at the dinner, but he really wanted to talk with the Father's sister and nephew.

Lawrence had many unanswered questions about Father Magnus, and they were just the people to answer them. Eventually, he was able to make his way over to India and Zachary and talk while the Father was off chatting with some other guests.

India was friendlier to Lawrence now than she had been when they first met in the church. Lawrence thought that perhaps meeting in the beautiful old church had set the tone for their meeting, and he was right. At the party, India was as bright and sharp as her son Zachary. She talked in broad terms about their lives in London and the Father's life in Oak Junction. As they talked more, many aspects of the Father's life were explained to Lawrence for the first time.

The fact that the Father came from a very successful, wealthy family and that he had been married and had a child in the past was exposed. Then Lawrence learned the story of the Father's own family being murdered. The story included details of his revenge on those who killed his family and the reasons he eventually left London. The siblings had no contact with each other for many years while he was on the run. Then, when he told them he was in the clergy, they were totally surprised. They had thought he'd been killed by bandits or caught by the sheriff's men. It still took more time for the rift to be healed.

These stories help to explain why the Father was never afraid to jump into the fray. He was not only completely sure that he was going to heaven; he was also a very brave man who stood up for what he believed in. He was apparently no stranger to violence and danger. If that included using a sword when necessary, he did so.

Lawrence began to understand better why he and the Father had such a special bond. They both saw the world very much the same light. Perhaps Father had more of the answers to those questions that Lawrence always wanted to ask him, but other than that they were very similar. They were men of action.

Lawrence answered many questions from India and Zachary about the Father and Lawrence's family. Zachary had no recollection of the Father and only knew him through the few stories his mother had told him. She, of course, had no contact with her brother for many years because of her stubbornness and failure to respond to the attempts Father Magnus made to reach out to her.

Lawrence told many stories about the Father to help them understand who he was now. They were amazed by what he had accomplished in the village through his ministry and by some of his more colorful exploits. In time as they talked, young Sam walked over and joined their conversation. Sam was seventeen now and very well built. He was slim but very strong from years of work on the farm. He was also very well-spoken and bright, like Zachary.

Zachary and Sam hit it off right away and had much in common though their lives were completely different. India and Zachary each asked Sam if he might be interested in coming to London sometime in the future, and he answered in the affirmative.

Sam wanted to see London, "the great city" that he had heard so much about. It was just an informal offer at the moment, but in time, that offer would change Sam's life forever. He didn't know it at the time, but it was the most important conversation he would ever have with anyone.

By the end of the evening, Lawrence knew that the story the Father had told him years ago was really about himself. It helped Lawrence to see the Father as more of a real person, not just a religious leader and his friend. The fact that he had suffered losses that normal, simple people suffered made Lawrence feel closer to Father Magnus. Lawrence had seen time and again what happened when he put his faith and future into the Father's and God's hands. There were still no guarantees in life, but the Father and God had been very good to Lawrence and his family.

As the cold night passed and their visitors left little by little, Lawrence was again reminded of how lucky he was. As he watched Catherine put their children to bed, they finally had some time to just sit together. Sitting under the stars, they counted their blessings and were content. Yes, they had suffered over the years—more than others, less than some—but at this pivotal point in their young lives, they both looked up into the dark night sky and counted their lucky stars. There were, in fact, too many to count.

It was a pleasant surprise for the Father and everyone else that in a few short months, India and Zachary returned to the village again. It had only been a short time since the wedding, and no one expected to see them so soon. That visit had been another chance for the Father and his family to heal and get to know each other better.

As the Father aged, he knew that he had no family except the monks and the nuns, although he was also close to Lawrence and his family. It was comforting for Lawrence and Catherine now to see that there might be a pleasant place in London for the Father to live when his working days were behind him. But there was another huge surprise for Sam and his family as well.

Another dinner was planned at Lawrence's house, and the Father and his family were to be there. India and Zachary spoke to Charles and everyone else about the plan they had in mind. They knew Sam was being educated in Themstead as Junior had been in Oak Junction. They wanted Sam to come to London when his education was finished. They had been impressed with his bearing and his intelligence, and because they were a very small family, they hoped he might want to come to London and join their shipping firm.

Charles and everyone else were stunned, but none more than Sam. He had thought that perhaps he might someday go to London for a visit, but never in his wildest dreams did he think it would be possible for him to ever live there. It wouldn't happen for a few years yet, of course. Not until he was finished with his education and his family felt comfortable with the thought of him leaving for the great city. But when that time came, there would be a place waiting there for him if he wanted it. Sam now had a goal and a destination in his life other than the mill. *Perhaps they might even come together somehow in the future,* he thought.

Lawrence had ordered a new wagon to be built well before the wedding. He planned on using it to move his meager belongings to Themstead and to use on the farm there. The old wagon would now stay at Oak Junction full-time.

Over the years, there had been many additions to the animals at Oak Junction. The cow had been bred several times, and the Smiths had kept three of the offspring. There were now two cows and a bull. Lawrence's horse had produced two fine offspring, and Junior's mare had been bred with a fine stallion from Langley's farm. The great stud that resulted from that breeding was now Lawrence's horse of choice. It was as black as any horse had ever been and stood a hand taller than any of the other horses in the county. It was a grand horse for any man to own, and it was Lawrence's.

He now could ride with the best of the gentlemen farmers around him, and that didn't always set well with some of them. That was their problem, as far as Lawrence was concerned. To Lawrence, it was just his horse. Charles started riding Lawrence's old mount when he wanted to go to Oak Junction instead of taking the wagon. There were now five horses on the farm, plenty for all who wanted or needed to ride somewhere or to plow the many fields. Elizabeth and Eli could both ride horses now. They never rode alone, but they understood how to ride and knew about the dangers that came with that activity.

By now, Lawrence was a man in the truest sense of the word. He had defended his family and others from certain death and tended to all of his family's needs. He took no pride in the killing of evil men but knew that it was necessary at times, even when he didn't want to do it, in order to survive.

Sometimes, men are forced to do things that are revolting to them due to circumstances. It's easy for some to stand by and let others do the dirty work, but Lawrence didn't have that luxury. He had been in battles and faced his mortality more than once, been married, and been given two wonderful children to protect and nurture. He had come into contact with many wealthy families and learned quickly not to envy them. That was because Lawrence was born and raised with the greatest gift a man can receive—poverty.

As Lawrence saw it, he could always try to improve his life and move forword without fear because at the end of the day, he had nothing to lose. His aspirations had always been quite modest. Because he earned his success a little at a time, he had little awareness of his growing prosperity and carried absolutely no guilt. He and his family had worked for everything they now owned.

Chapter Thirty-Seven

The move to Themstead went well. The women had planned it, and the men executed everything as expected. There wasn't much to take from the house, so the move went quickly enough. It was a tender time as everyone hugged and kissed and waved goodbye to each other. Father Magnus, as well as several of the nuns and villagers, were there to see them off.

William would stay with Charles and Martha in their house until he married later in the year. He spent much of his time at Halfway Farm now anyway to help with Joseph. After the illness, Joseph was getting better, but he still wasn't as strong as he had been in the recent past.

William could travel between the farms as often as needed and see Nancy when he didn't stay overnight. The Smith family spent the night at Halfway Farm on the way to their new home and new lives in Themstead. William rode with them and spent the night there as well. It already felt like home to him. In a few short months, it would be.

When the family reached Themstead in the early afternoon the next day, they could see their new home on the south side of the road as they traveled west. It was grand.

The first floor was made of river stone. A large entry opened behind a very strong, wooden-gated breezeway between the mill on the riverside and the house on the opposite side of the breezeway. The first floor also had narrow slots to shoot arrows through if needed. They faced the main road.

The second story was cedar planking with a shingled roof. No windows faced the road on the first floor of the house, which was impregnable. On the rear of the first floor, windows faced the farm to the south.

There were windows on all sides of the second floor. There was a fireplace in the mill and one in the house with hearths on both floors. It was a lovely home, a safe haven for Lawrence and his family. Lawrence and the boys had built most of it themselves with the help of Langley and all of his brothers. They had hired stonemasons for the walls of the first floor and the chimney and had worked with them through the entire project, fetching stones and stacking the smooth round rocks as they were needed around the house.

Two carpenters did the structural work, and Lawrence and the boys did the siding and the shingles on the roof. It was a far cry from the little house at Oak Junction. This house was a statement to everyone in Themstead that Lawrence and his family were there to stay. They called it "Mill House," and it would stand for generations. There was a large shed several yards south of the house full of large logs to be turned into lumber and some lumber already curing.

The first matter after moving into the house was to plant the crops for the coming year. Charles and Martha came up to Themstead to help. They brought the second plow and were ready early on a Wednesday morning. The cleared land was still small compared to Oak Junction, but soon they would cut down many more trees and clear that land for planting the following spring. Catherine was surprised to see several pieces of furniture in the house when she arrived at Mill House. Lawrence had ordered a proper bed frame and a dining room set as a present for her. It was the first furniture they hadn't made themselves.

Father Gregory and many of the same men Lawrence had met at that first meeting in the great church at Themstead came to the housewarming to see the completed house and the family. Father Gregory blessed the house and officially welcomed the family to the bustling town. Many of the men who came with Father Gregory were customers and friends of Lawrence by now, but few had met Catherine. They all talked and became acquainted with Catherine and the children. Lawrence took many orders on that first day that they had fully moved in. Father Magnus was there with Father Gregory. Lawrence remembered how Father Magnus had made all of this possible with the help of Father Gregory.

There was still a lot of work to do at Themstead. Several animal pens needed to be built along with a henhouse and a proper smokehouse. The larder was full, but Lawrence and Sam still spent a few early mornings hunting each week to keep their skills sharp. Sam was now as good as he would ever be with his bow. He was almost as sharp as Lawrence, but no one ever expected Sam to match Lawrence's accuracy and speed with a longbow. Sam was very skilled at stalking, and he enjoyed the silence of the forest as Lawrence did.

They had developed a very complex set of hand signals while hunting in the woods, and they often used them at home to tease the women. Sam also excelled at using another weapon while hunting, and that was the knife. He could gut and skin an animal as well as any butcher. He could also throw his knife and hit any target, large or small, within range. He had the eyes of a hunter just like the rest of the men in his family. Lawrence had also trained Sam to protect himself by wrestling.

There was seldom a day that Sam and Lawrence came home without something to eat. It wasn't always a turkey, but they would at least find a rabbit for the pot. Catherine was a great cook, and she never failed to create a decent meal for her husband and her children even when they didn't have every ingredient she needed. For the most part, however, the lean days were now behind them.

They had the money now to buy any spices they desired or anything else they needed or wanted. They often talked about the days when they first were together and all they had were rabbits.

They appreciated their lives more now for having endured those difficult times living off the land and sleeping under the stars in a lean-to. Lawrence felt sorry for people who never experienced difficult times. How were they to learn to deal with difficult times if they didn't experience them? Better sooner than later as far as Lawrence was concerned.

The new house was quite comfortable. There were five sleeping rooms upstairs, a kitchen area with a large stone-faced fireplace, and a great room on the first floor. Guests could sleep upstairs in one of the extra rooms, or even in the great room downstairs or in the mill. It had a fireplace as well, and there was plenty of room.

The days of the saw pit were over and Sam didn't miss them a bit, but they left their mark on him. He was very muscular with wide shoulders and thick arms. He didn't have an ounce of fat on him. He wasn't someone to trifle with, and everyone in the family knew that. He was a normal young man in all respects, but God help anyone who took him for a fool or an easy mark.

The mill had many orders to fill, and they were all hard at it as soon as the river was running again in the spring. There were still fish traps to set, but they now had nets as well. There were fish aplenty at Mill House, and all of the Smiths loved to catch and eat them.

Father Magnus had dinner and stayed at Mill House whenever he came to Themstead. He brought news from Oak Junction when he came to see Father Gregory on church business and when he just came to visit with Lawrence and the family.

Lawrence didn't travel to Oak Junction as he had in the past. His home was at Mill House now, and he had a business to run. Charles and Martha came to Themstead often to see their grandchildren. Father Magnus was like another grandfather to the children as well. There was always a room at Lawrence's home with Father's name on it, so to speak.

Junior and Ginger were busy with their lives as well in Oak Junction. Junior worked most days with Don and Ginger. They would walk with him to her parents' house where he worked.

Ginger would visit with her mother and little brother, and her father if he had the time. They all tried to make time to visit with Ginger when she came, and then she would leave to do what a young married woman needed to do in the village or at home.

She would purchase items that she needed in the village, and then she would enjoy the lovely walk back to Oak Junction under the shade of those giant trees and along the fence she had known since she was a young girl—the fence that Junior and Lawrence had made years ago along the road.

She was a woman now, with a husband and responsibilities of her own. She could close her eyes and follow her nose back to their farm. It smelled of the animals for sure, but it also smelled of the hay and the fruit blossoms and vegetables that had grown there for so many years now.

Don and Mary's life was perfect now with their only daughter well married and little Don walking, which made them feel young again. All was right with the world. And at her new home at the farm, Martha, Catherine's mother, and Ginger cooked and worked together in comfort and near bliss with happy hearts.

Everyone was awaiting the news that all inlaws excitedly anticipate. The announcement of a new family member coming in the not-so-distant future was finally made. Six months after the wedding, that wonderful announcement came. Both of the prospective grandmothers went to work making little outfits for the baby, and the time passed with great expectations and delight.

William rode out to Mill House, but never without stopping to see Nancy at Halfway Farm for lunch and a visit. Nancy was always happy to see William, but this time was different. Her father, Joseph, had been bedridden for three days, and she was worried. William talked with Joseph and was somewhat reassured by him that it wasn't life-threatening. He had experienced these symptoms before and had eventually recovered. He was in his late sixties now, so it wouldn't be as easy as it had been ten years ago, but he didn't see death knocking at his front door before his daughter was married.

The wedding was coming in six months. William and Nancy were worried all the same. If Joseph didn't recover, William would have to help Nancy with the planting at their farm as well as at Oak Junction and Mill House. He would have to add it to his list of things to get done. He was a Smith after all, and this was just another challenge to be met.

One day in the spring, Zachary arrived at Mill House. He was passing by on his way to see his uncle, Father Magnus, as he did quite often these days. He stopped to talk to Lawrence and Sam about Sam coming to London soon.

It had been over a year since they had talked about it in any detail. He knew Sam was almost finished with his studies and had done well. He knew that from his uncle, Father Magnus. Zachary had talked to Charles about Sam leaving as well, but Charles left the decision to Lawrence. At first, it wasn't an easy decision. Lawrence thought that he might still need Sam at the mill and the farm. Lawrence could surely use Sam, and he wasn't ready to send him out into the world and London yet.

It was agreed after a very long conversation over dinner in the new great room that Sam would go to London the following spring after the planting. Lawrence wanted Sam to leave with a clear memory of the hard farm work at home to remind him not to give up easily on his dreams while in London. He knew it wouldn't be easy for Sam to live in a giant city like ancient London. Sam was a bright country boy, but still a country boy. There was no doubt about that.

There was no shortage of young strong boys able and willing to work at the mill and the farm. Everyone knew that Lawrence was a fair man and paid a fair wage. But by having Sam stay a little longer, Lawrence sought to protect his brother one last time.

Lawrence had many connections in Themstead now through his business and Father Gregory. He would need an older boy or a strong young man to replace Sam in the mill. If Sam was leaving, which would happen soon, a new person needed to be trained to replace him. William came often and learned to operate the mill alongside Sam and Lawrence, but he was not going to be available full-time. He had his new life starting soon at Halfway Farm.

Charles had learned to operate the mill as well, but he was in Oak Junction most of the year. Eli would not be big enough to be of any assistance for a few years at least. So it was settled. They would hire a stranger to come and work at the mill.

Lawrence was very satisfied with his life and all that filled it now. He took his family to church every Sunday, and his relationship with Father Gregory grew as it had with Father Magnus. Father Gregory was not much older than Lawrence. Their relationship was more like that of brothers rather than father and son. Lawrence only missed church in Themstead when he was away in Oak Junction, and then he would sit in front of Father Magnus, listening and trying to put whatever message the Father was speaking about into action in his life.

After Junior and Ginger's announcement, Lawrence made a point of coming to Oak Junction whenever he could get away with the entire family. That always involved staying overnight at Halfway Farm, and everyone loved that. Elizabeth and Eli loved Joseph and Nancy and seeing the farm and all the animals. The two children grew up on farms, but to them every farm was different and a new adventure to be had.

Lawrence would often ride to Halfway Farm, meet them there, spend the night, and then ride back to Oak Junction with William. Eli would often ride on the horse with Lawrence. It was his favorite part of the journey. Lawrence and Catherine had more time to stay in Oak Junction and visit now, and everyone loved it.

When the planting was finished in Themstead, they could leave the mill for a few days and come to visit in Oak Junction. Lawrence was always current with their orders, and they had plenty. They had a vast supply of lumber already cut and stored in their sheds, and they had an older man to sit in the office to fill the orders while they were away. He wasn't much help loading the wagons, but their customers didn't mind that. They were just happy to have the lumber on hand to purchase. It worked out well for everyone concerned.

Lawrence now had time to speak privately with Father Magnus about those great questions that he'd had over the years and never asked. Before, he was too busy just trying to survive and then to create a life for himself and his family. He seldom had the time for long talks with anyone except Catherine.

Now the time had finally come. After services, Lawrence walked to the Father's office to talk with him while his family walked to their former home. The Father invited him into his little office, the small room where his life had been changed more than once, and they began to talk. "Father, can you explain to me why I have had the modest success that has come my way and why so many others have suffered? I can't explain it, and I don't fully understand it."

"That's easy for me, Lawrence. You're a very hard worker and an honest man. You are of above-average intelligence, and most of all, you believe in God."

"But Father, how much did God have to do with it versus my own endeavors?"

"Well, Lawrence, He created the world, the seasons, and all of us, including you. He seems very important to me in that equation."

"Then what about luck, Father? Why do I seem to have an abundance of good luck, and some others have less?"

"You make your own luck, Lawrence. You of all men should know that. You have always worked diligently and stayed out of trouble except when it came looking for you. You have always helped others and come to church as often as possible. What more should a man have to do?"

"What about Catherine's parents then? Why did they have to die at the hands of Jason and all of those other people?"

"I can't give you the answer to that question, Lawrence. I'm just a man like you and have many of the same questions. Only God knows the answers to those questions. Men do have free will, after all. God gave that to all of us. It isn't a perfect world, Lawrence, far from it. You of all men should know that."

"Where do we all come from then?"

"Oh Lawrence, I see you have been talking to Father Gregory again, haven't you?" With that comment, Lawrence cast his eyes to the rough stone floor.

"It's alright, Lawrence, you're only human like the rest of us. I think it may be time for me to answer those questions that have nagged at you for so many years. Perhaps you are mature enough now. In fact, I have no doubt.

"Even in London, terrible things can and do happen to innocent and evil people alike. I was nearly one of those. I mean that I was nearly innocent. I did have a great misfortune that cast me into the waters of despair. That man I told you about years ago was me. I lost everything. Yes, I lost a family rich with love and the promise of a wonderful future. I made a rash decision and took my revenge. I made the wrong choice and have had to live with those consequences ever since. I am truly sorry for what I did. I was young, not unlike you now. I am sorry, and still, those men are dead. I killed them, and I was lucky enough not to have gone to the gallows. But I live with that guilt and shame every day of my life. God saved me from the gallows and gave me a second chance. So, I gave my life over to God to do whatever he saw fit.

"Isn't it ironic that I sit here in front of you today as a priest? If I hadn't done what I did, we would never have met and had all of these adventures that we've had together. A priest should be allowed some adventure in his short life, even a priest like myself, as human as I am. And now my sister and nephew are back in my life, and your brother will be living with them in London shortly. Sam will be working with India and Zachary as my dead son might have if life had been kinder to him.

"You saved the lives of two children whose parents were slaughtered, you befriended the little brother, and you married the sister and made a family. You came from nothing, working the fields of another man, a lord, who set your entire family free from the land, and you wonder if God is watching over you? Could all of this happen by chance? Did the earth and the heavens happen by chance? I hardly think so, Lawrence. I lost a son and received you in exchange perhaps, plus all of your family.

"I was sent to help this village and become a part of it. My family now numbers in the hundreds, Lawrence. I miss my son, certainly, but we will meet again in heaven."

When the Father was done, Lawrence was truly stunned. He had answered many of his questions and more in a few short moments. Lawrence's head was still spinning when he stood up to leave.

"Have you discovered anything about the cloth?"

"I'm going north again on an adventure. I will tell you about it if anything comes of it."

"There's a rabbit in the hall, Father."

"Thank you, Lawrence, you're a good man."

Lawrence had heard some of this story from India, but not in such detail.

And of course, Father Magnus was right. No one had many answers that were certain. They all had to take everything on faith. And life was odd and strange and unpredictable, yet all of these wonderful and awful things had come to pass.

Lawrence's family was financially secure now. Lawrence was on his way, perhaps to great wealth. Only time would tell. Were the fortunes and futures of men drawn in the dirt with a stick to be changed by a harsh wind? Or, were they chiseled in granite, high upon a cliff by God where no one could change or alter them?

Lawrence surely didn't know, and he didn't spend much time or energy thinking about it. That was Father Magnus's calling after all; he had time for that and more. Lawrence only had time for his family, his work, and what good deeds he might be able to do as time passed. It now seemed that he had been away from his family for a decade, but it was only for a few years, and he had come home almost every weekend. But now he had his family with him at Themstead, and he had time to watch them grow and see his Catherine get more beautiful every passing day.

Father Magnus took a long ride on his wagon and ended up in the sheriff's town of Edgely. He spent the night in the church there. The next morning, he went out to the sheriff's estate. He knew the sheriff was in London on business. He walked onto the property and found the barn easily. An older man was working there with the horses. He was feeding them and cleaning their stalls.

"Hello Father, do you need my help?"

"Yes son, I would like to see the sheriff's saddle blankets. I am thinking of buying him a new one as a gift.

"Well, that might be a good idea, Father, as he covers a lot of territory riding all of the time in pursuit of those bandits and such."

"Yes, that's for sure. Might I look at his saddle blankets and see how badly he needs another?"

"Yes, they are over here in this box. The worst were used by my stable boy to sleep on."

"Oh, I see. Thank you for your time. I will look these over. Where is the stable boy sleeping these days?"

"Over there in that corner, Father."

"Thanks then. You have helped me immensely. You may go back to your duties. I will just look over these blankets and decide if he needs a new one. Keep it to yourself as it might be a surprise gift for him."

"No problem, sir, he never talks to any of us out here. He is too good for our sort, or so he thinks," the man said as he walked away.

The Father looked at all of the saddle blankets, which were in fine condition and not missing a corner. They were all red except for two, which were a bright royal blue. The Father then walked over to where the stable boy slept and found another red blanket on the ground. The right corner of the blanket was missing. Father pulled a small red piece of cloth from his pocket and placed it where the corner of the blanket should have been. It was a perfect match.

When the Father reached home the next day, he sent a letter off to London.

Chapter Thirty-Eight

Eventually, Lawrence hired two large young men to help him in the mill with Sam. They lived nearby and were happy for the work. Father Gregory had helped Lawrence choose them from a group of many worthy volunteers. Lawrence wanted two young men worth training who would stay on working in the mill for as many years as possible.

Having Father Gregory involved helped to remind these two that the Father had vouched for them so that somehow God was in the mix as well. Lawrence never wanted for orders, and he was soon able to purchase everything he needed to make the mill run more efficiently.

The first full year of the mill's operation was proving to be just as they had expected. There were startup costs, but once those were behind them, they would have a fine profit. They still had the income from the two farms, and soon the family was quite content and settled in.

The entire family was doing very well. Junior was working for his father-in-law, Don. Ginger was pregnant, Charles and his wife were happily working the farm at Oak Junction, and William was still working at Oak Junction but soon to marry and move to Halfway Farm. It was a happy family with two farms and a bright future.

Sam was seventeen now, and in the fall he would leave for London. He had written to India and Zachary often after the final decision was made to go to London. They were just waiting for him to come. They had a large townhouse with servants and ample room for him. His mother and father teased him no end about having servants to care for his every need. He would need to be trained, of course, but that was not going to be a problem. He could read and do mathematics as well as Junior. He was very well educated for a country lad, and that was unusual by the standards of the day.

Chapter Thirty-Nine

Lawrence invited all of the family to Themstead when it was time for Sam to leave. The house came alive when they were all there. The children ran around and played with their grandparents and the animals. The extra horses and the dogs that all of their friends brought with them made for a very chaotic but happy time.

Charles had some regrets about the amount of time he had spent with Sam, but Sam would have none of it. Sam thought that he'd had ample time with his parents and had some fine adventures as well with his brother Lawrence and his cousins. He reminded his father of the years they had worked together. The hunting adventures and all that his father had taught him were also discussed.

Sam loved them all and had no regrets. He was very nervous about going to London. It was a mysterious, giant city that he knew virtually nothing about. But he was not afraid. He reminded them all that Father Magnus's family would be there for him for warmth and protection.

It would be quite a change for a country boy like him. But he was looking at it as another great adventure. He was sad that he would not be there to help the family build their future on the gigantic wooded parcel to the west of their cousins, but he felt sure that Eli and Elizabeth would be able to take on that challenge in his place when that time came.

These were good times at Mill House. Father Magnus came at least once a month. Everyone had great memories to share and loved to visit and talk about what was happening in Themstead and Oak Junction.

Everyone was excited to see Father Magnus whenever he arrived because he would bring news of Ginger and Junior from the farm if Charles and Martha hadn't been up to visit for some time.

Ginger was able to help feed the animals on the farm and do her other chores well into her ninth month. Most women who lived on small farms had little choice, and they, for the most part, felt that it kept them fit. Most people in that time thought that it would help to ensure a successful birth. They saw it happen around them every day of their lives.

Late in the ninth month, Ginger felt her water break and sent Junior for her mother and the midwife. She had done all she could to prepare for the birth while waiting for her husband to return with the two women. When they returned, she was in hard labor, which was expected because it was her first delivery. But as time passed, she was in some distress and everyone agreed that it wasn't a good sign. After several hours of hard labor, the sun rose over the wooded horizon and a beautiful red-haired girl arrived. But she was dead. The umbilical cord was wrapped tightly around her neck, and she was gone. Her name was to have been Harmony.

The horror and heartache were immeasurable for all of the family. Junior and Ginger couldn't believe it. This happened very often all around them, in the lives of their friends and strangers alike, but to have to face this themselves was too much for them, or so they thought.

Father Gregory and Father Magnus knew there was never a satisfactory or easy answer for the families in times like these. All that Father Magnus could do was to promise that what God told his followers in his book would come to pass. The Bible had much to offer, and the Father knew all the passages to recite, but in the end, it was the faith of the survivors and time that made it possible for their lives to go on when it seemed to be impossible.

Their love for each other was tested. They cried and fought for no reason. They couldn't sleep. Their families did all they could to help. But life did go on. It wasn't as before, but the sun did shine. Not as brightly as before, and the birds did not sing as sweetly as before. But they did sing.

For Junior and Ginger, it would never be the same. The sky would never be quite as blue, and the flowers wouldn't smell quite as sweet as they did before Harmony came. But that was the way it should be for them for a while. They had lost their first child, and she was beautiful. She was put to rest in a corner of the cemetery at the old church in Oak Junction where all the Smiths would eventually lie. She was lonely, but she didn't wish anyone to join her too soon. She could wait. She knew that they would all be together there in due time.

Junior and Ginger, as well as the rest of the family, thought that for the first time they had been broken. What did this child have in store for the world and for them? What part would she have played in this beautiful growing drama and dream that Lawrence and Catherine and the rest of this family had created?

Junior and Ginger would eventually recover from the loss and death of Harmony. They had no other choice, but she would never be forgotten.

Chapter Forty

When the time came for Sam to leave for London, it was very difficult. If Harmony had survived, it would have been a joyous occasion, but now they were losing Sam just after the loss of Harmony.

Sam's leaving was a reminder to everyone that they had little control over what could happen to them at any moment. So what was supposed to be a joyous event was tinged with sadness and tempered with the realization of everyone's frailty and mortality. What dangers awaited Sam on the high road to London or even once in London were brought into sharper focus due to the family's tragic loss.

At least Sam had a warm home and a new surrogate family waiting for him at the end of his journey. He knew he wouldn't be seeing his family for some time. The hugs and kisses were stronger and meant that much more. He did have all of his memories to keep him company until he felt at home in London in the townhouse with India and Zachary and all their servants. In time, Sam hoped they would become a second family, like a suit of armor to store nearby in case of attack.

He didn't know how long it would take, but he was sure that he would do everything in his power to make that happen.

The ride to London was the first time Sam had traveled farther than from Oak Junction to Themstead. At times, the woods seemed to hold back all the evil and dangers in the world with their large black silhouettes, and at other times the forest itself seemed like a large animal waiting to devour Sam and his beautiful coach and team of horses, steaming in the cold air.

He slept a little that first night before they reached an ancient inn and spent the night. He dreamt of Lawrence and his family. He saw them calling out to him with outstretched arms and pleading faces. He heard Harmony telling him to carry on and take what he could from the world.

The second day, the forest was broken and even lovelier. Green fields and parks began to appear along with larger towns. Late on the second day as the sun was setting, the black edge of London appeared as a solid wall of towers and ramparts, and then bridges were crossed and churches were passed and bells were ringing in those churches all around him. Sam fell asleep again and dreamt of ghost ships and demons and a large blue ocean, and when he awoke in the evening, India and Zachary were looking into the carriage window at him.

"Welcome to London, dear boy," they whispered to him in unison, "You're home now, safe and sound."

When Sam walked from the carriage to the front of India's townhouse, he was still half asleep. He had his small bag of clothing, some silver coins in a small leather pouch his mother had made for him, and his hunting knife. He could smell the damp earth and the aroma of horse droppings.

Maybe London wouldn't be that much different from home, after all, he thought wearily.

He walked for a short distance on a hard rough surface as he left the carriage and then toward the large black front door of his new home. He was walking on the cobblestones of the large street that ran in front of India's residence. When he was about eight feet from the front door, he saw the small patch of dirt between the road and the townhouse that he had smelled. He was still keenly attuned to soil, still a farmer at heart.

Sam had slept a good part of the journey into town, but he had felt the turns of the road somewhere in his brain. He already knew that few of the roads in London were going to be straight.

He had awoken as the carriage made the final turn to India's house. He had slept but in bits and pieces. That was one of the reasons why he was so tired and disoriented when he finally arrived.

India and Zachary led him up to the giant black door that he would eventually see as the entrance to his safe haven in London. India unlocked the door with the largest brass key he had ever seen. He had very little experience with keys where he came from out in the country.

He was standing sleepily in the dark when that great door opened and revealed a beautiful, bright entry hall with a very high ceiling. With that flash of light, he was shocked back into the reality that he was no longer in his world of farming and hunting and was now in another world despite the soil he had smelled. He walked over the threshold with someone holding his elbow and leading him into a hallway with a high decorative ceiling painted with flowers and angels similar to those he had seen in church.

Then there was a smooth, shiny wooden floor under his dirty boots. Several strangers came running to meet him and his companions. One of them whisked his bag away from him as he was led into a large bright sitting room where he was seated in a soft leather chair that faced a formal fireplace that was ablaze. The room was as bright as day.

Sam could see paintings on the walls and several expensive pieces of furniture around the room. There was a beautiful carpet on the floor. It was yellow and trimmed with images of flowers that ran completely around the edge of the carpet. No two flowers were the same, and all the colors of the rainbow flowed through them.

He felt like he was in a dream, seeing things that couldn't really exist, but there he was, right in the middle of it all and trying to remember how he had gotten there. Perhaps the dream had placed him in a palace of some sort. As he was thinking about this, he could hear India somewhere far behind him giving orders to someone.

As he turned to look in the direction of her voice, a woman came floating in his direction with a silver tray and a pot along with four exquisite porcelain teacups. Sam's life in London began with a hot cup of tea and some biscuits. Eventually, he was led up to the second floor of the townhouse and to the bedroom that would be his.

That first morning after arriving, when he woke up in his new bedroom, Sam felt lost. He had little recollection of the events of the night before. He had some memories of the bright room, the tea, and the stairs, but it wasn't real to him yet.

There was a knock on his door, and a woman announced, "Breakfast." She waited for him while he quickly dressed and then led him downstairs to where he would eat. He found his new family waiting for him in a small nook off the kitchen. A round table was set for four, and he joined India and Zachary for their first meal together in their townhouse.

Sam sat stunned by the beauty of the house. It was so bright and sunny with windows everywhere. He could see more carpets on the rich wood floors, many more pieces of furniture, and more paintings on the walls. He had no way to prepare himself for how wealthy this family appeared to be. This was all beyond his wildest expectations.

"Yes Sam, we live a bit different here in the city." Sam could smell eggs and ham, and as he was thinking about how wonderful it smelled, an older woman placed a large plate in front of him.

"This breakfast looks wonderful."

"This is Becky, and she is our full-time cook and housekeeper. You met her last night, do you remember?" India asked.

"Not really, no."

"That's fine, Sam, you were very tired after the long journey. We have another younger woman who works in the house too, and Ralph, who serves as our butler and drives the coach. He answers the door, of course, and will help you with anything you need when he is in the house."

"I see, that will be very helpful."

"Today is Saturday. We will have Ralph drive us to the office and the warehouses so you can get a feel of everything while it's quiet on the streets."

"Thank you, I would love to see everything by the light of day. I fear I missed much while I was asleep in the carriage."

"Well, this is the best of London, and the docks are in a very different world, shall we say. We'll leave as soon as we finish breakfast. Perhaps you would like to send a note to your parents telling them that you arrived safely."

"That's a very good idea."

"We'll see to it before we leave."

"My father gave me some money for some proper clothes."

"That's fine. Monday we will go to the tailors and have some clothes made for you. We want you to make a good impression on your staff."

Just then, Becky approached Sam with an inkwell, pen, and sheet of paper.

"What do you mean by staff?"

"Well, you will have several people under you to help with your work, but more about that later. Ralph is bringing the carriage around to the front door." In a few minutes, they were finished with breakfast. "We'll be off as soon as he arrives."

They moved to the parlor and waited a few moments until the carriage pulled up in front. Sam could see it through the large windows facing the busy street and began to stand up.

"Sit down, Sam, we will wait until Ralph comes in for us. That's part of his duties, and we wouldn't want to disrespect him, would we?"

"No, India."

"Just call me 'auntie' when we're out in public. It will be easier for everyone. It will answer and stop all the questions about who you are and where you came from. You are family now in every sense of the word."

"You can call me Zachary," he said with a warm smile. "We're all in this together now."

Sam was surprised by their warm and casual attitude toward him, and their formal language to the servants. He soon realized that they were just trying to make him feel welcome and at home and at the same time show him the separation that was expected between the family and the servants. It was very interesting to be on the other side of that invisible line now. Sam wasn't sure how long it would take him to get used to this new lifestyle, but he thought with a smile, *not long.*

The ride to the river was a short one. The scenery shifted from grand to grim very quickly. Sam was quickly plunged into odors and sights that he didn't expect. The filth in the streets in and around their townhouse was nothing compared to the neighborhoods in the direction of the docks. It only got worse as they passed through the streets that led them down to the river.

As they stepped from the carriage, Sam was very glad that he had his boots on. There was a very large, red brick building on Sam's left as the street ended at the river. India explained to him that it was there that he would be working with them. To Sam's right were all the warehouses that India and Zachary owned. There were at least a dozen. There were ships with giant masts and sails as far as Sam could see in front of him. Some were tied up to floating anchorages; the rest were sailing in all directions in front of him. It looked like a world of chaos.

The ships were being loaded or unloaded by hundreds of men going in and out of the warehouses and then filling small boats that were soon paddled out to the waiting ships.

Painted on the red brick building and all of the warehouses was the name "Clark and Cook" in large red letters on a black field. Sam followed India and Zachary up the three flights of stairs and entered the building where Sam would be working. There were two high desks with stools to match and ten low desks in two rows of five behind the tall stools.

The room had windows on the three sides that faced the river. One set of windows faced north, the front of the building faced east, directly toward the river, and the third wall of windows faced south. All the windows looked out over the river and the ships. Looking to the south, one could see far off to where the river joined the sea. From that vantage point, the entire dock area and the river could be watched over.

Zachary walked Sam over to the tall desk in the northeast corner of the office where the two walls of windows came together.

"This is your desk, Sam. It was my father's. It's the best seat in the house. You can see most of what's happening on the river and at the warehouses from here." Sam was stunned. He had no idea of what he was to do, and they had given him India's husband's chair, the master's chair. It didn't make any sense to him, but perhaps in time, he would begin to understand.

"Thank you, Zachary, but what do I actually do?"

"There will be bills of lading and other paperwork brought to you to sign and file away for each of the ships that load and unload their cargo here." India sat in a large black chair as Zachary explained all of Sam's duties to him. She seemed anxious to be somewhere else, doing something else, anything else.

The floor of the room was made of rough wooden planks worn smooth from years of shoes walking over them and wearing them down. They were like the planks that Sam had made in the saw pit. He wondered who had cut them and where had they come from.

"You will also walk down to the docks and supervise the loading and unloading of some of the ships. Not all of them, but enough of them to make everyone certain that we are watching over them. Sadly, if you don't, these workers will rob us blind."

"Who will I work with down at the warehouses?" Sam asked as he pointed his right index finger at them.

"We have a foreman assigned to each of the ships as they arrive. He oversees the loading and unloading of his ship, one at a time, as they arrive. We have a main foreman who oversees the loading crews and has direct contact with each foreman. He will be your contact down there. He's a good man. Most of the foremen are alright, but they'll steal too if you don't keep your eyes on them," Zachary said with some sadness in his voice.

Sam stood listening to his list of duties and felt that in time that he would be up to the tasks at hand. He had dealt with people in the markets with his brother and his father and felt that he had the skills needed to accomplish this job. He felt that the best part of the job was going to be climbing the stairs. He already missed the physicality of his old life.

As Zachary finished speaking, India approached Sam with her gloved hand outstretched to him and touched his shoulder.

"Do you think you can do this?"

"I'll do my best, India. I think I'll be fine with the proper training."

"That's the spirit, Sam," Zachary shouted as they headed back to the stairs. Sam looked back over his shoulder and thought about how many ships were moored below him and across the river in the distance.

This is going to be interesting and exciting, he thought as he closed the office door behind him.

India was already in the carriage when Sam started down the stairs. She was in a hurry to leave this place. That was plain to see. Sam got into the carriage with Zachary and Ralph closed the green carriage door behind them. As they settled into their seats, India spoke to Ralph through the open window of her door. "Tea time, Ralph."

"Yes, ma'am." Sam heard the smack of Ralph's lips, and the horses began to move forward. India and Zachary looked at Sam and smiled warmly.

They headed east, away from the river and Sam's future. Back through the nasty buildings and neighborhoods for several minutes and never in a straight line. The streets were a maze. Children were playing in them as several carriages and wagons rushed by, the drivers hardly noticing them. Women threw dirty water and garbage into those same streets where their children played. Sam didn't know what he had expected London to be, but this wasn't it. The townhouse was the best example of what Sam had been hoping for when he left Themstead. He couldn't wait to get back to his new home. In short order, the streets were wider, a little straighter, and perhaps even a little cleaner.

The carriage stopped, and India and Zachary sat motionless. Sam started to open the carriage door, but Zachary stopped him. There was a rocking of the carriage, a grunt, and the carriage door opened.

Ralph was standing at attention as they left the carriage on the curbside. Sam had forgotten about letting Ralph do his job and felt stupid.

"It will take a while, Sam," said Zachary. "Don't be too hard on yourself." Sam looked up and down the broad street and was very pleased. It was like a different world again. There were many fine brick buildings with large windows and signs looking out on to the sidewalks and road. "This is the shopping district," Zachary explained.

They entered a fine two-story building with a tearoom on the ground floor and waited. They stood for a few moments until a young slender woman with dark brown hair came up to them and led them to a table at the window. Zachary looked at Sam as the young woman walked away. There was no need for them to speak. They shared a look that all young men had known forever.

She obviously knew India and walked away with a curtsy. Soon she reappeared with a silver tray as Becky had done at the townhouse. They each took china cups and saucers from the tray. She placed the tea, sugar, and cream on the table and left. Many well-dressed men and women were walking between the tearoom and the carriage.

"Don't worry, Sam, tomorrow morning we will go to the tailor. You will have proper clothing by Thursday." Zachary looked up from his tea and smiled. *How did she know what he was thinking?* Sam wondered. Zachary just nodded his head and winked.

As they drank their tea and talked, Sam noticed a sign over a shop door across the busy, wide avenue. It read "Clark and Cook" like their office sign at the river. Sam pointed it out to them, and Zachary explained to Sam that they owned several shops around London that sold imported goods. Their stores sold furniture and carpets to name just two items. Their shipping and importing business had made it quite easy to buy a few buildings and open up some shops. Sam said nothing more about it, but his mind was working.

This was the same model that his brother had used for success. Lawrence's was a rougher model perhaps, but very similar. "On Monday morning, Sam, you'll wear some of Zachary's clothes to the shops and then go on to the office. They should fit nicely." Zachary smiled and nodded his head again. "We are about the same size and age, aren't we, Sam."

When they finished their tea, India paid the young woman, and they walked to the door. The young woman held the door open as they went to meet Ralph at the carriage. India looked into Sam's eyes and spoke quietly when they reached Ralph.

"If you are ever in need of anything, and Zachary or I aren't at hand, Ralph will always be here to help you. We are all family, and we look out for each other."

"Thank you, auntie, and thank you, Ralph," Sam said to the driver. When India was finished, she turned to Zachary, who was still talking to the young woman at the tearoom door. "Zachary, come now, we are leaving." Zachary bowed to the woman and came quickly to the coach.

They left the tearoom and drove down a large busy street for some time, then down many larger roads and past many enormous and beautiful buildings of white stone and grey-tile roofs. Eventually, they passed a very large park that reminded Sam of his former life. He knew that if he needed to, he could live in that vast woodland.

They turned back toward the river, and in a few moments, they were back in front of the townhouse again. Sam had no idea where they had been or how to get back there.

"We will all ride to work together until you get a sense of where you are, Sam, don't worry. We don't know where we are half the time either. That's where Ralph comes in."

The carriage rocked, and soon Ralph was opening the door again, smiling.

"Let's have lunch, Sam," India said as the three of them entered the house and Ralph rode off with the coach. Zachary and Sam sat at the table with India where they had eaten breakfast earlier that morning. Becky brought them lunch with a smile and left them alone. It was served as before on fine china with silver utensils. It was a far cry from what Sam had grown up with.

"I understand how different this must be for you, Sam, but you'll get adjusted to it sooner than you think."

"I suppose so, Zachary, but it is a different world here. I guess it was the same for you when you came to Oak Junction the first time as well."

"Yes, but I had traveled some. So being in the countryside was not so difficult to adjust to. We have many friends with country homes, and we used to go to them quite often for short vacations before my father died. Since his death, we haven't had time for anything other than work."

They talked about Sam's family a bit as they ate, and then Zachary spoke about his relationship with his mother and father, and then about some of his friends in London whom he had gone to school with. Lunch was over in short order, and the two young men went up to the second floor and walked down the long hallway past Sam's room to the rear of the house and entered Zachary's bedroom.

It was identical to Sam's room, with a bed, a chest, and a large armoire. In one corner of Zachary's room stood a very large armoire with two grand, intricately carved doors. Zachary opened the huge doors, and Sam could see several jackets, a few pairs of pants, dozens of shirts folded on shelves, and many pairs of beautiful shoes.

"Pick what you want, Sam. We're about the same size, I think, so any of these should fit you just fine. Well enough for a week anyway."

"Thank you, Zachary, that's very generous of you. I know my clothes aren't suited well for the city."

"They're fine for town, Sam, but not for your new life in the office."

"I see, Zachary. May I ask you something?"

"Of course, go ahead."

"Who were Clark and Cook?"

"Oh, they were the original owners of our company. Joseph Clark was my great-grandfather, and William Cook was his best friend. They started in business as young men with a small shop and saved their pennies until they could buy a warehouse. They had their office in that warehouse for many years and became very successful merchants. They saved more money, worked hard, and eventually bought two more warehouses.

Finally, they bought an older ship, and over some time and hard work they became wealthy traders. It took them twenty-five years. Mr. Cook never married and outlived all of his family, which he attributed to the prevalent belief that London's "night airs" promoted disease. So it all came to my great-grandfather."

"What was your mother's maiden name?"

"Why Clark, of course, why?"

"Just curious as there are many Clarks about."

"That's for sure, Sam, that's for sure. But none of them are family?"

"No, all of my mother's family is gone except for her brother Magnus."

"But what about Ralph?"

"Oh, that's a story for sure. He was in some kind of trouble, and my grandfather brought him into our home as a young man. He has a mysterious past for sure, but I haven't looked into it much. He is like another uncle to me."

"And what about Becky?"

"She came to us when her previous employer died. She had no place to go, so mother brought her on as our cook and housekeeper. She lives on the third floor."

"With Ralph? Are they married then?"

"No, Ralph lives in the carriage house most of the year. He only comes to his room in the house in the winter when it's cold, and not all the time even then. He likes his own company best, I think.

"So they are like family then?"

"Absolutely, they are completely trustworthy and will do anything for us. Anything that happens or is said in this house will never pass the threshold of our front door. You can be assured of that. This was my grandfather's house, and when he became ill, my family moved in to help my grandmother Abigail. She eventually died, and we inherited everything. I was born after my grandmother died, so I never met her."

So here was this line of Clarks and their servants. Living in this townhouse until death took them quietly away in their old age. Sam was enthralled with the stories of this family and thought he was beginning to understand them.

It was a wonderful house, and the Clarks were a wonderful, giving family. He was the outsider trying to fit into this now small family, and they were doing everything they could to make him a part of it. As he stood wearing Zachary's clothing and shoes, he felt it was possible for him to become a small part of it. All he had to do was put away his fears and button up his shirt.

On Monday morning, Ralph sat parked in front of the townhouse as usual. He climbed down from his lofty perch and entered the front door of the residence as if it was his own. It was

173

a foggy day. India had many things on her mind, and this thick cold fog was not a help to her.

Ralph would take all of them to the river and drop Zachary off to open the office. Then they had to go to the tailor's shop to have some proper clothes made for Sam. The drive to the office was much longer in the fog. Sam couldn't see how Ralph was able to find his way there, but he did.

It was then another forty minutes to the tailor's shop in the high street. Sam was still trying to get his bearings, but it was impossible on a day like this. He tried to see the sun to figure out what direction they were traveling, but it was useless. The roads were no straighter than they had been the day before. This entire city was lacking in straight roads as far as Sam could tell.

After forty minutes of leaving the river and passing through ugly, grimy slums and eventually passing beautiful white mansions and townhouses, they arrived in front of a small shop with a large black sign in front that read in gold letters, "Levi and Sons, Tailors."

Ralph helped Sam and India from the carriage, and they walked briskly into the shop. India removed her suede gloves and sat down in a comfortable chair. A very old, white-haired little man with pale blue eyes approached them and spoke to them by name. "Hello, Mrs. Clark, Zachary sir," and then he noticed that it wasn't Zachary after all. They were his clothes, he knew that as he had made them, but the face was different.

"I'm sorry, sir, my eyes aren't what they used to be. I saw Mrs. Clark and my handiwork and assumed you were young Zachary. Please forgive me." India smiled at him as he bowed and she quietly spoke.

"This is my nephew, Sam Smith. He has come to work with Zachary and I. He needs a proper fitting and several suits of clothing, including a dinner jacket or two."

"Yes ma'am, let me measure young mister Smith while one of my sons shows you some fabrics." Sam was led over to a carpeted box and asked to stand on it. As he was measured for clothing for the first time in his life, he smiled at India and she smiled back affectionately.

She had obviously taken Sam under her wing and was treating him as another son. As he stood in front of a full-length mirror for the first time in his life, in Zachary's clothing, he couldn't see how his life could get any better.

After the measuring was finished, India spoke to the old tailor again, and she and Sam left his ancient shop. They got into the carriage with Ralph's gentle help and drove a short distance to another shop. This one was a shoe shop.

They walked in and quickly sat down. Again the proprietor knew India by name, and she explained to him what she wanted. He went for his measuring stick and came back and knelt in front of Sam. Several men and boys were working in the small shop making shoes and boots of many colors and styles. He noted the size and asked India how many pairs she wanted.

"Five, I think. Four pairs of shoes and one pair of boots will do, thank you."

"Thank you, Mrs. Clark, give me the week, and Monday they'll be here waiting for you." After that task was finished, India informed Sam that it was time for lunch.

They walked back to the carriage through a throng of smartly dressed men and women busy with shopping and the like. They seemed to be walking against the tide, but eventually, they were at the side of the carriage, and Ralph helped them in. Sam was now getting a sense of what Ralph looked like as he saw him at least twice a day now under the bright sun. They were for short periods of time as they either entered the carriage or left it, or went into the house or came from it.

Ralph was not an unattractive man, but you could tell that those deep-set grey eyes had seen more than most men. He was tall, strongly built, and walked with a sense of self-assuredness that came from years of various adventures. At least that was what Sam thought.

He had seen this type of man before in the country riding a great black horse and covered in armor with a huge sword at his side. "Lunch, Ralph" was all India said, and the coach lurched forward and was off down the busy road again, the two horses leading the way.

In twenty minutes, the carriage stopped and Ralph helped them down to the street where they walked into a pub. India was recognized instantly. An attractive young woman took the two of them to the rear of the pub to a more private area of the establishment. She smiled at Sam as they were seated away from the most crowded part of the room.

The large room was dark with wood-paneled walls and black-leather, high-backed seats. The tables were a deep brown color with a candle in the center. The ceiling was almost invisible due to the black soot that had built up on it from the candles and all the tobacco smoke from the guests of the past two centuries. Sam began the conversation with a question: "How did you get the name India?"

"It was my father's favorite place in the world other than here in London. He only went there once, but it left a lasting impression on him. My mother wasn't happy about it, but he would allow no other name for me. My name has always set me apart from others, but that hasn't always been a bad thing. I was always noticed and had to prove my worth to the students around me and the teachers who had contact with me.

"I don't know if my father knew that was going to happen, but somehow I think he did. You see the results seated in front of you. What do you think?"

"Well, you are very successful, and you do make an impression on everyone around you. As you said, that isn't always bad."

"Thank you, Sam."

"What was Father Magnus's name before he entered the clergy?"

"He was known as Clifton Clark here in London. My mother named him after the village where she was born." Sam didn't realize that Lawrence had been wondering about this for years, but when Sam wrote to him at the end of the week, that long mystery would be solved.

They ate a leisurely lunch of chicken soup and bread and talked about London and Themstead. Eventually, they ambled out to where Ralph stood at attention waiting for them in his red jacket and tall black hat.

"To the office please, Ralph."

"Yes, my lady." And off to work they went. India never seemed rushed or flustered. She had the air of a princess and seemed to live in her own world. And yet she was friendly and approachable when she needed to be. She was indeed separate from those around her when she needed to be the boss, but that would soon come to an end.

When they reached the office after lunch, they climbed those stairs, and Sam's new life really began. He saw Zachary there and was introduced as the new floor manager. Sam met with several men and women, young and old, who he would soon be managing. Zachary led Sam to his chair and sat next to him.

For that entire day, Zachary sat with Sam and showed him what to do with the paperwork brought up to him from the warehouses below. Zachary helped Sam learn which papers went to which people after Sam signed off on them. It was the only day Zachary would ever help him in the office, but Sam was a smart lad and a quick study. It didn't take very long for him to figure things out. The next day he would spend at the warehouses and learn that portion of his new job.

India was nowhere to be seen in the office after Sam started to work that day. He wondered where she went as he signed papers and watched countless ships pass by below him. Sitting on his tall oak stool behind lofty windows, he could see for miles in opposite directions as the beautiful, ever-changing river flowed below him.

Sam could see several dozen ships moored below him being loaded and unloaded by hundreds of men. He wondered where they had all come from and where on earth they were all going.

On the far side of the wide river, he could see great ships in many different stages of construction. The river was a bright blue when he sat down that first morning, but it was a cold black when he walked down those stairs with Zachary that evening and climbed into the coach for the bumpy, jarring ride home.

As they settled into their seats, Sam was surprised that India wasn't in the carriage waiting for them.

"Where's India, Zachary?"

"Oh, she seldom rides home with me in the afternoons. You won't see her much now that you are settled into the office. She has other duties that she must attend to in town."

"What duties are those, Zachary?"

"She has to keep her eyes on our shops. The salespeople must be cajoled into doing their work, and the inventories need to be checked. She spends most of her days with that. You have freed her up from that cage that is the office, and she has gladly flown from it."

"I find the office exciting and the view beautiful, Zachary."

"That may be, Sam, but you now sit in the seat where her husband, my father, died."

"Oh, I obviously had no idea. You had not explained that to me."

"By taking that seat, Sam, you have truly become one of us. My mother didn't give it to you lightly. There are many people in that office who wanted that position and some who felt that they deserved it. You may find some difficulties there because of that. But I'm sure the two of us will make it work."

"I will do my best, Zachary."

"I know. That's why my mother picked you. She saw what your family has done and knew that you were the one person who could fill that chair."

"But it was your father's."

"Exactly, and don't ever forget that. There is a great deal of power and respect that comes with that seat, and you must earn it and prove that whatever happens, you are worthy of it. I will be next to you most days to help you do just that."

"Thank you, Zachary, I didn't realize all of this in the beginning."

"Of course you didn't. If you had known everything, you might not have come. Then we might still have been looking for someone who might not even exist. It was meant to be. My mother is no fool, after all." With that sentence, they pulled up to the wonderful townhouse that Sam called home now—number eleven, Castle Lane.

"Good night, gentlemen," Ralph spoke up as he helped them from the carriage. They walked away and headed upstairs to their rooms to wash and dress for dinner.

A week after Sam left Oak Junction, William and Nancy were married. The wedding was in the village of Oak Junction that had grown into almost a town now. As with the previous Smith weddings, Father Magnus was there to marry the young couple. Joseph was able to attend as he had hoped and prayed to do. Most everyone from the village came to the wedding as expected. They felt that they were family after all that Lawrence and Catherine and all of them had been through. William would move to Halfway Farm and start his new life there with Nancy and Joseph.

Sam wasn't at the wedding, but everyone knew that he was too far away to come back after just leaving for London. His life in the city came with a different set of responsibilities. Sam had left a letter and a gift for his brother and his new bride. Now William was married, and Sam was the only Smith son left without a mate. He was on the young side, but his mother was still concerned. Charles and Martha wanted to see their last son married and happy before they passed on. They weren't that old, but they knew that anything could happen to either of them before the wedding that they hoped to see, sooner rather than later.

Harmony was always present in their lives to remind them of that. Since her death, the entire family had been shaken to the core and was still in the healing process. Their false sense of invincibility created by their good fortune had been shattered and was now buried with her.

Sam started to feel comfortable in his new position after a few weeks. Zachary had taken him down to the warehouses the second day that Sam came to work. He met the main foreman, Lester. He ran the crews that loaded and unloaded the giant ships. He was responsible for sending young "runners" up to the office with all the necessary paperwork. Sam would need to learn Lester's job as well.

If Lester missed a day or left, or died, Sam would need to cover for him until a replacement could be found. Lester had a hard face created by his outdoor work and his life. His eyes were bright, dark-brown orbs, set deeply in a leathery square face. They were constantly shifting their gaze on the men working under him. His hands were huge and strong. They showed the years of handling ropes and crates before he became the master of all these men.

His personality was the complete opposite of his physical appearance. He could be tough on his men certainly, but that was an act. His men knew it, and his reputation for fairness got most things accomplished for him on those ships.

As Sam talked with him, he came across as direct and honest. Lester and Sam liked each other from the start. Sam thought that that would make his life much simpler in the long run. To be friends with the leader of all of those men loading and unloading the ships would be a great help. Sam now thought that he had at least one friend down on the docks that he could depend on, and he was the most powerful man of all.

Sam met several of the men who worked under Lester and who managed the gangs of workmen. Sam hoped he could just deal directly with Lester. It would make Sam's life much easier. Those other men that he met were a rough bunch and seemed like they might be hard to control if he was put in that position.

After those first few weeks, Sam's new life seemed to be coming together. He sent another letter to his family that included the real name of Father Magnus, and he received a letter as well. As Sam became more comfortable with his new situation, he understood that he could leave his chair for some time and go down to the warehouses whenever he wanted.

He wanted to get a sense of where things went and belonged. As long as his paperwork was done by four-thirty, he was free to get acquainted with the equipment and the buildings. He felt that the more he understood the workings of the docks and warehouses, the better he could do his job. Zachary felt the same and had no problem with that at all.

Their partnership was working very well, and India seldom came to the office. It was a blessing to her. It was always difficult for her to come and see that chair where her husband sat for so many years. Now Sam had made that unnecessary for her, and she felt blessed for that.

Chapter Forty-One

India now spent most of her time working in town and planning parties at her home for the coming "season." She was now thinking of which woman her son would marry and a bit about who might show an interest in Sam as well. He fit in nicely at the office, and she was sure that he would pass the inspection of her friends and clients. He was very bright, nice looking, and had adapted well to the city. It was not an easy task for most ordinary country folks, but Sam didn't come from an ordinary family. He was, in fact, extraordinary.

Sam sometimes felt a little guilty for his now comfortable life, but as with most things, it came with a price. India was completely satisfied with Sam at this point, so there were only two in the carriage with Ralph on those early morning rides now. Sam worked five days a week from seven in the morning until his work was done each day. They usually finished by four-thirty or so. On those chilly mornings, Becky would send the boys off with hot tea, coffee, or chocolate to drink on the ride to the office on the river. It was a challenge to drink from those cups on the bumpy ride through old, crooked, narrow streets. Usually, Sam and Zachary tried to finish the drinks as fast as possible or they would end up wearing them on their clothing.

Ralph would drive the horses in the early morning light through these streets that he now knew like the back of his hand. He had been making this journey for more years than he could remember. He always wore the same thing on these cold mornings, including a long black muffler wrapped around his neck to keep the cold out and his ever-present black hat and red blazer. He always wore his black leather gloves as well.

Ralph would return from the docks, eat a small breakfast, and wait for India to come down from her room. Some days, she would have Ralph drive her to all of the stores around London to pick up the receipts and check on their inventories. On other days, she visited with friends and went out to lunch with them in fine cafes or went out to the nearby parks for a picnic or a stroll.

India was a little spoiled, but she carried her weight when her husband died, and all of her friends and clients respected her for that. She thanked God every day for her son and for the fact that he made it possible for her to keep the business going as well as they did. She had many sleepless nights worrying about what the future held for both of them right after her husband died.

Zachary had turned out to be a good and honest man, and all had turned out well after all. She was one of the lucky ones, a woman with a good son. He wasn't perfect; she knew that. That was one of the reasons that Sam was in London, after all.

Over time, Ralph and Sam began to get close. When Zachary left work early or had other duties that took him away from the office, Sam would ride up on the bench of the carriage with Ralph. Ralph wasn't comfortable with Sam next to him at first, but eventually, he learned to enjoy it. He didn't see any harm in it as long as India didn't know. Ralph knew that Sam had experience with driving and riding horses. He knew Sam's background and was sure Sam could take care of himself when it came to horses and coaches.

Eventually, Sam learned all about Ralph's life history. He had been a wanderer and an adventurer from the time that he was a very young man. He had been married once, but his wife died, and he vowed not to enter into those murky waters again. Not because his wife, who he missed, had been so wonderful but for the opposite reason.

He showed Sam several scars she had given him, and there was a horrible story to go with each one. Each story he told Sam was worse than the last. Sam didn't know how many of

Ralph's stories were true, but they all were very enlightening.

He had shipped out on many vessels at an early age, and over the years had seen many things. But eventually, he decided that the sailing life wasn't for him. He went to work in the warehouses for Mr. Clark's company. Ralph, who Mr. Clark finally noticed after a number of years, was eventually rewarded for his toughness and trustworthiness and came to work in the house as a reward of sorts.

Threats had been directed at the family as well as Mr. Clark many times and for several reasons. Some of them came from the laborers on the ships and others were misunderstandings between Mr. Clark and his clients. The clients were usually easier to deal with due to their level of education and civility. The laborers were something else altogether.

James Clark carried a heavy, brass-topped cane with him at all times as many men did at that time. But over the years, Mr. Clark had soured on his workers and seldom thought twice about using his cane on them if he felt justified. He was often in the wrong, and he soon gained a reputation among his men of being a real bastard. Eventually, he quit going down to the docks for his own safety.

It was a sad state of affairs because he had at one time been loved by his men and enjoyed mixing with them unlike many of his contemporaries. Sam had been told of the problems down on the docks and soon experienced it for himself. When he walked on the docks with Lester, he had heard some men whisper, "Where's your stick, bastard?" Sam didn't take it to heart; after all, some of these men had been mistreated long ago. But if things got out of control, he did have his knife. He just hoped he wouldn't have to use it.

After a few weeks of hearing the moans and grumbling on the docks, Sam talked with Zachary and Lester about the state of the morale of the men and asked for a meeting with all of them.

It was held on a Friday afternoon. Lester spoke first to get the men's attention, and then Sam stepped up on a crate to be able to see all of the men and for them to be able to see him. He told them, "I'm not here to tell you how to do your jobs. You already know them or Lester would have tossed you into the river. I trust Lester to run the docks. I trust your foremen to treat you fairly, but this is hard work. If any of you aren't happy here, tell your foreman, and he'll talk with Lester. Talk to your foreman about your issues or leave. There are hundreds of men out in the streets waiting for you to leave so they can take your jobs—and women as well."

The men watching Sam laughed at that last remark or groaned. Zachary was looking down from the office windows above the docks. "When I come down to the docks, have your foremen talk to me about your grievances. I'll take them upstairs, and we'll try to work something out. But remember, this isn't a party, and if you aren't man enough to do your job, go on home and explain it to your wives. I'm sure they'll straighten you out if Lester or I can't."

Many of the men stood up laughing or clapping, and those who didn't were seen by everyone for what they were—troublemakers. They now had a choice to make. Go on back to work and change their attitude, or pay the consequences. Sam didn't hear much grumbling after that. Some issues that did come to his attention and they were dealt with—not always to the men's satisfaction—but they felt that they had at least been heard.

Zachary liked the way Sam handled the situation and so did India after Zachary recounted the events to her that night. They were both reassured that they had made the right decision regarding Sam. The mood on the docks changed virtually over the weekend, and Lester was very taken with Sam. Lester became more open with Sam about what was happening with the men, and more importantly, the men were impressed with Sam's apparent fairness and willingness to listen to them.

Eventually, everyone on the docks became aware of Sam's family history, and things improved even more. They had all thought that Sam was another snob or high-society know-it-all. When the warehouse workers heard where he came from and what his family had accomplished, it gave them all hope. It gave them hope that their lives could somehow improve, and if they worked hard enough and saved their pennies that they too could eventually move up and out of their current situation and on to something better.

Sam was a constant reminder of that possibility, and the men couldn't dispute it. Sam learned a lesson as well from this experience. His workers had decided who he was based on what he wore and how he spoke. Sam vowed never to make that mistake in his life again, and he constantly tried not to make assumptions based on someone's appearance or speech.

On the Sunday after Sam's speech to the men, he went to church with India. Zachary wasn't interested in spiritual matters. Young Sam could clearly see that. It was a pleasant chance to visit with India again in private since she didn't come to the office anymore. Sam would have been too busy to visit with her even if she did. He was constantly busy now that he had learned his duties and had started to discharge them in his capacity as office manager.

The ride to India's church was to the north and away from the river. It was in the opposite direction of the shops they had gone to in the past, but the neighborhoods were still grand that they passed through. The buildings were large and well kept with white stone facades and beautiful rooflines. There was nothing like these fine buildings where Sam came from except for the two churches he had grown up in. Sometimes he thought that many of the fine buildings he was seeing were churches when in reality they were just old mansions or office buildings.

There were still no straight roads as they traveled to their destination, but Sam was finally getting used to that. He created a game in his mind by trying to figure out where he was and how to get to the church, but he usually failed. Sam knew that, like his job, if he worked at it hard enough and long enough, he would eventually figure out this city of mysteries and fog.

As they traveled away from their beautiful townhouse with the great black door, Sam decided to ask India about something that had been bothering him since he had arrived in London. "Why am I sitting in your husband's seat and not Zachary?" he asked.

"I was wondering how long it would take for you to ask me that, Sam. I'm surprised that it took so long."

"I was determined to learn the job you have given me and not to ask personal questions about your family. You have given me a great opportunity, and I didn't want to jeopardize my new position, but I feel sometimes that Zachary should be sitting where I am."

"Well Sam, it's a fair question, and I will answer it as best I can. Zachary will be a good man, but he isn't mature enough now to do what you are doing. He may be able to complete the tasks at hand, but his heart isn't in it yet. We spoiled him to some degree, and he has an eye for the ladies of the worst sort. And the combination of those two traits could put our company in danger and disgrace if Zachary were left to run things now.

"In time, I hope he will be able to take on your job and remain here in London with me to run the company. I have other plans for your future with us."

Sam was startled by India's answer. "What other plans could you possibly have for me?"

"In good time, Sam, in good time. You are like another son to me now, and you will never have to worry about a thing if you will put your trust in me. Zachary is no threat to you now and never will be, I will make sure of that—and besides, he cares for you as much as I do, perhaps even more.

"We have talked at great length about your future, and it will be wonderful if you will just let us help you. You have saved my life in more ways than you could know or understand by coming to live with us and help run the business. My brother was right about you and your family, and I owe him a great deal as well.

"I was locked in grief and hopelessness after my husband died. Now I am able to see more than just the grave that I was longing for. You have done that for me, and I thank you."

Sam was still reeling from this disclosure from India when they arrived in front of the largest building he had ever seen. It was India's church, and they entered as Ralph drove away in the carriage. They eventually reached a pew near the front and sat down among a group of very well-dressed men and women. Sam thanked the Lord and prayed like he had never prayed before.

After the church service of an hour or so, Sam and India walked out to the front of the church to wait for Ralph to return with the coach. As they waited, several women and couples came up to India and spoke with her. Sam was introduced as her nephew and listened to the conversations as these wealthy people spoke about the issues of the day and coming social events. He was startled to hear his name mentioned in the conversations and couldn't understand why he was coming up so often in them.

When Ralph finally appeared and helped them into the coach, Sam's heart was racing again. India could see the queer look on his face and understood immediately what was troubling Sam. "You are in this family now, Sam, and there will be many things you will have to do other than your work to become a success. None of them will be against God's decrees, and most of them will become quite pleasurable to you in time.

"You will have to learn to become a gentleman, but you are nearly one now, so that won't be much of a problem. That also includes an understanding of the fine arts, architecture—which I notice that you already seem interested in—and you will have to learn to dance. I will take that duty on myself. Zachary is a fine dancer. He was one of my first pupils, after his father, of course. I will have you floating around the dance floor in no time." Sam felt sick to his stomach, but he knew that would pass as would his ability to keep from learning to dance with India.

Sam got used to wearing his fine clothes soon enough. His armoire was full of the fine suits, shirts, and shoes that India had purchased for him. He had more shoes in front of him in his closet than he had worn in his entire lifetime. He was always amazed when he opened those great curved wooden doors. It was like a temple to Sam. It was filled with wonderful gifts from India. It wasn't that she was trying to buy Sam's loyalty. She knew that she already had that. But money was plentiful, and she wanted her wealth to bring him a little pleasure. And besides, these suits were his uniform for the office. They gave his underlings the sense that he was in charge. He looked the part of a successful leader and boss when he was properly dressed.

India didn't own a giant mansion in the country. She had no need to, though many of her friends did, and she was often away now that Sam had arrived. When she went on those "little trips," Ralph would drive her, and she would take Becky with her as well. When India was away, Zachary would hire a coach to take Sam and him to work and back. It was when she was away that Sam noticed the Zachary that India had described. Zachary often spent more time away from the office without any reason that Sam could understand. And Zachary would often send Sam home alone at the end of the day as he had "matters to attend to."

On a few occasions, they walked to the office to get some fresh air and exercise. It wasn't far, but they knew they would have to pass through those same nasty neighborhoods that they traveled through in the carriage. As they walked to the river, many men and women called to them for any number of reasons.

Zachary knew that Sam wore his hunting knife on his belt, and he had asked Sam about it a few times. Sam had mentioned that it was the last piece of home that he still owned. All his clothes were long gone as were his one pair of old shoes. His knife couldn't be seen under the long jacket that he wore to work, but he often took his jacket off in the office and there was some talk about it among the employees.

On one occasion while walking through one of these rougher areas, they were accosted by two large dirty men. One was a little larger than the other, and they looked disagreeable enough to keep an eye on as Zachary and Sam walked on toward them. As they approached them, Sam knew instantly that trouble was coming their way.

As the larger man began to speak, he reached out and tried to hit Sam. Sam swept his feet out from under him and hit him where his jaw and ear come together with the butt of his knife to disable him. The man lay perfectly still on the pavement. Sam then stood up and moved toward the smaller man with his knife at the ready. That man yelped, turned quickly on his heels, and ran away as fast as he could. Sam placed his knife back where it belonged and knelt down to check the man at his feet.

"He's still breathing. He's alive at least, thank goodness." Sam looked up at Zachary and could see that he was in shock. He couldn't move or speak. Sam sat him up against the building closest to them and waited for Zachary to come around. There were many onlookers, but they stayed away from the two men. After some time passed, Zachary came back to his senses and asked Sam what had happened, and more importantly, how he had done it.

"I grew up in a dangerous place where life is fragile. I learned never to let a man do harm to me, and there was no doubt about what those two had on their minds." From that day on, Zachary and Sam never had a problem the few times they chose to walk to work through those neighborhoods.

Word traveled quickly in the area about Sam. He had disabled one of the most dangerous men in the neighborhood with a single blow, and all of the onlookers were highly impressed. He didn't think much about it though. He was a Smith, after all.

Zachary and Sam swore an oath of secrecy to prevent India from finding out what had happened. They were never going to speak of the matter again. But in a few days, Lester asked to come up to the office to speak to Sam and Zachary at the end of the workday.

"There's talk about the two of you on the docks."

"What kind of talk, Lester?"

"It seems the two of you were attacked down there on the streets where no fools like you should have been. Apparently, Sam took care of a couple of troublemakers."

"What if it is true?" Zachary asked.

"Well, the men have a much higher opinion of Sam than they had before if that's possible."

"Then it was us, but we won't make a habit of getting into trouble in that neighborhood again. Perhaps they should try to keep their friends in line down there."

"It wasn't anyone held in high esteem by our crews, that's for sure. Those men were preying on all of them as well."

"Then we are happy to be of service to them, Lester. Thank you for the information," Zachary said with a sweep of his arm and a slight bow.

Ralph heard the news in The Noose and Stool soon enough while waiting for the boys to get off work. He kept it to himself but filed the information away for use at perhaps another time. India heard it as well at her favorite tearoom one afternoon near her home. She knew it had to be Sam and Zachary by the location of the altercation and by the descriptions of the two men involved. She wasn't happy. She didn't need Sam or her Zachary hurt or in trouble with the law.

She made her feelings very clear to both of them over dinner the next night, and there were few walks to work after that. She had great plans for both of them, and she would tolerate no nonsense from them. Things between England and America would be changing for the better, sooner or later, and she wanted them all to be ready when the time came.

One afternoon after dark as Sam rode up on top of the carriage with Ralph, they began to talk once more. "So is your brother *the* Lawrence Smith."

"Yes, he is Lawrence Smith of Oak Junction and now of Themstead."

"Why didn't you ever mention that to anyone before?"

"India and Zachary know. I didn't see any need to mention it to anyone else. Who would care about a small farmer and his family in this big city?"

"Well, many men have heard the stories about your brother and your family, even here."

"Well, I was living with my parents when Lawrence received his great gift from the king. He left soon after, and we didn't see him again for some time. When we rejoined him, he had already started his family and had built his house and cleared the land for his first farm.

"Eventually, when I came to live with him, I spent many hours hunting and working with him. He taught me how to use a bow and how to farm and build things. He taught us all how to dream about a future we would be able to create in our own lives without the interference of nobles or kings. He taught us to love God, be unafraid, and work as hard as we dreamed."

"You seem to have learned a lot from him."

"We are just peasants, Ralph."

"But you and your family are rich now."

"We were always rich. We were raised to work hard and not to complain even when we had nothing. We can read now, we own land, and we have some income from the mill and the farms, but we earned every bit of it. In our family, hard work shows what a man is made of. The wealth is the result, not the goal. A hard-working honest man will usually do well, but good luck never hurts."

"I see, Sam. You seem to have learned a good deal from your older brother. What do you think the future holds for you?"

"It's hard to say. I'm still very young, and I see the world through my eyes and experiences. I was raised to think I can do anything I set my mind to and that I have as good a chance as the next fellow to succeed. This job at the river has shown me that. But you are older and wiser than I. You have had much more experience at this life than I have had. Perhaps you have a different opinion of my fate based on your knowledge."

"Well, no one can see their own fate, thank God, but I don't doubt that you will do well," Ralph replied. "Just remember that everything that happens to you makes you smarter and better prepared for your next adventure."

"You sound like my brother."

"Thank you, Sam, that makes me very proud."

Ralph and Sam became very close over time, and Sam learned a great deal from Ralph. As noted, Ralph preferred to stay and sleep in the carriage house most of the time even though he had a room in the house upstairs. He had a small tidy room in the carriage house with an iron stove and his store of food. He had lived for years aboard ships so he needed little room. He ate most of his meals in the townhouse and came and went as he pleased when he wasn't needed. He was treated as a member of the family, as were Becky and Carol. They all had their own rooms up on the third floor.

Chapter Forty-Two

Ralph had seen more in his lifetime than most men. He had gone to sea many times. He fired cannons in battle and fought more than once with his saber in the king's navy. He had been across the vast Atlantic a few times and had even seen North Africa. He had fallen in love with an African woman who was as dark as the night and who had beautiful blue eyes. He knew she would never be happy in cold foggy London, so he ended their romance after some time. He remembered her kindness to him even though he was a stranger in her country. He remembered her sweet voice and touch. She was someone he would never forget for all the years of his life. Ralph had few regrets, other than not staying with her, and endless stories.

He had many scars not only from his demon of a wife but from his naval career. Ralph offered to teach Sam how to fight with a saber, and Sam was eager to learn that new skill. But Ralph made it very clear to Sam that India must never know about what they were doing out in the carriage house. She tended to worry a bit. Sam agreed with Ralph about that. So they began to practice in the evenings after work and when India was away. Sam made quick progress, mostly due to Ralph's skill and patience. Sam was impressed with Ralph and soon came to believe most of what Ralph had told him about his life. Sam still had some doubts about Ralph's stories, but he kept them to himself.

There was no doubt that he had been a soldier and a sailor. Zachary and Becky both said those stories were true when Sam asked them. They both thought that some of Ralph's problems with people came from his time in battle and being away from his home in England. He had spent far too much time away from civilized society according to India.

After several weeks of practice, Sam learned the basics of saber fighting and felt some satisfaction, as did Ralph. Sam was his "protégé," Ralph would say as they rode together on top of the carriage on the trips to the river and home again. Sam asked what that word meant more than once.

Luckily, India never knew what they were doing in the carriage house in the evenings when she was reading or writing letters to her lady friends about Zachary and Sam and their need for future wives. Sam's life had fallen into a comfortable routine of work and his saber practice with Ralph on those evenings when he had the good fortune of having time to spare. Sam needed something to keep himself fit, after all. Sitting at his desk and walking down to the docks on some of his days wasn't enough to keep him in shape. His life at home with Lawrence had always been very physical, and they never overate. This life in London was many things. It was interesting. It could be dangerous, as Sam had discovered. But it wasn't physically taxing.

That was the reason he started to walk to the docks in the first place. Sam hadn't been looking for trouble. He just needed the exercise, like any animal. That hadn't changed. He needed to be active. That was who he was.

Sam loved the back garden of his new home, and seeing Ralph in the carriage house always gave him a reason to walk into that narrow, deep wonderland. It wasn't Oak Junction, but it was a miniature version to be sure. There were few plants or trees in the front yards of these beautiful homes in London, but the rear gardens could be fantastic. India's garden was just that. She had the wealth to create a divine space where she could spend her early evenings before it got too cold and sit with friends or family to sip drinks and eat lovely meals prepared by Becky.

Sam loved those times almost as much as the time he spent with Ralph. There were many trees along both sides of the garden and plants that flowered in front of them and along the path that meandered into the middle of the yard.

There was a small fountain in the center of the path. The path passed by it and went on out to the rear of the yard where Ralph lived his solitary life. It was an oasis for Sam, a country boy brought into the big city like Ralph. Like Ralph, who had been to North Africa, he was a stranger in a strange environment. All he lacked was a lover to keep him company and to speak softly to him in those lonely nights away from home.

As for the carriage house, it looked like a small chalet with fancy wood trim on the eves and window. The walls were covered in dark wooden shingles as old as London. A large window made up of several small panes of glass faced the garden from Ralph's room, and giant doors opened onto the alley that ran behind all these great houses.

Each house in this neighborhood had a carriage house of some sort behind it for the horses and their carriages. Some of these carriage houses contained as many as six horses, but Ralph had only the two horses and the carriage to care for. As Ralph said often, "Taking care of two stupid horses and a carriage is nothing after working and taking care of the rigging on a proper sailing vessel."

Ralph told Sam many stories about having to do maintenance and repairs on large ships of war and commercial ships. If these stories were true, Ralph was indeed suited to care for the carriage and two fine horses. Sam often helped Ralph clean and feed the horses, but Ralph never allowed Sam to touch the carriage. That was Ralph's domain alone, and no one was allowed to enter it. Sometimes Ralph would let Sam wash the spokes of the wheels, but never the coach.

When Lawrence received the latest letter from Sam, it solved the final mystery of Father Magnus's true name. After all those years of wondering, it was anticlimactic. He would always be Father Magnus to Lawrence, and that was the end of it. Lawrence had matured and realized that there were more important things to focus on.

The farms were doing well as was the lumber mill. Lawrence now was able to feel a comfort that he hadn't known before. He had ample time now to be a part of his children's lives as well as his beloved Catherine. He still took time to hunt and dream, but it was different now. He had the time to teach his young son to hunt and shoot, and Grandfather Smith would often go with them into the still, deep, and dark forest on Lawrence's land.

His brothers were doing well and didn't need him to watch over them any longer. Junior was a success in his own right now. He was doing much of the work in the blacksmith shop with Don Jr. watching him and learning as Junior had done before him. Don came into the shop occasionally to see if Junior had any questions about a project at hand, but he seldom had any. So Don would join his wife and visit friends and even do a little traveling.

Since Harmony's death, everyone had been trying to recover and get their lives moving forward again. Don took his wife to southern England and into London once to see Sam. It was just a short visit, but it helped Sam feel less homesick.

Junior and Ginger focused on the blacksmith shop and tried to heal as well as anyone can after the loss of their firstborn.

Lawrence's energies began to focus on his aging parents and their future. They would soon be too old to be able to do physical work on the farm, and Lawrence wanted them to have an easier life.

Lawrence decided to build an inn at Oak Junction and a new larger house for his parents. Junior and Ginger would then have the house at Oak Junction all to themselves, and perhaps they would try to start a family again. Lawrence put his idea into motion after talking with his family and Theo, the innkeeper at Oak Junction.

Lawrence wanted to be sure that there was enough traffic now for two inns, and Theo was sure there was. Lawrence's inn would receive trade from all the traffic that didn't come west into the village or proceed on into Themstead. Theo would still get trade from those coming and going to Oak Junction and going on to Themstead, and those coming from Themstead or on to places farther to the north.

They all agreed that it was a good plan. Lawrence had the perfect location at the crossroads at the old oak tree. There would be ample money to build it, and Lawrence's parents were looking forward to running an inn and pub. They would use the inn where they had stayed on the way to Chesterfield as a model.

Back in London, Sam was finishing up his apprenticeship under the watchful eyes of Lester, and to a somewhat smaller degree, from Zachary. Sam was completely comfortable with all of the tasks that anyone would put to him. He was now more proficient at his work and had a little more time to pursue some of his own dreams.

Sam realized how much he owed India for his new life, and he was determined to make her faith in him pay her dividends. One of his ideas was to send more products to America when the time came. Yes, there were difficulties right now with the war, but soon, he had no doubt that trade would resume. He wanted Clark and Cook to be a part of this new relationship with America, even if only in a very small way.

Every morning as Sam sat in his office chair, he saw the sun rising over the Thames and watched all the great ships leave on the tide. He wondered about all those places Ralph had talked about. He saw all the rough wooden crates leaving the warehouses and getting loaded slowly on to their customers' ships and eventually floating silently off to distant ports around the world.

He would venture down to the ships as often as time would allow and climb up into the rigging. He climbed higher each time he went up into the sails until he felt comfortable at last. He wasn't a sailor yet, but he was learning his limits and stretching them. Sam didn't dream of all the distant ports where these ships sailed. His dreams began and ended with Boston and America.

Ralph was tall compared to his friends and was seldom accosted by strangers. He was strongly built with large arms created by his hard navy life and a face that revealed his adventurous life in the form of dark-brown skin, creases, blotches, and wrinkles. He was about in his mid-forties, but he was still very fit compared to most men of his age. He appeared eager for anything that came his way. He wasn't a rabble-rouser, but he never backed away from a difficult problem or person. This was to his detriment on more than one occasion.

He had seldom been beaten in a fair fight, but drunken brawls were seldom fair. He wasn't a big drinker, but he enjoyed the atmosphere of his favorite pub. He loved to sit at the bar of The Noose and Stool and soak up the ambiance around him.

He was self-educated for the most part, having read a good deal while on his travels, but he would rather participate in history and great adventures than read about them. He never started trouble and was always welcome in his favorite pubs. His presence alone often kept things from getting out of hand. Ralph had a few friends from his navy days and the docks. They met most weekends at The Noose and Stool for lying sessions and a few dozen harmless drinks.

The Noose and Stool was typical of most pubs with a long, dark wooden bar and a few friendly men or women behind it to serve everyone at the bar and a few tables. As long as customers were well behaved, that is. When strangers or the regular troublemakers started anything, the mood could change quickly.

The locals wouldn't put up with much foolishness, and they felt protective of their ancient retreat. It had a few small windows in the front, facing the river, and a very large, heavy entry door that could keep anyone or anything out or in as needed. It had a low-beamed, plastered ceiling that made it feel smaller than it was. A large fireplace in the corner warmed everyone on cold London days and nights.

It had a very long history as most of the establishments along the river did. They were some of the first buildings erected and some of the most cherished by the sailors and the shipwrights. Zachary had been taken there by his father a few times as a youngster and had become friends with the owner and his wife.

Zachary didn't come back often, but when he began thinking of his father or missed him, he would sometimes return there for a bit of reminiscing over a pint or two. The owners were always glad to see how he was doing after the loss of his father. The fact that they didn't see him too often meant that he was getting on with his life.

It was Ralph's second home. He could drink a lot and get into trouble, but he seldom did that anymore. Time and experience had shown him that that didn't always end well for him. He was older now, and he healed slower than in his youth of days gone by. He just liked being with his few good friends and the people who he had something in common with now. He hadn't had the greatest luck with women in his life, and he didn't interact with the staff at the townhouse very much. He was pleasant but didn't have much to talk to them about. He wasn't much of a talker to start with, and he would rather sit on a stool and listen to his friends tell their tall tales than chat with women.

He did feel a connection with India, however. India had been badly neglected by her father. He had spent all his time building a business instead of caring for his family, and her mother was often too busy with her friends and social activities.

Like India, Ralph had been neglected by his parents so he felt compassion and was protective of her. Ralph had run away from his family when he was quite young due to his father's drinking and his abuse of all of them. His mother was no bargain either. He had many siblings and half-siblings about but had little contact with them. He was essentially alone in the world except for this woman and her son. He had little idea of what a real family looked like and felt safest and most comfortable alone.

Zachary would see Ralph occasionally at the pub during lunch, but they seldom spoke there. Zachary understood that it was Ralph's private time and tried never to intrude. Zachary may not have been much of a drinker, but he did enjoy the ladies. He had gained a reputation with them over time, and it wasn't a good one.

He did his best to confine his activities to the neighborhoods away from the river. He liked the women from the better areas for the most part, but he didn't always confine his lust there. He was twenty-one and had some time to fill. If his mother hadn't kept Zachary busy at the office, he would surely have been in trouble by now.

Sam was nineteen now and so busy at work that he was living the life of a monk again but without receiving the training or the salvation that he received at the feet of Father Gregory. Sometimes he wished for a young woman to come into his life, but he knew that at some point that would happen whether he was ready or not.

He noticed the beautiful young women with their snow-white skin and pink lips who worked in the various pubs and shops in his geographical sphere. It was a small sphere, but there were many young beauties. He couldn't help but wonder what the rest of London might hold for a young man like himself.

He was amazed at the possibilities that lay waiting for him out in the world. It was a very big place, most certainly. Little did Sam suspect that India was trying to answer his dreams and Zachary's dreams regarding young, beautiful women.

India was constantly flitting among her social contacts when she wasn't working. She had arranged several invitations for her and her two young bachelors for the coming season. Zachary and Sam had no idea what was in store for either of them, but that wasn't unusual for the young 'upper-crust' men of the day. If India's plans worked out as she hoped, they both would have a fine choice of young women who wished to marry.

Zachary and Sam, to some extent, were wealthy enough in their own right to be able to choose any of the women presented to them. Zachary was a known quantity to most of the women and their daughters in India's social circle. Sam had his family's reputation and growing wealth on his side to attract young, beautiful women as well.

Sam was very much like his brother Lawrence, and that wasn't a bad thing. He just needed someone to point out his virtues and to advertise them a little. That was going to be India. She would be his champion and coach. All this planning of hers was going on as the boys kept busy at the office watching shipments arrive and sending off shipments of goods from their warehouses out into the world beyond the distant horizon.

Sam kept busy reading books from India's ample shelves. There were many books in the house, and Sam would eventually read most of them. India had history and science books, books about sailing and geography, and many more. Sam was indeed fortunate to live in such a place.

Zachary had other pleasures on his mind and was seldom seen around the house. This troubled India terribly, and she wanted to put an end to Zachary's debauchery as soon as possible.

Chapter Forty-Three

It had been a long, difficult, and interesting ten years for Lawrence. Lawrence was now nearly twenty-nine years old and Catherine was twenty-six. Elizabeth was a cute, slender nine, and Eli was almost eight. He was husky with tousled blond hair and a very strong opinion about most everything.

The times had been, for the most part, good for the Smiths and the farms at Oak Junction and Themstead. Both farms were on the same main road. What came through Oak Junction would most likely pass through Themstead or visa-versa.

Good or bad, the two towns mostly shared the same fate. Oak Junction was at the crossroads, so it received more of the trade from the large north-south road. It was mostly the same products, but the location was better. Eventually, it appeared that Oak Junction might surpass Themstead in traffic, but only time would tell.

Farmers' produce, fabrics, furniture, and leather goods, along with fresh meat and salted fish, were the main items of trade. Themstead had more fresh fish due to the river that passed through it, and it was on a route from London so it received more manufactured goods.

There had been some hard winters and dry springs, but life had been good for Lawrence and his family. They had prospered and were in good health. Lawrence and his father Charles discussed the plans for the new inn at Oak Junction on many evenings and at some length in front of the fireplace when Lawrence visited Oak Junction or when Charles came to Themstead.

This building project was a big endeavor for them to undertake as the mill had been, but they feared little in their lives. The women brought up ideas as well and were listened to quite seriously. After all, it would be Lawrence's mother and Ginger doing the lion's share of the work after the inn was finally built. Lawrence would be working at the mill along with his family. Lawrence's mother and Ginger would be cooking and cleaning until they had enough money set aside to hire help if there ever was any extra money.

The building materials would cost next to nothing. They had an entire forest for the lumber, but they would need laborers to help build their dream. They now had the mill to process most of the timbers they would need. Their land was still only cleared for the house and the fields. It was still a huge forest just waiting to be harvested.

Anyone passing by would hardly notice their little house and fields for the forest that was all around Lawrence and his small family's old house in Oak Junction. As far as one could see to the south and the west the land was still covered in ancient trees. Lawrence wanted to clear the land near the south road next to the fields that they had already cleared. This would be the area where the inn would stand. The ground was very wide and flat.

Most of Lawrence's land at Themstead was still a mystery to him and his family. They had lived there full-time for nearly three years, but Lawrence had little time to explore it. He had to go into town to sell his crops and build up future trade for the mill. The farms in Themstead and Oak Junction were doing well, but Lawrence wanted the mill to be the main source of income for his family. If the weather turned bad or the farms failed for any reason, he would have the mill to tide them over.

Come frost or drought, he would survive if nothing else. All the forest lands that he owned would guarantee that at least. There was always a need for wood in the towns, and Lawrence had plenty of that even if only to burn in the homes around him. But he had dreams of much more. Since Sam had left five years before, Lawrence had constant thoughts of how he could get his lumber to London for shipbuilding and the like. He hoped it was possible, but he had no idea how to do it.

As the years passed, Father Magnus aged well. He still walked to his pub and had a pint often enough. "It's God's gift to man" was his favorite response when asked about his consumption of ale. No one argued with him about that, and everyone drank his or her share—men, women, and children alike. It was an essential part of their diet and always had been.

Father Magnus went into London often to visit with his superiors as the years passed and always stayed with his sister India whenever he could. It was a grand time when he did come to stay with them. His visits changed the routine of the house, and some great meals were eaten there when he came to visit. He wasn't as concerned about the meals as the cook was. It was her time to shine, and she felt she was showing God her respect by feeding the Father and his family well.

Father Magnus always took the time in the evenings to tell Sam about what was happening with his family at home. And Sam filled the Father in with the details of their lives in London. The Father had been away from London for a long time. It was nice to come back and revisit his former life despite his memories of the losses that occurred there.

He refused to dwell on the sad and evil aspects of the past. He had prayed, and he knew God had given him a second chance and the strength to move forward with his life. He might still end up in hell, but he did and would continue to do everything possible to be forgiven and see the smiling faces of his family in heaven when he died.

Father Magnus was glad that Sam and Zachary had become such good friends. And he hoped that some of Sam might rub off on his nephew Zachary. Father had seen the Zachary who was drawn to the rougher side of life. He had hoped that someone or something might intercede before it was too late. India and the entire family could lose everything if one of them did something foolish. Father Magnus knew that all too well from his own mistakes, and it didn't look like Zachary was going to care about what happened inside a church very soon.

Back in Themstead, Lawrence and the entire family decide that eight guest rooms would be just right for their new venture in Oak Junction. The kitchen and the pub would be on the first floor and the eight rooms on the second floor. The building would be set well back from the corner of Oak Junction so wagons and carriages could move easily on and off the main highway. There would be a barn, a corral, and a blacksmith shop in the rear. Perhaps Don Jr. could work there when he was older, but for now, it was a convenient place for Junior or Don to make more money if their business in Oak Junction was slow. Surely there would be plenty of work on the wagons and other equipment that would pass by in the future.

As Father Magnus spent more time with Zachary and Sam, he could see that they had much in common. They were both energetic and driven. But the problem was clear to Father Magnus after several visits with the two men in London that their ambitions were very different.

Zachary was a stallion wanting carnal knowledge of every mare in London while Sam used his vast energy to learn and work. He was the far more mature of the two young men. Sam was heading toward wisdom and adulthood while Zachary was heading for disaster and heartache. Someone or something would have to intervene, hopefully sooner rather than later.

Father Magnus caught India one late afternoon at home while visiting, and they finally had a chance to talk about Zachary. India was often away checking on her shops or visiting with friends, so they didn't have many chances to sit and visit.

They walked into the beautiful room where Sam had been seated on his first night at the house. It was brightly lit, and the windows were open on this day. "I'm afraid for your immediate future, India," the Father said. "I think Zachary is headed for certain disaster and is going to take you and everything you have worked so hard for these many years and destroy it. His appetites are not those of the Lord, and you are going to pay a heavy price when the inevitable happens."

"I'm afraid you're right, brother. I had hoped that the friendship of Sam would somehow save Zachary, but that friendship has only given him more time to find mischief."

"Perhaps you could send him away on a voyage on one of your ships for a year or so."

"Believe me when I tell you that I have thought of that, but I feared that would only make the problem worse. You know what the sailors are like onboard those ships."

"Sadly, India, all men crave the pleasures of the flesh. It was a necessary part of God's plan, but sometimes it takes on a life of its own. Zachary seems to have fallen into that trap, and there may be no good escape."

"I'm actually trying to get him acquainted with some nice girls from some of the most prominent families that I know of in London as we speak. Perhaps that may save us yet. It's the best plan I've been able to come up with so far. I need Sam to do some traveling for the firm soon. I would send Zachary, but I can't trust him to represent me in Europe without supervision."

"I see your point, India, but you must act quickly before disaster strikes. I see how he leers at some of these shop girls."

"I know, Father, it's disgusting. Ralph and I try to keep him on a short leash when we're with him, but that's not often enough. He has far too much free time on his hands."

"That may be. Perhaps you could give him more duties at the office."

"I've been thinking about that, but I need to speak to Sam first. He needs to know what's going on and be a part of our plan."

After a few days of work and visiting, Father Magnus left for Oak Junction. India finally had a chance to meet with Sam and Lester while she had sent Zachary on some errands. The three of them talked in the office, and it was decided that because India was still the "boss," she would explain Zachary's new and very important duties to him.

India coming to the office that following Monday piqued Zachary's interest. She hadn't been there for several months. The three of them sat in the office in a quiet corner and talked.

"Zachary," she began, "we are coming up short each month now from pilfering, and it has to stop. You are going to have to double- and triple-check your paperwork against the inventory in all of the warehouses until this has stopped. And you will have to watch the men on the docks closer as well." She looked at Sam and then spoke to him next.

"It is your responsibility to make sure that Zachary completes these important tasks so that we can see what and how much of our products we are losing and who is responsible."

India, Sam, and Lester had created this "plan" that India explained to Sam and Zachary. The false story that there had been some shortages in the warehouses and on some of the ships was just to keep Zachary busy and out of trouble. India stressed that she needed Zachary to take the inventories more often and with greater care and to watch the men working on the ships and the warehouses. Zachary wasn't surprised that these common men in the warehouses had been stealing from the family.

Of course, Sam was in on the plan. He knew that this story was just a ruse to keep Zachary busy and that their business was doing fine. Even with the war in America and the loss of those exports, the business was in good shape. Sam tried to have lunch with Zachary more often, as did Lester once in awhile. The plan helped to keep Zachary out of trouble. He was now constantly patrolling the warehouses with his pencil and paper, looking for anything out of the ordinary that he could find.

Lester began to enjoy this new plan. He created many time-consuming activities for Zachary to do around the warehouses and in the dirtiest places he could find for him aboard the ships in port. These were some of the best days for Lester in a long time on the docks. Work was much more enjoyable for Lester after this new plan was initiated.

Lester's wife became a little suspicious when he left for work early every morning and with a new spring in his step. He finally had to let her know the secret when she accused him of having a mistress.

India had the most important part to play in this drama. With the social season starting, she had to redouble her efforts at finding a match for her son. As part of that plan, she continued teaching the boys to dance. Ralph was learning as well, albeit with some reluctance.

She kept the three of them virtual prisoners for several weeks in the evenings after work and put them through their paces until she was satisfied that she wouldn't be embarrassed by their dancing when they were finally invited to a party.

The other benefit of this part of the plan was that any of the young women waiting for Zachary in one of his favorite pubs would surely find someone else to take his place while he was spending so much time learning to dance with his mother. This was exactly what India hoped for. Indeed, there was only one woman who was trying to contact Zachary of late, and she would be dealt with as necessary. When Zachary did meet a decent woman at one of the upcoming parties, India's only problem in her life would be solved.

India had a harpsichord, which had belonged to her father, and she played it for the boys as she tried to show them the latest dances. She had taken lessons on the harpsichord as a young girl and was still an adequate player. She was often at her friends' homes for the weekend parties, knew the current dances, and had been well taught in the social graces by her mother. She was a charming companion, and many fine men were interested in her as a wife. However, Zachary was her prime concern at this time in her life.

Her social life was a means to only one end at the moment. She was completely content in her present life except for Zachary's bachelorhood. India knew she had to find the right woman for her son. She would have to be beautiful because her son was shallow, but more importantly to India, she had to be smart, strong-willed, and willing to push Zachary in his work. India also felt that any woman who wanted to be with her son would have to agree with her vision of his future. Such a wife and daughter-in-law would be well rewarded for her patience and skillful teamwork.

Zachary asked Sam several times about why Sam's routine wasn't changed as well, but Sam reminded him that India was the head of the firm. "We all do as we are ordered," he told him. Whenever Zachary complained to Lester about what he had Zachary had been doing all day at work, Lester just answered, "Ask your mother, she's the boss."

Zachary finally did go back to his mother and asked her what was really going on, but she stood by her story and mentioned that his hard work was, in fact, showing up in her ledgers, and he could look at them any time that he wished. She maintained that he had slowed the loss of their inventory by his hard work and hoped that he would continue his diligence as needed.

India knew that Zachary couldn't and wouldn't try to check the books, but the invitation to do so added to the appearance that he was indeed making progress. The plan seemed to be working for the time being. Soon, the season and the parties would start. Ralph was glad that it finally was. He hated dancing with Zachary when he could be sitting in a pub with a glass of ale in front of him, and he didn't like the looks that the ladies of the house were giving him whenever they saw him dancing with Sam or Zachary.

Many of the parties took place in London. On those occasions, both Sam and Zachary would attend them together. If there was a party that would take India away from London for more than a day or two, only Zachary would go with his mother.

Sam ran the office now, and he had to be there if Zachary was gone. Zachary could go and not be missed very much. Zachary always came back with interesting stories to tell Sam. Sam was always more interested in work than in dancing.

There were two telescopes on the office floor, one at each end of the long room. Sam and Zachary could use them to watch for the ships coming up the river from the ocean or to see which vessels were sailing downriver to the sea. They looked for the names of the ships on their bows as they sailed into port and would send word down to the men who were going to have to unload them when they were spotted coming up the river. It helped the men prepare for the individual ships and their cargo.

Sometimes when Sam had the time, he would watch the men building new ships in the shipyards across the river and follow their progress. He didn't have the time very often, but he enjoyed it when he could. Eventually, between his reading and his watching the construction of sailing vessels, he began to understand how these great ships were created. From rough timbers by equally rough men. He was always surprised that the ships came together as well as they did.

He worked with the men who created those ships and who worked the docks, and he knew that they were generally a wild and uneducated group. Then he would think of Lawrence, and he would be reminded that perseverance was almost always the key to any possible success at anything. It was sometimes equal parts hard work and intelligence, but hard work often trumped intelligence.

Sam loved to wander late in the day among the rough wooden crates of all shapes and sizes in the giant warehouses. He could smell the fragrances from faraway lands as he checked his inventory on long sheets of paper or just roamed in a daze among the imported products that came to England from all of her many colonies and other countries. Sometimes he could swear that he smelled America on some of the older battered crates even after that trade had ended years before.

Sam hoped, no, he knew that one day he would sail to America and work for India there when they were able to open up their offices again. He wasn't sure of many things in this life of his, but he was sure of that. Perhaps he would have to travel to many other countries first for her, but he knew his destiny was in the West.

He sometimes thought that he could smell America on the wind that came through the often open windows of his office overlooking the Thames.

When the social season was finally in full swing, Sam often found himself arriving at a lovely apartment or grand home with India and Zachary to meet the elite families of London society. Ralph would help India first from the carriage, then Zachary and then Sam.

Ralph always gave Sam a good-luck wink as they walked away from the carriage and into another encounter with the young women who India hoped would find Zachary attractive and wealthy enough to want to marry. Sam would shrug his shoulders and follow his new aunt and cousin into these remarkable dwellings with a sense of adventure. To him, it was all like a dream.

He had become well known in these circles now and could pass as a city dweller. His manners were perfect, he was dressed to a "T," and he spoke perfectly. Few people knew that he was a country boy outside of these high society parties. India made sure of that.

Of course, many people knew who his brother was from the tales of his exploits told around the counties and in London. It had been a hot topic when the news first came to London. And that just added to Sam's popularity at many of these parties. Zachary would pick the cutest girls and dance the night away to the disappointment of his highly focused mother. Sam danced as well, but he enjoyed talking business and politics with the older businessmen who he was now beginning to recognize and even to know.

He enjoyed this much more than dancing with the beautiful young women who were all around him to India's great dismay. She wanted and needed these two young men to be settled with decent, wealthy young women as soon as possible.

It was now her primary concern, and everyone in the household understood that. India knew as only a woman can that once they were married—domesticated, one might say—the two young men would become much more suitable in her business. She wasn't getting any younger, and she couldn't leave two randy bachelors to run her long-dead father's business concerns.

Several parties took India and Zachary away from London for several days at a time when they were out in the country at one of her wealthier friend's estates. Sam was fine with that and enjoyed spending a day or two at work without having to worry about or watch over Zachary.

Lester was also quite happy when Zachary was away. But he did miss telling him what to do all day. When India and Zachary were out of town, Sam had more time to spend with Ralph as well. There were always Ralph's stories to listen to, but he also taught Sam some practical things. He had already shown Sam how to fight with a saber and foil, and now he was showing him how to tie several sailing knots in the ropes that he still kept out in the small barn. Ralph was teaching Sam basic seamanship in his carriage house too. They both enjoyed passing the hours of the evening in that way. It helped their friendship grow.

Sam would not be walking onto the deck of a ship without some useful knowledge to see him through the many difficult situations that he would encounter. If it were up to Ralph, Sam would know nearly every knot and term used onboard a ship before he sailed on one.

Ralph knew that if Sam came aboard a ship without some basic knowledge and skills, he would never gain any sailor's respect. Sam already knew about most ships' construction and had climbed into the rigging of many and lost his normal fear of heights. That wouldn't be a problem for him when he set sail for the first time.

It was a different story altogether for Sam when it came to women.. Sam was now well aware of what India was trying to do. He had no qualms about her getting Zachary married off. He knew that it would turn Zachary into a responsible man at last or destroy him. Sam thought that it was completely proper for Zachary to marry a fine, young, educated English girl.

But Sam wasn't quite sure about what he wanted for himself. Ralph's stories had made him well aware that there were many smart and beautiful women throughout the world. Sam knew that if he stayed in England, he would marry an English or European woman, but perhaps he might get to America and marry an American girl. Maybe he would marry one whose parents or grandparents might have been English or European in the not-so-distant past. Perhaps he would end up marrying a woman who was truly an American, a woman born and bred there.

These possibilities caused him many long sleepless nights. He eventually decided to let India worry about his future wife so he could get the rest he needed to function at work. Unlike Zachary, Sam couldn't drink and play all night and come to work and do his job. Sam's life had fallen into a pleasant routine with work, the parties, and much of his time, reading or studying with Ralph.

Lester was very much like Ralph in history and disposition. They had both seen more than any man should have to. They had seen the deaths and sometimes useless sacrifices of sailors and soldiers as well as some of the positive things that happen when one lives in a wartime environment and only with men. These events were carved into both of their memories.

They had both spent years away from their families, and they and their families had suffered for it. Lester's wife even had a son who was magically conceived while he was sailing off of North Africa. It was an unpleasant surprise for sure, but it came with the sailor's life. It didn't destroy his marriage, but it certainly put more pressure on him and his wife to survive a difficult situation.

Lester surely had children of his own around the world, but he didn't bring them back home to meet his wife. Yet this special son, as he was called, was always well treated and loved. He never knew Lester wasn't his father, and as time passed, they became very close. As it turned out, he was the cleverest of all of Lester's children. His wife did have very good taste in men, Lester would often say. Everyone in Lester's neighborhood knew the situation, of course, but no one ever told the child that Lester wasn't his father, and Lester was given high marks for his behavior toward his wife and his "son."

Chapter Forty-Four

Sam was very fortunate to have Ralph and Lester in his life. They both were living depositories of sea lore and sailing knowledge. They were older and wiser friends who might be available to offer important advice. Ralph was more of a common sailor while Lester was definitely officer material. Lester was more sophisticated and social, but by most standards, he too was far from perfect. Both of these men became true friends and protectors of Sam and were endless resources for him.

They were perfect examples of how men should not behave around children or in proper society. Thankfully, they were seldom inflicted upon either one due to having jobs that kept them away from both.

Lester's work kept him among rough and dangerous men for most of the day, and then he went to the pub or home and kept to himself. Ralph was out in society quite often, but in his job, his most important and valuable quality was his silence. No one suspected what his past had been or what type of person he really was.

Their imaginations would fill in those blanks as needed as they were driven by him or helped into and out of the carriage. He seemed like a perfectly normal person on the surface, but of course, Sam knew the truth.

Sam had started a new life with that long foggy carriage ride from Themstead to the great maze that was London. He had been totally ensconced in a poor farmer's rural English life his whole life with all of its rewards and dangers until he was transported to this completely new environment and new age that was London. London, with its paved streets and beautiful homes, lit at night to look like the sun was still shining from within them, was so different from his rural home. Well-dressed and educated people were all around him now. Their speech and accents were different as well. His ability to adjust was a testament to his strength of character and personality.

Whenever Sam ventured down to the river and the ships from his office, he always made an effort to talk with the loading crews. He listened to them complain about their working conditions as usual, but he would also always ask them questions to learn something about their work and the individual ship that he was visiting. All the ships were different from each other, some in small ways and some in ways that made them very different from others.

By December 1778, Sam had spent a good deal of time in London and on the docks. He was quite comfortable onboard ships and very knowledgeable as well. He was almost a sailor. He had not yet gone to sea, but that wasn't his decision to make.

India still had Sam and Lester watching over Zachary as much of the time as possible and trying to keep him out of trouble. As the days passed, the old Zachary that everyone knew was indeed slowly changing into a slightly more responsible and mature version of himself.

He was coming to realize that the women of his social strata had much more to offer him than just the physical attributes that all women possess. He began to realize that those women he pursued in the past were for the most part more interested in his wealth and not in him as a person or a man.

It soon became clear to Sam that perhaps all the time he spent reading about history and sailing and war, and the time he spent with Lester and Ralph, might come in handy sooner rather than later. Sadly for Sam, Zachary's behavior was the key to Sam's future at sea and eventually going to America.

For Sam, the marriage of Zachary to a woman from a fine family was in his best interest.

And to that end, he began to speak to every available young woman he would meet about Zachary's endless list of virtues, true or false though they might be.

Sam would tout Zachary to every woman he danced with at the parties he now attended. In the past, he had been quite content to visit with the older businessmen at these gatherings and listen to them discuss politics or the news of the day. But now he began dancing up a small storm and "chatting up" all the beautiful young ladies he could corral to put a good word in for Zachary.

India was puzzled by this interesting turn of events until she was finally able to overhear a few of Sam's conversations at a party one night in town.

"Oh yes, he's as smart as a whip and works like a dog," Sam went on saying to a very beautiful young woman about Zachary. India couldn't believe her ears when she heard the conversation. She couldn't think who Sam was speaking of. It surely wasn't anyone she had run across lately.

"He's the first in the office in the morning and the last to leave at night." India thought Sam was speaking about Lester at first, but why would these young girls want to hear about Lester, a man of at least forty? And then she heard it, a blatant lie from Sam.

"Yes, Zachary keeps all of us on our toes down at the docks. He's the man who keeps us all afloat, so to speak."

It was the first lie India had heard to come from Sam's mouth since she had known him, and she was amazed by it. None of what Sam was saying was in the least bit true, though she wished it to be so with all her heart. But her next thought was, *what is Sam up to and what is his motive?*

India felt that Sam was in need of a wife just as much as Zachary was. So why would Sam tout Zachary so stridently to all these beautiful young women. As the night passed with wonderful food and drink and a festive air, India was beside herself.

Finally, as the evening was coming to an end, she noticed that more girls were standing near her son and trying to gain his attention than ever before. She was pleasantly surprised. But she was having some trouble trying to figure it out. Zachary himself was aware of the increased interest in him and what he had to say. It made little sense to him. As the three of them finally walked out to their carriage at the end of the night where Ralph stood waiting, India knew that she would have to have a very serious talk with Sam and the sooner the better. Sam was just trying to further his own plan for sailing away.

Chapter Forty-Five

India was extremely busy for several days after the party. But she surely needed to talk with Sam about that night and his behavior. India didn't have a chance until their ride to church on the following Sunday.

It was a beautiful morning with a slight breeze from the east. Sam was thinking, *what a beautiful day to set sail for somewhere, anywhere* when India startled him.

"What were you up to at the party last Friday?"

"I'm sure I don't know what you're talking about, auntie." Sam often called India 'auntie' when he wanted to soften her wrath.

As their carriage traveled through the damp London air, Sam tried to formulate his thoughts into a coherent theme. It was still very early in the morning, and he was not yet completely himself. He had been up most of the night before reading *The Adventures of Marco Polo.*

"I heard you speaking to several young ladies about Zachary at the party, Sam. You needn't lie to me."

"I think my stories about Zachary will be more believable coming from my mouth than from his mother's, that's all. I want to travel to other countries and see how other people live and work. I want to see the date trees in Morocco and the tea fields in China. I don't want to just smell those aromas in the warehouses any longer."

"I know, Sam. So are you trying to free yourself by getting Zachary married and making him grow up at long last?"

"I guess it sounds stupid when you put it that way, auntie, but it's my best hope, perhaps my only hope, of going to sea."

"Perhaps, Sam. We are both intent on the same future for Zachary, but so far I think you have been more successful than I have."

"India, most people will listen to a young man's mother speak of his virtues, but they may not believe everything that she has to say. In my case, many may see me in competition with Zachary for a wife. What I say may carry more weight than what you say."

"You may be right, Sam. As Zachary's mother, I may be at a disadvantage when I speak of his merits."

"I meant no harm, auntie. I just want to be able to be more valuable to you and the firm as well as experience some things that are more exotic than London society."

"I understand completely, Sam. You come from a family that makes its own luck and future, and you haven't had much of a chance to do that here as far as Zachary is concerned. But I promise you, Sam Smith, that your chance will come as soon as we get Zachary married. And to that end, we must join forces and land a suitable wife for my son. We must create interest in someone who is not that interesting, after all."

India and Sam talked as their carriage passed through the most beautiful neighborhoods of London before arriving at the most splendid building in town, their church, St. Paul's Cathedral. They visited with all of India's friends who found church a worthwhile endeavor and soon entered. Sam sat among them, the country boy, now a young man, surrounded by the elite of London society.

After the church service, the two of them talked more about their plan for Zachary. India and Sam were soon being carried home by Ralph in their fine coach, powered by those two lovely dark horses that he knew so well.

Ralph dropped the two off in front of the house and drove around the block to where he lived out back in the carriage house with its black shingled walls and little red chimney poking out of the grey slate roof.

The horses were most of Ralph's life now. Not his complete life but perhaps the best part of it except for India and her family, which after so many years of service had now almost become his own as well. The horses accepted him, respected him, and perhaps even loved him as only horses can.

He had missed his chance to be a great husband and father, but at least he could endeavor to be the best groomsman, driver, and family servant he could possibly be. He wouldn't make the same mistakes he had made with his wife and family with this one. He would work every day to gain and keep their respect, perhaps even their love.

The green-and-gold carriage was one example. It would continue to look as good as the day that India's father had bought it those thirty long years ago. After all, Ralph was its captain, so to speak, and it was his duty to keep it safe, sound, and splendid looking.

As the months passed, the family's routine continued without change. Sam worked during the week and went to parties on the weekends. He tried to attend as many as possible, but sometimes work interfered. He now understood he had a partner in India.

Sam finally understood that he did have some control over his future in London, and with India's help, he could make everything he wanted a reality. He just had to be careful of what he wished for because he just might get it.

All Sam had to do was find Zachary a mate. And now with he and India definitely on the same page, his chances at freedom were doubled. It was a good feeling to have a sense of control over his destiny again.

He had always felt that at the farm in Oak Junction but had lost it upon arriving in London. He had been plucked from his pastoral life and whisked away to this giant unknown. Granted, it was a long time in the making, and he was always kept abreast of what was happening between his family and India, but it had still been a shock when his chance finally came.

It might be a challenge to find a young, smart, and beautiful woman who would find Zachary to be a good catch, but Sam hoped it wouldn't be impossible. There were many families with young women who might fit the bill. All the parties of this season would give those women a chance to meet Zachary and size him up. Zachary, likewise, would have a chance to meet many young women of prominent families and see what was on offer.

That was what all the parties were about, after all. Trying to get the best deal or best family for your child to marry into. Zachary came from a family of some means. He was as handsome as the next man as far as Sam could tell, and he didn't have a lurid past. He had tried to have some misadventures, but had been mostly unsuccessful.

There were some tales about Zachary's sometimes crude behavior but nothing that compared to most young men of his age and station in life. He regretted his rather staid history, but it was to his advantage when looking for a wife. Of course, Zachary didn't think he was looking for a wife for himself at these parties, but Sam and India surely were.

After several months and many wonderful parties, and after what seemed like endless mothers and daughters, Emily finally appeared.

On a beautiful evening after a long and cold ride in their carriage, the three of them, India, Zachary, and Sam, arrived at yet another lovely mansion in the north of London. It was obvious that the owners of this beautiful home were a very successful and sophisticated family.

The party itself was one of the largest and finest they had attended in some time. It was almost as sumptuous as those they had gone to out in the countryside. This was not a country estate, but it was lovely.

A long circular driveway at the front of the house arced off the wide street. And that long driveway led up to grand front doors recessed between two enormous, beautifully carved, white, two-story-high columns.

The doors were the blackest black Sam had ever seen. He thought at first that there could be something almost foreboding about them as Ralph's brown gloved hand helped him and India from the carriage. Behind those dark doors was the most beautiful entry hall Sam had ever seen.

It was full of just the right amount of flowers, paintings, busts, and white light. There was a perfectly crafted staircase in the center of the tall, bright hallway. Only the fortunate few were allowed to climb it and enter the private living quarters of these wealthy people. And that would be only after a very long time and if they were lucky enough to become friends. Sam had no idea of what the night might bring, but he would be satisfied just to see the ground floor of this seemingly perfect abode.

Only after years of fawning and bowing time and again were some of the people invited to this party allowed to ascend to the upper reaches of this fine house. It was a wonder to behold. Simple, but everything inside and out was perfectly presented.

The master of the house was a well-known judge who had inherited his wealth from his family. But no one who knew him held it against him. His wealth assured everyone that he was an honest judge, a rare thing in these times, and that he could not be bought or tainted. His reputation was spotless. He was a man of great charm, character, and charisma in the world of London society.

His name was as simple as he was rich: Joseph Hass. His family was English to the core but perhaps had come from Germany or farther east in the ancient dark past. The family name had been well known in London for generations and was held in high esteem.

They had come from humble beginnings and worked their way up the social ladder and into their fortune and security. They were the living embodiment of the reality that hard work and planning could produce more than broken bodies and heartache, even in a place like London, which held pedigree in such high esteem. Sam was at ease with the idea of this family at once; it sounded just like his.

There were many fine young men and women along with their families at this function. Sam and India did their best to mingle and chat with as many of them as possible. They both knew many of them from the parties of the last two years. And of course, India knew most of these families, or the women anyway, from their business associations and social events.

India and Sam saw Emily and her mother exactly at the same moment and approached them with broad smiles and hands reaching out to make their acquaintance. They had great hope that soon one of these young women would be married to Zachary. Though they would argue about it later, Sam and India had played equal parts in the success of that special evening. Zachary followed closely behind them as they began perhaps the second-most important conversation of Sam's life.

He didn't know when, of course, but he had always hoped that this moment would come. "Good evening," India began. "We are the Clarks, this is my son Zachary, and this young man is my nephew Sam Smith."

"Good evening, I'm Mrs. Stanley and this is my daughter Emily."

"Very nice to meet you," the Clarks answered. And so it began, the feeling out, the pleasant interrogation, to determine pedigree and status.

Mrs. Stanley was a pleasant and open woman of average appearance but with beautiful, bright blue eyes. Her husband was a doctor of some prestige, well known in London circles. The family had four daughters, Emily being the eldest, who had just turned nineteen.

India could tell instantly that Zachary was showing an interest in young Emily. She was beautiful and poised, and obviously well trained at appearing comfortable and relaxed at these balls. Why she hadn't been snapped up yet was a mystery to India, but she was glad of it. Perhaps it was her age, but India saw that as an advantage.

India thought that perhaps in the future, if all things worked out as she hoped, Emily might become her daughter-in-law. India hoped she could be of some influence over her.

Emily was quite attractive with the narrow waist and plump bosom that was in style at the time. She had clear, beautiful blue eyes like her mother and seemed quite sensible as they talked. There was little doubt in India's mind that she was smart and could portray the proper amount of femininity when necessary with a large dose of the type of intelligence needed for her husband to succeed. India saw a rendition of herself standing in front of her and liked Emily the more for it.

The two young men talked with Emily as India talked quietly with her mother while trying to put in a good word to Emily about Zachary whenever she felt it necessary. It wasn't necessary. Zachary saw Emily and was interested in her at once. Emily was very interested in Zachary for some unknowable reason.

Sam's heart was beating faster than India's or Zachary's. He was sure of that. It seemed like it might be a match, and Sam was beside himself. He tried not to get too excited. They had just met, after all, but part of Sam could already see himself sailing away from London as the two young people talked to each other. Perhaps he would soon be free at last. India and Mrs. Stanley set a luncheon date at India's home while the youngsters chatted and gossiped about their mutual friends. Both of the mothers could see that there were sparks aplenty.

They would meet the following week for lunch and some conversation at India's townhouse. India, Zachary, and Mrs. Stanley stood together talking for some time in the entry of this grand home. India had made eye contact with Sam, and she left no possibility for misunderstanding: Leave quickly and let these two talk alone.

He did just that, wandered throughout the beautiful home, and wondered what was happening at home in Themstead. He hadn't been home in more than two years. He wrote and received letters from his family often, but it wasn't the same as being there and working with them in the fields or the mill.

His visits with Father Magnus were enlightening and interesting. He enjoyed hearing the news from home, but he also wanted to see his family and smell the forest again. He couldn't do that in London.

Zachary and Emily danced together often as the evening passed. They did truly seem to enjoy each other's company. Eventually, the party ended and everyone said their goodbyes and began the long drives back to their respective homes, each family wondering if this had been the night when their sons or daughters had found someone interesting at long last.

Ralph was glad the night had finally ended. He wanted the family to find someone for Zachary to be sure, but it was a cold night and he was worried about his horses. He didn't like them out in this damp London air any longer than necessary.

When the three of them reached home that night after the party, it was clear that Zachary was a changed man. After the boys kissed India good night and went upstairs to Sam's room, they talked for some time about the evening.

Zachary was taken with Emily. That was clear. He talked about her as he had never talked about another woman before. He was respectful and spoke of her beauty and intelligence. Sam was thrilled as he fell asleep. He dreamed of seeing London sink in the distance behind him as he sailed south with a strong wind pushing him away from London.

Chapter Forty-Six

Sam was sailing most of the night in his dreams and left London more than once as his two families waved him off to distant and exotic ports of call.

He was sorely disappointed the next morning when he awoke to find himself lying in his huge, comfortable bed in India's house just a few blocks from the Thames. It had all felt so real. He didn't know whether to curse or bless those dreams of the long night that had just passed. They had made him so happy. And then he awoke to such a great disappointment in his large, warm, soft bed. He knew instantly that he wasn't on a ship.

As the days passed, Sam's hopes grew, and then he would talk himself down to realistic expectations. Then he would see Zachary smiling as he walked from the ships and up to the warehouses below Sam, and his hopes would rise again.

Sam knew Zachary's attention span when it came to young ladies. It was very short. But perhaps Zachary really was a changed man now, and this young woman had truly captured his heart, after all. By the time Sunday afternoon was at hand, Sam was as nervous as India.

When that knock came on the front door, they were both ready to collapse from lack of sleep and anticipation. Zachary seemed fine as usual. He seldom worried about anything. That was his charm and his greatest shortcoming at the same time.

"How do I look, Sam?"

"You look lovely as always, India. You look perfect. How about me?"

"You look like a fine young gentleman, Sam."

Ralph opened the thick wooden door and led the pair of ladies into the parlor. Even Ralph, who had sworn off women, was impressed by the two of them. The two women were dressed in fine dresses and looked like perfect ladies. Ralph hadn't seen them at the party days before. They were polite, pleasant, and attractive. He led them into the parlor and made sure that they were comfortable. As he left the room, India and the boys entered, followed by Carol and Becky carrying silver platters of small sandwiches and a gleaming tea service.

They talked pleasantly for half an hour or so until lunch was served. This was, of course, a chance for Mrs. Stanley to examine Zachary's prospects as displayed by his mother's home, staff, and manners. She was pleased by India's apparent wealth and social skills. She could see by the neighborhood and the furnishings that the family was well situated.

Mr. Stanley and his male business acquaintances knew of the Clarks even though the wives did not. After all, they owned a medium-sized shipping company. The wives, if they had heard of them at all, would probably know of them through the shops they owned in London and many other large cities.

They were held in some esteem, and their wealth was ample. They would not likely find themselves on hard times anytime in the near future. There was the question of the nephew and how he fit into the family dynamics. But he seemed pleasant enough at first glance a few nights ago, and he seemed pleasant enough today.

For Mrs. Stanley, it wasn't a question of whether Zachary wanted to or would marry Emily, but now whether India would accept them into her family. Mrs. Stanley was quite ready to marry her daughter off into this seemingly pleasant and wealthy family as soon as possible before someone else might get the chance to marry Zachary. Thankfully, Zachary's shortcomings were not apparent at first glance, and he had passed muster at the party.

Eventually, Ralph called everyone into lunch, and the two servants served the guests first. Mrs. Stanley could see that there were three servants in the household. She only had two in her home and was glad to see that her daughter would have more help than she did.

The afternoon went very well, and most everyone learned something about each other that they hadn't expected.

Mrs. Stanley learned that Zachary's father had been dead for many years and that India had run their family business for many years with the help of Zachary. That impressed her to no end. She learned, as well, that Sam also worked in the firm. She learned who Sam's brother was and wondered which of her daughters might find Sam interesting enough to perhaps marry him in the future when they were a little older. They were close to a marriageable age now, and who knew what the future might hold for them? She hoped that she might marry one of them off to Sam if it was the least bit possible.

India learned that she and Mrs. Stanley had several friends in common and that they had actually met once at a party several years ago. India had done her homework since the party and now knew quite a lot more about the Stanley family than she did the night they met. She now was certain that they were of the right social status and were indeed quite comfortable owning many properties in town and a larger home in the country with some acreage.

It did seem like a perfect match if there ever was such a thing. Zachary learned that Emily had several horses and that she smelled rather nice. Sam learned that he should spend more time at the office and less time with women eating lunch. No matter how lovely they were. Except in this case. Sam's freedom depended on Zachary's ability to convince Mrs. Stanley that he was the man for her daughter. He wasn't so sure that would come to pass, and he sat with worry under a forced smile.

In the end, the lunch was a success, and there were many more meetings throughout the rest of the year. At each of the lunches and dinners that followed, things kept looking even better.

As the encounters with Emily and her mother continued, Zachary's attitude toward work improved. His mood was better, and he worked much harder at the river. He had more interest in what he was doing at long last. Zachary seemed to be looking into the future now with some sense that this was actually what he would be doing for the rest of his life.

It had never occurred to him before that he was the heir apparent to this vast enterprise. He had only thought about his nights on the town until he was introduced and entranced by this young woman, Miss Emily Stanley.

Zachary began to come home with Sam now after work while before he might have stayed at the river and sat in The Noose and Stool drinking and pestering the girls three or four nights a week. Unaware as Zachary was, he didn't know how happy most of the women at the pubs were now that he was otherwise occupied.

Lester spent some time with Zachary at work, talking to him at India's insistence. And even hard old Lester was impressed by Zachary's modestly improved thinking and behavior. Zachary was still far from perfect, but he was now truly a work in progress, and the light might now be just over the horizon, so to speak.

As the months passed, it became clear to everyone who saw them that Zachary and Emily had become a couple. The families spent much more time together, and Zachary had even become close to her father, which was rather difficult. Her father spent most of his time working in the city or reading in his library at home. He seemed to have little time for anything else. Eventually, that began to change as Zachary came to the house more often and the two families spent time together over meals and visits.

Doctor Stanley, it turned out, had lost his mother at an early age and never learned to talk with or feel comfortable around women. He was able to eventually find a wife, but it had been an arduous and unpleasant task, to say the least.

Eventually, all of Zachary's and Emily's friends and relations were waiting with anticipation for the announcement that they knew would surely come. By January of the following year, that announcement did come, and it was of little surprise to anyone. Congratulations were flying between friends and relatives of the prospective bride and groom. The wedding was to occur in July with high hopes for clear weather and happiness for all concerned.

Happiest of all was Sam. India was thrilled at finally finding someone for Zachary. Mrs. Stanley was beside herself, and even Dr. Stanley showed how happy he was in his own quiet way. But their happiness could in no way compare to that of Sam's. He wrote his family often as a good son should, but the letter announcing the marriage of Sam and Emily was almost indecipherable.

His hand was flying from ink to paper like perhaps no other in history. He remembered watching Father Gregory and the monks writing with him so long ago with calmness and certitude. Sam's hands, in contrast, trembled with the excitement of being one step closer to his ultimate dream of freedom and going to sea.

He cared little for adventure if the truth was to be known. He'd had plenty of that in his young life already. But freedom was a different matter. He didn't hate his life with India and Zachary in London or the one he had with his family in Oak Junction and Themstead. These had both prepared him for his ultimate challenge. Sam's dream of getting to America and bringing India's company to those shores with him at the head of it was what pushed him.

Chapter Forty-Seven

The wedding was a grand affair. Everyone who was anyone in the two families and their large circle of friends and relations were there. The weather was perfect. Only the two horses attached to India's carriage and Ralph seemed uninterested. Ralph knew the perils that this young couple would face in their new venture together and was apprehensive, to say the least. His past experiences clouded his ability to be joyful for his employer and friend's son.

Father Magnus conducted the service, and Father Gregory was there to help if needed. Everything went off without a hitch. India had made sure of that. She had been planning for this occasion for several years. It had just been a matter of finding the proper bride. That had now happened. Everyone in attendance seemed to be pleased with the choices the two families had made regarding the mate of the other young party involved. Everyone could also see that there was a real affection and even love between the two young people. Many of India's friends mentioned that Zachary seemed to be a changed man over the last year or so, and they were right.

Sam had started packing long before the wedding. He packed, and then he unpacked. And then he packed again. He wasn't sure what he should take and what he should leave behind. Ralph tried to help him, but in this case, Sam seemed to be at a loss.

Finally, a day before the wedding, he had packed again and seemed to finally be satisfied. By the time Sam was finished, Ralph had no idea what his duffle bag held, and he no longer cared. He resolved that Sam was a man, after all, and should know what he might need on a long ocean voyage.

Sam had read almost every book on the subjects of sailing, seamanship, and navigation by then, and if he didn't know what to pack now, he never would. He had packed a few books that he thought might be both interesting and important to him on his first voyage as well. Some he had read before, and he thought they might be helpful in times of emergency or leisure. The others were of different subjects that he was interested in or that might make him a better sailor or person. He had several books on the theory of navigation and the history of sailing.

The married couple was soon gone for a week on their honeymoon. That was ample time for all of Sam's family to reach London and have some time to visit with him before he left on his journey. There was a new apprentice in the office now that he and Zachary had been training, and that made it easier for Sam to have some free time.

Sam talked with his family, and they said their goodbyes over the week that Zachary was gone. When Zachary returned, he would start back at the office as soon as possible. He would now be sitting in his father's chair. He had no choice. He was a new man and the new man in charge. He was the rightful heir to that seat, and he would fill it properly or die trying. His new wife would make sure of that. India, his mother, was now completely confident that he was ready for the tasks that he would have to deal with.

Sam would be somewhere on the other side of the globe. Sam had talked to many captains and first mates down on the wharves and found one sailor who might put in a good word for him on his ship. They were short a few men and needed replacements, skilled or not. When asked, the captain agreed to let Sam come on his next voyage, sight unseen. Sam's last and most important task had been completed.

Most everyone down at Clark and Cook who had known Zachary were amazed at his transformation since meeting Emily. She and India had several pep talks with him during their engagement, and he was now well aware of what he was going to lose if he failed and what was expected of him. Sam knew that Zachary would not fail; he had too much to lose, and Zachary finally understood that.

After the week visiting with his family had passed and the newlyweds returned home, it was time for Sam to leave the great city that was London.

He had learned much about the city and had learned to appreciate it. Sam was looking forward to leaving, however. He could appreciate those beautiful mansions now. He enjoyed the beauty of the large parks that reminded him of home. He found the neighborhoods near the docks that had so much character—and even danger for those who went into them unaware—to be interesting and even exciting.

He still didn't know where he was half the time, but even those born in London often found themselves in that same predicament. Thank God that he had Ralph to drive him wherever he needed or wanted to go. But in the end, he was still drawn to the sea and America.

Chapter Forty-Eight

On a fine, unusually warm sunny day, Sam and all of his family piled into Ralph's coach and one that had been hired for Sam's final ride to the docks and the ever-changing river that would soon carry him away from everyone he knew and loved. That river would carry him into the unknown and the unknowable.

Sam and all of his family members stepped out of the carriages when they arrived at the riverside for their last embraces and words of encouragement. Everyone knew or hoped that Sam would be fine, but they were all very sad nonetheless.

Lawrence had ample time to talk about home and family with Sam. He had been doing well as usual, and his only issue was the threat from the sheriff. That had not been resolved to his satisfaction yet, but things had mostly remained calm in Oak Junction. Lawrence was relying on Father Magnus and the proper authorities to look into the matter.

The ship that Sam was to sail away on was in front of them. It was tied with mighty ropes at anchorage out in the river that Sam had worked and walked along for so many years. Sam knew the ship that he was to be on for the next year or so. He had climbed the rigging and helped to load it several times over the past few years. It held few surprises for him.

It was the Ever Ready. She was a fine ship, and the crew took great pride in keeping her fit. She was a three-master—a three-masted ship—with a club-footed jib. She made good time under sail and complained very little when she was pushed hard, so he had been told. The ship was black with golden-yellow trim. She wasn't the best ship to leave these docks, but she was far from the worst.

The two families embraced time and again, and too soon, Sam had to leave. He walked away from the bosom of his family. Perhaps not for the last time but for the last time for at least a few months. He stepped into the waiting dinghy and placed his small parcel of belongings next to him. He waved as he was rowed to his ship and new home. He turned around one last time to see his family and his second home, London, still behind him.

He wasn't sad. He was excited for his new life to start. Everyone was on the shore except for Ralph. Sam thought that perhaps he was on the other side of the carriage when he turned around one last time. They had said their goodbyes out in the carriage house privately while Ralph gave him a few last-minute pointers on shipboard etiquette and safety.

The small, worn dinghy rocked and swayed as it was rowed out to the Ever Ready. The man rowing paid little attention to Sam as he sat and wondered what lay before him. In a few moments, the small craft came to rest at the side of the giant ship. It had looked smaller to Sam than it was. A rope net hung over the port side of the ship for Sam and another man in the boat to climb on board. He was not warmly welcomed.

Sam was soon on board and settled. He took his belongings below and was shown where he was to stow them and where he was to sleep. It was very different from India's beautiful, bright apartment. He then returned to the deck to help get the ship ready to leave. As he came up from the depths of the ship, it finally hit him that he was truly on his own now.

It made his stomach tighten a bit, but he had felt that before. He had felt it in the Battle of Themstead and when he had learned to first ride a horse. The feeling would pass as soon as he was busy with his new endeavor. He looked to where the coaches had been onshore, and they were now gone.

Sam was soon following orders from the first mate that were relayed down through the chain of command and then yelled up into the sails. He had little time now to think of anything except what he was ordered to do. He moved quicker than most of the other new sailors, and he was soon sent up into the rigging as a test by the first mate who was trying to get a sense of his new recruits and their abilities.

It was a tricky piece of sailing to get out into the Thames and head down to the sea without an unwelcome accident.

"Release the braces," an old sailor working next to him yelled up at him, and Sam did as he was ordered. The old fellow seemed surprised that Sam knew what the braces even were.

"That's right son, you've got it." He seemed surprised by Sam's knowledge.

"Been to sea before then, lad?"

"No sir, but I know my onions," Sam answered back.

"Good job, you slack-jawed landlubber," he said with a little surprise in his voice. "Your fresh outfit tells me you're new at this life, but you got that bit right."

"I may look like I'm wet behind the ears, Billy, but I've prepared myself for this life over the last few years as best I could. I've been on this ship a hundred times when she was moored, and I've climbed this rigging a thousand times. I know her better than you do, you can count on that."

"My name is Thomas, young man, not Billy."

"Fair enough, Thomas, I'm Sam Smith."

"The same Sam Smith from Clark and Cook?"

"One and the same, Thomas."

"Fine then. We'll have a grand voyage, I'm sure of that, but I want to hear all of your stories, and I'll tell you mine."

"I think I'll get the best of that arrangement, Thomas, but so be it." Sam had quickly made his first friend on the ship. That was a relief to him. At least he would have one man to keep company with at meals and quiet times on the voyage.

As Sam was climbing higher into the rigging and preparing to let more sails loose, he heard a voice that sounded familiar. He looked around and up but didn't see anyone he knew. He climbed higher and was working on some lines when he heard it again. This time, it seemed to come from above him.

He looked up and saw a familiar face looking down at him. It was Ralph. He had been too high in the rigging for Sam to see him before. Sam started to climb higher and finally reached Ralph.

"My God, Ralph, what are you doing here?"

"We couldn't let a pup like you go to sea without a nursemaid, could we?"

"I can't believe it. You said you were finished with this life."

"You forgot your saber, Sam. I had to bring it to you. It's in my chest below."

"I didn't think I would need it."

"That's what I'm talking about, Sam. You can't come on board without one."

"Thank you, Ralph."

"I might have spoken too soon, Sam. There's a woman in Morocco I think I might want to see again. She might even have a little sister."

Sam's dreams of expanding his horizons and learning new ideas could never happen in London. His father Charles had thought he couldn't change his fate. Lawrence, his older brother, knew he had to change his life. And luck gave him that chance. Sam knew that he had to go to America sometime to create his new life in Boston. England wasn't going to be big enough for him. This was Sam's first step to America in what would turn out to be a long process. He was headed to Europe and Africa on his first voyage at sea. This would be another test of his endurance and fortitude and the strength of the Smith family.

It would be a long while before he would see the great buildings of London again. Sam would see all the things that he had wondered about and smelled in those warehouses that he had walked and dreamed about at Clark and Cook, and more. But when he would return with Ralph at his side, as he always was, he would be a more mature and even a stronger Sam.

This is an original work created between 2015 and 2020.

To contact the author, send emails to cowboyproductions52@gmail.com or R. C. Hand, P.O. Box 213, Sunset Beach, Ca. 90742-0213.

Made in the USA
Middletown, DE
28 May 2024

54964413R00128